Walk Me Home

4/13

Walk Me Home

catherine ryan hyde

amazonpublishing

Published by Amazon Publishing

P.O. Box 400818
Las Vegas, NV 89140

ISBN-13: 9781611097979
ISBN-10: 1611097975
Library of Congress Control Number: 2012948673

For my mom, Vance Hyde, 1922-2012.

Sorry this is the first one you won't get to read.

PART ONE

Right Now

NEW MEXICO

May 1

They creep along, walking their bikes past the big house in the pitch dark. There are no lights on inside. But Carly can't help thinking there will be. Suddenly. If they're not quiet enough.

Too much depends on this moment. Everything.

Carly hears the clicking of the spokes of Jen's bicycle wheels. She reaches over and slaps her hand down on Jen's handlebars to stop the bike—and her sister—in their tracks.

"We have to carry the bikes till we get past the house," she hisses in Jen's ear.

"Easy for you to say. Yours is light."

Carly sighs and trades bikes with Jen. Jen's bike is a heavy old beach cruiser. And it has no headlight. So Carly duct-taped a flashlight to the handlebars.

The driveway is uphill, and Carly struggles for breath as she trots for the freedom of the road. It's a long driveway, and her chest is beginning to ache. She feels she can't keep going. But she does anyway. Because she has to.

Any minute now, a light might come on in the house. And Wade's brother might appear in the window. Then it will all be over.

But it doesn't. No light comes on.

Suddenly they're on the road and free.

Carly trades bikes again with her sister.

As they straddle the bikes, prepared to launch down the hill into the night, Jen switches on the flashlight.

Carly reaches over and slaps her hand over the light.

"Turn it off!"

"But I thought—"

"Not till we're farther away. Not till we can't be seen from the house."

"Carly…"

"What?"

"I have to tell you something."

"Oh, my God, Jen. Not now."

"Has to be now."

"Jen. Listen." Carly grabs Jen's bike and shakes once, hard. To stop all foolishness once and for all. "Listen to me. We have to get out of here. Now. And you have to stop acting like we have all kinds of options. We have Teddy. He's the only option we've got. Now I hate to pull rank, but I'm older. And I'm in charge of the family now. What's left of it. And we're going. Now come on."

They're making incredible time. And they don't even have to pedal.

They coast down the mountain, a few scattered lights in the valley below. The thin beams of light reveal the road in front of their bike tires. Carly can faintly see the headlights of cars on a two-lane highway below. Headed west. Well, headed both ways. But she focuses on the traffic headed west. The direction of Teddy and home.

The only challenge of the downhill run is applying the brakes just right, and just frequently enough, to keep the bikes from speeding out of control.

No car has come down the road for ages. So they ride side by side in the traffic lane. The edge of the road is too scary. Just a drop-off. Not enough light to see where that would take you. But Carly can pretty much figure it wouldn't take you any place good.

"What's that noise?" Carly asks. "Is that your brakes?"

"Yeah. I think the pads are low."

"Well, stay off them as much as you can."

"I'll try."

Jen begins to pick up speed. Carly eases off the brakes to catch up with her, but it scares her to go that fast. Too many curves. Too little shoulder. Not much margin for error.

"Maybe you need to slow down," she calls to Jen.

Carly hears a ghastly metal-on-metal noise.

"Oh, shit!" Jen shouts as she flies over the handlebars and disappears into the darkness off the side of the road.

Carly steers her bike to the spot where Jen disappeared and jumps off, dropping the bike on the narrow shoulder.

"Jen! You OK?"

"I think so."

"Keep talking so I can find you."

"I'm right here," she says, tugging at Carly's jeans. "Where's my bike?"

"We should be able to see the light from the flashlight."

"It must've broken."

"I'll get my bike, and we'll shine a light down there."

Carly carefully walks her bike a few steps down the hill. In the thin beam of the headlight, they see Jen's bike crashed up against the side of a squat, gnarled tree.

Jen scrambles down the hill to retrieve it.

"Oh, this is messed up," she calls back up to Carly. "I think the frame is bent. Yeah. I can't even roll it."

"Well…just leave it then. Just sit on my handlebars, and we'll keep going. We can't afford to slow down."

Jen climbs back up to the road. "Hmm," she says, looking down the grade. "Can I sit on the seat instead? And you pedal standing up?"

"Sure, whatever. Let's just go."

"Before we go, can we say a little prayer that your brakes don't give out?"

"I don't pray," Carly says. "But you can if you want."

They walk the bike through a small town shortly before sunrise. Carly doesn't know what town it is.

"We need an Internet café," Carly says. "Or a library."

"Library wouldn't be open this early. Why do you need that?"

"To get Teddy's new address. He promised he'd e-mail it to me."

Jen never answers.

"Never mind. We'll just keep going. By the time we get to the next town, something will be open. The farther away we get, the better off we'll be."

She wants to think of this place where they lived with Wade and her mom as a horrible dream. But it still feels vividly real.

They mount the bike again and pedal along the main drag to the highway. And run smack into a highway sign that says: NO BICYCLES. NO MOTOR-DRIVEN CYCLES. NO PEDESTRIANS.

"Now what?" Jen asks.

"Oh, shit, Jen. I have no idea. Let's just stay here until we figure something out."

Collapse seems appealing. It speaks to her, promising relief. Carly regrets having already ruled it out as an option.

They sit on the library steps. Waiting. Watching the town wake up. People bustle by in both directions. On foot, in cars. Pedaling in the bike lane.

Carly's bike leans up against the brick of the building a few feet away. Unlocked. They didn't bring a bike lock.

Jen has a little scrape on her cheek. And her eyes look faraway. Like there's no Jen at home inside. Like she's locked up and left the premises of herself. Carly wonders if she looks the same way. Then she decides it doesn't really matter.

A boy a little older than Jen rides by on an ancient and dilapidated old bicycle. On the sidewalk. Looking their way. A few minutes later, he rides by again, going the other way. Still staring.

"He keeps looking at my bike," Carly says.

"You think he's going to try to steal it?"

"I wouldn't care if he did. It's no use to us now. I think we're going to have to ditch it and hitchhike."

On the boy's third ride by, Carly calls out to him, "You like that bike?"

He skids to a stop, his unlaced sneakers braced on the pavement.

"It's a nice bike. Is it yours?"

"Yeah. And it's for sale."

"I couldn't afford it."

"I'd let it go cheap."

"How much?"

"How much've you got?"

He carefully empties his jeans pockets. Separates out a few noncash items. Carly can't quite see what they all are, but one looks like a red rock and another like a guitar pick. He counts a few bills, then digs back into his pocket for a handful of change. Adds it up, pointing to each coin, his lips moving.

"I only have twelve dollars and thirty-five cents."

"Sold," Carly says.

Carly's the first to sit down at one of two library computers. She pulls up her e-mail on the Web. She hasn't checked it for ages. Eleven pieces of spam mail. One e-mail from her friend Marissa in Tulare. It says, "Carly, why didn't you tell me you were moving? Where did you go? Write back, OK?"

Nothing from Teddy at all.

They get their first ride with a sweet middle-aged woman. Plump, with thin, graying brown hair.

"Where are you girls going?" she asks when they pile into the backseat.

"West," Carly says.

"Well, I know that. But where?"

"Um. Home."

"But where's home? You girls seem awfully young to be out hitchhiking by yourselves. I usually never pick up hitchhikers, but I was worried about you. How far do you have to go?"

Carly kicks herself for not anticipating this problem in advance.

"It's just down this road about twenty miles," Carly says.

"Does your mother know you're out here alone?"

In her peripheral vision, Carly sees Jen begin to cry quietly.

You're in charge now, Carly tells herself. There's nobody else. If a problem comes up, there's no one to run to. You have to solve it yourself. So go ahead. Save the day.

She glances at the odometer. Memorizes the number plus twenty miles.

"It's like this," Carly says. "We went out last night with some friends. And they drove us way up into the mountains. We didn't know we'd be going so far. And we didn't want to go back with them because they'd been drinking. Our mom would kill us if she knew. So we're hitchhiking home—I know. I know it's a bad idea.

We're never going to do it again. It's scary. But if you'll let us off twenty miles up..."

The woman sighs. "I'm just glad it was me who picked you up."

"Yeah. Me, too. Thanks. We appreciate it."

Then the potential flaw in Carly's plan sinks in. What if twenty miles goes by and they're exactly in the middle of nowhere? No houses as far as the eye can see?

She sits on the edge of the backseat, peering through the windshield. Trying to be nervous without looking nervous. They pass intersection after intersection of long, paved roads crossing the highway. A scattering of ranch homes in each direction. If that changes, Carly will need to pretend she was wrong about the twenty miles.

Her luck holds.

When the odometer hits the magic number, Carly says, "Next intersection. If you'll just let us off right up there..."

"I can drive you all the way home."

"No. Please. That'll just get us in trouble."

Another big sigh from the front seat. The driver pulls over and lets them out.

"You girls take care, now."

"We will. Thank you."

They stand at the side of the little highway and watch her drive off.

Jen waves.

"Shit," Carly says. "That was close."

"Close to what? She was nice."

"Too nice."

"How can you be too nice?"

"She wanted to help us."

"We need help, Carly."

"You know what she would've done. Don't you? If she'd known we don't have anybody? She'd have called child protective services. I don't want to get put in a foster home, Jen. We don't even know if they'd keep us together."

"So what do we do, then? Do we still hitchhike?"

"Yeah. I think so. I think we have to. But this time let's have our story ready."

The man who picks them up next doesn't seem interested in their story. He doesn't express any concern for their well-being. He's maybe forty. Thin and pale, like his skin has never seen the sun. He wears heavy, black-framed glasses. He won't stop looking at them in the rearview mirror.

They drive for well over an hour without any questions. He doesn't even ask where they're going.

Then, when he finally speaks, all he says is, "You're making me feel awfully lonesome. Up here all by myself."

Carly doesn't answer. Neither does Jen. But Jen shoots Carly a look. A silent question. Are we in trouble? Carly doesn't know. But it doesn't feel good. There's an "ick factor" in the car. That was something Teddy used to say. This ick factor has hovered throughout the ride, Carly realizes. She just hadn't looked it in the eye. Until the man spoke.

She reaches into her backpack and feels around for her hairbrush, a round brush with a narrow round metal handle. The handle has a plastic cap on the end, but Carly pries it off with her thumb.

They're coming through a town. Thank God.

"Let us off right up here," Carly says. "Please."

She can see an intersection. And a stoplight. But the light turns green, and the driver speeds through it.

Carly looks over at Jen, who's gone stonelike again. Carly worries her sister's bones might melt, the way they did last night. They can't afford that kind of collapse now.

"I'm sorry," he says. "I wanted to make that light."

"Well, you made it. So pull over. Please."

"Next light. You can walk back."

Carly squeezes her eyes shut and prays for the next light to turn red. It does, and the driver has to stop. Only then does Carly remember how she told Jen she doesn't pray.

Jen's on the passenger's side. The safe side to get out. She tries to open the back door. "It's locked." She tries to pull up the lock button. It won't pull.

Ick Man is watching in the rearview mirror. "The child safety lock is on," he says.

"Then take it off!" Carly shouts. Just at the edge of panic. "And let us out!"

No answer. Nothing moves. Carly watches the blood drain out of Jen's face, leaving her skin white like a porcelain doll.

"Open this door or I'm getting the gun," Carly says.

The light turns green.

Carly pulls the hairbrush out of her pack, careful to keep it behind his head, where he can't see it in the mirror. She presses the round metal of the end of the handle to the back of his head.

"Do *not* step on the gas," she says.

The back door locks click up. A beautiful sound. Jen swings the door wide, and they bolt out of the car. The man drives away with his rear door still open.

"Oh, my God," Jen says. "Oh, my God, oh, my God, oh, my God."

"Relax, Jen. Calm down. We're OK."

"I can't do this, Carly. We can't keep doing this."

"OK. We won't, then. No more hitchhiking. I promise."

"So what are we going to do, then?"

"We'll walk."

"To *California*?"

"Not to California. Of course not. Just from one phone booth to the next. And when Teddy picks up the phone, he'll drive out and get us. Or he'll wire us money for a bus ticket or something. But the more we walk, the closer we'll be to home, and the faster he can get us there. And we won't be in one place long enough for anybody to decide they want to help us by putting us in foster care. We'll just walk along like we know exactly what we're doing. And if anybody asks, we'll just say we're walking home. That's true. Right?"

"We're walking home," Jen says. As if the story needs rehearsal.

"Right. We're walking home."

They walk until dark. About ten hours.

Carly calls Teddy four times that first day. Teddy doesn't pick up.

NEW MEXICO

May 9

Carly is keeping a close eye on Jen. Maybe even more so than usual. She's watching Jen walk on the shoulder of this skinny, raggedy little blacktop road, kicking at the scrubby grass and gravel at the edge of their path.

For a time, Carly doesn't know why she's keeping such an eagle eye on Jen this morning. In most ways, it's a morning like any of the last nine. It's just their new normal.

She looks up ahead to see the black road dip down into a valley. And in this valley is…nothing. Just more scrubby weeds. A line of low mountains at its far end, mountains they will have to walk across in time. In the far distance, a few rock spires in different shapes and sizes, like the classic desert formations she's seen in old cowboy films. And the clouds are edging the sky in great puffs, dense at the mountains, more sparse above their heads, white on top and copper at their bottoms, unable to crowd together and cover the steely blue sky.

Too bad, Carly thinks. Because they're fresh out of sunscreen as of yesterday.

The clouds move on the stiff breeze. They scud, Carly thinks. She's not certain why—or from where—she remembers that odd word, but she's quite sure the clouds scud.

Jen does another exaggerated kick step, and Carly puts her finger on what she's been noticing. Where's all Jen's energy coming from? They're both exhausted. Sure, they've only been walking for less than an hour so far today. But when you put in the miles they do, day after day after day, you wake up tired. There's no such thing as rested. There's no such animal as fresh.

Jen stops and looks all around them, 360 degrees. She's been doing that all morning. Thoughtfully. As if there were something out here to see.

"Pretty here," Jen says.

"What's pretty about it?" Carly asks, clear in her tone that the kid is talking crazy.

"Well," Jen says, looking all around again. Breathing in a piece of that sky. "There's that."

She points at the wind-whittled formations just in front of the mountainous horizon.

"You're nuts," Carly says. "It's rocks."

"Pretty rocks."

"No such thing."

They walk a few steps more, Jen kicking a few more times. The crunch of their footsteps and the click of kicked gravel is the only sound. That and the wind in Carly's ears.

"The sky," Jen says.

"We have clouds at home, you know."

"Not the clouds. The sky."

Carly stops. Jen walks a couple more steps, then notices and also stops.

"You're being stupid," Carly says. "It's the same sky everywhere."

"No, it isn't. I never saw a sky like this one."

"Don't they teach you anything in school? The sky is the sky. Each place doesn't have its own sky."

"I know that. But this sky is bigger."

"You're just seeing more of it. You just can't see so many miles of sky where we come from."

"Right," Jen says. "That's what I mean. That's what's different. That's what's better."

Carly sighs and walks again, and Jen joins her. A bit more subdued. And though it ignites a pang of guilt in her gut to admit it, Carly is more comfortable with Jen that way. That's what's been eating her about Jen all morning. How could she act...almost... happy? At a time like this?

Out of nowhere, startling Carly, Jen squeals and breaks into a run, her backpack bouncing wildly. Carly looks up to see what Jen has seen.

Horses.

Three horses graze in a field, behind a fence almost laughable in its construction. It's made with branches for posts. Some straight, some curved, some forked. Branches standing straight up out of the ground, at intervals, strung with three strands of wire in between. Not barbed wire. Just wire. And it goes on forever. Two of the horses are white, but not as pretty as that makes them sound. Dirty white, with long yellowish tails and ribs showing just a bit.

But the third one is a beauty. A brown-and-white paint, with a brown tail and a thick white main so long it trails down below the bottom of his neck. Carly never thought much about calling a pinto horse a paint, but she sees now why that description fits. It's as though someone took brown paint to a white horse in big, broad splotches, then got bored and stopped halfway through.

The paint looks younger. And he acts younger.

As Jen gets closer to his fence, he's infected with her energy. He runs the fence line toward her, then turns and runs away, bucking as if trying to shake off something invisible, kicking out his heels.

Jen squeals laughter.

Carly stops and watches, trying not to sort out the parts of her that both do and do not like what she's seeing.

Then Jen breaks stride and hops on one foot, four hops, yelling, "Ow, ow, ow, ow," one "ow" for each hop.

She hops over and stands at the fence, holding one branch post, and looks at the bottom of her filthy white sneaker. The horse has stopped running as well and seems to be trying to decide whether he dares approach her. Jen drops her foot and leans over the ridiculous fence, trying to entice the paint to come close and be patted.

Carly breaks into a trot.

"Don't," she says. "Maybe he bites."

"He won't bite me," Jen calls back.

"And you know this *how*?"

"He won't."

By the time she catches up to them at the fence, the horse is rooting around in Jen's palms with his muzzle, twisting his lips and showing yellow teeth. Carly stands close enough to smell him. That deep, musty, not-at-all-unpleasant horse smell.

"You want some food, don't you?" Jen says to him, the way you'd talk to your pet dog. "But if I had some food, let me tell you, I'd eat it myself. You can eat grass. You're lucky. Wish we could eat grass. And sleep standing up in a field all night and not mind."

Carly sits gingerly on a big tire that's half buried in the dirt against the fence. Extra big, like a tractor tire. She has to use her hands to ease herself down.

"We have food," she says.

Jen comes and sits with her.

"What do we have?"

"Two more Snickers bars."

"Breakfast! Score!"

Carly takes off her own backpack and roots around in there until she finds the two candy bars at the bottom. She hands one to her sister.

"Make it last," she says.

"I'd rather have it all now."

"But then you'll be sorry later."

"But maybe we'll get more food later."

"But maybe not."

"I'll take my chances."

"Look. I'm the grown-up now. And I say just eat half."

Jen rolls her eyes, but she breaks the candy bar in half, folds the wrapper over the half she's been told to save, and slides it into her shirt pocket.

"You're as bad as Mom," Jen says.

Carly can feel the darkness in the air between them, the sense that Jen would snatch the words back inside if only she could.

"I can't believe you just said that, Jen."

"I'm sorry. I didn't mean—"

"But you didn't mean it in a good way, right? When you say I'm as bad as Mom, that's not a compliment to Mom. You're saying Mom was bad."

"Hey! You're the one that—"

"That's called speaking ill of the dead, Jen. And it's a thing nobody is *ever* supposed to do, *ever*. And you're the superstitious one, so I'm really surprised you would speak ill of the dead."

Jen looks up and around, as though trying to identify a particular area of sky.

"Sorry," she whispers.

Then she takes a bite of her breakfast.

The paint horse leans over the wire, snuffling his muzzle in the direction of the food. His lips make a popping sound that causes Jen to turn around, and she laughs out loud to see him there.

"Horses don't eat Snickers bars," she says.

But a minute later a strong breeze upends the long, dark strands of Jen's curly hair, and both of Jen's hands fly up to her head to brush it back into place. And the horse, seizing an opportunity, leans farther over the fence and nicks the candy with his teeth.

Jen screams laughter again and holds the treasure close against her chest.

"Ick," Carly says. "Now you have to throw away the part he touched."

"No way. I'm not wasting it."

"You'll get a disease or something."

"People don't get diseases from horses."

"How do *you* know?"

Jen raises the candy bar and chomps off half of what's left in one big bite.

"If my neck starts getting longer," Jen says, her mouth full, "and my feet get hard, you can throw a saddle on me and ride me all the way to California."

"We're not walking all that way. Teddy'll come get us."

Jen doesn't answer.

Remembering something, Carly grabs one of Jen's ankles and pulls her leg out and up, until she can examine the bottom of Jen's sneaker. Even though she can't remember which foot it was.

"Ow," Jen says. "What?"

On the bottom of Jen's sole is a hole about the size of a quarter, worn clear through. Carly can see the dusty dark green of Jen's sock. She drops that ankle and grabs the other. The bottom of that sole has a hole the size of a dime. Carly gives Jen her feet back.

"Why didn't you tell me you had holes in your shoes?"

"It's not like you could have done anything."

"We could put cardboard inside or something."

"Oh. Yeah. I guess."

A minute later Carly stands up, using her hands for support, and tugs on Jen's sleeve.

"More miles," she says.

"Right," Jen says. "I know. More miles. How did I guess? Because it's always more miles."

Jen leans over and kisses the horse on his nose before they walk on.

The paint ambles the fence line with them, loose-kneed and confident, until he runs out of pasture.

Jen waves sadly to him.

"Bye, pretty."

"He's not your boyfriend."

"Says you."

Jen gazes over her shoulder at him three more times before the road dips, obscuring their view. Then she looks one more time, as if it helps her remember.

Half a mile later they pass a ranch house with a garden hose coiled on the side. No cars. No garage to hide a car. No one seems to be home.

They drink their fill before moving on. It's the first day they've been without a gas station bathroom for more than half a day. It scares Carly to be so far from a source of water. And a phone.

They make it over the low mountains that same day. They crest the top and look down into the next valley. Carly expects to see more of the scant food, water, and shelter sources that have lined their path at intervals so far.

What they see is more nothing.

They stand on a sidewalk together, Carly marveling at how long it's been since they've had a sidewalk to stand on. Carly appraises what thin opportunities this place has to offer. Gas station with tiny convenience store. Thrift shop. Ice cream stand. Hardware store. Native American blankets, Hopi and Navajo, both.

"What town is this?" Jen asks.

"I don't know. I never saw a sign, did you?"

"I don't think so. But I was busy looking at those rocks. They're pretty."

Beyond this stretch of highway imitating civilization, the landscape is made up of tumbled rocks, big and small, some forming tumbled rock mountains, others going it alone. All the same shade of ordinary rock brown.

"What's with you and rocks all of a sudden?"

"I dunno."

"Maybe it's too small a town to even have a name," Carly says.

"All towns have names."

"How would you know? You're twelve."

Jen says nothing, and Carly knows she's crossed a line. And then she knows she's been crossing a line with Jen for days, being meaner than situations require. But she's not sure she has the energy to fix it just yet. Or even knows how.

There's a rough bench on a dirt lot near the sidewalk, made with a plank on two cut tree stumps. They hobble over to it and slide off their packs. Carly eases herself down and unties her shoes, pulling one off.

Jen flops on her back in the dirt and puts her feet up on the bench.

"You're lucky you're not a redhead," Carly tells her sister.

"Don't take your shoes off. Why is that lucky?"

"I have to take them off. My feet are all swollen."

"You'll never get them back on."

"I can't help it. They're killing me."

"Why is it unlucky to be a redhead?"

"Because they burn so easy. They have that fair skin. Can't take any sun at all. Like my friend Marissa. You didn't know her. She was from my high school."

"Which one? New Mexico or California?"

"California. We can buy more sunscreen."

"With what?"

"I'll get somebody to give us some money. I always do."

Jen has the back of one hand thrown across her eyes. Probably to shield them from the sun, but it makes her look dramatic. Like one of those old-time movie actresses depicting angst. Though angst was never Jen's style.

"Carly," she says. "I'm hungry. I don't care if I burn to a crisp. I don't care if I burn till I blister. Do not waste…like…*four dollars* on sunscreen. You know how much food we could buy for *four dollars*? You want more miles—I need more *food*."

The holey soles of Jen's sneakers keep calling Carly's eyes back.

She squeezes her eyes closed, and when she opens them, there's the thrift store. Right in front of her. As if she's been trying to conjure something, and now it's arrived, just as ordered.

She pushes her feet back into the shoes, but they barely squeeze in. It hurts. It would be easy to cry out, but she doesn't. She can't even bring herself to lace them up again. She'll just have to be careful not to trip.

"Come on. Walk with me."

"We're resting!" Jen howls.

"No, I don't mean that. I mean we're going in that thrift store."

"For what? We don't have any money."

"Just shut up and walk with me."

"You go. I'm tired."

"No. You have to come, too."

Jen sighs deeply and rolls over, pulling to her feet. A couple in their twenties strolls by. Each has an ice-cream cone. Two scoops apiece. The woman smiles at them. Jen stares at the ice cream until it's too far away to ogle.

They cross the street together to the thrift store. The window is hand-painted and says all proceeds go to benefit Saint Ignatius Hospital.

A bell jingles when Carly opens the door.

"How're you girls doing today?" the woman asks.

She's maybe forty, reading a paperback book. She looks Indian. Native. Native American, Carly should start saying. Indian might offend somebody. They're getting close to Navajo country, the big reservation, but Carly doesn't think they're quite there yet. But at least they're finally over the border into Arizona.

Carly never answers.

"Anything special in mind?"

Carly sees a birdcage hanging near the woman's head, with two blue-and-green parakeets. They make a chirping racket, almost like singing.

"Shoes," Carly says. "We were looking for some shoes for my sister."

"Go all the way down that aisle and then left. They're on the floor in the corner back there. All two dollars unless they got a tag says they're more."

"Thanks. Want us to leave our backpacks here?"

People don't like for kids or teens to come in their stores with backpacks. They've learned that for sure.

"It's fine. I'll trust you. Let me know if you need help."

Then Carly feels bad. The lady's trust makes her feel extra bad.

Jen tugs at her sleeve as they walk down the aisle, but Carly knocks her hand away again. She shoots Jen a warning look. The shop is small. The woman won't be able to see them once they're back in the corner with the shoes. But she might hear.

Jen runs straight to a pair of cross-training shoes about her size. She has her hand on them before Carly even sees them. They're scuffed up pretty good. But when Jen picks them up and turns them over, the soles are nice. Not worn much at all. She turns them back upright, and they both look at the tops of them. They have a tag that says they're five dollars, not just two.

Carly takes a quick look over her shoulder, then pulls off the tag, breaking its string. Jen sucks her breath in, and Carly shoots Jen another warning with her eyes.

"Try them on," she whispers.

There's no place to sit, so Jen sits on the floor and pulls off her holey old sneakers. Meanwhile Carly spots a pair of lace-up boots. She picks them up, considering. She turns her foot over and holds them sole to sole with the shoes she has. They look about right. A little big, maybe. But that would give her feet room to swell.

She puts them on and laces them snug to make up for their bigness, then looks up to see Jen sitting up straight on the floor, the new shoes on. Her eyes seem extra wide. Carly catches Jen's eye, and Jen nods. Those are the ones, all right.

Carly picks up her old shoes and Jen's old shoes, and arranges them in the line on the floor with all the others. They don't look much worse than some of them, at least if you don't turn Jen's over.

"OK, well, we looked, anyway. You happy now?" Carly asks in a normal volume and too cheerful.

"I guess," Jen says, sounding nervous.

Carly reaches a hand down to Jen and pulls her to her feet.

She looks down at the new boots. They're sturdy. That'll help. But they're a risk because they're more one-of-a-kind than Jen's trainers. The lady might spot them walking out the door. She looks back at her old shoes and almost decides to take them back. But her feet have swollen even more by now. She probably wouldn't get them back on.

"Don't look at her," she whispers in Jen's ear. "Don't talk to her. Let me do all the talking."

Jen is a terrible liar. Jen is so honest she busts herself every time.

Carly tugs the sleeve of her sister's shirt, and they walk. God knows if there's one thing they know how to do by now, it's walk.

"Thanks anyway, ma'am," she calls, prepared to keep walking right by the counter. Then she realizes that's not the best thing to do. She should stop and talk. Because that's just what a person who's stealing something would never do.

"You girls have yourselves a good day."

Carly stops, close to the counter, where the woman can't see their feet anyway.

"What's the name of this little town?" she asks.

"Not really a town exactly. Just part of McKinley County. The mailing address is technically Gallup, though that's a pretty long way south of here."

Carly looks to Jen, happy to have been proven right. But Jen is staring up into the birdcage, oblivious. Either hypnotized by the birds or paralyzed by fear. Or both.

"But that's a different state," Carly says.

"Not sure what you mean," the woman says, sounding patient.

"Gallup is in New Mexico, and this is Arizona."

"No. This's New Mexico."

Carly feels Jen's reaction, at her left side, without even looking. She's been promising Jen they've already crossed over the line into Arizona at long last.

"Really?" As though it could still turn out not to be true.

"You girls lost?"

And then Carly realizes her mistake. She's raised a red flag, just what she's been teaching herself not to do.

"No, ma'am. Not at all. We're on a road trip with our dad. He's out gassing up the car. He told us we were over the line into Arizona. Wait till I go tell him how wrong he was. How far from here to the state line? You know. Just so I can tell him."

"Twenty miles or so. Maybe a little more."

Carly is careful not to look at Jen, knowing how hard that news must be settling in. More than a day's walking. Just to get to where they thought they already were.

"OK. Thanks, ma'am," she says.

"You girls have a good day."

Then the woman puts her nose back down into her paperback book. She doesn't look at Carly's or Jen's feet as they walk out the door.

Carly watches Jen walk down the shoulder of the road with her backpack balanced on her head to keep the sun out of her face. There's more of a spring in her sister's step.

"We didn't end up getting to rest much," Jen says. "These are really bouncy."

She bounces more stridently, to emphasize the point, but carefully, so as not to drop the backpack.

"I just wanted to get a little farther away from there first," Carly says. Which is phrasing it mildly. They ran scared, but at a fast walk.

She's using the jacket-held-over-her-head method. Her backpack is heavier.

"Did you get their address?" Jen asks.

"Yeah, I'm holding the number in my head till I can write it down."

"These sure are a whole bunch better. Can we rest now?"

But there isn't much of a place to stop. Nothing like that nice bench they'd had before.

"There's a rock," Jen says.

They walk to it and sit.

The sun is off at a slant already, and Jen's still doing that thing she's been doing, looking around as if there's something worth seeing out here.

Carly slips off her backpack and digs around in it until she finds the little blank book, its pen still clipped on. She flips to the first blank page and writes:

> We owe $7.00 to the St. Ignatius Thrift Store at 3397 Route 264, McKinley County, sort of near Gallup, New Mexico. Look up zip code.

She sees Jen peeking over her shoulder.

"How much do we owe by now?" Jen asks.

"Over thirty dollars. But it's OK. Teddy'll give us the money."

"You act like he has money. He doesn't have money."

"Well. Some. Not much. But that doesn't matter. He'll give us what he has. Teddy's like that. He'll know how important this is to us, and he'll find a way."

"You act like he never did a thing wrong in his life."

"He didn't. It was Mom—"

She tries to stop herself. But the word *Mom* slips through the gate.

Jen's mouth forms a small, tight O.

"Now who's speaking bad at the dead?"

"Sorry."

Oh, shit, Carly thinks. We should have called him again in that last town.

And that's more than true. They should've done a lot of things in that last town. They should've gotten someone to give them a little money, in that special way Carly's learned how to do without raising big flags. And bought food. And bought sunscreen. And rested. And, yes, called Teddy again. Because Teddy will buy them a ticket to ride a bus or a train. Or maybe he'll drop what he's doing and drive out to get them. They only have to walk until Teddy answers the phone. It was never supposed to take nine days.

"We'll call him again. Next phone," she says. "We have to walk if we're gonna get someplace by sundown."

Jen doesn't even complain. Just unfolds her skinny legs and brushes off the back of her jeans.

They start off down the road again.

They hear the first engine they've heard in a while.

Carly looks over her shoulder to see an old motor home lumbering up the hill. Her heart falls when it slows and then stops in the road alongside them. A middle-aged woman leans out the window. Carly can feel air-conditioning pouring out of the rig. It feels weirdly comforting, something she forgot existed.

They've been lucky with the weather. Warm but not hot by day and cold but not freezing at night. But it's getting warmer now.

"You girls OK out here all by yourself? Need a ride?"

Just for a minute, Carly considers that it might be safe, just this one time, to break their no-ride policy. This woman can't be dangerous. But Carly can't get a good enough look at the driver.

Then it hits her, the lunacy of what she's considering. She must be more tired than she realizes. Even if they're trustworthy and nice, they'd ask questions. They'd want to know where the girls were headed. Carly couldn't just say, "Take us up the road as far as you're going and then we'll walk some more." No, they'd get involved. They'd want to help. All grown-ups want to help.

This trip would be so much easier without all these grown-ups wanting to help.

"No, ma'am, but thanks. We live right around here."

"Around *here*? Really? Thought there wasn't another thing clear to Arrow Rock. Nothing much out here."

"Well, it *looks* that way," Carly says, pasting on a smile. "But our house is down a dirt road just a quarter mile up."

"Want a lift?"

"Thanks just the same, ma'am, but you wouldn't offer if you'd seen our dirt road. You'd never get down it in this big thing. Need four-wheel drive. It's fine, though. Really. We walk out here all the time."

Carly can hear the tapping of the driver's fingers on the steering wheel. Good, she thinks. He wants to go.

"Long as you're OK," the lady says.

Then she rolls up her window, and the motor home takes off uphill with its engine groaning.

The girls walk on.

"You're getting to be a good liar," Jen says.

"Thanks."

"I didn't mean it like a compliment."

The woman turns out to be right. There isn't another thing clear to Arrow Rock. Not even an old house with a hose coiled on its side. Not even a tree with wormy crab apples.

"We could sleep standing up in a field," Jen says. "Like a horse."

"They probably have coyotes and stuff out here."

"Oh."

They stop and put their spare shirts on right over the ones they're wearing, and their jackets. Now Carly's pack is lighter, and she wears it like a hat, the way Jen always does. To keep the setting sun out of her eyes.

Half a mile down, Jen runs off the road a few yards to pick up a walking stick. She doesn't say it has anything to do with coyotes. Then again, she doesn't need to.

It's getting dark fast, and cold, so they walk off-road to a rock hill and find a space to tuck in. That way there's only one side of them vulnerable to coyotes. And they can hold some of their heat in that small space.

That's where they sleep.

Well, Jen sleeps. Carly stays awake most of the night, teeth chattering, stick at the ready. But so far as she can tell, there's nothing awake out here in all this nothing. Except for her.

She wonders if it's possible to freeze to death out here. Probably not, but she can't help worrying. This is the first night they haven't found some kind of shelter, if only a dumpster. She wraps herself over Jen, just in case.

Jen cries in her sleep through most of the night. Carly makes up her mind that she will never mention this. Like it never happened. Like she never saw. Because she would be humiliated if someone witnessed her crying in her sleep. And she wants to spare Jen the humiliation.

Then it hits her that it might already have happened. And she would never know.

ARIZONA

May 10

"Bus station!" Jen shouts. "Score!"

It's after seven in the evening, and the sun is all but down. A bus station is the best thing that could have happened to them. In fact, a bus station's the best thing that's happened to them in a long time. Though neither has said so out loud, that one night out in the cold was something they don't want to try again.

Not that they can take a bus. Until Teddy answers the phone, there's no money for any option but the one they've been using. Sometimes Carly wonders if walking is really the only way, or if it's just the only way that doesn't scare her too much, make her think they'll be caught and handed over to child services. But she feels like she can't rely on any new thinking, so they've just kept walking. It's worked so far. Next call to Teddy will be the one. This will be over soon.

They step up onto the wooden porch and read the sign on the door to see when's closing time. Nine o'clock. That's good. Earlier than some.

"Wait here," Carly says, knowing a few steps saved at the end of the day would have to feel good to Jen. "I'll go inside and see what time a bus comes in."

"Maybe last bus already did."

"Then they'd close earlier."

She swings the wooden door open, and the arrivals and departures board is right there. She doesn't even have to go inside to read it.

"Eight thirty," she says. "Last bus is at eight thirty."

Which still leaves a lot of logistics and problems. If there's a crowd at eight thirty, even a small one, they can get lost in it. If not, this might or might not work. Like everything else in life lately, it's hard to know until they try.

At a little after eight, they go inside and wait by the gate, as if expecting someone. Then they get a break, and the only guy who seems to work here goes into a back room. Carly runs to the door and pushes it open, letting it swing shut again with a bang. As if they've gone outside.

They slip into the tiny, two-stall ladies' room and sit on the toilets, one in each stall. With their feet pulled up. For a long time.

They can hear the bus come roaring in, but as far as they can hear, nobody gets off and comes through the station. All they hear is the man who works here punch the ladies' room door open. Carly's blood freezes, thinking maybe he comes in and cleans in here after hours. But his footsteps retreat, and the door swings closed again.

Then they hear him lock up for the night. Probably a little early.

It fills Carly with an exaggerated elation. As if they've just been locked into a five-star hotel. With room service. Something at the back of her brain registers the sadness of this. But if she focused on that, she'd lose this moment. So she pretends she doesn't know it's there.

The first thing Carly does is unlace the new boots and ever so carefully ease them off. She has blisters on her heels. Bad ones. She can see that the heels of her black socks are soaked through, but she doesn't know if it's blood or clear fluid from the broken blisters or both.

They're good boots, as far as that goes. They give her feet a lot more support. Overall, her feet feel better than usual. But the boots are too big, so her heels don't lock down right. They lift up and sink down with every step, rubbing against the stiff leather. Maybe they'll break in. Maybe she'll get protective calluses. Maybe tomorrow's miles will be a nightmare, and she won't be able to hide the pain anymore. Lots of things could happen from here.

She peels off her thin socks.

A big, ugly flap of skin drapes off one heel.

She washes the worst foot first in one of the ancient pedestal sinks, yelping out loud when the liquid hand soap touches her heel.

Jen sticks her head through the door. She's been out in the main waiting room, kicking, and trying to bump and jiggle, the vending machine.

"You say something, Carly?"

"Nope," Carly says.

She washes her other heel, then wraps both feet in toilet paper and slides her clean pair of socks over that.

Then she goes hunting.

"Look what I found," Carly says, holding the wire coat hanger behind her back.

She walks to where Jen is sitting cross-legged on the floor, staring longingly into the only food-related vending machine. There's also a soda machine, but Carly has no magic keys for that and no ideas. Both machines have been centered over a spot where the linoleum flooring is missing.

"Money? You found money?"

"Next best thing."

She shows Jen the wire hanger. It seems to take a minute to compute in Jen's head. Carly thinks she can see raw data rattling around in there, waiting to fit. But Jen gets there eventually.

"Get those corn chips," she says.

"I doubt it. They're on the top row. I think we have to go with bottom-row stuff."

"OK, let's see. Trail mix. Peanuts. Licorice. Potato chips. Peanut butter crackers. Which one should we get?"

"*Which one?* Are you kidding me? We're getting everything we can knock out of there."

In fact, Carly's thinking maybe she can get multiple packages of each thing. But when she bends the hanger properly and pokes the peanuts down into the tray, she realizes that the one behind it will not mechanically push forward where she can get to it.

Still, five items. That pretty much makes this Thanksgiving.

She looks up through the high, dirty window. The station has outside lights on all four sides, making a nice glow for them to see by, while at the same time making it darker inside than out. So they can move around unobserved. Not that anything or anyone seems to be moving out on the street.

She briefly wonders what day of the week it is.

A huge tan moth beats his wings against the window from the inside. She can hear him. Tapping on the glass. She knows in her head it's the light he's after, but she can't imagine wanting to get outside when you could sleep here. Even if she were a moth.

"Where'd you find a hanger?" Jen asks, startling her.

The peanut butter crackers finally fall, and Jen dives her hand into the tray to grab them.

"In the office back there. There's this pole where they can hang up their coats. And there was one wooden hanger and two wire ones. The money's all locked up, I guess."

Jen eats peanuts in silence for a minute, then dives a hand into the tray when the trail mix drops.

Then she says, "Hey. Carly. Just this once, can we…you know…just eat everything we've got? All at the same time?"

"Sure," Carly says. "Just this once."

Truth is, Carly needs this moment, too. Even sixteen-year-old grown-ups sometimes need a celebration. Especially when times have been hard.

She takes out her little book and stands, examining the machine until she finds a shiny silver label. It says this machine is serviced by Harmony Vending, 21900 Navajo Boulevard, Holbrook, AZ 86025.

She copies down the address.

"Are all five of those things seventy-five cents?"

"Yup," Jen says.

She pauses. Doesn't write anything for a minute.

"Three dollars and seventy-five cents," Jen says.

"I knew that," Carly says.

It's half true. She *would* have known that. Given a little more time.

"I also found one other thing," Carly says. "There was a first-aid kit back there. And I opened it up and took out two big adhesive bandages. You know. In case I get blisters from these new boots. Just in case. My heels are feeling a little rubbed."

"OK," Jen says.

"Are *your* feet OK?"

"The best. These cross-trainers are the bomb."

"Good. So…"

"So…what?"

"So, should I put that in the book?"

"Hmm," Jen says. Her mouth is full of black licorice. "We don't know what they would cost."

"I was just thinking, if the guy were here and I said I had blisters, he'd probably give them to me. I mean, I think they're to hand out. Not to sell."

"I guess."

"So you think it's OK?"

"Probably. Yeah."

"You don't think it's sort of…breaking a promise to ourselves? Like our honesty system is breaking down some?"

Jen chews in silence for a moment, her eyes closed.

Then she says, "Maybe a little bit. But I don't think it's a very big deal."

Carly nods a few times. Then she looks down at the wire hanger and carefully bends it back into wire hanger shape. It looks a little worse for wear. But she hangs it back up on the pole in the back office. It'll still hold coats, which is the main thing. And then only the adhesive bandages are a little over the line.

Carly calls Teddy's cell phone number from the pay phone while Jen washes up in the ladies' room, an odd bathing system with paper towels, liquid hand soap, and water. Jen always seems to find a way to be gone while Carly calls.

She braces herself for the recorded announcement of how much is left on the prepaid calling card she bought herself on that miserable Christmas in New Mexico with her mom and Wade. She doesn't really want to know. She knows it can't be much. She shouldn't be leaving messages every time. She's been running it down too fast.

It's just around two minutes. It's running out.

It rings. And rings. And rings. The way it used to when Teddy was out of minutes on his cell phone. Then Carly hears a click, like Teddy picking up the phone.

"Teddy? Teddy, is that you?"

Silence.

"Teddy?"

It's a recorded message. A woman with a robotic, irritating voice. She says, "I'm sorry. The cellular number you have reached is not in service at this time, and there is no new number."

Carly hangs up fast. In case the woman was planning on saying more.

Jen is all dressed again in her clean shirt when Carly gets back into the ladies' room. She's washing out her socks and underwear in one sink. She looks up, apparently startled by what she sees in Carly's face.

"What's the matter?" Jen asks.

"Nothing. He just wasn't there."

Carly leans over the other sink and drinks her fill of cold water.

"You look like something's wrong."

"No, everything's fine," she says, then dries her face on her sleeve. "We'll just try him again. He must be working a second job or something. I'm sure he's in his own place by now. And I just bet he has to work a lot."

She's hoping Jen won't ask why working two jobs would prevent him from answering the cell phone in his pocket.

"Maybe he's out of minutes. And can't afford more."

"Yeah! Maybe."

"What would we do then?"

"I could call his work tomorrow."

Until she hears herself say it, she doesn't realize it's that simple. Of course. She can just call Ralph. The guy he's been working for. Ask him to get a message to Teddy. She's a bit shocked, in fact, that she didn't think of it until now. A weight lifts from her full belly, leaving her feeling light and clear again.

"Do we know his work number?"

"No, but we know it's Ralph Martin Construction. So we can get a listing."

"Doesn't that cost a dollar? Or two? How much is left on the phone card?"

"I don't know, Jen. We'll figure it out. Want me to wash your hair?"

"Yeah. Definitely."

She leans Jen forward into one of the sinks and wets her hair thoroughly under the tap. This station is so old that there's actually hot and cold running water, both coming out of one tap, so you can make it just as warm or cool as you like. And you can leave it running. Not like those new ones where you press down and the water blasts as long as it feels like blasting, then stops on its own.

She soaps Jen's hair with liquid hand soap because it's all they have.

As she's rinsing it out—and it's no small job to get all the soap out of Jen's thick, coarse hair—she says, "Wait till we get home. Till we're living with Teddy again. We'll get that hair conditioner that smells like mangoes. And shower gel."

"I hate that foofy stuff," Jen says. "It's for girls."

"You're a girl. Stupid."

"I'm not a girl like *you* are."

"And we'll have clean sheets every few nights…"

"How do you figure?"

"Because I'll wash them myself. And we'll put lotion all over ourselves every night, and we won't have scaly elbows and flaky shins."

"I couldn't care less about elbows and shins. I just don't want to ever walk anywhere ever again. If you say go get the mail at the end of the driveway, I'll hook up some kind of little cart to take me down there. Like an old lady cart. Or I'll get one of those bikes with the 'chicken power' motors. And we'll have wieners and beans every night for dinner and candy bars for dessert. Not candy bars for dinner."

"You'll get sick of wieners and beans."

"I could never get sick of wieners and beans."

"OK. I think I got all the soap out. Squeeze out most of the water over the sink. And then dry it with paper towels as much as you can. I'm gonna wash up now. Don't look."

"Why would I look?"

"I don't know. Just don't. And don't leave your socks and underwear hanging on the stall doors like that."

"Why not?"

"Because we might need to scram out of here fast in the morning."

"Oh. Right."

Carly strips out of everything but her socks, then looks up to the milky glass window into the alley. It has a hole about twice the size of a baseball broken out of it. In the outside light, she can see a light mist of rain falling.

"It's raining," she says.

"You're kidding." Jen's combing her wet hair and can't seem to immediately break away from that to look for herself.

"Just a little bit of rain."

"Thought it never rained in the desert," Jen says, popping up.

"Sure it does. Just not as much."

They stand side by side a moment, staring.

Then Jen says what Carly hasn't quite gathered together yet.

"Damn. The one time we can't stand out in it."

They stare awhile longer, then Jen makes herself comfortable— at least, as comfortable as one can get on a tile floor, curled in a fetal position, using her pack as a pillow.

Carly jumps up, bracing her hands on the windowsill, and reaches her face up to the hole in the window, still naked, a mist of light rain on her sunburned face.

She wakes knowing she dreamed about Teddy in the night. But, try as she might, she can't remember *what* she dreamed about him. She scrambles for it like something precious pouring down a drain. But it's already gone.

ARIZONA

May 12

"Hey, a gas station," Carly says. "With a little food store. Finally. Finally we can get something to eat."

"But there's nobody getting gas there," Jen says.

Carly's special system relies on people. People who can be talked out of a little money. The trick is to be clear that their parents are only slightly lost or briefly delayed. That they can rejoin their parents right here, right at this station, if they simply stay put. All they need is a little something to eat while they're waiting.

"Somebody will come."

Jen looks around nervously. Surprisingly few people have passed them all morning.

"What if they don't?"

"Well. There's somebody working in the store. That's as good as anything."

But when they get there, there's nobody working in the store. Just a hand-lettered sign on the locked door.

CLOSED THURS MAY 12 OWING TO FAMILY EMERGENCY.

They sit down on the curb by the door.

"May twelfth," Jen says. Like it's a thing that couldn't possibly be true.

But Carly knew that already. She's been counting days.

"The pay phone is outside," Carly says. "I'll call Teddy's work." But she knows she probably can't. Not with the time she has left on the card.

She marches over to the phone, dials in the numbers for her calling card by heart. And finds out the card is less than a minute from spent. Not enough to call directory assistance. She walks back to where Jen is sitting, careful to feel as little as possible.

"What happened?" Jen asks.

Carly sits down beside her. "Card's used up."

"Oh."

They sit awhile longer. The sun is almost directly overhead. It's warm for May. Nothing like summer desert heat. Just warm. Maybe eighty. But when you're walking in the sun all day, it adds up.

Carly looks up into the sun, squinting and watching light radiate out from that yellow beast. Somewhere inside herself she knows it's desert straight through Arizona and halfway into California. And that it will be summer soon enough.

Except Teddy'll come and get them. Teddy will save them. They won't be walking by then.

"Know what really burns my butt?" she asks Jen. "If Wade hadn't had to order steak and eggs, I'd be making that call right now. Takes a special kind of son of a bitch to ruin your life even after he's dead." She squints up at the sun again. "Think he did it on purpose?"

It's that thing nobody's said. So far. Carly wonders if Jen will think she means the steak and eggs, and the way it robbed her of phone card money. But no. Of course not. Jen won't think that. Jen will know exactly what she means.

"I've been trying not to think about it."

"Oh. Sorry."

"I don't know, Carly. I don't know what to think about that."

"Never mind. We'll just worry about what's right in front of us."

Carly levers to her feet and walks over to the water and air island, the place where people fill their radiators and tires. To check and see if the water hose is running. It is. So she waves for Jen to come.

Maybe it's not the kind of water you're supposed to drink, she thinks. But she tries it, and it tastes normal. She gulps it down for a good minute, gorging herself, then hands it off to her sister.

"I'm going to dial the operator and tell her it's an emergency. That I'm a minor and I'm stranded and I don't have any money and I have to make a call and get help."

In other words, exactly what she's so carefully hidden from everyone but Jen since this journey began.

She doesn't wait for an answer. Just marches to the phone and follows the instructions for dialing the operator.

"Hello?" she says. "Operator? I have to find a number and I have to make a call and I can't pay for it. I'm only sixteen, and I'm out here with my twelve-year-old sister and our mother is dead and I have to call my"—a quick flinch, as she reminds herself to lie—"father and he'll come pick us up. I don't have any money to put into the phone, but it's an emergency, OK? We're in trouble."

Humiliatingly, in the middle of the last sentence, she starts to cry. Because she's not lying. It hits her as she hears the words come out of her mouth. Teddy is not their father. But everything else is true.

"I need to call Ralph Martin Construction in Tulare, California."

The operator doesn't even connect her with directory assistance. Just gets hold of the number somehow. Even dials it for her. And it must not be collect, either, because Carly doesn't have to give her name.

Next thing she knows, she's talking to Ralph. Just like that. It makes her stop crying. She feels thoroughly rescued.

"Ralph. It's me, Carly. Is Teddy there?"

A long silence. Too long.

"Jocelyn's kid?"

"Yeah, Ralph, it's me. Can I talk to Teddy? It's really important."

"Honey, Teddy doesn't work here now."

"Where does he work?"

"I don't rightly know, hon. He just up and left. Couple months after your mom moved you guys to New Mexico. Said he couldn't stay in this town another minute."

"Did he say where he was going? Think hard, Ralph. Please. Really, please. This is really, really important."

Ralph doesn't think hard.

"Not to me. He didn't say a thing to me. But let me ask Jud. Teddy was pretty good friends with Jud. Can you hold a minute?"

"I think so. I'm on a pay phone."

"I'll be as fast as I can."

Carly chews on her thumb while she's waiting. Not her thumbnail, but the whole thumb. She watches Jen, who's staring in fascination at something in the window of the gas station convenience store. As if she's reading something written there.

Ralph's voice makes her jump.

"You there, Carly?"

"Yeah, Ralph. I'm here."

"Jud says Teddy went up to Trinidad. But that's all he knows."

"Trinidad? That sounds like another country or something."

"Naw, it's up in Northern California. On the coast. Little town up in the Redwoods. Up by Eureka. Nice up there. You could probably track him down, 'cause I'm thinking there can't be more than a dozen contractors up in that neck of the woods. But Jud doesn't know where he settled."

"Oh," Carly says.

"You good now?"

She begins to cry again. No. She's not good. But there's no point telling Ralph that because Ralph has already given all the help it was ever his to give.

"Yeah, thanks," she says, trying to keep the crying out of her voice.

Then she hangs up fast because she knows she failed.

She walks back to Jen, who's still staring at the window. Jen's looking at a map. There's a map of northeastern Arizona taped to the inside of the window.

"Smart, huh?" Jen says. "I bet this way they don't waste so much time giving directions. Operator wouldn't put you through, would she?"

Jen doesn't look away from the map and see Carly's tears, so maybe Carly has an extra minute to wrestle them back in.

"No," she says, wiping her eyes roughly on her sleeve.

She'll tell Jen. She will. But right now she has no idea how. She needs time to think.

"S'what I thought. I could've told you. Money makes the world go round." She looks over at Carly. Takes in her condition. "Don't get all bent about it. It's no big deal. We'll get some money soon."

"Yeah."

"Now look at this. This'll kill you. This highway's been going partly north. West, yeah. But also north. And if anything, we need to go west and south. We've already gone probably ten or twenty miles out of our way. And now look. This's where we are." Jen points to a roughly drawn red arrow that marks their location. "And in just a couple miles, it turns and goes even farther north. And then it loops around and goes south again. I don't want to go all that way out of our way. I think we need to cut through. You know. On these little roads. We need to get off this highway and go this way again."

The pay phone rings. They both turn and look at it. But neither girl moves. It's unsettling to Carly. As if the phone knows she's here. But she forces her attention back to the map.

"But those roads...they're so..."

They're small and confusing. They're such fine lines on the map. They're probably just little residential dirt roads. Reservation roads. For locals. And not a one goes straight through. Or even straight. It's a maze.

"So...what?"

"I feel like we'll get lost."

The phone is still ringing. It's on what may be its twelfth ring. But Carly hasn't been counting.

"We'll just keep going west," Jen says. "We'll watch the sun."

"Why is that phone ringing?"

"I dunno. Answer it."

"Come on. Let's just go."

But as they're walking out of the gas station lot, it hits her that maybe Ralph or Jud is calling her back. Maybe they know more after all. Maybe they found out, right after she called, that somebody else knew more.

"I'm gonna get that," she says.

She grabs it up but doesn't say hello. It feels too volatile to say hello.

"Are you there?" she hears. "Is somebody there?"

It's not Ralph. It's the operator. Her belly ices over with panic. "Yeah..."

"Did you get the help you needed, honey, or should I call somebody for you?"

"No!" she shouts. Way too loud and defensive. Badly played. She just gave away a lot. "No, we're fine now. He's gonna come pick us up."

But just as she says it, it hits her that maybe the operator stayed on the line the whole time she was talking to Ralph.

"Honey, do you and your sister have someplace safe to go right now?"

Carly slams the phone down.

"Come on," she tells Jen. "We're going. Fast."

"Why? What?"

"The operator's going to call somebody to come help us. We're going to do just what you said. First road goes off to the left, we'll take it. Get as far away from the highway as we can."

"Maybe—" Jen begins.

Carly doesn't let her finish. She can't afford to. She can feel where this is headed. She grabs Jen by the sleeve, and they set off down the road double-time.

"We didn't come all this way to get picked up by child services," Carly says as they nearly jog. "If we're gonna get put in different foster homes or something, we could've just sat where we were and waited for them to come and get us. We wouldn't have had to go through all this. We didn't go through all this for nothing."

Jen never answers.

A road appears to their left. They have no idea what road it is or where it goes.

They take it.

By sundown they could be anywhere. They're headed for the setting sun, but then the road keeps curving. They could be going around in a circle for all they know.

They're in a different sort of neighborhood now. Reservation residential. A fence made of old discarded tires. Squat stone houses with three or four pickup trucks out front, stone mesas towering behind. Tiny wood or stone shacks with old motor homes or trailers parked nearby, often more than one, like inexpensive housing compounds. And though they don't see a soul close-up—just plumes of dirt rising from tires on the next road over, or people sitting outside too far away for Carly to confirm her theory in their eyes—she's nursing the distinct impression that they don't belong here. They are outsiders in this place. She can feel it.

"Maybe just cut straight through," Jen says.

They try that. But it's brushy. Hard going. And Carly keeps getting a bad feeling they're on private property. "Maybe we could sleep there," Jen says, pointing.

There's an old yellow school bus, sitting mostly down in a gulley. No tires. No windshield. No grill.

It's cold. And they want someplace sheltered to sleep. They haven't said so out loud. They haven't needed to. It's just a thing that's there.

"Maybe," Carly says.

Because it's cold, but also because it's more important than ever that they sleep somewhere. Because they haven't eaten in over twenty-four hours. And Carly is running out of steam. The walking is hard with no road. And she's upset all the way through her insides, and that's sapped what little strength she had to begin with. But something bothers her about the school bus. It has towels or sheets or something over the back windows.

"I think maybe somebody lives there."

"How could somebody live there?"

"Same reason we're willing to sleep there, I guess."

"Let's at least go see."

"But if there's somebody in there…"

"Let's just go a little closer."

Carly tries to angle around toward the front of the bus so they can look through the missing windshield. But it's hard to see. Especially in the dusky light. They creep a little closer.

"There's a sheet across it on the inside, too. Somebody must be in there."

"I'm just going to ask."

"Don't, Jen."

But Jen cups her hands around her mouth and calls out, "Anybody there?"

A dog bursts out of nowhere and charges, teeth bared, barking and snarling at the same time. Filthy white with brown patches and a bib stained rusty red. Not huge but big enough. Carly can see his teeth flash in the fading light.

She turns and tries to run but immediately catches her foot and falls flat, scraping her palms and face on the gravelly dirt. She covers her head with her arms and waits to be savaged, praying Jen got away. But though she can still hear the dog's fury, it's not getting any closer.

In time she sits up and sees that Jen is standing her ground, holding one hand out in a stop sign for the dog. Talking to it.

"I'm going," she says. "You don't move." She takes a step backward, never breaking eye contact. The dog moves in a step, snarling and barking. "Ho!" Jen shouts and holds the hand out again. The dog stops moving but does not stop howling with rage and flashing its teeth.

Go help her, Carly thinks, but she's frozen. She just sits there in the dirt, watching Jen hold the dog at bay as she slowly backs away. To her humiliation, she thinks, Who's the grown-up now?

A big male voice breaks the dusk. "Chua! Shut up and get in here!"

Silence.

The dog shrinks, turns, slinks back toward the school bus.

They run all the way back to the dirt road.

By the time they manage to get there, it's nearly full-on dark, and Carly can't stop crying. Literally can't stop.

"It's OK," Jen says. "It's fine. I'm OK. We're both fine."

But these tears are coming out. There is no reasoning with these tears. There is no logic to which they'll respond.

Nearly an hour after sundown, picking their way along in the dark, they pass a property they can tell is deserted. Because it would be physically impossible to live there. The house is in pieces, its own roof having caved in on it and brought it down. In the overgrown yard is a turquoise Pontiac from the forties or fifties. A big old boat with flat tires and one cracked window.

"We could sleep in there," Jen says. "Carly, you can stop crying now. Are you ever going to stop crying?"

"We could look."

But those are just words. She can't bring herself to go any closer.

Jen marches over and peers inside, then motions for Carly to come.

"It's perfect," Jen says. "Great big bench seats front and back."

Jen opens the back door, and the metal of the body and door grind together, then snaps free with a report like a gunshot.

Carly jumps the proverbial mile. But then she steadies herself and approaches the car.

Jen is already bedded down on the backseat, the door wide open for Carly.

She tries to open the front door, but it's locked, or rusted shut, so she climbs over Jen into the front and curls in on herself, shivering and letting go. Crying as if the crying she's been doing up until now was nothing. A mild intro.

"I'm worried about you," Jen says.

"I just need some sleep."

But she thinks she won't get much. She's cold, she's too upset, and she has a spring poking into her side.

She's wrong. She sleeps.

ARIZONA

May 13

Sun pours through the dusty windshield onto Carly's face. A door has opened on the car, waking her.

It must be late. The sun is nearly overhead. Still her teeth chatter.

Shooting pangs of emptiness radiate from her stomach. Her mouth is cotton dry. She winces as she opens her eyes.

On the passenger side floor of the old Pontiac, on a surprisingly well-preserved rubber mat protecting the faded carpet, is a coiled rattlesnake, apparently fast asleep.

Carly pulls back in slow motion and eases over the seat and into the back, expecting to land on Jen. But the backseat is empty, the back door wide open. She can feel the cool air of the desert morning. It feels colder inside the car than out.

She bolts out of the car, vaguely aware of the clanging of bells. Tinny bells. She slams the door fast.

She looks back through the window at the rattlesnake. It hasn't stirred.

"Hey, Carly!" she hears. "Come and look at this."

Jen is standing in the dirt road, completely surrounded by sheep. White sheep with big woolly bodies and skinny legs and elongated, droopy ears. Well over a hundred of them, moving along the road like a sheep river, parting to flow around Jen Island. About every fifth sheep is wearing a bell around its neck.

Now and then part of the procession leaps or bolts or turns suddenly, and then Carly sees they're being herded from behind by a dog. A yellow dog with bizarre yellow eyes. She looks around for the person who goes with the sheep, but there's no person. Only the dog.

When the dog pulls level with them, he stops cold, puts his head down, and barks at them. But not as viciously as the last dog. More bitter complaint and less flat-out assault.

"Why are Navajo dogs so mean?" she asks Jen.

"They're not. They're just doing their job."

The dog looks to his sheep and sees they're too far ahead. He abandons his complaint with the girls and runs to catch up.

"You're not gonna believe this," Jen says. "There were mice in that backseat with me. Three of them. Either that or I saw the same mouse three times."

"I believe it."

"Bet you didn't have a mouse up front with you."

"That's true," Carly says. "I didn't have a mouse."

They set off walking down the road together. Carly's heels hurt, and she feels like she might be about to black out. But she doesn't say so. She doesn't even limp.

Jen says, "Remember when we were at that gas station yesterday?"

Carly feels a lurching in her stomach, like something trying to come up. As if there were something in there to lose.

"Yeah…"

"Remember that sign on the door?"

Carly has no idea where this is going.

The sheep are still clanking along in front of them down the road, and now and then the yellow dog stops, turns, and shoots them a disapproving look.

"What about it?"

"It said it was May twelfth. But didn't it also say a day of the week?"

Carly suspects she knows where this is headed now. And she doesn't want to go there. More precisely, she doesn't want Jen to go there.

"I don't remember," she says, which is a lie.

"Was it Thursday?"

"I don't remember."

"Because if it was Thursday the twelfth, then this is—"

"Right. I know. Friday the thirteenth. But I don't think it said Thursday. And even if it did, there's nothing we can do about it anyway."

"Maybe we should go back to that car."

"No!" Carly shouts, too harshly, remembering the snake.

"We'd be safer there."

"Jen. It's just a dumb superstition."

"But it can't hurt to be safe."

"Can't hurt? To spend the whole day without food or water?"

"Oh," Jen says. "Right."

Carly notices Jen chewing on her lower lip.

About half a mile later, Jen says, "Where're we supposed to get food and water out here, anyway?"

"Good question."

"Isn't it weird that I didn't think of that day-of-the-week thing the minute I read the sign?"

"Not really," Carly says.

But it is. It's very weird. For Jen.

"Normally I'd be all over that, right away."

"This is not normally, though," Carly says.

Carly's arms hurt so bad they feel like they might be about to drop off at the shoulders. And maybe that would be better. Maybe that would hurt less.

They're walking into the low afternoon sun, holding their spare shirts over their heads—holding them out in front, like the visor of a hat—to keep the sun off their faces.

Jen has a line of dried blisters across her forehead and over the bridge of her nose, cheekbone to cheekbone. Carly can only imagine what her own face must look like. Her lips are agonizingly chapped and split, and licking them only makes it worse. Last time she opened her mouth to talk, it made them bleed.

But a couple of good things can be said about this walk, down this road, on this afternoon. The road is straight. And it points west. Right into the slanting sun.

On their left is a rock face, but it doesn't provide any shade because it's on the south side. On their right are some homesteads, maybe four or five to a mile. Off in the distance behind that is a long mesa, the facing side horizontally striped and whittled into what looks like wavy, uneven columns. Thick on the bottom and tapering as they go up.

Jen stumbles. Catches herself.

"I can't go much farther," she says.

Carly can't, either.

But she says, "Just a little, then."

Just until they come across some kind of option, though Carly can't imagine what option that might be.

"Oh, shit," Jen says.

"What?"

"Look."

"*What?*" But she thinks she sees.

"This road just ends."

"No, it doesn't."

"Yes, it does. Look. It ends right up there."

"I don't think so," Carly says.

But she already knows Jen is right. She just doesn't want her to be. She wants to fight the truthfulness of that observation. Fight it so vigilantly that it will give up and stop being the truth.

They reach the end of the road. It's still true.

They stand in the wide dirt turnaround and look west. Going cross-country looks all but impossible. It's too brushy and full of long gashes where the earth has cracked open into deep gullies with sheer sides. On a good day, it might be only barely navigable. In the shape they're in, it might as well be a fifty-foot brick wall.

Jen sways wildly, and Carly catches her before she falls right over onto her face in the dirt.

"Whoa," Jen says. "Got a little dizzy there."

Carly walks them both over to the rock face and clears away pebbles with her boot, making them a spot to sit down. She helps Jen down. They sit with their backs up against stone.

They're still in the sun. There's no way to get out of the sun.

They drape the spare shirts over the left sides of their heads.

Across the road from them is a tiny, modest brick house with a few dilapidated outbuildings, and a tall metal windmill with what looks like the fan from an old car or truck, spinning squeakily in the light breeze. And a pink trailer. An old, bubble-shaped trailer in bright hot pink, with a horizontal white stripe. It seems to have no tires or suspension. The body of it sits right on the dirt. The brightness of the pink looks absurd against the earth tones and man-made drabness all around it.

There's an old truck parked under an open corrugated carport. Somebody must be home. Too bad. Otherwise she'd look for a hose. Even take a chance on a dog at this point.

Neither girl speaks for a long time. Maybe half an hour. Maybe only two or three minutes.

Carly watches chickens scratch around in the yard. A few dozen of them. And there's a skinny baby goat tormenting a tabby cat. Bouncing around as if trying to entice the cat to play. All it gets him is one of those big Halloween-cat hisses, with the fully arched back and raised hackles.

"You see that?" she says to Jen.

"Yeah," Jen says flatly.

It rattles Carly, deeply, that reply. Because it means Jen sees but doesn't care. Doesn't find it delightful. Or funny. And that's a very bad sign.

They don't talk for a while longer.

Then Jen speaks, startling Carly.

"In case we don't get out of here, there's something I need to tell you."

"Stop," Carly says, pressing a hand gently over Jen's mouth. "We're getting out of here. We're not going to die here."

Then she wishes she hadn't used the word *die*.

She takes her hand back.

"Your lip is bleeding," Jen says. "People die when they don't eat or drink."

"But we won't."

"How do you figure?"

"If I thought we were gonna die, we'd just knock on the door of that little house and throw ourselves at the people's mercy, and they'd call the cops to come get us, and we'd get locked up into the child protective system. But we wouldn't die."

Long silence.

Then Jen says, "I think maybe it's time."

"No."

"What, then?"

"I'll think of something," Carly says.

It's meant to end the conversation. It doesn't.

"Maybe we could knock on the door and tell the people the truth and say we're desperate and we need a glass of water and some food, and maybe we can trust them not to turn us in."

"I don't trust anybody," Carly says. "Except Teddy. I trust Teddy completely."

A silence that feels different from all the other silences.

"You shouldn't trust anybody completely," Jen says.

"Why not?"

"They're still just people. They can still let you down."

"Teddy never let me down."

"I can't walk anymore."

"I know. We'll just sleep right here."

"No. I mean I can't walk anymore."

Carly pulls in a few deep breaths and lets them out again. Carefully. Care is so important now.

"You'll feel better when we've had something to eat. I know you feel that way now. But we're just hungry. We'll get a second wind."

But, oddly, Carly doesn't feel hungry anymore. Empty. Shaky. Scraped out. Less than real. But it's almost as though she's moved beyond hunger.

"And where are we supposed to get something to eat?"

"Right there," Carly says.

She doesn't know it until the exact moment she says it.

She points across the road.

"What? The chickens?"

"Yeah. The chickens."

"I'd rather die than kill a chicken and eat it raw."

"That wasn't what I meant. Chickens lay eggs, right?"

"Can't argue with that."

"So when it gets dark, I'll go over and get some of the eggs."

"Get? You mean steal?"

"We need them."

"There's no address, Carly. This road doesn't have a name. The house doesn't have a number. And you don't know what the eggs cost. So it's over our line. It's not honest."

"It's life or death."

"How would we cook them?"

"We couldn't. We'd have to eat them raw."

"I might vomit."

"You could just swallow them whole, really fast."

"Maybe. But—"

"Jen, eggs only cost around three dollars a dozen. That's only... like..."

"Twenty-five cents each," Jen says.

"So if we have two each, that's only a dollar."

"Maybe a dollar is a lot to those people."

"But chickens probably don't lay the same number of eggs every day anyway. Maybe some days they lay less. So four eggs...it's just like a day when they laid less. It's a good plan, Jen. It'll work. When it's dark, I'll go over there."

"I'm going with you."

"You don't have to."

"Yes, I do have to. There might be a dog. You're no good with dogs."

"OK. Fine. Come with me. We'll get two eggs each and swallow them, and then in the morning we'll walk straight through west and find the highway again. I think it's close. We'll find a way to walk around those cracks. Somehow. Or jump over them. And then maybe when we get to the highway and know where we are again, maybe we can find a place to hole up for a few days. You know. Really rest up. And use the phone more. It's a good plan. It'll work."

"Not if it's Friday the thirteenth, it won't."

"It's not Friday the thirteenth. I think that sign said Tuesday. Tuesday the twelfth."

They fall silent again.

Carly watches the young goat pick his way back to a dozen adult goats grazing on scrubby grass in a corral. He squeezes between the rails and finds his mother. He butts underneath her belly like he wants to nurse. It makes Carly wonder if she could figure out how to milk a goat. If it's even safe to approach one.

She lifts the shirt off her face and looks west, trying to judge how long before the sun goes down. Looks like another two hours of light baking at least.

She leans back again, closing her eyes.

"Jen," she says. Quietly. "I have to tell you something. I have to tell you I'm really sorry I've been extra grumpy with you lately. It's just that I've been so scared."

She waits for a time. In case Jen wants to answer. Apparently not.

"And I have to tell you something else, too. I should've told you this before, and I'm sorry. Teddy doesn't live in Tulare anymore. He's up in the redwoods in Northern California. We're gonna have to find a way to call every construction company anywhere near this little town called Trinity. But we'll find him. We will."

She waits. No reply.

She lifts the shirt off Jen's face to see that her little sister has already fallen asleep. Sitting up. Head back against the rocks. Dry mouth open, as if hoping.

Just before sundown, an old Native American woman wanders out of the tiny house. She's tiny, too. Short and round. She waddles slowly around the yard with a bucket, strewing something for the chickens. Some kind of feed.

Carly knows the woman will spot them sitting across the road. But there's nothing she can think to do about that. So she just holds still.

There's a pattern to the old woman's strewing, she realizes. She's leading the chickens along. Dropping a few bits of something good, waiting for them to come get it, then dropping more farther on. Moving toward an outbuilding.

A henhouse, she realizes.

With a sinking in her belly, Carly gets the picture. The chickens are being put away for the night. But maybe that's better, she thinks. Because where will she find their eggs outside in the dark? No, this is OK. This is good. They'll be on their nests all night, with the eggs underneath them.

This will be easy.

Come nightfall, she'll simply break into the henhouse.

The woman turns her head in all directions before locking up the hens. Carly goes cold, waiting for the woman's eyes to stop on them. Waiting to be spotted. It never happens. The woman looks right past them. As if they're not here. Which seems odd.

Then she waddles back into the house.

Just for a moment, Carly plays with the idea that maybe they're not here.

A nearly full moon rises, just one angled edge off round, yellow, and breathtakingly huge at the top of the mesa. Carly can't decide if all that moonlight will be a good thing or not. Makes it easier to see. But also makes it easier to be seen. But it seems she's invisible now. Anyway. So maybe it doesn't even matter.

She's halfway across the woman's yard when something grabs at her shirt. She jumps and lets out a near-silent scream. A mere puff of air when all is said and done.

She whirls around to see Jen at her heels.

"I told you I'm coming with you," Jen whispers.

"Why did you even wake up?"

"'Cause you weren't there. You're always there. Even in my sleep I knew you weren't there."

Carly puts a finger to her lips.

They creep around to the henhouse door, but it's padlocked.

"Shit," Jen hisses.

"We'll find a way."

Bent over and scuffling, they move around the side of the building. Carly examines the windows to see if they can be opened. But they don't even appear to be built that way.

"Look at this," Jen whispers.

She motions Carly to a corner of the henhouse where the wood has rotted away near the dirt line, leaving a space maybe two feet high and a foot and a half wide at the bottom. A triangle of rot. The gap has been patched with chicken wire.

Carly crouches down and examines the wire patch closely. It's attached with those big staples you shoot from a staple gun. She grabs one edge and pulls hard. Three or four staples pop free, and the wire breaks at those that hold firm. She pulls again, and then the wire is attached at one side only. She can peel it back like a door.

"Can you fit through there?" she whispers to Jen.

"Sure. Easy. You can, too. There's lots of room."

Jen sinks to her belly and shimmies through, leaving her backpack outside in the dirt. Then she reaches a hand out to Carly.

Carly strips off her pack and falls to her belly, shivering at the thought of snakes. She inches through the space, but halfway in her jeans get hung up on the wire. She has to shift into reverse and move completely out again, then bend the wire much farther back, out of her way.

Her hips just barely make it through the rot triangle. Jen has to grab hold of her hands and pull while she turns mostly sideways. Now they're both inside, but Carly doesn't like the feeling one bit because there's no fast escape.

She looks around.

The hens are dozing in straw nests in two layers, the lower layer on the hard-packed dirt floor, the second on a shelf at waist level. Their eyes are closed, heads drooped downward. They either don't know they're being invaded or they don't care.

The big yellow moon shines strong through the windows, bathing the room in light. Nearly as strong as daylight, but seemingly in black and white, like the negative of an old photo. All this light's not good, she thinks. She motions to Jen to get down, where they can't be seen through the windows.

She crawls on her hands and knees to the first nest and reaches under the bird's warm, feathery belly. The hen squawks a sharp complaint.

"Shhhh," Carly says.

There's no egg.

She crawls to four more nests. The hens only scold in quiet clucks. Then she finds one. An egg! She wraps her hand around it and pulls it free. Looks at it in the moonlight. It's brown and medium size. It's the most beautiful thing she can remember seeing. It looks like salvation.

"I got one," she hisses to Jen.

"I got one, too," Jen whispers back. "But it's really little." Jen examines the little egg in her palm. "It's sort of light green. Is that normal? Or does that mean it's bad?"

"Just the color of the shell, I think. Hurry up. Two more, and then let's get out of here."

She wonders briefly how they'll shimmy through the rotten triangle without breaking the eggs. Maybe they should eat them before they go.

A loud, metallic click nearly stops her heart.

The henhouse door swings open with a spooky creak. Carly jumps up and spins around, and then she's staring down the muzzle of a shotgun. On the other side of the weapon is the old native woman.

The old woman's spotted brown hand is so clear in a beam of moonlight, strong and unbent as she chambers a round with a grave, deadly "shuck-shuck" sound. It sounds like death. Like the last sound you hear before dying.

Jen lets out a sound, halfway between sucking in her breath and screaming, and the woman spins and turns the gun on Jen. As if she hadn't known Jen was there until Jen gasped.

"Who goes there?" she asks. Her voice is accented. Strong for a woman her age. "Name yourself! Stand closer together!"

Jen runs to Carly so fast that she slams into her, nearly knocking her down.

"That Fred Na'akabayo's boys?"

Carly's heart is pounding so hard she thinks it might kill her. Literally. Maybe it'll just break and stop. She opens her mouth, but she's too scared to speak. The first sound just cracks and comes out a cross between a little squeak and nothing at all.

"Speak up for yourself!" the old woman barks.

She looks like one of her eggs, the brown one. Both in shape and color. Her skin is the exact same color of brown as the egg in Carly's trembling hand. Her fluffy white hair is pulled straight back. Her cheeks are fat and drooping, deep diagonal caverns on either side of her mouth casting shadows in the moonlight. Her eyelids droop down on the outside, so far they must make it hard to see.

"No, ma'am. We're…just…two girls. Just passing through."

"Should of known," the old woman says. "Even Fred's rotten boys ain't rotten enough for this. They got more respect than to come in my henhouse at night. You're Anglo, ain't you? Sound Anglo."

"Anglo?"

"White."

"Yes, ma'am. We're white."

"Well, don't that just figure. Got some neighbors think there ain't no such thing as a good Anglo, and here I always argue for judgin' 'em one Anglo at a time. That's what I get for bein' such a lib'ral thinker. One thing I can say for every Anglo I ever met— they got no respect. Don't respect their world. Don't respect each other. And they sure as hell don't respect no Wakapi."

Carly breathes, disjointed, yet sure now that she and Jen are not about to die. She knows it's bad. But not how bad. But she knows it's not death. Meanwhile she wonders why she had to tell the woman, in all this moonlight, that they are white. And not boys.

"Wakapi," Carly says. "I thought this was Navajo reservation."

"It was, but now it ain't. Navajo Nation goes all around Hopi and Wakapi like a donut, but with two donut holes. So whatever direction you come from, you was on Navajo land. But now you ain't. Now you're on my land. Now you're in the private henhouse of Delores Watakobie, where you got no earthly right to be. I don't take no truck with Anglos, but I don't need 'em, neither. I sure's hell don't need no trouble from 'em. I don't come to your house and take what's yours. I never done nothin' to you or your people. And this's how you pay me back for that respect."

"I'm sorry, ma'am," Carly says. And she means it sincerely.

But Delores Watakobie huffs. "That ain't hard, to be sorry. That don't amount to much."

"We're starving. Literally. Starving. We've been walking fifteen miles or more a day. Sometimes twenty. And we got lost out here, and we didn't have anything to eat or drink, and we didn't want to die."

Delores Watakobie does not lower the shotgun. She continues to sight down the barrel of it as she speaks.

Carly can hear Jen quietly crying beside her.

"Had no choice. That what you're saying?"

"Yes, ma'am. That's what we're saying."

"We? I only hear one of you open your mouth so far."

"That's what we're saying, ma'am," Jen squeaks, sobs evident in her voice.

"You didn't have a choice to knock on my door and say you was hungry and thirsty and near about to die?"

Carly doesn't answer. There's too much to explain in the answer.

"'Cause if you had, here's what I'd of said. I'd of said, 'You girls want two scrambled eggs each with your fry bread? Or can you handle three?' But that ain't the situation we got ourselves in now, is it? That choice is water over the dam now, ain't it?"

"We'll just go now," Carly says, backing one step away.

"No you will not," Delores Watakobie says, raising the muzzle of the shotgun a little higher.

Now Carly starts to cry, too.

Delores says, "You could do me a favor and try not to act like it's so damn mean, me havin' a problem with this."

"We didn't take anything," Carly says, half sobbing. "We each have an egg in our hand, but we'll put them back."

"Yes you will."

Both girls set their eggs carefully on the straw.

"So there's no harm done," Carly says. "Right?"

"Let's do us some supposin'. Shall we? Supposin' I aim this here shotgun at a place right between your eyes and squeeze off a shot.

And supposin' I ain't so good with this gun, except I am and don't you doubt it, but we're just supposin'. And I let the kick raise the shot and all them pieces of buckshot sail clean over your head. No harm done, right? You call the police, but I say I didn't do a thing wrong. 'Cause there's no harm done. Right?"

Carly only swallows hard. Doesn't speak.

"Answer!" Delores barks.

Jen sobs harder.

"No, ma'am. It'd still be attempted murder. But trying to steal eggs isn't as bad as trying to murder."

"Never said it was. But it ain't as good as respect and honest behavior, neither. And nothin' to your credit that you didn't get clean away. That's my good ears alone. None of your own doin'."

Jen pipes up for the first time, at least voluntarily. "Carly is real honest," she says. "She keeps a book with anything we took in it and how much it costs and the address to send the money to as soon as we can."

"That a fact?" Delores says. "And where was you gonna send my egg money? What's my address?"

By the time the old woman finishes these questions, Jen has deflated into a squat. But the old woman keeps speaking to a spot above her head. She never lowers her gaze to where Jen is hovering now.

Something breaks through in Carly's mind. Things makes sense now. Delores Watakobie can't see. Or can't see much.

Carly raises her arms, slowly, silently, and waves them around in big sweeping arcs above her head.

"Uh-huh," Delores says. "That's what I thought. Plus, bet you ruined my chicken wire patch. Didn't you? Bet you bent it or tore it off to get through, 'cause there ain't no other place to get through. And now the coyotes'll come 'n get my hens, at least till I can get Alvin or Virginia to come patch it up for me, and I could lose half my hens before the sunrise. And another thing, little missy. I may not see so good, but I can see good enough to see you wavin' your arms around like a dang fool."

Carly sinks to the hard-packed dirt floor. Thinking, It's over. She doesn't know exactly what "It's over" will look like in this case. But she knows it's true.

"What're you gonna do with us?" she asks the old woman.

"What do you think I should do with you?"

"Let us go?"

"Not on the list."

"What's on the list?"

"Keep you here till morning and then turn you over to the tribal police, or keep you here a few days and make you work it off."

"We'll work!" Jen shouts. Hopefully.

"Make that a week."

"A week!" Carly says bitterly. "That's too long. We didn't do enough harm to be here working for a week!"

"Take it or leave it," Delores Watakobie says.

PART TWO

Seems So Long Ago

TULARE

December 17

Jen walked into Carly's bedroom with a history textbook, pushed a pile of Carly's clothes off the corner chair and onto the rug, and plunked herself down. It was a thing out of place and then some.

Carly glared for a time, thinking that would be enough. But Jen never bothered to look up.

Carly cleared her throat with exaggerated volume.

Nothing.

"Excuse me…"

Jen looked up, but not all the way. Not enough to actually break eye contact with the text of her book and transfer that contact to Carly. "Yeah?"

"What are you doing?"

"Reading."

"Why in my room?"

"Teddy's putting up the Christmas lights."

"And that's supposed to explain it how?"

"Right outside my bedroom window."

"So?"

"So…it's very…distracting."

"Don't look."

"He keeps talking to me."

"Poor baby."

"He's trying to tell me all those same corny jokes again."

"I like his jokes."

"Nobody likes his jokes. Besides, I'm trying to study for my history test."

"It's Christmas vacation."

"Not forever, it isn't. And not everybody puts everything off to the last minute. Like *you* do, Carly."

"Why not study downstairs?"

"This was closer."

"Right. It's also mine. That's why we call it my room."

"Why does he have to put, like, ninety percent of the decorations right outside my bedroom window?"

"Um. Maybe because your window faces the street? Where people will actually see them? And my room faces a vacant lot? Where nobody will see them?"

"You want me to go downstairs? Fine. I'll go."

But Jen didn't move.

"No, never mind. It's OK. I want to go talk to Teddy anyway."

Teddy was on a ladder just outside the window. He didn't see Carly come in because he was looking down, his head lowered, untangling a string of colored lights. It seemed to Carly that the untangling would be better done on the grass at the bottom of the ladder. But that was Teddy. He did things the most direct way. Not always the easiest or safest.

A half-drunk brown bottle of beer rested on the sill of Jen's open window.

Carly walked closer, noticing the beginnings of a small, round bald spot near the back of the top of Teddy's scalp. His hair was always so shaggy and long that the spot had never been noticeable before. Besides, he was tall. How was Carly supposed to see the top of his head?

"You need a haircut," she said.

Teddy jumped a mile and grabbed the ladder with both hands, dropping the tangled mass of lights.

"Geez Louise, kiddo! You trying to kill me?"

"Sorry. Didn't know you'd be so jumpy."

"I thought there was nobody in there. Where's Jen? She was here a minute ago."

"She bailed. She's studying her history in my room. She says you were distracting her."

"I was telling her some jokes."

"Jen hates jokes."

"It was my best material."

"That explains why she left, all right."

Teddy looked right into her face. Carly examined the little crinkly laugh lines at the corners of his eyes. The way they deepened when he was amused.

"You're getting to be more like your mother every day. And I don't mean that in a good way. Talk about a chip off the old block..."

"And I'm telling her you called her an *old* block."

"Only if you want to see me speed-pack my bags."

And, on that line, nothing was funny anymore. A couple of months ago, it might have been funny. But since Carly's mom had been working longer hours, staying out late, acting like she had better things to do than Teddy...hanging out with that guy...

"I don't want you to go, Teddy," Carly said, shifting the whole energy of the conversation.

"I was kidding. It was a joke." Again with the broad smile, the laugh lines.

"Right. I knew that."

"I'm going down for my lights."

Carly walked to the window and watched him climb down. Watched the way the smile faded from his face the minute he thought no one was watching.

She waited, expecting him to untangle the lights before climbing the ladder again. He didn't. He just threw them over his shoulder and marched back up.

"You didn't forget about my driving lesson. Right?"

"Driving lesson. No. Did not forget. Why do you think I'm already drinking so early in the afternoon? Getting ready for your driving lesson."

"So...today?"

Before he could even answer, Jen shouted in from the other room. From Carly's room.

"Not today!"

"Why not?" Carly shouted back.

"Because I have that soccer game."

"Oh," Teddy said. "That's true. I have to take Jen to her soccer game."

"Why is her soccer game more important than my driving lesson?"

"Because soccer games have dates and times. Soccer players have to show up when all the other soccer players show up. Driving lessons are anytime."

"True," Carly said, more than a little resentfulness bleeding through in her tone. True, but it didn't kill the feeling that Jen was always the priority in this house. "But you shouldn't drive her. Because you already started drinking."

"One beer."

"Three."

There had been two more empty bottles down on the kitchen table. Carly had recycled them for him.

"I bow to the beer counter," Teddy said with a sweeping gesture of one arm. Christmas lights swung from his hand. Clattered against the siding on the house.

"Let me drive us to the soccer game."

"It'll be dark. You can't drive after dark on a learner's permit."

"Not on the way there, it won't. Let me drive there."

"If your mom says it's OK."

"She won't be home from work yet. She won't even know."

Teddy frowned. Pinched his lips in a weird way. Then he threw her one end of the string of lights. Tossed them right through the open window.

"Here, help me untangle this. OK, fine, you can drive there. But if she finds out, you have to tell her *you* told me you were sure it would be OK with her. And *you* can take the heat from her. I can't take too much more heat from her, Carly. Any more and I'll have to get out of the kitchen."

That cooled the conversation. They untangled the lights without another word spoken.

"Oh. My. God," Jen said, stopping in her tracks in the driveway. "Tell me this isn't happening."

"Sorry," Carly said, slipping behind the wheel of Teddy's car.

The passenger's side door was still hanging wide open, the seat tipped forward to allow Jen to climb in the back. Which Jen was still refusing to do.

"*Teddy...*" Jen whined.

"It'll be fine, Jen. Just get in."

"Great. I have to choose between missing a soccer game or ending my own life."

"You're such a drama queen," Carly said.

It was different when you were behind the wheel. The inside of the car looked different. The words you said to your kid sister sounded different. Everything changed when you got to drive.

"*Teddy...*"

"She's half right, Jen. You *are* a *little bit* of a drama queen. Now are you coming? Or should Carly and I just go to your soccer game and cheer for everybody else on your team?"

"Aren't you the goalie?" Carly asked. "Won't the other team score an awful lot of goals?"

Jen sighed and plunked herself into the backseat with an overblown sigh. "Goalkeeper," she said.

She slammed the seat back into place much harder than necessary.

"No destroying my car," Teddy said.

"Goalkeeper," Carly said. "Right. My point exactly."

"You said goalie."

"Which is short for goalkeeper."

"You don't call them goalies in soccer."

"I'll write that on my hand. That way I can never make such an earth-shattering mistake ever again as long as I live."

Carly started the engine. And all was right with the world.

"Put your left-hand turn signal on," Teddy said. "And look in the side mirror before you pull away from the curb."

"Wait!" Jen shouted. "I have to put my seat belt on. It's all that's standing between me and death."

"I know to put on my signal, Teddy," Carly said. "I know to look in the mirror. You think I wasn't paying attention on my first two lessons?"

"Well, you obviously don't need me," Teddy said. "So I'll just take a nap. Shut up, Jen. Don't say what you were just about to say. It was a joke."

"Hmm," Jen said. "I'll have to remember that. 'Shut up. Don't say what you were just about to say.' I think I'll use that next time you decide to go over your corny joke routines."

Carly shifted into drive and pulled away from the curb. Fairly smoothly.

"Stop sign at the end of the block," Teddy said.

"Right. Because I've only lived on this block for three years. I only walk past that stop sign every day."

"Those jokes are my best material," Teddy said.

When Carly pulled into the parking lot of the middle school, near the athletic field, it was almost dark. But not quite. And a couple of guys from her school were there. Popular guys. Dean Hannish and Jerry DeVries. Which was weird because…well, this was a soccer game for twelve-year-olds. Why would they want to see it? Carly wouldn't have been caught dead at the middle school if it hadn't involved a chance to drive.

Dean Hannish looked at Carly. Looked right in at her. Carly's face immediately went hot, which probably translated to beet red.

Dean waved.

Carly waved back.

She barely knew Dean.

He peeled away from Jerry and walked right in her direction as she settled the car into a parking space.

Carly hit Teddy on the arm, harder than she meant to.

"How do you roll down this window?" she whispered.

Teddy said nothing at all. But it was the look on his face. The hint of a self-satisfied grin. He reached over her and pressed a button, and the window powered down.

"Shut up, Teddy."

"I didn't say a word."

"Dean," Carly said. Too loud. And definitely not smoothly enough. "Hey."

He was more clean-cut than most of the guys Carly found herself crushing on. His hair was short enough to get him into the military. Blond and barely long enough to lie down flat. Which was a minus. But the piercing light-blue eyes were a plus. Along with that huge, blocky jaw.

"I didn't know you drove," Dean said.

It struck Carly for the first time that he was impressed. By her. She casually leaned her arm on the edge of the open window. No words came out of her mouth, though. But maybe he would think she hadn't intended any.

"This your car?"

"Uh…" She might have said yes, if the owner of the car hadn't been two feet away and staring at her with his laugh lines crinkling. "No. It's Teddy's car."

It could have been worse. She could have had to say "my mother's" or "my father's." But Teddy was just Teddy. She didn't even have to say who he was to her. She could have adult friends for all Dean knew. Besides, her mother's car was a dorkmobile. Teddy's car was ten or fifteen years old, but it was a Firebird. Firebirds were always cool, as best Carly could figure. The older they got, the cooler they got.

Dean leaned down and peered across her to Teddy.

"Nice ride, man."

"Thanks."

Just then Jen kicked the back of Teddy's seat, hard, with the bottom of both feet, rocking the whole car.

"Let. Me. Out," Jen said.

"OK, see you in there," Dean said.

He turned and wandered off again.

Carly sat there, watching him walk away.

Next thing she knew, Jen was standing in front of the open driver's window, snapping her fingers in front of Carly's eyes as if to release her from a trance.

"Earth to Carly."

Carly didn't even tell Jen to shut up. She was just happy enough with the moment that she didn't need to.

It was nearly halfway through the game, and Jen hadn't allowed one single goal to get past her.

Now it was Jen's fourth and most dramatic block. The kind that forced her to throw her whole body up into the air and sideways to get in front of the ball. But get in front of it she did.

Teddy leaped to his feet, belting out a chorus of whooping noises.

Jen picked herself up, dusted off her uniform, and glanced over her shoulder uncomfortably. In Teddy's direction.

"What was *that*?" Teddy asked Carly, plunking himself back on the bleacher seat again.

"I think that was Jen's ever-so-tactful way of saying you're embarrassing her."

"You'd think she'd appreciate a little enthusiasm."

"You'd think."

"She's just such a hell of an athlete. I've never seen anything like it."

"Seriously? You never saw Pelé? Or David Beckham?"

"I didn't mean that. I meant for someone her age."

Then Carly felt a tiny but very distinct sting on the back of her ankle. She pulled her foot up reflexively. Rubbed the spot. Then, not knowing what else to do, she put her foot back down again.

Not three seconds later, it happened again. This time on the back of the other calf.

She bent over at the waist and peered under her seat, between tiers of the bleachers. Dean and Jerry and some other boy she didn't know were under there. In the dim. Toward the back. In the shadows created by the bleacher seats, hiding them from the stadium lights. Smoking cigarettes. Dean was winding up to throw another pebble at her.

At first she thought he was being mean, and it twisted into her stomach, the way it did when boys teased her at school. But then he made a hook with his index finger and beckoned her. He was trying to get her attention, she realized. He was trying to get her to come down.

"I'll be right back," she told Teddy.

Teddy gave her another one of those looks. Then he bent down to see what Carly had just seen. He straightened up and gave her the look again.

"Try not to come back pregnant."

"Ha ha."

"That was *not* my best material."

"Which explains why that one was actually funny."

Carly didn't wait for him to answer. She just trotted down the bleacher steps, along the aisle, ducked under, and joined the three boys, nursing an unfamiliar feeling. Like actually being part of something.

"Hey," Dean said.

The other two boys just stared into space. Stared and otherwise pretty much ignored her.

"Hey," Carly said back.

Carly sat with them, cross-legged in the dirt. They formed a sort of ragged circle. Carly heard a sudden cheer come up from the crowd, and she wondered if Jen had committed another act of amazing athleticism.

"Want a smoke?" Dean asked, extending the pack in her direction.

"No, thanks," Carly said. "It just gives me a headache."

Then she realized how incredibly stupid that must have sounded. And how she should have just taken one. Let it burn in her hand. Or, better yet, she should have said she'd just take one hit of Dean's. That would have been…well…better. She couldn't fit the words to how much better it would have been and why. But it would have been more like they knew each other. Maybe almost more like…boyfriend and girlfriend.

Then it dawned on her. It wasn't too late.

"I'll take a hit of yours, though," she said, sounding more confident than she felt. "I won't get a headache from one hit."

Dean smiled. It was a smile she felt in a low place in her gut. Scary but nice.

He held the cigarette in her direction. Their hands touched when she took it from him.

"Thanks," she said. "Don't take this the wrong way, but…what are you doing here?"

"My dad's the coach."

"Seriously? Your dad coaches my kid sister?"

"Which one is your sister?"

"The goalkeeper. Jen."

Imagine if she'd said "goalie." How humiliating would that have been? Every now and then, things worked out.

"Oh. Jen. Yeah. My dad says she's his best player."

"So…you go to all his games?"

The other two boys snickered, and Carly didn't know why. She took a hit off the cigarette. Barely inhaled, so she wouldn't humiliate herself by coughing the smoke up again.

"Naw, I almost never do," Dean said. "But we're trying to get my dad to let us go up to the cabin. So I'm playing the model son."

"Actually," Jerry DeVries said, "we're trying to get Dean's dad *not* to go."

"I don't get it," Carly said.

Another rush of crowd noise. Clapping and cheering. Carly glanced down at the cigarette in the half-light, vaguely surprised to see it still burning in her hand.

"Oh," she said. "Guess you want this back."

"Naw, it's fine," Dean said. "Keep it." He shook another out of the pack and lit it with an expensive-looking silver lighter. "Usually he won't let us go up to the cabin without adult supervision. We're on a crusade to convince him we're mature enough."

He shifted back slightly, which brought his face into better light. Into a slat of stadium lights, filtering in from between the tiers. His eyes locked on her, burning their way in. It lit up that spot in her gut again. A weird mix of excitement and fear.

"You should come," he said. Suddenly and enthusiastically. As if he had only that moment thought of it. But, for some unknown reason, Carly didn't feel that was the case. "You should totally come."

"Not sure if my mom would let me."

"Tell her there'll be parents there."

"I could try."

"It's gonna be great. Three guys and two girls so far. See? We need you to make it perfect. It's up in the Sierras. Not even that far a drive, but it's like another world. It's right by this little lake. It might even be snowing up there. We might need to take my dad's four-wheel drive. Ever seen snow before?"

She had. But not for a long time. Not since her last grandparent died. She never answered the question.

"When?"

"Day after tomorrow. We'll be back the day before Christmas Eve."

"I could ask Teddy. Maybe he'd back me up with my mom. He's really cool."

"Ask him," Dean said. "And then call me. I'm in the book."

Carly sat still a moment longer, not sure if that meant she should go ask Teddy right now. No one said a word.

"OK," she said, pulling to her feet. "I'll go ask him."

It wasn't until she'd picked her way back out into the light from the stadium that Carly realized she was still holding the cigarette high in the crook of her first two fingers. She looked up to see Teddy watching her. She dropped the cigarette into the dirt and ground it under her heel.

She climbed back up to where he was sitting. The crowd exploded into shrieking and applause again, nearly deafening her. She craned her neck to see what Jen, or Jen's team, had done. But it was too late. The play was over.

She plunked herself down next to Teddy. So close that her hip accidentally bumped up against his.

"I didn't know you smoked," he said.

"I don't."

He leaned in close and sniffed her breath but said nothing.

She opened her mouth to ask him about the lake, the cabin, then lost her nerve. She would seem too anxious, it would seem too important, if she asked him now. She should wait until later and bring it up almost as an afterthought. As if it were so minor she'd let it slip her mind.

As if it were nothing, really. Almost nothing at all.

"I call shotgun!" Jen shouted on the way to the car.

And it was already too late.

Carly turned her best pleading gaze on Teddy. "Seriously? You're going to make me sit in the back?"

"Come on. You drove on the way here. Besides. She called it."

He opened the driver's side door and folded the seat forward. Carly climbed in with a theatrical sigh.

"I was good," Jen said, fastening her seat belt.

"You were amazing," Teddy said.

Carly only stared out the window as the car pulled out of the dirt lot. She saw Dean on the corner and ducked her head down. So he wouldn't see her sitting in the back.

"I'm starving," Jen said. "What time is it?"

Teddy looked at his watch. He wore it on his right arm because he was left-handed.

"Little after seven thirty."

"That explains it. Let's stop for pizza," Jen said.

"Nope."

"*Teddy...*"

"I made my world-famous spaghetti and meatballs. Well. I mean...I didn't make the spaghetti yet. But I made the sauce from scratch. And the meatballs. So that's what we're having."

Carly's eyes shifted away from the dark streets and found the back of Teddy's head. Something was coming together in her brain.

"Mom's favorite," she said.

"Yup."

"She'll be bummed she has to work late."

"Maybe she can get away."

Then it all clicked.

"Oh, my God!" Carly said. "I know what day this is. This is your anniversary."

"Of what?" Jen shot back. "They're not married."

"Tell her, Teddy."

"It's nothing."

"It's not nothing. It's the anniversary of when you moved in with us. Two years."

"It's not a big deal."

"It *is* a big deal. It's, like, two or three times longer than any of those other losers lasted. And you're the first one who's not a loser. It's a *very* big deal. Does she know you're making spaghetti and meatballs? With extra Parmesan?"

Carly's mother liked lots of Parmesan.

First no answer. For a long time.

Then Teddy said, "Yeah."

He made the word sound short. Even more so than it normally would.

"We should go by the bar. Tell her to get somebody to cover her shift."

"She'll come home if she can."

"We should go get her."

"Look. Carly. With my back giving me trouble again, and all the work I've missed, she's doing everybody a favor picking up extra shifts. We need the money."

"But—"

"Drop it, Carly."

It made something burn in Carly's stomach and behind her eyes. Teddy almost never snapped at her.

She decided to talk over it.

"You think Mom would let me go up to a cabin on a lake, up in the Sierras, with some friends from school? There'll be parents there."

"Boy-type friends?"

"Both. Besides, what difference does it make? There'll be parents there."

"And what difference does it make if I think she will or not? How does my opinion on the matter help you with her?"

"You could put in a good word for me."

He glanced halfway over his shoulder at her, then back at the road.

"Carly...you're a smart girl. You can't possibly think I can make your mom do anything she doesn't want to do. If I could, we wouldn't be eating spaghetti and meatballs without her tonight."

And that shut down the conversation. And it stayed shut. All the way home.

Carly sat in front of a steaming plate of spaghetti and meatballs. There were flowers on the table, clusters of little miniature pink roses and a spray of fuchsia, both from their front yard. And two long white candles in their late grandmother's antique silver candleholders. It struck Carly as almost unbearably sad.

Jen plunked down hard into her chair and grabbed up her fork. Without even waiting for Teddy, who was serving up his own dinner at the stove.

"I am *so* starved," Jen said.

Then she stuffed her mouth with the equivalent of about three bites' worth.

"Well, don't wait for me," Teddy said. "Just dig right in."

The sarcasm sailed well over Jen's head. She just nodded, her mouth too full to answer.

When she'd managed to swallow, Jen said, "This is better than pizza, Teddy. I'm sorry I gave you a hard time about pizza."

Carly watched Teddy's reaction, the look on his face, nursing an unpleasant and uncomfortable feeling that she had never made Teddy as happy as Jen just had.

She wound spaghetti around her fork and took a bite.

"You're a good cook, Teddy," she said, her mouth still full.

Teddy smiled as he sat down. But it still couldn't hold a candle to what Jen had said. Nothing Carly said ever did.

Carly opened her mouth to say, I can't believe Mom didn't come home for this. She actually almost said that. But she stopped herself just in time. The last thing she wanted was for Teddy to snap at her again.

They ate in silence for what seemed like a long time.

Then Teddy said, "I'd be willing to tell her I met the boy and he seems like a good kid. Even though it's a slight exaggeration."

Carly looked up at him, but his eyes remained trained on his plate.

"You're the best, Teddy," she said. And she had never meant it more sincerely.

"I'm not even in the top forty percent," he said.

They finished dinner in silence, Carly's eyes fastened to the flowers and the candles. An idea formed, almost without Carly needing to think it through. It just sort of bypassed her brain and came together on its own.

By the time she set her fork down, it was fully formed. Definite. Done. There was no getting around it.

"I'm going for a walk," Carly said, jumping to her feet.

Both Teddy and Jen looked up at her. A little strangely. Because Carly wasn't the "I'm going for a walk" type. She waited for one of them to put their thoughts into words. They never did.

Carly grabbed a warm jacket on her way out the door.

It was fifteen blocks from their house to her mom's work.

Only trouble was, she could walk there, but she couldn't go in.

She paused under the neon sign. It was supposed to say Leopard Lounge. But the big *L* and the little *g* were burned out. So it read more like "eopard Loun e."

Carly pressed her fingers to the glass of the front window, forgetting for the moment that her mom would yell at her for doing so. It was her mom who had to clean any stray fingerprints off the glass. In between serving drinks.

Her mom was not serving drinks.

She was sitting at a table with that guy. Wade, his name was.

Carly watched the way they leaned in close to each other. Not completely overt. They weren't hugging and kissing. But there was an intensity about the exchange. Like a short, live wire connected their eyes and faces. Transmitting something impossible to ignore.

Desdemona, the other cocktail waitress, was on duty and serving drinks.

Desdemona looked up and waved at Carly through the window. Carly quickly took her fingertips off the glass.

She stuck her hands in her pockets and waited while Desdemona tapped her mother on the shoulder, breaking the transmission between her and Wade. Carly's mom spun around to see Carly standing at the window.

She did not look pleased.

Carly reflexively took two steps back as her mom stormed toward the door. She looked back in at Wade, whose face looked dark. Wade had a darkness to him, an edge. Like all the guys her mom went for. Except, of course, Teddy. Sweet, sweet Teddy.

Carly's mom burst out into the cool valley night, wearing only a strappy, low-cut sleeveless top.

"Want to tell me what you're doing here?"

She was tall, which could have been part of why Carly found her intimidating. But there was more. If indeed height factored in at all. Her hair was a different color every month. Right now it was a sort of mahogany. Nothing quite like the color of hair a woman might actually grow on her own. Her eyelashes were long and thick, clumping with mascara. She wore a lot of makeup. Too much, Carly thought, but she knew better than to say so out loud.

"Thought you had to work late," Carly said.

It was brave. And she knew it. But it was something Teddy couldn't say. Or anyway, didn't feel he could. So Carly was going to do it for him.

Carly's mom rocked her head back a little. A defiant gesture. She crossed her arms across her impressive chest.

"I'm here," she said.

"But you're not working. Desdemona's working."

"We're both working."

"But you never both work at the same time. Besides. You're not working. You're just sitting there. Flirting with that guy I hate so much."

Carly's mom's hand came up, and Carly flinched and pulled back, expecting a slap. Instead, a long fingernail just pointed at her. Close to her nose.

"You're on thin ice with me, young lady. I'd move along if I were you."

But Carly couldn't stop. She could use more caution, but she couldn't leave things where they were. It was too late for that.

"It's your anniversary."

"Of what? I'm not married."

"It was two years ago today that Teddy moved in with us. Did you know that?"

"That's not really an anniversary."

"It is to him. Did you know that?"

"I'll be home when I can."

"He made your favorite dinner. Spaghetti and meatballs with extra Parmesan. And he picked flowers for the table. And he put white candles in Grandma's silver holders. And then you called and said you had to work. And you're not even working."

"I'm on a break."

If she felt anywhere near as guilty as Carly meant her to, she hid it well.

"Maybe Desdemona would cover for you."

"Thin ice, Carly. You got your nose where only my nose is supposed to be. Now you get on home. And don't ever come back here again when I'm working. Not ever. I don't need a spy in the family. And don't say a word to Ted, or you'll have me to answer to."

Carly just stood a moment, feeling slightly dizzy. Probably a fear reaction brought on by what she was about to do. She was about to say something brave. Something that might get her hit. Or grounded. Or some worse punishment, some torment she didn't even know existed.

Before she could, her mom spun on one high heel and stamped back into the club. Carly watched as she sat down with Wade. She seemed able to pick up right where they'd left off.

Carly had no idea how she could do that. Or why she'd want to.

She walked home, surprised by how much longer each block seemed now.

When Carly let herself into the living room, Teddy and Jen were sitting on the couch together, watching an old black-and-white movie about a mummy. Except Jen wasn't watching. She was fast asleep, tucked under the comfort of Teddy's left arm.

It made Carly feel left out, in a deep place in her gut.

The feeling must have shown on her face because Teddy said, "I've got another one on this side."

He lifted his right arm. Carly dove in and sat under it, feeling him wrap her up in warmth. She didn't even bother to take off her jacket first.

"*The Mummy?*"

"Hey," he said. "This is a classic."

"Whatever you say."

"Where'd you go?"

"I just wanted to take a walk."

"No. Really. Where'd you go?"

"I walked, Teddy."

She'd started to say, "I just walked." But that wasn't true. She did more than *just* walk. But she did walk. So she stuck with that.

"This have something to do with that boy?"

It relieved Carly to hear him guess wrong.

"I didn't see him," she said. Hoping he might think she'd tried.

"Better luck next time."

They sat for a time. Watching the horrible film. How long a time, Carly wouldn't have been able to say. Could have been five or ten minutes, or it could have been half an hour.

Then the front door opened, and Carly's mom came through. Something came up and filled a big hole in Carly's heart, from the inside. Maybe Carly really had made things better. Maybe it really was possible to advocate for what's right. And get it.

The look on her mom's face was hard to read.

She came and stood over them, hands on her hips.

"Don't you three look comfy."

"Because we are," Teddy said. "I hope you're hungry. I made your favorite dinner."

Carly watched the look on her mom's face change. Soften. And Carly didn't think it was about spaghetti and meatballs with extra Parmesan, although that may have been a contributing factor. Carly realized then that her mom had been waiting to see whether Carly had ratted her out.

"You're a sweetheart, Ted," she said. "I'm starved."

"Oh, good. I was worried maybe you ate at work."

"Just nibbled on the French fries all night. But that didn't get me much of anywhere. Carly. Wake up your sister, and you girls go upstairs to bed. If you're not sleepy, you can tuck in and read. Me and my beau have some celebrating to do. Three's a crowd."

Teddy's arm disappeared. So did Teddy.

Carly shook Jen awake, gently, and half held her on her feet all the way up the stairs.

Then she snuck back down and watched from the landing. Just for a minute. Watched through the open kitchen doorway as Teddy poured her mom a glass of red wine. Then he disappeared again. She heard that deep, throaty laugh that Teddy only used when her mom was around. Heard her mom say, "There's no music, you big dope." A minute later they waltzed past the doorway in each other's arms, Teddy humming a tune.

Carly withdrew up the stairs. And slept. Well. For the first time in a long time.

TULARE

December 18

"Absolutely," Carly's mom said. "Absolutely you can."

It didn't feel right. It felt too easy.

They were sitting at the breakfast table. Just the two of them. Jen had ridden her bike to her friend Krista's house, and Teddy wasn't even up yet. Carly's mom held on to her coffee cup as if it contained some life-saving serum for exactly what might be about to kill her. Her face looked ragged and tired without all that makeup.

"Seriously? You're really going to let me go?"

"Oh yeah. Absolutely. Best idea I ever heard. You just keep an eye on the weather reports and give a yell when hell freezes over."

Carly absorbed the news the way she might absorb a slap.

She stood and marched out of the room.

She could think of a dozen things to say, but she couldn't untangle them, one from the other. Besides, it wouldn't do a damn bit of good. Suggesting that her mom was being unfair would not bring about fairness. And it didn't help to be angry. Because Carly's mom could out-angry Carly. She could out-angry anybody. She could bully Teddy, and Teddy was a big, strong grown man.

Carly made her way upstairs, into her room, and slammed the door behind her.

She picked up the phone, then realized that the phone book was downstairs. Rather than risk it, she called directory assistance.

"What city, please?" the operator asked.

"Tulare."

"What listing?"

"Hannish. With two *n*'s. I think. I don't know the first name."

"I have a Dean Hannish Senior on West San Joaquin Avenue."

"That's it. Thanks."

She wrote the number on the inside of her hand in red pen. Her heart thrummed lightly. The ink absorbing into her hand made it feel important, like tattooing a guy's name on her skin. The redness of it made it feel forbidden. It was both of those things and so much more. She didn't know what, specifically, the "more" was. But she was determined to find out.

She dialed the number, and Dean—her Dean, not Dean Senior—picked up on the second ring.

"'Bout time you called, you big asshat," he said, in that place where "hello" would normally have fit.

"Um…"

"Oh. You're not Jerry. Uh-oh. Sorry. Sorry. Especially if you're calling for my mom. Extra sorry."

"No, I'm calling for you."

"Carly?"

"Yeah."

"Hey. Carly. Hey. Glad you called. Wasn't sure if you'd call."

A long, awkward silence.

Then he said, "You coming to the cabin tomorrow?"

"Yes," Carly said. "Absolutely I am."

"Great. We'll leave at eleven. Give or take. We'll swing by and pick you up around eleven."

"No!" she said, far too stridently. Nearly giving it all away. "No, that's fine. I'll come to your house. Your address is in the book, right?"

"You sure you don't want to get picked up? Parents like that."

"Positive."

"Slight problem. You can't come to the house. The only reason my dad's letting us go alone is because he thinks it's all guys. Tell you what. Pick you up in the parking lot behind the middle school."

"OK."

"See you tomorrow."

Carly set the phone back into its cradle. Gently. The way she'd handle live ordnance.

It was pretty simple, really, in her head. One of two things would happen. Teddy would work with her, and for her, persuading her mom to change her mind. Or Carly would take off in the morning, leaving a note. Her mom wouldn't find the note until after work, when Carly would be long gone.

The note could say something like:

After I get home you can punish me for the rest of the history of civilization. But right now, for once in my life, I'm going to be the one who gets chosen.

When Carly came downstairs around lunchtime, Teddy had three friends over. His usual guy friends. Ernie and Paul and Javier. They were playing poker in the kitchen.

Teddy had bowls of tortilla chips and salsa in the middle of the table. Amid the poker chips. Carly stuck her head into the kitchen just in time to watch Paul call a raise and toss a blue poker chip right into the salsa. It splashed. All four guys made audible noises of disgust. Ernie almost stuck his hand in the salsa to retrieve it, but

Teddy yanked the bowl out of the way before that disaster could happen.

As he was carrying it to the sink, he saw Carly over his shoulder.

"Hey, you," he said.

He tossed Paul a dish towel, and Paul set about swiping at the stacks of poker chips to catch the salsa splashes.

Teddy took a fork out of the drawer and fished the poker chip out of the salsa. Rinsed both under the tap.

"At noon?" Carly asked.

"What better time to have chips and salsa than at noon?"

"I meant the poker. Isn't poker sort of like drinking? Don't normal people do it after five?"

Her eyes settled back to the table, where she noted that each of the four men had an open beer going.

"When you're unemployed," Teddy said, "every hour of the day is after five."

All three of the guys nodded. Ernie and Javier clinked the mouths of their beer bottles together in a toast to the sentiment.

Teddy sat back down and rearranged the table so that the tortilla chips and salsa sat between Teddy and Paul. Where they would be safer.

Javier took a cigar out of his pocket and clamped it in his teeth.

Teddy set his cards facedown on the table.

"I will kill you with my bare hands," he said, staring down Javier.

Javier was searching his pockets for a lighter and didn't notice. Finally Paul jabbed him in the ribs.

"Oh. Who? Me?" Javier asked, meeting Teddy's eyes.

"You're the one with the cigar, so, yes. I will kill you with my bare hands if you light that thing in this house. And I won't even have to face legal retribution because my lovely and delicate lady friend will murder me in cold blood the second she walks through the door and smells what you've done."

Carly leaned on the kitchen door frame and tried not to smile. It was fun to watch the men interacting. Especially with her mother playing an offscreen role as the attractive-yet-wicked witch.

"Teddy—" Javier began.

"Get thee to the back porch."

"I don't want to miss any rounds."

"Great," Teddy said. "Nice priorities. It's not worth missing a round, but it's worth signing my death warrant. I'll be sure to come back and haunt you. Now put the stinky thing away."

Javier sighed and slid the still-unlit cigar into his shirt pocket.

"Teddy," Carly said. Suddenly. Surprising even herself.

"Yeah, hon?"

"I need to talk to you about something."

"OK, but it'll have to wait till after the game."

"It's important, though."

"I got real money riding on this game, Carly. You know how little real money I've actually got?"

"I just…Did you talk to Mom about Dean?"

"I'm sorry, hon. Last night was not the right time."

"So…you'll talk to her today?"

"Um…Hmm…Things were better when I made that offer. I'm on thin ice with your mom right now."

Carly just leaned a moment, marveling at how Teddy and her mom could be in trouble again so quickly. Last night they'd been sweethearts, just like the old days. Still, Carly couldn't help but register that her mom's swing back to Teddy was abrupt. Abrupt even for Carly's mom, who only made sudden turns, with no notice or signaling. And if the number of towns and houses Carly had lived in over the past sixteen years was any indication, her mother didn't stay in anything very long.

"You promised me, Teddy," she said. Quietly. No overt emotion. But it was in there. Hiding.

"If I'm on her bad side, it could do you more harm than good, Carly. If she's mad at me, and I say I think you should go, she'll be a hundred times more sure you shouldn't."

That was true, and Carly knew it. Then again, "when hell freezes over" times a hundred might not be all that much worse than the original. Like multiplying zero by anything and still getting zero.

Carly peeled away from the doorway and sat on the big, overstuffed chair by the front window. Looked out at the empty street. Every now and then a car drove by, one of them pumping out that gut-shaking bass from its sound system. Teddy had set up a fake snowman draped with Christmas lights on the lawn. It made her feel like a little kid to stare at it. To like it. To be comforted by it.

Maybe she was just a little kid. She wasn't sure anymore.

She also wasn't sure she was going.

Watching Teddy quake at the very idea of her mother's wrath had shaken her. Wakened her senses. Was she really brave enough to do something her mother had expressly forbidden her to do?

She envisioned her mother marching over to Dean Senior's house to find out where the cabin was located. Or calling the police and having them ask the questions. Dean would never speak to her again, never forgive her. None of them would. Word would travel. No one she went to school with would ever trust her for anything. Here Dean might have finally convinced his dad that they were mature enough to go up there alone. Carly could ruin everything.

She couldn't go. There was no other answer. She just couldn't go.

But she had told Dean she could.

Maybe she could feign illness.

It twisted into her stomach so tightly, so sickeningly, that it occurred to her that she might not have to fake it. Making a fool of herself in front of those three popular boys might be enough to make her sick for real.

Teddy came in about an hour later. Sat on the rug by her chair, arms wrapped around his knees. Looked out the window with her.

Carly listened and realized she couldn't hear Teddy's three friends in the kitchen anymore. Could they really have walked right through the living room and out the front door without her noticing? And why hadn't she noticed when the voices, the slap of the cards, the clinking of the chips stopped? She tried to track where her head had been but came up empty. She literally didn't know.

"Are the guys gone?" she asked, her voice sounding as though it had been in storage for days.

"Yup."

"I didn't hear them go."

"They went out the kitchen door."

"Oh. How'd you do?"

"Bad."

"How much did you lose?"

"Let's just say…everything I had to lose and then some."

"Ow."

"I'm on thin ice with your mom."

"I know. You said that. Those were her words, weren't they? She said that to you, right? Pointed her fingernail at your nose and said, 'You're on thin ice with me, Ted.' Right?"

"Pretty much."

Then they stared out the window for a few moments in silence.

It was right there, right in front of them, the specter of Teddy having to move out. But she refused to make room for it. She refused to shift out of the way and give it a place to sit.

"You like the snowman?" Teddy asked after a while, startling her slightly.

"It's a little on the tacky side."

"Thanks. Knew you'd like it."

"I actually sort of do," she said. "I feel like you're the only one who cares about me."

For a long moment—longer than she would have liked—Carly just listened to the sound of his breathing. Exaggerated, like a series of sighs.

Then he said, "You have no idea how much your mom loves you."

"You're right. I have no idea."

"She'd do anything to protect you. Why do you think she won't let you go? She doesn't want anything bad to happen to you. Her love for you girls is…just…what's the word? Fierce."

"Yeah. Fierce. I feel the fierce. It's a little harder to feel the love."

Another series of sighs.

Teddy levered to his feet.

"I'm going out for a little while. You OK here by yourself?"

"Sure."

She was disappointed, but she didn't say so.

"You going to be around for a while? In case Jen comes home?"

"Yeah. I'll be right here."

She really didn't have the energy or the enthusiasm to be anywhere else.

Jen came bouncing in about five.

Carly was still staring out the window. Well, again. She'd made and eaten a tuna fish sandwich. Gone to the bathroom. Then resumed staring.

"Where's Teddy?" Jen asked, hanging up her jacket.

"Out."

"Where'd he go?"

"He didn't say."

"That's weird. He always says where he's going. Oh, God," Jen added, peering into the kitchen. "It was poker night? I mean, day? They played poker in the middle of the day? How'd he do?"

"Not well."

"Maybe that's why he wouldn't tell you where he was going. Maybe he has to go out and borrow some money. Or steal it. Or do something horrible for somebody. You know. To pay off the gambling debt."

"Would everybody leave Teddy alone?" Carly shouted. She'd set out to say it in a normally irritated tone, then lost control. "Geez, Jen! He's the nicest guy mom ever brought home. You've seen some of the losers she's paraded through here. Teddy is the sweetest guy in the world. And everybody dumps on him for it. I'm sick of it!"

She stared out the window a few seconds more, composing herself. Then she risked a glance at Jen. The kid looked a little shaken.

Carly looked back out the window again.

A minute later Jen appeared behind her chair. Carly felt the hard bone of Jen's chin rest on the top of her head.

"I'm sorry, Carly. I was really mostly kidding."

Carly sighed.

"I know. I'm sorry I got so upset. I'm just in a lousy mood."

"What happened?"

"Nothing. Nothing happened. That's just the problem. Nothing ever happens around here."

Teddy came through the door at six with a pepperoni pizza.

"Your mom's working late again," he said.

Carly never thought, at the time, to ask how he knew. Her mom would have called the house before trying Teddy's cell phone.

And Carly had been sitting ten feet away from the phone all afternoon. If that phone had rung, Carly would have known it better than anyone.

In deep sleep, in a deep dream, Carly was somewhere in the mountains—some mythical and unrealistic mountains—with Dean. She could feel his presence beside her, but the details felt fuzzy and indistinct.

Then she felt his hand on her forehead. Rubbing. Pushing the hair aside and rubbing her warm skin in wide, smooth strokes.

She bolted awake, suddenly knowing it was a real hand, in the real world. In her bed in the middle of the night. She instinctively slapped the hand away. Sat up straight, gasping.

It was only her mom. Carly could see her mom's bright lipstick in the sliver of moonlight that shone though the filmy bedroom curtain.

"Sorry, honey," her mom said. "I didn't think that would startle you. I used to wake you up like that all the time when you were a little girl. You'd wake up real gentle that way. Guess I have to remember you're not a little girl anymore."

Her mom's voice was cigarette-gravelly and deep, even though she hadn't smoked for years.

Carly breathed deeply a few times, then set her head back down on the pillow. Looked up at her mom in the dim light. It seemed weird to have her there. It felt different. Her mom's energy felt like something she'd either never witnessed or had long ago forgotten.

Carly's mom stroked her forehead again, and Carly closed her eyes.

"Know where Ted was from three o'clock today to almost six?"

The question should have made Carly nervous. But the softness in her mom's tone did not allow it.

"No. Where?"

"He was sitting at the restaurant with me. I gave him a free piece of pie, and he just kept nursing the same coffee mug, refill after refill. Probably poured him seven cups of coffee. He might never get to sleep tonight. Hell, he might never get to sleep again. And every time I had a minute in between orders, he'd tell me more reasons why I should think about letting you go. Like he'd remind me how it felt when we were sixteen. Not that we were sixteen together or anything like that. But still. He'd tell me stories of all the crazy sh…stuff…he did, and then he'd ask me about some of the stuff I did that your grandma and granddad—God rest their souls—never found out about. I think he was trying to remind me that kids get into all kinds of…what's the word? Adventures. Half the time it's OK, and the other half the time it's not but they live to tell about it, and probably that's how we learn to grow up."

A brief silence.

"So…" Carly said, barely above a whisper, almost afraid she might jinx it. "Are you letting me go?"

"Ted told me you need to feel like I love you more."

Her voice cracked just a little bit when she said it, and it brought a lump to Carly's throat and tears to the back of her eyes. The only times her mom had ever cried, so far as Carly knew, was when they'd buried Grandma and then, two months later, Granddad.

It had to be a pretty serious thing if your mom was half about to cry.

"I shouldn't have said that," Carly said. "I'm sorry."

"No, it's OK. Don't be sorry. It hurt, but maybe I needed to hear it. I work so hard, two full-time jobs to keep food in our mouths and clothes on our backs. And I work extra so I can say yes to about ten percent of what you girls want, even though it's stuff people can live without. But it's stuff your friends have, and I know how that feels. And I say no to things like the lake 'cause I know what can happen to girls your age, and I want you safe. And I feel like that proves it, you know? Like, why would I do all that if I didn't love my girls more than anything? But then Ted said something that stuck with me. That maybe there's more love in trusting your kid to be OK than in keeping her in a cage so you know for a fact she will be. Guess I'm used to having little kids. Little girls. Just being a plain old momma bear. I'm not so good at the other part yet. The later part. Letting you get older and not need me. Letting you girls go off and look after yourself."

"I'll be really careful and smart if you let me go."

"One condition. If things go a way you don't like…if anything happens you can't handle, call. Right away. I'll come get you, or Ted will, if I'm working."

"There'll be parents there," Carly said, even though she was pretty sure it wouldn't turn out to be true.

"Parents can't be everywhere at once. Just be careful."

Before Carly could even gather herself up to answer, her mom kissed her on the forehead and slid over to the door. Carly could see the shape of her, framed in the light of the hall. It was a good shape. Ask nearly any man who'd ever seen her.

"You really like this guy?" her mom asked.

"I don't really know him all that well. Yet. But he wants to know me. And that's something. Right?"

"If he's a nice guy, then yeah. That's a lot."

"And if he's not?"

"Then…I'll kill him."

She slipped out, closing the door behind her.

CRADLE LAKE, THE HIGH SIERRAS

December 19

Just on the other side of a tiny town with the memorable name of Fish Fork, Dean stopped the SUV at a little store along the forest road up to the cabin. It called itself Ned's Bait & Tackle, announced with neon signs that seemed out of keeping with the gray-white granite mountains and the cone-laden firs. Ned's also loudly announced cold beer and snacks.

Carly glanced over her shoulder at the fishing rods loaded in the back, their long, springy ends sticking out the rear window. But she didn't look for long. Jerry was in the backseat with two girls from her school. They all looked at her as though she wanted something special from them. And as though that something was an imposition, whatever it was. So she straightened out and stared through the windshield again.

She was sitting in front between Dean and that guy she didn't know. But she'd figured out through conversation that his name was Hunter and he was a senior. Not through her own conversation.

She'd done nothing but shut up and listen throughout the hour-and-a-half drive.

"Almost there," Dean said to her. It was only the second time he had addressed her directly. The first time being "Hey" when she first got in at the middle school. "This'll just take a minute."

Dean turned his attention on Hunter, leaning and talking over Carly in a way that made her feel awkward and uneasy.

"Two cases," he said. "Heineken. And three cartons of those night crawlers. Make Ned open the lids and really look at 'em. Make sure they're fat and peppy. He'll sell off the old half-dead ones if you're not paying attention. And…wait…do you have split-shot sinkers?"

"Not many." Hunter always seemed to say as few words as humanly possible.

"Get some, then."

Hunter let himself out with a grunt, leaving Carly with a refreshing sense of owning enough room to exist again.

"Hunter's twenty-one?" Carly asked Dean.

A chorus of snickers rose from the backseat. Carly kicked herself hard. Why did she always say exactly the wrong thing?

"According to his picture identification, yes indeed," Dean replied.

"Ned doesn't look too close, huh?"

Dean polled the backseat for an answer. "What do you say, guys? If you want two cases of beer, how many questions does Ned ask?"

"Depends," Jerry said. "On whether you have enough money for two cases of beer."

It did not turn out to be a quick stop. Apparently no one had anticipated that a car—even a big SUV—containing six humans, the luggage of six humans, two tents, two coolers of food, and enough fishing gear for an army would not also accommodate two cases of beer. Hunter had to borrow a length of rope from Ned and lash them to the roof between the rails of the utility rack.

When they finally got under way again, Dean made a formal announcement.

"Listen up, guys. We have two neighbors up there close enough to see us or hear us, depending on whether we're inside or outside and how loud we are. My dad made it clear he'll check with them. So anything that would get me in trouble should be done quietly. No beer bottles left around. They go back in the cases, and we'll lose them in a dumpster on the way home. Here's the report I want: 'Mr. Hannish, your son is an absolute angel, and his friends are so quiet and respectful. Why, they give young people a good name.' And another thing. If you're a girl, you're not staying at the cabin as far as the neighbors are concerned. You're visiting from a cabin on the other side of the lake. You ruin this for me, you're on my shit list forever."

"Maybe the neighbors won't even be there," Jerry said.

"Christmas vacation? They'll be there."

"Did I tell you we're maybe expecting snow tonight?" Dean asked.

He'd told her. Or rather, he'd told the group at large. Three times.

"That would be kind of cool," Carly said.

They'd been sitting by the lake for over an hour. Carly and Hunter and Dean. But Carly and Dean sat close together, with Hunter a few yards away. The boys were fishing. But not catching.

Everybody else was back at the cabin. Or somewhere.

"They're just not biting this afternoon," Dean said.

He jumped to his feet, set down the fishing pole, and began to take off his flannel shirt. Which struck Carly odd. It was only maybe ten degrees above freezing.

"Wouldn't it be cool if we got snowed in?" Dean pulled off his T-shirt. "We'd have to stay here for Christmas. Till they got around to plowing that road."

Carly stole a glance at his bare chest, then looked away. He was bulkier and more athletically built than she'd realized. It felt exciting and intimidating, both at the same time.

"My mom would freak."

"Naw, it'd be cool. I'd grab those snowshoes out of the shed and walk down to Ned's bait shop and call everybody's parents from the pay phone. And I'd say, 'We're just fine here, but we're stuck until they plow the road. Not our fault. Nothing we can do about the weather.'"

He unzipped his jeans and dropped them. Underneath, he was wearing what could have been boxer shorts, or they could have been swim trunks. Carly couldn't really decide. His thighs were almost hairless—either that or the blond hairs barely showed—and thick and solid, like scaled-down telephone poles. He levered off his shoes and stepped out of the jeans.

Surely he didn't intend to go in. The water must have been cold enough to kill a person.

"What are you doing?" Carly asked, finally.

He grabbed up his fishing pole again.

"See that rock?" Dean pointed with the pole. A domed rock formed a tiny island about thirty yards offshore. "That's in much deeper water. I could probably cast almost to the middle of the lake from there. When it's cold like this, that's where the fish'll be. In the deep water."

Dean took off, running a few dozen crazy steps into the lake. When he got in to about his knees, he dove forward. Disappeared entirely. Then his head and shoulders came up again. He let out the most blood-curdling bellow Carly could ever remember hearing. Horror films included.

"Oh, *shit*, that's cold!"

Carly wondered if the neighbors could hear. Probably not. It was a pretty good walk from the cabin to the lake.

Dean kept swimming.

Carly looked over at Hunter.

"Is that...even..." But then she didn't know where to go with that sentence.

"Sane? Not really."

"I think I was going to say 'safe.'"

"Nope. Not that, either."

"Think he'll be OK?"

"He might be. Or he might get hit with hypothermia before he can even get out to that rock, in which case he'll sink like a boulder and drown."

It was more words than Carly had ever heard Hunter string together. And none of them were spoken with much emotion.

"And another thing," Hunter said. "He's got it exactly backward. When it's hot, and the lake is warm, the fish go into deep water. When it's cold, they stay near the edge, where it's warmer. Gets more sun toward the bottom there, you know?"

"But you weren't catching any at the edge."

Hunter shrugged. "Just 'cause they're there doesn't mean you'll catch 'em. And he knows that. No doubt about it. Dean is insane."

On that note, Dean popped up at the rock and climbed barefoot to the top of its dome.

"Hmm," Hunter said. "He made it. I'm surprised."

Carly watched Dean hold the fishing pole between his knees and rub his own arms briskly. She could see him shuddering even from the shore.

Then he set up to cast. Drew the pole back and then snapped it forward with amazing force, trying to propel the baited hook to the center of the lake. The worm broke free and flew, landing a good twenty feet beyond the spot where the bare hook hit the water.

Hunter let out a derisive laugh. "How many beers you gotta drink before you don't see that coming? And of course he didn't bring any extra bait. No way to carry it. Stupid, stupid fuck."

Dean dove into the water and swam back.

He stepped out of the lake, his skin a cross between gray and blue. He looked around as though disoriented. His teeth would not stop chattering.

"Now we gotta go back," Hunter said. "Now we gotta get you warm. Stupid fuck."

"It's only about five thirty," one of the girls said. Carly didn't know either one by name, and their names had not come up. "And it's pitch dark. That's so weird."

"It's the third-shortest day of the year," Dean told her. "Solstice is day after tomorrow."

Then everybody argued about whether the solstice was the twenty-first or the twenty-second. Except Carly. Carly listened in silence.

They were sitting around a campfire, a few yards downhill from the cabin. It was a spot with a great view of the lake, but it was pitch dark, as the girl had pointed out, and the sky was overcast. So no stars or moon. So no lake view.

Carly was sitting with her back leaned against Dean's chest. They were both wrapped in the same blanket. It felt good. That he would be with her that way. Right in front of everybody. That they were together. And it was no secret.

He had only recently stopped shivering.

Both of the other girls were roasting hot dogs on sticks, then placing them in buns and handing them around. No ketchup, no mustard, no nothing. Just hot dogs and buns. No drinks except beer. Carly had already had one beer, and that felt like enough.

Jerry said, "Hot dogs are OK and all, but not when you had your mouth set for grilled trout."

"Fine," Dean said, pretty much right against Carly's ear. "You go catch some trout, then."

"Forget it," Jerry said. "Did I mention the hot dogs are good?"

Dean fished a pack of cigarettes out of some pocket somewhere—Carly could only feel him shifting around—and offered one to her.

"No, thanks," she said.

"Headache."

"Right."

"Here," Hunter said, and handed her a half-smoked joint in the firelight. Carly hadn't seen it going around or smelled it burning. "This won't give you a headache. Hell, if you got a headache now, this'll fix it."

She accepted it from him. Drew in a long hit of the smoke, which was stronger and richer and more tar-laden than she'd expected. She'd smoked the stuff a couple times before, when she was fourteen. Her half-friend/half-boyfriend Emilio used to have some. Cheap ragweed that didn't taste like much and didn't do much. Just made her hungry for potato chips and ice cream.

She passed it to Dean, who was lighting a cigarette for himself, both hands outside the blanket now. It partly uncovered Carly and made her cold. She missed the warmth immediately.

Warmth was always a hard thing to come by. In any form.

Then he mostly wrapped them up again, just his one hand with the cigarette poking out. Carly watched the tip of the cigarette glow in the dark. She could hear people talking, but the words refused to penetrate. Like she'd lost the ability to either hear or understand. Also the ability to tell hearing and understanding apart.

Then the joint came back around, and she hit it again.

A few seconds later, the top of her head suddenly threatened to come off. Her senses felt heightened, so much so that it startled her, and the physical sensations were unbearable, and it was all too much.

She sat as still as she could, focusing on making it stop. Over and over she thought, How do you turn this off? How do you go back again? But in the undercurrent of her mind, she knew you didn't. It had to wear off on its own. And she was still getting higher.

She opened her mouth to speak, but no words came out.

She struggled out of the blanket and made her way to her feet. The world did not hold still as she did so. The ground did not stay level, and neither did she.

"Hey, hey," Dean said. "Where ya going?"

She heard someone distant say, "Not feeling so good. Gotta go lie down."

A few steps later it dawned on Carly that the someone had been her.

"I'll come with you," he said.

He caught up with her and put his arm, along with the blanket, around her shoulder. Wrapped her up again and supported her as she walked.

That felt better.

"You OK?"

"I need to lie down."

"No problem. I'll show you where we're gonna sleep. There's only one bedroom in the cabin. Guess who gets it?"

They stood before the three steps up to the cabin's back porch. Carly looked at the steps, vaguely unclear as to how one surmounted such an obstacle.

"Who?" she asked.

It was coming on stronger now. And it was way too much.

"Whose dad owns the cabin?"

"Oh," she said. Grateful for a riddle she could solve. "*You* get the bedroom."

"*We* get it," he said. "And everybody else has to fend for themselves."

A few light, dry flakes of snow began to swirl. Carly watched in fascination, wondering how to tell if they were real or if her imagination had created them.

"Ah, cool," Dean said. "Maybe we'll get snowed in."

He walked them up the stairs together. It was easy. It went OK. Carly thought, I have a boyfriend now, to help me do hard things like that. Maybe now everything will be fine.

He walked her into the bedroom, where she slid out of the shared blanket and sat on the edge of the bed. She wasn't sure for how long. But when she turned around, Dean was almost entirely out of his clothes. He had his thumbs in the waistband of those boxers—or swim trunks—and was about to take them down.

"Oh," Carly said. "Wait. Whoa. Whoa."

The words sounded weird to her. She wondered if they sounded weird to Dean. He came and sat on the edge of the bed with her. Put his arm around her. Leaned his mouth close to her ear.

"What? What's wrong?"

It seemed if she willed words, they failed. If she let the faraway Carly speak, that worked better. So she waited. To see what that other Carly would say.

"We don't even know each other," it said. "We said, like, ten sentences to each other before you asked me to come up here. And maybe another ten today..."

She couldn't pull all that into a conclusion. She hoped he would.

A long, long silence. It felt like more time than should have existed in the world. Or, at least, more than ever had before. And she was still getting higher.

"You're right," Dean said.

"I am?"

"Absolutely. You're absolutely right. We're up here for days, and I'm rushing you. Why am I rushing you?"

He took her gently by the shoulders and lifted her to her feet, then pulled back the covers and laid her back on the bed. Still fully dressed.

"Shouldn't I sleep…I don't know…somewhere?"

"Yeah," he said. "You should sleep somewhere. You should sleep here. I won't do anything. Not if you don't want."

He got in beside her and tucked up close behind. Still in just those big shorts. But the top half of him was closer than the bottom half. She felt him shift his bottom half even farther away.

"Yeah, that won't work," he said. "That's not a good idea at all."

He rolled onto his back and draped one big hand casually on her hip.

It struck Carly that it was probably not bedtime yet at all. But here they were. And Dean was asleep—or passed out—in a matter of minutes. She could tell by the rhythm of his breathing.

She lay huddled that way, on her side and close to the edge of the bed, for most of the night. Wide awake. The thin mattress made her hip ache. But she didn't roll over. Because she didn't feel she had a right to displace Dean's hand.

Hours later, when the high had almost worn off, leaving her feeling like herself again, but more jangly and unsettled, she looked over at him in the mostly dark. And she thought, this is what it's like to have a boyfriend. A real one. Not a half one.

Oh, there had been a couple of others. But they didn't seem to know how this being-a-boyfriend thing was supposed to be done.

Dean seemed to know.

CRADLE LAKE, THE HIGH SIERRAS

December 20

Carly woke, surprised she had ever been asleep. She guessed she might have dozed off for maybe forty-five minutes. Dean's hand was gone. She rolled over, easing the pressure on her screaming hip. The mattress was about as comfortable as sleeping on the ground.

Dean was not in bed with her.

"Hey, you," he said.

She sat up. He was standing in the corner. Dressing. In the dark.

"What time's it?" she asked, the grogginess of the words surprising her.

"Four."

"Where're you going?"

"Hunter and I are going hunting. Funny, huh? Hunter the hunter. He says it's the role he was born to play."

"When are you coming back?"

"When we've got a deer strapped to the hood."

"Oh," Carly said.

Then, without realizing it, she must have drifted off to sleep again. Because when she opened her eyes, it was light. And Dean was gone.

Carly stepped out into the main room of the cabin, still blinking, and noticed two girls sitting in the kitchen area. Thing is, they were not the same two girls as last night, as had been on this trip with her all along.

They were Janie and Heather, girls who were in a lot of the same classes with her. Girls she actually knew a little bit. But not really in any very successful way.

"There's coffee," Janie said.

It sounded friendly enough, so Carly walked over and sat at the table with them. But the minute she did, Heather jumped up and flounced away.

"Sorry," Janie said when Heather was out of earshot.

"What's wrong with her?"

It was a question Carly would normally have thought but not asked. But since Janie was actually talking to her, she experimented with actually talking back.

"She thought Dean was up here alone until we got up here and heard about you."

"Oh." Which led Carly back to the fact that they hadn't been there before. "When'd you guys get in?"

"Last night. Late. We came up in Heather's car. We got completely lost. Don't take this the wrong way. I'm not leaving 'cause you got here or anything. But I'm gonna go look for Hunter. You know where he is?"

"Off hunting with Dean."

"That's funny. Hunter is hunting."

"The role he was born to play," Carly said.

"Yeah, huh? That's bad, though. Because I'll never find them."

"And if you did, they might accidentally shoot you."

"I'll just go down by the lake with Heather. There's toaster waffles in the freezer."

She rose from the table. Stretched as if just now waking up, showing a bare midriff with a silver belly button ring. Then she wandered away.

Carly ate two toaster waffles with artificially maple-flavored syrup. She drank two cups of coffee. No one came around. She had the place to herself, which felt like a relief.

She staked out a spot where she could sit in the sun to keep warm and see the lake if she looked down and see the road to the cabin if she looked up. That way she would know when Dean came back.

Trouble was, the sun moved directly overhead, then slanted distinctly to the west, and still Dean did not come back. And still Carly sat. For lack of any other ideas.

It was only about an hour before dusk when she admitted to herself that she had never in her entire life been so thoroughly bored.

Dean and Hunter came back at early dusk. Carly watched them drive in. Watched the plume of dust the SUV kicked up on the long dirt driveway.

There was no deer strapped to the hood. Carly felt a clear sense of relief.

She got up, brushed off the seat of her jeans, and walked up the hill.

Jerry was out in the driveway when she got there, raising a fuss over their coming home empty-handed.

"Hot dogs again," he said.

Dean held out the keys to the SUV. "Go shoot a deer, Jerry."

"Did I mention the hot dogs were good?" Jerry asked.

Carly shifted slightly, and the movement caught Dean's eye.

"There you are," he said. "Just who I wanted to see after a lousy day." He reached into the back of the SUV and pulled out a stiff tan blanket. "You can be the only good thing to happen all day. Let's go for a walk by the lake."

Dean held Carly's hand on the walk down. It felt good. Then he let go, and Carly had no idea why. And she couldn't bring herself to ask. A moment later she felt his hand slide into her back jeans pocket. She smiled to herself and returned the gesture.

When they found a nice spot to stop—private and in the trees—Carly expected him to wrap them up in the blanket. The way he'd done the night before. Instead he spread it on the ground.

"What are we doing?" Carly asked.

"What do you think we're doing? We're lying down."

"Oh. OK."

She settled herself on the blanket. Well, physically settled. Inside, she felt more than a little unsettled.

Dean lay down beside her. But less than half a minute later, he rolled on top of her, his full weight resting on her. He didn't even kiss her first. He had never kissed her.

"Wait. Whoa," she said, wondering if that had even been enough volume to get his attention. It was hard to talk with a big guy resting on your chest.

Carly felt him back off her some. She heard the zipper of his jeans come down.

"Wait!" she yelled.

This time she had her lungs back, and the volume was strong. Too strong. Carly wondered if a wandering neighbor might have overheard.

Dean climbed off her and sat up. She sat up beside him and looked at his face in the dusky light. His eyes were closed-down and dark.

"What is your *problem*, Carly?"

She received it the way she absorbed tongue-lashings from her mom. Like a blow. She didn't feel the urge to cry, because it felt more like a physical wound. Like he'd punched her in the gut. With a knife in his hand.

"I thought we agreed we didn't even know each other."

"That was yesterday," Dean said, not one tiny scrap of friendliness left over in his voice. Not one.

"Yeah. Exactly. That was yesterday. I said we'd barely said ten sentences to each other. You thought I meant I wanted to wait *a day*? I haven't even seen you today."

"I didn't think you were so high maintenance."

Carly sat and breathed for a minute. Thinking about transporting herself home in some magic way. But then the minute was up, and she was still at the lake with Dean. And she had to say something. So this is what she said.

"I always figured it would be...you know...more...special."

Dean looked at her as if she'd just spoken Dutch.

"You're a virgin? You're trying to tell me you're a virgin?"

"Yes and no," Carly said. She'd meant only to think it. Yes, she was a virgin. No, she hadn't been trying to tell him so. "Technically." It really wasn't all that technical. It was really pretty clear. But "technically" sounded better than "completely." "I'm just...not...I don't feel ready. You know? I'm just not quite ready."

"You're sixteen, right?" A flat indictment. Judge, jury, and executioner.

"Yeah. But...that's not so weird. Is it?"

A long wait. Carly already knew she wouldn't like the answer.

"It's very weird. It's, like...freakish." He levered to his feet. "I can't believe I wasted all this time with you. Shit. Nothing's right today. I hate this fucking day."

Another knife punch to the gut. But now Carly's gut was ready. She had shut off all the nerve centers, and the blow landed in a field of nothing in the darkness inside her.

Dean walked away.

"Where are you going?"

It sounded so thin and pathetic and lame that she'd gladly have pressed an off switch on the entire universe if that would have deleted it.

He stopped. Looked down at her over his shoulder. In more ways than one.

"I'm gonna go make some time with a girl who's not looking for something so...special." He imitated her voice on the last word.

The final insult.

Or so Carly thought.

Halfway back up to the cabin, Carly passed Dean and Heather. Walking down to the lake. Hand in hand.

Dean grabbed the blanket off Carly's shoulder.

"We'll be needing that," he said.

Heather flashed Carly a smile of smug and utter victory.

Carly quickened her steps and trotted double-time up to the cabin.

There she grabbed her suitcase from the corner of the bedroom floor. Threw in any of her clothes she happened to see lying around. Latched the bag with the sleeve of a long-sleeved T-shirt still hanging out.

She marched out the front door of the cabin and up the driveway, shifting the heavy bag from hand to hand as she walked down the road. In the direction of somewhere that wasn't the lake.

It was already nearly pitch dark.

Ned's Bait & Tackle stood out in neon in the night, the only man-made object for a mile. There was a pay phone out front. Just like she remembered. Just like Dean had said. It made her feel saved.

She followed the directions on the phone to place a collect call, punching in her home number by heart. When a recorded voice asked her to say her name, she said, "It's me, Carly," in a slightly shaky voice. Then she decided she could say she was only cold. That maybe it had sounded like she was trying not to cry, but really her teeth had just chattered slightly.

The line rang six times. Then the answering machine picked up.

Carly hung up and pressed her forehead to the phone. Closed her eyes. Snow began to swirl. Lots of it. Big flakes, quite suddenly. She glanced over at her shoulder and watched the flakes settle on her jacket in the neon glow.

She scoured her pockets for quarters and found six. If she hadn't found any, she had no idea what she would have done. Even dollars would have been of no use. She dialed Teddy's cell phone number by heart.

He picked up on the second ring.

She said his name, but it was noisy wherever Teddy was. She could barely hear him. He could barely hear her.

"It's Carly," she shouted into the phone, though he probably still couldn't hear her. And she didn't have much time. Not for six quarters.

"Wait," he said. "Let me take this outside."

The background noise faded, then sharply cut off, replaced by almost complete silence.

"Teddy, it's me. Carly."

"Carly. Where're you calling from?"

Only then did she realize how close she'd been to losing it. To falling apart.

"I'm in trouble, Teddy. I need to get home. Can you come and get me?"

In the midst of those words, Carly couldn't hold the tears back any longer.

"How much trouble? What kind of trouble? Should I be calling nine-one-one here?"

"First I need you to call me back. Before we get cut off. Let me read you the number of the pay phone."

"Wait. Let me see if it comes up on my cell phone. Yeah. I've got it. I'll call you right back."

Carly set the phone gently in its cradle and pressed her forehead against it again. When it rang, the vibration made her jump. She picked it up.

"Now where were we?" Teddy asked. "How much trouble? Should I be calling nine-one-one?"

"No. Not that much trouble. I just couldn't stay there. I just walked away. And now I'm at this little shop that's closed, and it's snowing, and I can't go back there, and it's cold, and I have to get home somehow. Nobody answered at the house. Why didn't somebody answer at the house? Where are you? Where is everybody?"

A long silence. Then Teddy said, "When it rains, it pours."

"What does that mean?"

"It means we've got ourselves a situation here."

"Still not following."

"OK, I'll say it clearer, then. My whole world's falling apart here, Carly. Yours, too, you just don't know it yet. Everybody's world is falling apart. And here I thought it couldn't get any worse. But if you need to get home, fine. Of course I'll come get you. Where are you?"

"I don't know."

Another long silence.

"You do realize that doesn't help our situation."

"I don't know the name of this road. But I'm in front of this little store called Ned's Bait & Tackle. It's near a town called Fish Fork, which is like the tiniest town in the world, hardly even a town, but this is sort of on the other side of it. It only took us an hour and a half to drive up here from Tulare."

Silence.

"Fish Fork? No. Never mind. This's no time to make jokes. Besides, it's too easy. Ned's Bait & Tackle. OK, fine. I'll look that up. I'll try to get the address from a listing on the business. And I've got the number of the phone booth in case I can't find you. Hold tight, OK? I'll be there as quick as I can."

"Teddy? What's going on there?"

"Please, Carly. One disaster at a time."

When she'd let him off the phone, Carly sat down on her suitcase. Leaned her back against the bait shop window. Waited. Set her internal clock so she'd be prepared to wait a long time.

The snow covered her in light veils as she sat.

It might have been a cold ten minutes or a cold hour later when Dean's dad's four-wheel drive SUV pulled up. Pulled off the road and into the dirt parking lot in front of Ned's Bait & Tackle. Carly didn't figure she could handle seeing him until it came clear why he was here. Maybe to apologize. Maybe to share more thoughts on what a freak and a loser she was. So she kept looking up into the falling flakes. It was a world she could almost live in. If she just never looked down again.

The engine shut off. For a few moments, it had been the only sound in her world. It felt good to get back to all that snowy silence.

In the absolute still, Carly heard the window power down.

"You OK?"

It was not the voice of Dean. It was not even the voice of a boy. Carly looked down.

It was Janie. Janie had gotten the keys somehow and driven all the way out here to find her. To see if she was OK.

"I'm fine," Carly said and tipped her head back up to the sky again.

"You need a ride or something? Want me to drive you back down to Tulare?"

"That's a nice offer," Carly said. Still without looking down. "But I called my friend Teddy, and he's on his way up here to get me."

A long silence. Carly listened to it with great care.

Then Janie said, "You know. I dated Dean about three times. Sophomore year. He's a total jerk."

Carly said nothing for a long time. Right up until the time she said, "Thanks." Without even knowing she was about to. "Why'd you even come up to his cabin, then?"

A question she probably had no right to ask. But it was too late.

"Because Hunter was here."

"Oh. Hunter's nicer?"

"No. Hunter's a total jerk, too. But he's so hot, who cares? You sure you're OK? You want to sit in the car till your ride gets here? Are you freezing?"

Yes and no, she thought. She'd almost gotten used to the cold. Accepted it as normal. She thought of the inside of Dean's car, the ride up. She should have known, even then, that she was never a part of anything. Now *that* had been cold. This was fine.

Carly wanted nothing less than to go backward into any part of that world. And Janie's pity made her uneasy. Made her feel like even more of a jerk.

"No, I'm good," Carly said. "Thanks, though."

Flakes swirled down into her face for a couple of moments more. Seconds or minutes, Carly didn't know. She'd lost the ability to judge. Swirling flakes against a black sky gave no frame of reference. For anything. Life was not demarcated in any way. Not anymore.

The engine of the SUV fired up again.

"Merry Christmas," Janie said.

Then she powered the window up, backed out onto the snowy road, and disappeared around a hairpin curve.

Carly looked down, briefly, watching her go.

Yeah, Merry Christmas, she thought. 'Tis the season to be jolly. Oh joyous night. Oh wondrous freaking everything.

She leaned back even farther, so that the crown of her head rested on the cold front window of the bait store.

At some point, without realizing it, she must have drifted asleep.

A slamming car door brought Carly bolt upright. Her neck screamed complaints when asked to suddenly straighten out again. But she didn't voice that pain.

Teddy was standing right in front of her.

She looked up into his face for what seemed like a long time. Watched the swirling flakes gather on his shaggy hair. She couldn't see his face well enough to gauge the look in his eyes.

"Now you know why your mom didn't want you to go," he said.

With some effort, she pulled herself stiffly to her feet and threw her arms around him. He sighed. Wrapped her up in warmth. Not just physical warmth, either. Every kind of warmth. Every version of warm that existed anywhere in the world.

A moment later he held her at arm's length by the shoulders.

"Question number one: Should we be making a stop at a police station? Or a hospital?"

Carly shook her head.

"Nothing happened against your will?"

She gathered herself up to speak. It wasn't easy.

"He stopped when I told him he had to stop. But then he just…
he just…He totally turned on me."

Teddy sighed and pulled her close again. Carly let the tears
flow. She could feel her teeth chattering and couldn't figure out
why she should be colder now, all wrapped up in Teddy. Maybe it
was because of the truth. Letting the truth back in.

Teddy held her at arm's length again.

"Let me tell you something about boys. It's a subject I happen
to know a thing or two about. Because I used to be one. In fact,
there are those who'll tell you I still am. So take it from a pro.
A surprising number of boys are assholes. Not all. But a surprising number. Total assholes. Well, no. Not total. Assholes, but not
complete assholes. This is the part I'm trying to tell you. They're
actually not trying to be assholes. They're trying to figure out how
to be men. And, let me tell you, it's not as easy as it looks in the
directions. And all the different ways that man thing gets mod-
eled for them…well, that's definitely not helping. I'm not trying
to let them off the hook. I'm not saying it's not their fault. Exactly.
Because if it's not their fault, then whose fault *would* it be? I'm just
saying they're trying to figure out something tricky. How to be a
man is a tricky thing to figure out on your own."

Carly sniffled. She could barely see Teddy through the snow-
flakes that had gathered on her eyelashes. Carly had her mother's
thick eyelashes.

"How old were you when you figured out how to be a man?"

"When I get there, I'll be sure to let you know. Now come on.
I don't have snow tires, or chains, or four-wheel drive. I'm in a low-
clearance vehicle here. And it's really coming down. We need to get
out of here while we still can."

"I don't like this," Teddy said. "I don't like this one bit."

He maneuvered the car around a series of tight turns, at about five miles per hour. Every now and then the rear tires fishtailed dangerously on the icy road. It made Carly lose her stomach, like a sharp drop on a roller coaster.

"I can't really touch the gas or the brake. Or it tries to spin out. And it's steep here. I'm putting it in low."

Teddy shifted the automatic transmission, and Carly heard and felt the deep thrum of the added engine compression.

"We'll be down soon," she said.

Somehow she knew, or at least felt with all her being, that in a minute they'd return to a reasonable altitude. To something like the world she'd always known. Then this nightmare would be over. Unfortunately, that reminded her there might be other nightmares. Waiting.

"What was going on when I called, Teddy?"

"Oh, God," he said.

Then, for an extended and difficult moment, she thought he might not be willing to say more.

"You know," he said at last, "I was about to offer to go find this guy and beat the crap out of him for you. If that would help your situation. I don't mind doing the ninety days or whatever the law would give me. I'd be happy to. Except it wouldn't help your situation, and we both know it. Word would get around, and then no boy in the whole school—hell, the whole town—would ever come near you again."

"Why are you changing the subject?"

"I'm not. I'm trying to tell you, Carly. I was just thinking…you know…the part I just said. And then it hit me that you really don't have a problem at all. I mean, not an ongoing one. Because you're never going to see that guy again. Because your mom is home packing you guys up to go. She's not only moving to another town, she's talking about another state entirely. I think she said New Mexico."

Carly waited for some emotional reaction from herself, but all was still and calm inside. Probably because she didn't believe a word she was hearing.

"New Mexico?"

"I think it might have something to do with that guy."

"What guy?"

"You can drop the act, Carly. I've known for a long time."

"Wade."

"Yeah. *That* guy."

"She'll change her mind."

"Not this time."

"She always changes her mind."

"Not this time, Carly. This is a whole different ball game."

"What happened while I was gone?"

The back wheels spun with an alarming whirring sound and took on a life of their own, drifting close to the edge of the road. And the path of the headlights illuminated what lay beyond that edge. Not much. Just a long way down.

"Shit," Teddy said and took his foot off the gas.

Carly instinctively braced her hands against the dashboard. The car stopped sliding with maybe a foot to spare.

"I better concentrate on what I'm doing," he said.

They navigated the twisty mountain road in silence for several minutes.

The car didn't slide again. The snow was letting up some. Thinner hitting the windshield and a thinner buildup on the road in front of the headlights.

They were coming down into the valley.

"There were no parents there," Carly said.

"Now there's shocker," Teddy said calmly. "I can't imagine how anyone could've seen *that* coming."

"You think my mom knew there wouldn't be?"

"I think it crossed her mind."

Silence. Until the road looked familiar again.

"Just one more thing I wanted to say," Teddy said, startling her. "I think you know better than to believe everything you hear about me. About anybody. Right?"

She waited to see where he was going with that thought. He didn't say more.

"That's it?"

"Yup. That's it. Just don't believe everything you hear. Just promise me you won't believe everything that's said about me. That's all I'm asking, Carly. Seems like a small price to pay for the ride."

Teddy pulled up in front of the house and shifted into park. He didn't pull into the driveway. He didn't turn off the engine.

"Do me a favor," he said. "Do us both a favor. Do the whole world a favor. Jump out quick before she sees me. And don't tell her I brought you home. Tell her one of the guys drove you down, or that everybody came back early."

Carly just stared at him. None of this seemed willing to click into place.

"You're not coming in?"

"No," Teddy said, as much an expelled breath, a rueful laugh, as a word.

"When will I see you?"

"Well, that's a problem."

"You're never coming in the house again?"

"When your mom moves you all out...rent's paid till the end of the month."

"I'm not going. I want to stay with you."

"That's not an option, Carly. That's never going to happen. She'd never allow it. No way in hell. Besides, I can barely look after myself right now."

Carly felt the tears pressing again. She pushed back. Hard.

"So I just never see you again?"

"When you get settled, call me on my cell and let me know where you are. That way I can let you know when I find a place to live. But don't let her find out we're in touch, or there'll be hell to pay. Now hop out. Quick, Carly. There's going to be trouble if she looks out that window."

"It couldn't possibly be as bad as you're making it out to be."

"Kid," he said. He had never called her kid before. "You have no friggin' idea how bad it is. Go quick. And don't believe everything you hear."

Carly stepped out onto the curb and watched Teddy's Firebird speed away. Part of her thought she might never see him again. Another part of her firmly believed this would all blow over by tomorrow. Lots of stuff blew over in her mom's house. Bad stuff. All the time. This could blow over, too.

Whatever "this" was.

When she got inside, Wade was there. In the kitchen with her mom. They were wrapping dishes together. Her mom was up on a step stool, taking Grandma's good dishes down and wrapping them in sheets of newspaper, then handing them down to Wade, who fit them into cardboard cartons.

Only then did Carly realize how unreal this had all seemed. Until just this moment. And how real it all was. How real it had been all along.

She stood in the kitchen entryway, her shoulder leaning on the doorframe.

They both looked up.

"What's *he* doing here?" Carly asked.

Wade's stare darkened.

"We're leaving," Carly's mom said.

"I can see that. But why?"

"I'll tell you later."

"Tell me now."

"OK, fine," her mom said. Like it was Carly she was mad at. Like Carly had caused all this trouble. Like her mom had forgotten that Carly hadn't been here a minute ago, wasn't supposed to be here now. "You want to know? You want to talk about it right now? Fine. We'll talk about it right now. We're leaving because Teddy tried to rape Jen."

Carly felt her head rock back a little. Teddy's voice echoed in her head. *Don't believe everything you hear about me.* So all her mom had to do was tell this vicious lie out loud. Then Teddy was out and Wade was in. And nobody would think any the worse of her mom for it. She'd be the heroine. The momma bear. Carly wondered why she hadn't seen something like this coming.

"You're unbelievable," Carly said.

"I don't know quite what that means coming from you right now, but go pack."

"I'm not going."

"Oh, hell yeah, you are. Now go pack up your stuff."

Her mom stomped down off the step stool and grabbed up a box of dishes. Wade had barely finished taping up the top. The end of the tape hadn't even been torn off the roll when she whisked the box away. She paused briefly to let him finish, then carried the box to the garage.

Wade stared into Carly's eyes in a way that made her uneasy. She looked away.

"If I'd talked to my mother like that, I'd have been sorry."

"Like I care," she said, feeling brave.

"If you were my kid, I'd teach you some respect."

"I'm not, though."

Carly peeled away from the doorframe and marched upstairs. Halfway up, it hit her what she should have said. You can't teach respect. The person who wants it has to earn it. Those would have been the right words. But by then it was too late.

She marched into Jen's bedroom. Jen was packing the clothes and shoes from her closet into cardboard cartons.

"Don't," Carly said.

"What are you doing back already?"

"Don't pack."

"I have to pack. We're moving."

"I'm not moving."

"You have to, Carly. We can't move without you."

Jen's eyes looked too wide. Like a spooked animal. Carly tried to remember if she had ever seen Jen spooked before. Nothing came to mind.

Carly flopped down on Jen's bed.

"Can you believe this? How much does this suck?"

"I know," Jen said. She stopped packing and sat on the edge of the bed. Near Carly's hip. "All my friends are here."

"She's unbelievable. I can't believe she did this. Wade's going with us, isn't he? She didn't need to do this. She should have just told the truth. If she wanted to be with Wade, she should have said so. I'd hate her for it, of course. But not like this. Nothing could've been worse than this. She wants Teddy to be the villain, not her. Teddy could never be a villain. He's too damn sweet. Nobody's ever going to believe this, so I don't know why she even tried."

Jen opened her mouth to speak.

At that moment, their mom appeared in the doorway.

"Don't talk. Pack."

"I'm not going," Carly said.

"Here's how it's going to be, Carly. You *are* going. That's a legal fact. I can enforce that. The only question is whether you're going with or without your stuff. When Jen and Wade and I get all packed up and ready to go, whatever of your stuff isn't packed stays here. You don't own it anymore. Now is that some kind of motivation?"

Carly sat up and looked straight into her mother's eyes. Carly was set, planted as firmly as she had ever been in her life. But the look in her mom's eyes matched all that. And raised it. Carly should have known. She could never out-angry her mom. Nobody could.

The moment stretched out.

"You're a liar," Carly said. "And I hate you for it. And I'll never believe another word you say. And I'll never forgive you for this. As long as we both live, I'll never…ever…forgive you."

TULARE

December 21

It wasn't until late the following day that Carly's mother looked at her as though she were some kind of alien life-form and said, "Aren't you supposed to still be at the lake?"

Carly told her they'd all come down early so they wouldn't get snowed in for Christmas.

It was the first time she'd spoken to her mother since the previous night.

It was the last time she spoke to her mother in months.

In fact, for all intents and purposes, it was the last time she spoke to her mother.

PART THREE

Now Again

WAKAPI LAND

May 13

"Your first job..." Delores says as they file out of the henhouse like a chain gang of two.

Carly doesn't even give her time to finish.

"Now? We don't even get to wait till morning?"

"Nope. You don't. Not in this case. You're gonna get on over to that rock pile and haul a bunch of them big rocks and put 'em at the corner of the henhouse. Build it up there, so nothin' can get through where it's open, thanks to you. Otherwise I'll just have to charge you another week for every hen I lose. But first lemme show you where you'll bed down."

Carly looks at Jen, who looks back wild-eyed. They were ready to drop from exhaustion before they ever crossed the road to this hell. And the adrenaline has drained away now, leaving Carly trembling from her belly out. She feels like she couldn't lift an egg. How are they going to lift big rocks?

Jen sighs.

Carly sighs back.

The door of the hot-pink trailer screeches when Delores opens it. They barely have to step up to get in.

"Go on in an' get settled. Gotta go get Roscoe."

Carly's stomach tingles in fear. There's a man here after all. She prays the man is even older than Delores and can barely move. She looks out the little round window in the trailer door, waiting to see him.

But when Delores Watakobie reappears, there's no man. The old woman is just leading an ancient dog along by the collar. He's liver-colored and white, with liver spots on his white legs and a big, lumpy mass on his hip.

There's no glass in the little slit of side window. Just a screen. So Carly can move over and speak to the old woman from there.

"How come your dog didn't bark at us?"

"Old Roscoe's deaf as a post. And don't we just make a great pair? I can't hardly see, and Roscoe can't hardly hear. Gotta put the two of us together to get one good observation. Guess our creator figures we deserve each other. You. The little one. Come along with me to the well out back and we'll get you girls a bucket of water and a couple of cups. Got to drink plenty of water so's you don't die."

Jen slips out into the night.

Delores leads the old dog to a spot by the trailer door, where he happily sets his rump back down.

She lifts one of Roscoe's heavy, droopy ears and shouts straight in, "Watch the trailer, Roscoe!"

Roscoe curls up and goes back to sleep.

Delores Watakobie waddles away with Jen following behind.

Carly lets Jen drink her fill first, even though it seems to take a year. Then she gorges herself. The water is vaguely warm and has an aftertaste like metal. But it's still the most welcome sensation her body can imagine.

There's a bare mattress at the other end that looks just big enough for both of them. Jen is already making herself comfortable on it.

"We'll get away," Carly whispers.

Now that they've had their fill of water, they have half a chance to make it. Then again, Carly thinks, is half a chance good enough? What about the other 50 percent of their possibilities?

"Might be nice to be someplace for a whole week," Jen says.

"Yeah. Someplace. But not here."

"But we're here now. So this is as good as any place."

"Are you kidding? At hard labor?"

"But maybe she'll feed us at least."

"Shhhh. I think she's coming back."

Carly leans over to the window and watches the old woman waddle across the dirt to the trailer. She's holding something, a different something in each hand, but the moon is behind her, casting shadows, and Carly can't see what she has. But she can clearly see the muzzle of the shotgun angling up from the crook of Delores Watakobie's right arm.

Knock, knock.

"What?" Carly says.

"Open up. Move it, Roscoe!" With an accompanying nudge of her foot.

Carly does as she's told. So does Roscoe.

Delores hands in a woven basket with something inside it, but it's wrapped in a linen towel and Carly can't see what it is. Then she hands in a white glass bottle. Or a clear glass bottle with something white inside.

"Couldn't see fit to cook eggs after you tried to get 'em on the help-yourself plan. But I got to thinkin'...even the worst jailer in the world gives bread and water. I ain't the worst jailer in the world. So I'm givin' fry bread and goat's milk."

"Thank you, ma'am," Carly says.

"Thank you, ma'am," Jen echoes.

"You're welcome. Part humane and part selfish. Gotta put somethin' in you girls to get some good work out. Now hurry up and eat 'n then get on out here. You got a lot of work to do."

Before she can hobble all the way back into the house, Jen runs to the window screen.

"Ma'am?"

"Yeah?"

"You know what day of the week this is?"

"Friday, I think." The old head bobs thoughtfully. "Ninety-five percent sure it's a Friday."

"I knew it," Jen whispers under her breath. "I knew it all along."

Not ten minutes after the food is gone, they're out hauling rocks in the moonlight. Delores Watakobie supervises. As does her shotgun.

About an hour after Jen begins snoring lightly, when she's pretty sure Delores Watakobie will be asleep, Carly checks the trailer door. To see if they're locked in.

The door squeaks open a few inches, then hits an obstacle. She sticks her head partway through to see what the trouble is. It's Roscoe. He's sleeping in front of the door, which has hung up on his rump.

He lifts his head and growls at her, a low, meaningful rumble in the depths of his throat.

Carly gives up. On everything. This trip. Her life. Everything.

She curls up behind Jen and tries to get some sleep.

WAKAPI LAND

May 14

A knock on the trailer door startles Carly out of a deep sleep and a deep dream. But she doesn't know what the dream was. The knock sends it flying. She finds herself sitting straight up, looking around, literally not knowing where she is or why. And she can't seem to figure it out, either. It's almost as though she's still sleeping but with her eyes wide open. It's a panicky sensation.

A few seconds later it rolls back over her, like a wave that had only briefly pulled away from shore. It feels heavy and ugly, a twist in her belly.

She looks around for Jen, but Jen is gone.

Another knock, startling her just as deeply.

She walks to the trailer door and opens it to that same horrible metallic scream. Looks into the face of her dreaded captor.

"What?" Carly says, already defensive. "Am I not working hard enough?"

She notices that Delores Watakobie has no shotgun in the crook of her arm. Carly could just run. But in the next breath she knows she can't because she doesn't know where Jen is. She can't leave without Jen.

"C'mon'n the house for breakfast," the old woman says, then turns and waddles away.

Carly looks around for Roscoe, but he's nowhere to be seen.

She crosses the dirt yard and ducks into the little house. It has an oddly low doorway. It doesn't literally force her to duck her head, but it's lower than usual, so she does anyway. Like a reflex.

Jen is sitting on a faded old couch with a colorful blanket thrown over it as a cover. She's holding a woven basket in one hand, examining it carefully. With the other hand she's scratching Roscoe behind the ears. Such a dirty, smelly old dog. It makes Carly's stomach do a quarter turn just to watch it. Or maybe that's not the reason. Maybe it's the fact that Jen looks relaxed and at home. Almost…content. Sometimes the moments that bring happy responses from Jen make Carly think she doesn't know her sister at all. And her sister is all she has left. That is, until they get home to Teddy.

Jen looks up, and Carly sees it in her eyes. Something like guilt. For being caught liking these miserable surroundings.

Be patient with her, Carly thinks. That was a pretty close brush we had with…she still doesn't want to use the awful D-word. With being nowhere. With never being found. Not in time. Jen is probably just happy to be alive and to smell breakfast cooking.

Carly sits in the kitchen—though there's no formal division between that and the living room—at an old Formica table that looks like a throwback to her mother's childhood. Hell, her grandmother's, maybe.

Jen sits down, too. Without a word.

Delores sets a heavy pottery plate in front of Carly, with three small fried eggs and a disk of the same bread they had last night.

"Thought we didn't rate eggs," Carly says. "You know. Since we tried to get them on the help-yourself plan."

Delores sweeps the plate away again.

"Fine. Don't have 'em, then. You just made Roscoe's morning."

"Wait!" Carly shouts.

The old woman stops, plate at about her chest level. Which isn't very high, in the world of average-height people.

"I'm sorry. I really do want them. I'm sorry."

The plate clatters down in front of her again.

"Thank you," Carly says. "Thank you for making us eggs."

Delores wrinkles her already wrinkled brow. "You got a lot of attitude, you know that? Darn shame it's all bad."

"My attitude's no worse than yours." The words come out before Carly can stop them.

She looks down at the eggs, ready to watch them disappear again. She briefly mourns their loss.

Then she looks back at the old woman's face, just in time to see Delores toss her head back and shake, seemingly to her bones, with a weird laughter.

"Now there's a true thing," Delores says. "No arguin' with you there."

She fetches a second plate of eggs and bread and sets it more gently in front of Jen, who smiles up at the old woman. As if with some kind of affection.

First, Carly thinks, Don't bother kissing up. She probably can't even see well enough to tell. Then she wonders what happened while she was sleeping. How long was Jen in the house with the horrible old woman? Do they somehow know each other already? And, if so, can that be anything to smile about?

Carly waits for the old woman to sit down so she can start.

Delores only putters around at the porcelain counter. After a moment, she turns her head, as if listening for something.

"Well, don't let it get cold," she says. "Eat."

Carly grabs up her fork and does as she's told.

The more real, more permanent fix to the henhouse involves first moving away all the rocks they so carefully stacked last night.

It's still early-ish morning, with the sun on a long slant, but Carly can feel sweat running down into her collar as she works. The cores of her arms and legs feel shaky, and she can't tell if it's a physical or an emotional response.

Delores Watakobie is sitting in the shade, watching them. Or, at least, following with her eyes. Carly has no idea how much the old woman sees. She can never be quite sure what the old woman's vision will hide, will allow Carly to get away with. Maybe nothing that Delores's unusually sharp hearing won't take back again.

Roscoe is sitting in the shade, leaning on one of the old woman's legs, panting amicably.

The more Carly moves around the dilapidated property, the more she sees it's not as clean as it looked from the road. Behind the house, there's junk stored. Behind the henhouse, more junk. Old bedsprings and rolled metal fencing material. Rusted paint cans. Behind the little barn, it looks like somebody tore a vehicle of some sort apart with their bare hands.

It seems wrong to Carly to just throw or stack all that stuff behind something. Like that solves it. Out of sight, out of mind. Carly is anything but a neat freak, but it argues with her sense of order.

Someday, she thinks, I'll have a sweet little piece of property. But not here. Someplace that's nothing like here. Someplace that's not so hot. And dry. And empty. And depressing. And I'll keep it nice. Not like this.

"What's wrong with your feet?" Delores asks. Suddenly.

It startles Carly out of her thoughts. She stops and drops her rock, careful not to drop it on her foot. Jen keeps hauling.

"Who, me? Or Jen?"

"You."

"Nothing's wrong with my feet. Why would you ask that?"

Her blisters are killing her. But she doesn't want to admit it. She feels like a wounded deer being watched by two coyotes. I am not lame. I am not lame.

"C'mere a second," Delores says.

Carly inches closer to her.

The old woman's hand darts out and grabs her by the calf, pulling her foot up, pulling it closer. She's surprisingly strong for her age and stature. Carly almost falls but catches her balance again. She thinks the old woman is going to somehow look at her foot very close-up. The better to see it. Instead, Delores shakes the foot up and down. Carly can feel the oversize boot slip back and forth.

"These boots're too big."

"I know it."

"Don't they give blisters?"

"Maybe. What's it to you?"

"Nothin'," Delores says. "Nothin' at all. You want blisters? Fine. Keep 'em."

She drops Carly's foot. It hits the dirt with a *whump*, raising a miniature puff of dust.

"What choice do I have?"

"I was gonna offer to fix 'em. But you 'n that attitude..."

"How can you fix them? They're just too big. You can't make them smaller. You can't make my feet bigger."

"You wanna argue about it? Or you wanna see?"

Carly looks over her shoulder at Jen, who is clearly listening.

"You didn't tell me you had blisters," Jen said.

"Sure I did. Remember at the bus station. I…" She started to say "took." I "took" those bandages. She changes it. "…got those adhesive bandages?"

"You said that was 'in case' your heels got rubbed."

"Well, they did."

Delores Watakobie lumbers to her feet. It's quite the production. "C'mon'n the house," she says to Carly. "Little one," she calls to Jen. "Wanna take a break?"

"Naw, I'll keep going," Jen says.

Which seems weird. Hauling rocks if you've just been given a chance to stop hauling. That's outside Carly's understanding of the world.

Carly follows the old woman into the house.

She sits on the couch while Delores rummages, mostly by feel, through boxes in the closet. Most are the size of shoe boxes.

"How did you know I had blisters?"

At first, no reply. As if she doesn't rate the attention. As if answers were something like cooked eggs. Something Carly might not deserve.

The old woman grunts deeply and straightens up, clutching a shoe box to her chest. She crosses the room to the kitchen and plows noisily through a drawer.

"Could hear it," she says.

Carly laughs out loud. Not an amused laugh but a judgmental one. A laugh that discounts. Criticizes.

"You can't hear blisters. They don't make a noise."

"People's steps sound one way when all's well, another way when there's pain. Person walks different in pain. Hard to explain. But I know it when I hear it."

She sits down next to Carly on the couch. "Take 'em off," she says.

Carly unlaces her boots, sighing slightly as she slips one off. It feels good to have nothing pressing against the bloody disasters that are her heels.

Delores opens the box. Inside Carly can see small, narrow scraps of what look like thick sheepskin. None of them look wide enough to line a shoe.

The old woman sets the box top on the rug, sets a big pair of shears on top of it. She runs her hands through the scraps until she finds the biggest, widest one. Then she holds it to the bottom of Carly's boot and begins to cut the scrap, feeling the edge of the boot sole as she goes along.

It seems like a process that will take a little time. Carly has no idea how to pass that time. Where to look. What to say.

She wants to say something halfway nice.

"No shotgun today."

She knows that wasn't it.

The old woman only grunts.

"How do you know we won't just walk away?"

"Up to you."

That sits in the air for a moment. Carly has no idea what to do with it.

"What do you mean, it's up to me? You're forcing us to stay here for a week."

"Nope."

"What do you mean, nope?"

"You don't know what 'nope' means?"

"This is not voluntary."

Carly's getting heated now. She can feel it. Something about this old woman brings out the fight in her.

"Honor system. You two say you're all about honest. If so, you'll do what you promised. If not, you'll go."

Delores has already finished cutting one sheepskin insole. It has something like a long sheepskin tail at the heel end. Maybe an inch wide. Carly wonders when the old woman will cut it off.

"Last night you were holding us at the point of a gun."

"Last night if you'd of taken off, you'd be dead. Nothing clear to Arkoba Village the way you was headed. And even that's only if you know how to get there."

"That's bull. You don't even know which way we were headed."

"Yeah, I do. Your sister told me. Besides, it don't matter. Nothin' in a day's walk in any other directions, neither. If I hadn't put some food and drink in you, you wouldn't've had a chance. Don't like your chances now, but that's up to you. Pigheaded enough to chance it, you will. Your sister got more sense, though."

Carly can feel her jaw hanging open. Dropped. She doesn't know what to counter first. The part about Jen was over the line. So she leaves that part alone.

"Oh, right. So this is all for us. Not for you. You're just being helpful. Is that what you want me to believe?"

"Believe what you want," Delores says. "Ever'body always does."

Carly stands at the kitchen sink, her left leg weirdly angled up, watching Delores wash one of her blisters by feel. It makes her wince a little. Partly from pain, partly from a squeamishness about being touched with those spotted, wrinkled hands.

Delores is using a rough bar of soap that doesn't exactly look like soap you buy in a store. It stings, a sting exceeding any logical expectation for soap in a wound. Delores is not gentle, either. Anything but. In fact, when the old woman feels the flap of skin dangling from Carly's heel, she pulls it off. In one quick rip, the way you'd take off a bandage you know is stuck to the wound. All at once, just to get it over with.

"Ow!" Carly shouts. Really even a little louder than necessary. "You want to ask before you start removing pieces of me? Maybe I wanted to keep my skin."

"You don't want that."

"Really. Why don't I?"

"'Cause it's infected. Last thing you want's for a flap of skin to seal back over an infection."

"Oh. Still. Can you warn a person?"

"Put your foot down and gimme the other one."

"Right," Carly says. "Sure. Whatever you say. Thanks for answering the question."

She takes her still-wet left foot out of the sink and sets it on the kitchen floor, presenting the second disaster to Delores and the sink.

Delores washes by feel again, her head slightly tilted.

Then she says, "I'm thinking to take this flap o' skin, too, so you might be wantin' to brace yourself now."

Without waiting for an answer, Delores pulls.

Carly does not say ow.

"What about this thing?" Carly says, indicating the long strip of sheepskin that protrudes from the top of each boot. "You're not going to cut that off?"

"Now why would you want me to go 'n do that?"

"Well. When I stick my foot in, it'll get all smashed down into the boot, and I'll be walking around on that all day."

Delores just shakes her head. As if Carly has brought a level of silliness into the house that doesn't even warrant the old woman's attention. Instead she takes hold of Carly's shoulders and plunks her onto the couch.

"Sit," she says, when Carly is already down.

"I'm not a dog."

"I noticed."

"You don't say that like it's a good thing."

"If you was a dog, all you could say to me's 'woof.' That'd be some improvement."

Carly decides not to escalate things any further.

Delores picks up Carly's feet, one at a time, and slathers her heels with a thick, evil-smelling, translucent ointment. Carly expects it to burn like hell, and she braces for that pain. Instead it's soothing, which leaves her speechless and feeling, for some inexplicable reason, like she might be about to cry.

Delores tears strips off a length of clean white cotton fabric and wraps it twice around each foot like a bandage. Then she lumbers to her feet.

"Those socks you got are worth next to nothin'."

She hobbles over to a chest of drawers.

Carly looks around, wondering where the old woman sleeps. It's all one big room. No bed in sight. Maybe the couch folds out.

Delores comes back with a pair of thick gray socks. Weirdly thick, like boot socks or hiking socks. Nothing like any socks Carly's ever worn before.

She drops them in Carly's lap.

Carly just stares at them, as if she doesn't know what they are or how to use them. In fact, she simply doesn't know if they are a loan or a gift, and if she can accept either one from this horrible old woman without being obliged to tone down her hatred and resentment. At least by a notch or two.

Delores says, "Waitin' for directions?"

"Why are you acting like you like me? I know you don't."

"So...you don't like somebody...you see 'em sufferin'...You just let 'em suffer?"

Carly has to think about that for a minute. If it was a stranger... Maybe. She's always thought of other people's suffering as entirely outside her realm of influence. Not so much like she's withholding assistance. More like she's on a different planet from the suffering.

As if I don't have enough trouble with my own life, she thinks. What could I possibly do for a stranger? What do I have that could rescue anybody? I can't even rescue Jen. Or me.

"So you admit you don't like me."

"I like your sister," Delores replies, without missing a beat.

That just hangs in the air, leaving Carly at a loss for what to say, or even what to feel. But a moment later, something breaks through. Something that hurts. Everybody likes Jen better. Why does everybody like Jen better? What did Carly ever do that was so wrong? She tries so hard to make everything work out right. Jen just floats through the world, through her life, and people spark to her. Just like that.

Teddy liked Jen better.

The thought slices up her gut like a rusty can opener. She's always known that but never formed it into words. Not even in the privacy of her own head.

"Sister thinks like a Wakapi," Delores says. "Picks up the feel of the land. First thing she did this mornin'...when she got out of the trailer...hold still 'n look around. Said she was lookin' at the way the sun hits that big mesa back behind the place, and then she sniffed the air. Smelled the mornin' to take the measure of it. She knows where she is. She's payin' attention."

"She thinks this is someplace," Carly says, her heart as cold and dark as frozen mud. "I know better."

Delores levers to her feet, a little faster this time.

"Put your boots on 'n get to work."

She waddles out of the house.

Carly looks down at the boots and suddenly gets it. The sheepskin liners have been cut to extend all the way up the back of her heel. There's even enough to fold over the top of the boot, a little tab to hold on to, so they stay in place as she slides her foot in. Not only do the new liners make the boots fit better, they include a soft cushion for her damaged heels.

Just for a moment she wants to follow Delores and say something. Somehow leave the conversation on a better note. But instead she just sits. Their talk, this morning, is like the suffering of others. Well out of her sphere of influence. Life just keeps happening to her. If there were a way to make it work out right, to take it in a better direction, she would have veered down that road a long time ago.

Jen is mixing plaster of Paris with a hoe, stirring it back and forward in a low metal trough. As if she's mixed plaster every day of her life.

Carly is walking back and forth, stacking the last of the rocks on the pile again. Feeling the difference in her ability to walk without pain. Oh, the broken blisters still hurt. Some. But the boots don't rub against them anymore—they fit normally now, plus there's that extra cushioning in back.

When the rocks are all stacked, Carly squats down next to the trough, looking in. As though nothing could be more fascinating than watching plaster mix.

"How much did you talk to her while I was sleeping?" she asks Jen.

"A little," Jen says, already on the defensive. She seems to know what Carly wants to hear. Apparently it doesn't match with what she's got to tell.

"What did you say?"

"I don't know."

"How can you not know, Jen? You were there, weren't you?"

"I don't remember. She weaves her own baskets. I was looking at the baskets. We were talking about how she gets the different things she needs, being so far away from a town and all. Nothing, really."

"She's already decided she likes you."

Jen's face lights up. "Yeah?" Then she catches the look in Carly's eyes, the daggers Carly is quite purposely throwing, and her face falls again. "Well, that's dumb. We don't even know each other."

"Stay away from her, Jen."

"Why?"

"Because I don't like her, that's why."

"*I* like her."

"I thought you didn't even know each other."

Jen's mouth moves briefly, but no audible words come out.

Then, suddenly, the old woman is back. She's carrying two straw hats across the dusty yard. One is a cowboy hat with a curved brim. The sides of the brim curl up close, like a roper's hat. It's battered and old. And small. The other is floppy-brimmed, like an old lady's gardening hat. Which is probably exactly what it is.

Delores says, "How the two o' you was so dumb as to come all this way with nothing to keep the sun off you, I'll never fathom. Mad dogs, you know? Like that old sayin' about mad dogs. 'N Anglos. Plain common sense to stay out of the sun."

The sun is closer to overhead now, and Carly feels as if every drop she drank from the bucket last night is sweating out of her. But she wants to tell the old woman where she can stuff her floppy old gardening hat. She just knows that hat is for her. The ridiculous one. She knows Jen gets the good one. The fact that the good one is likely too small for her doesn't make her any less mad.

She doesn't want the hat because she knows she'll feel stupid in it. But even more, she doesn't want the hat because she doesn't want to accept any more helpful gestures from her enemy.

"Thanks," Jen says, and grabs for the good hat. The cowboy hat.

Delores says, "That one belongs to my great-grandson. He's the only other one I know got enough bad sense to come out here with no hat. So it might fit you, or it might be a little big on account of him bein' a boy and all."

Jen puts the hat on, and it drops down over her forehead, nearly obscuring her eyes. Despite the smallness of the hat, Jen is smaller.

"OK, OK, just hold steady," Delores says. "I'll get you a bandanna to wrap your head in. Catch your sweat and hold that thing up a little more."

"Thanks, Delores," Jen says, almost cheerfully.

Delores turns to Carly, her face darker, and holds the floppy gardening hat wordlessly in her direction.

Carly's mind floods with images of yesterday, their last day out in the sun. The way the rays of heat seemed to bake right through her spare shirt when she held it over her head to create shade. The way her lips cracked and bled when she spoke. The line of dry, peeling blisters she can feel on her forehead if she runs her hand across it.

She takes the hat.

"Thank you, ma'am," she says.

Delores only grunts. Then she waddles inside to get Jen's bandanna.

Carly feels like an idiot in the hat. But that's really no surprise. That's probably exactly what the nasty old woman had in mind for her.

"We need to use your phone," Carly says, loud and strident, the minute the old woman comes out again.

"I don't think so," Delores says.

"Well, that's just not fair. If I could call my stepfather, he'd come get us. And he'd pay you enough to cover what you're trying to work off us all week. And then we could get home. You act like you care so much about us and all. But I know you don't. If you did, you'd help us get home."

There are other problems, but Carly wants not to think about them now. She'll need to call directory assistance. Maybe as many as a dozen times. To get the numbers of all the contractors, all the building firms in Trinity. Then she might have to call every one. Or maybe she'll get lucky and hit it on the first or second try. But it could get expensive. Still, a whole week of hard labor has to be worth something. Something more than two eggs.

Delores opens her mouth to speak, but Carly cuts her off.

"Fine, if you're worried about money, we'll work even harder. We'll work longer days. We'll work an extra day. Or my stepfather, he'll pay you back for the calls when he comes out here to get us. If you're worried about the damn money."

Delores waits a moment. As if to assure herself that Carly is quite done.

Then she says, "I ain't worried about the damn money. I don't never worry 'bout money. Don't use much out here anyways. Trade the eggs or milk for most of what I need, and if I got nothin' to trade I still get what I need 'cause I'm an elder, and the Wakapi take care of their elders. Besides, money's a gift from the creator, like ever'thin' else. No point worryin' over what you get for free."

"Then we can use your phone?"

"Sorry—" Delores says.

Carly cuts her off again.

"I don't believe you! You're just being mean! You just want your slave labor. You don't care about us at all. I bet this is illegal. I ought to call the police."

But then she realizes the absurdity of her threat. Because to call the police, she'd need access to a phone. Besides, if they could afford a run-in with the police, they wouldn't have wound up here in the first place. Talk about being stuck. Every road she tries to take to freedom loops right around in a circle. Drops her right back here. In hell.

At her left side, she can feel Jen stiffening, feel the stress rolling off her. But Carly can't stop her own agitation. She feels like a trapped animal. Panicky. Anything to get away, even if she has to chew her own leg off.

She's halfway aware of a cloud of dust and the sound of an engine. A pickup truck is pulling up the old woman's dirt driveway. But it can't seem to break entirely through Carly's panic and rage.

Why is the world conspiring to keep her from getting back to Teddy? Such a simple request to make of life.

Delores is standing with her hands on her hips, a posture probably designed to remind Carly that she can't match the old woman's life experience in the field of indignation.

"First off," Delores says, "I told you once already. Honor system. Stay or go. I ain't holdin' no gun on you. Second of all, you're in luck. Wanna call the police? Lucky you. You don't need no phone for that. He's right there. Just yell the name Alvin, nice 'n loud. Wait'll he turns off his truck, though. Give 'im half a chance to hear you."

Carly turns her full attention to the truck. It's about ten years old, well maintained. Dark blue. It stops in front of the henhouse, and the driver cuts the engine. Carly can hear the gears of the hand brake being set.

The man who steps out is Native American, probably Wakapi like the old woman. He's maybe in his late twenties. Handsome, with shiny black hair pulled back into a neat ponytail under a wide-brimmed hat. He smiles at Delores, and his teeth are brilliant white.

Carly snatches the silly hat off her head. Because now there's a boy watching.

He's no cop. He's just a man in a pickup truck. Delores must be playing some sort of mind game on her.

"That's a cop?" Carly asks, sarcastic.

She means to hurt the old woman, but then, too late, she realizes she's also insulting this man she's never met. He might be nice. He might be their salvation. Maybe he'll yell at Delores for taking indentured servants against their will. Maybe he'll take them to a phone they can use.

"Pleased to meet you, too," Alvin says. "Who're your friends here, Delores?"

"Well, the one with the mouth calls herself Carly. This nice little one is Jen."

"And what brings these lovely young ladies to our neck of the woods?"

"Just passin' through," Delores says. "Little Miss Mouthy here don't believe you're with the tribal police."

Alvin says, to Carly, "What, a policeman can't even take a day off?"

Carly doesn't think either one of them is telling the truth. He's just some guy. A neighbor or a friend or a grandson. Or something. They just want her to think he's a cop to scare her into line.

Carly says nothing. Everyone says nothing.

Finally the old woman says, "Alvin, tell Little Miss Mouthy here why she can't use my phone."

"Oh, that's easy," Alvin says. He looks up over the roof of the tiny house. Points. "How many wires you see up there?"

Carly looks up. One thick wire comes down at an angle from one single pole. It enters the house from the back, out of Carly's line of sight.

"Just one," she says.

Then it hits her. Old Delores has electricity. But no phone.

"That's crazy," Carly says. "What if you need to call someone?"

"Like who, for example?" Delores asks.

"Like if you needed help or something."

She doesn't want to add the part about how old Delores is. She's not sure if it goes without saying or not.

"Alvin comes by here ever' mornin'. See if I'm OK. Or if I need anythin'. Ever' mornin' like clockwork, on duty 'r off. You could set your clock by Alvin here."

"I could drive you girls to a phone if you need one," Alvin says.

"Or she could use your cell phone," Delores chimes in.

"Well that's only for official business, I'm afraid. But I could run 'em into the village."

Delores says, "Yeah, there's a pay phone at the gen'ral store."

She puts the emphasis on the word *general*. Not the word *store*. As if they sell generals there.

Carly is all ready to jump in his truck and let this nightmare be over. Then it hits her. Pay phones need to be paid.

"Um. Thanks. Maybe tomorrow."

She can feel Jen trying to catch her eye, but she refuses to look.

Alvin exchanges a few sentences with the old woman, right in front of them, but in a native language Carly can't begin to understand. Then slides into his truck and waves. Jen waves back. Carly doesn't. Her arm is too defeated, too completely out of hope.

Alvin starts up the truck and backs out to the road in a swirl of dust.

Delores waddles back inside.

"You should have gone with him," Jen says.

"Me? Why not we?"

"I'm OK here. But you should've used the pay phone. I don't want to walk anymore, Carly. I'm not walking all the way to California. When we're done here, I want a ride. Even if…"

But then she never finishes the sentence.

"Even if what, Jen?"

No answer.

It's funny how Jen has these boundaries. Like hidden walls. You never see one coming up. You just hit it. And that's that.

It's like there are two of her little sister. The one she's known since she was four. And then this one. This other person.

"You know why I can't use the pay phone, Jen. You know that, right?"

"Maybe he would've loaned us the money. You know. If he knew how much trouble we're in."

"Jen. If he knew how much trouble we're in, he'd call child protective services and get us picked up and thrown in the system."

"Oh," Jen says. "Right. I didn't think of that."

"Right. You don't ever think of those things. You never think of anything important. I have to think of everything. That's why it's a good thing I'm the one in charge."

Jen sighs and goes back to work, cutting a piece of chicken wire to form a base for the plaster. Just the way Delores showed her.

Then Jen says, "You think that Alvin guy was really the police?"

"No. Did he look like a cop to you?"

"I don't know. What's a cop look like?"

"Well, they wear a uniform. For starters."

Carly can hear herself talking to Jen as if Jen were an idiot. And she doesn't like her own tone. But she can't seem to break it.

"He said it was his day off."

"They're just trying to scare us, Jen."

"I guess," Jen says.

They work on the henhouse for at least another hour without talking. Without interruption of any kind. It's almost a relief. Life may be miserable, but at least for one blessed moment the damned thing holds still.

The sun is overhead when the old woman comes out again.

"Take a break," she says. "Get out of the midday sun. You can do more later. After lunch. After four. Too hot now."

Carly straightens up. Leans on her hoe. Stretches her sore back. She looks around the property as if gathering complaints. Making a list of things to criticize.

The junk. She feels like making a big deal about the junk. The rusty bedsprings and the rolls of chain link fencing. The old car or truck parts.

"I don't see how you can stand to keep all this crap around," she says. "Place looks like a junkyard."

It's harsh, but it feels good. Carly wants to lash out. She wants somebody else on the planet to hurt even 1 percent as much as she hurts. Especially if that somebody is Delores.

But the old woman only laughs. That strange laugh.

"Helps when you can't hardly see it," she says.

"Other people can see it."

"Well, that's their problem, then. Ain't it? It bother you?"

"Yeah. It bothers me."

It's only half-true. Carly doesn't feel much investment in this place. In a little over six days they'll be gone. Sooner if she can call Teddy. What does she care what the place looks like, as long as she can get away?

"That'll be your next job, then. When you got that patch fixed, haul all that stuff over to my truck and load what you can in the bed. You drive?"

"Yeah, I can drive."

"OK. I'm comin' with you, though. Don't trust you with my truck all on your own. But there's a guy about three miles west. Buys scrap metal, just about anythin' you got for 'im. Don't pay much, just a few cents a pound, I think, but you can keep whatever he pays. Should be enough to make your phone call, at least."

She disappears back into the house.

Carly starts gathering up the chain link. It's heavier than she realized. She looks up to see Jen standing near the door to the house.

"Come on," Jen says. "We're on a break."

"You go. The faster I get this done, the faster we can get out of here."

Jen shrugs and goes inside.

But after ten minutes or so wrestling heavy rolls of chain link in the midday sun, the break starts sounding good. Besides, she doesn't want to leave Jen alone with the old woman anymore. Not for long. Not if she can help it.

Delores is casting some kind of spell over Jen.

Carly is already infected with an eerie worry about the situation. About that brand-new bond. She feels as though she's lent her sister to the old woman, very much against her will, and now, somehow, she can't be entirely sure she'll get Jen back again at the end of the week.

Well, that's not true. In fact, that's stupid. Right?

But that's still the way it feels.

"Hey. Jen. You awake?"

"Shoot," Jen mumbles. Barely enunciating the word. "I guess I am now."

Carly's been lying awake in the old pink trailer for hours. The longer she lies awake, the bigger her fears and worries grow. Like she's been feeding them some kind of super-grow worry food as she tosses and frets. And they're eating it right up. And it's doing everything the label claimed it would do, plus a whole lot more.

She even worries about all the work she has to do in the morning. How it will feel on no sleep. The more she tries to will herself to sleep, the more the pressure builds and cements her sleeplessness.

She tried to tell herself, before waking Jen, that she was doing it for a better reason than misery loving company. She hopes that was the truth.

"I've got to tell you something."

"I hope this is not bad news."

"It's...not real bad. It's fixable. Just sort of inconvenient. You've got to trust me to fix it."

Carly waits. But Jen only sighs.

"I tried to tell you this before. Before we even got caught in the henhouse. But then you were asleep, or maybe you were even passed out or something, and I went through the whole speech, and now I don't know if you heard a word of it. If any of it sounds familiar, say so."

"Just tell me, Carly. Just tell me what it is."

The moon is more than three-quarters round. Carly can't see it through the little trailer window, but she saw it less than an hour ago. And she can see the moon shadows cast by the henhouse and the spooky light the moon throws directly on the big mesa.

"Teddy doesn't live in Tulare anymore."

"That doesn't sound familiar," Jen says.

"He moved to a little place called Trinity in Northern California."

"You got his number?"

"No. But I'll get it. I'll find him. You'll see."

A long silence falls. Jen rubs her eyes. Yawns.

Then she says, "Maybe we just forget about Teddy."

She might as well have driven an elbow into Carly's gut, without warning or provocation, knocking her to the floor. That wouldn't—couldn't—have been any more of a shock.

"What did you just say?"

"Did you really not hear it?"

"Jen. Teddy's all we've got. Who the hell else is going to take care of us?"

"Maybe Delores would."

Carly whips back the rough blanket and jumps to her feet, pacing barefoot on the cold linoleum floor. She felt this coming, saw it somehow before it even showed its face, but convinced herself it was impossible. That she was being paranoid and foolish. What does this say for her other worries? Are they all a possibility?

"We've known her for, like, one day, Jen."

"I like it here, though. I really like it."

"She's not going to take care of you."

"How do you know? She likes me."

"She's not going to take care of *me*. She doesn't like *me*. And besides, I won't allow it. I wouldn't let her. And you want us to stay together, don't you?"

Jen sits up. "Sure, Carly. Yeah. Of course I do. I didn't mean what I said. I'm just sleepy, OK? You just woke me up and I didn't know what I was saying. Come back to bed, Carly. Please. I didn't mean it."

Carly sits down on the edge of the bed, and Jen tucks back in again.

Finally, when she's settled herself a bit, Carly climbs back under the covers. She doesn't get to sleep for hours.

Jen is snoring lightly in a matter of minutes.

WAKAPI LAND

May 15

Delores Watakobie has a time getting into the passenger seat of her own truck. Carly sits behind the wheel, both doors open, in the shade of the carport, feeling a sense of minor power for the first time in a long time. Driving does that for her. She watches the old woman reach up, reaching for a handle above the doorframe. Delores steps up onto the running board of the truck and grunts out an odd series of sounds as she attempts to pull herself in.

Carly is about to jump out. To go around and help. Push or something. But she's only just barely flinched toward doing so when Delores stops her with words.

"Don't you dare." Her voice is even—doesn't rise in volume—but the words pack a lot of power. It's a stern warning. "Day I can't step up into my own truck's the day I let my creator put me six feet under. No point hangin' around if you can't even do for yourself."

With one final grunt, she drops into the passenger seat.

Carly looks in the rearview mirror. Checks, again, the way she and Jen have stacked the first load of junk in the truck bed.

"Sure we don't need to tie that stuff down or something?"

"Can't go that fast on these roads anyways. Should be OK. You disconnect the batt'ry charger?"

Carly says nothing for a beat or two. She doesn't even know what a battery charger is or how to spot one, not to mention how to disconnect it.

Delores sighs heavily. "You think I'm gettin' down 'n then up again, you got another think comin'. You can do this. Get out. Open the hood. It's unlatched. See two wires goin' in. One's clamped on the batt'ry, one on a strut. Take 'em off one at a time. Don't touch 'em together whatever you do. Slam the hood real good. Leave the charger where it lays."

Carly climbs down. Circles around to the front of the truck. Approaches the charger the way she might approach a venomous snake. It's sitting in the dirt, about the size of a car battery or a little bigger, with a wide, black molded handle.

She opens the hood of the old truck. The squeal of the hinges sounds just like the door of the pink trailer prison. Maybe a little deeper. More bass. But close.

She reaches for the clamp on the battery. Squeezes it. As she's pulling it off, it sparks, startling her. She drops it into the engine compartment.

"Ain't gonna bite you," Delores calls. "Just don't touch 'em to each other, whatever you do."

Now there's a mixed message if Carly ever heard one. It won't hurt you. Just be careful not to get hurt.

She takes hold of the insulated cable and carefully pulls the clamp back up and out again. Sweat drops off her forehead, and she wonders how much is the heat and how much is that jumpy feeling, like she's disarming a bomb.

She throws the clamp in the dirt. Realizes the other probably has no charge now. She pulls it off and throws it into the dirt as well, near the first one. As it falls, she remembers. They mustn't touch. Her heart stops beating for the half second it takes to watch it land. Two inches from disaster.

She breathes out her relief.

Mentally, she kicks herself hard. Why are you always so afraid, Carly? Damn you. Why can't you just do things? Why can't you handle these simple little things that other people handle all the time?

She looks across the yard at Jen, who's happily feeding the goats.

Jen could have disconnected the battery charger. No problem. No fear.

Carly slams the hood hard. Too hard, maybe. Climbs back into the truck. Looks down at the gearshift.

It's a stick.

Carly doesn't know how to drive a stick. Teddy's car was an automatic. She only knows how to drive an automatic. She can't believe that observation didn't break through in her brain until just this moment. As she was actually ready to start it up and drive.

The moment stretches out.

"What?" Delores croaks.

Carly doesn't answer.

"Speak up, girl. What's it this time?"

"How much harder is it to drive a stick shift than an automatic?"

Silence.

Delores rolls her head back, as if attempting to seek heavenly guidance right through the roof of the old pickup. Then she drops her head into both spotted hands and shakes it—and the hands—back and forth three or four times. Slowly.

"Trade places," she says, dropping her hands hard into her lap.

Carly's one tiny bit of power is lost. Figures. That's been her lot for as long as she can remember.

"Maybe I could learn it."

"Oh, no. No, no, no. Not on my truck, you don't. Not on my clutch. This clutch's lasted since 1973, 'n it needs to keep goin' long as the truck does. Long as I do. Won't do to have you strippin' my gears, no thanks. Trade places."

"Can you see well enough to drive?"

"Nope. You're gonna have to see for me."

Carly sits still a minute. Lets that filter down. She's been asked to take a ride on a dirt road with a blind woman driving. Sure, she wants that phone. Badly. But she needs to survive long enough to get back to Teddy.

"That sounds...dangerous."

"That 'r stay home and forget the whole deal."

Carly looks again at Jen. Jen's scratching a goat on the forehead, between its eyes. The goat is trying to rub its head against her. Jen doesn't seem afraid of the horns. She's laughing. Carly can't hear it, but she can see it. She can see Jen's face, laughing.

They'll go slow. Even if they crash, it probably won't be fatal.

Carly sighs. Climbs down. By the time she goes around the back of the heavily loaded bed, Delores has slid into the driver seat and is gunning the old engine to life.

"You're going in the ditch!" Carly shouts.

They're not literally driving into the ditch on the right-hand side of the rust-colored dirt road. Not yet. But they will if Delores keeps going the direction she's going.

Delores adjusts right, steering them even closer to the ditch.

"The other way!"

Delores stomps the brake, sending Carly slamming into her shoulder belt. She bounces back again, hitting the ripped vinyl bench seat. She can feel an exposed spring against her lower back.

"Let's get somethin' straight," Delores says. "There's two ditches. One on my right. One on my left. If you yell at me I'm gettin' too close to one, don't you think it might be wise to specify?"

"Sorry. You were too far right."

"Now that's a little clearer."

"Sorry."

Delores sits a minute, as if waiting for her patience to catch up. Then she reaches out and feels around close to Carly, grabs hold of Carly's left wrist and pulls her hand over to the steering wheel.

"You steer," she says flatly. An order. "I'll go slow. You tell me if there's anything to hit, 'n I'll go even slower."

Delores downshifts from second to first and hits the gas again. Accelerates all the way up to five or six miles an hour. It makes Carly nervous at first because she's never manned a steering wheel without sitting directly behind it. It requires some adjusting.

Within a minute or two, she finds it far less nerve-racking than watching the truck she's riding in head straight for a ditch.

Delores rides with her left elbow out the open window, right hand in her lap. Carly quickly learns not to look. It's alarming to watch a driver who hasn't got the wheel. Even if your brain knows you've got it yourself.

They're about to pass two little houses now, one on each side of the road. First…anything…they've come to.

"There's a dog up there," Carly says. "And three little kids."

"I know it."

"You can see that far?"

"Didn't say I could see it. Said I know it. That's Hal and Velma's three girls. I know how far down the road they live, and I know what time they wait for the school bus ever' mornin'."

"Then what do you even need me for?"

"Well. If you see one right in the middle of the road, lemme know."

As they pull closer, Carly sees the faces of the three little Wakapi girls. They look an even year or two apart in age and size. They're waving. The littlest one is smiling widely, showing missing front teeth.

"Hi, Delores," the oldest girl calls, cupping her hands around her mouth. "Be careful, Delores."

The old woman leans half out the window as they roll by.

"Don't you worry none about me, Hannie," she says as they pull even. The dirty white dog stands up and wags its tail. "Got me a borrowed pair o' eyes."

"Who's your friend?" the little one asks.

"Don't matter," Delores says, then pulls her head and torso back inside.

They drive another minute in silence.

Carly looks back at the kids and the dog, suddenly feeling like, if only she'd had a dog who waited for the bus with her each morning, everything in her life might've turned out OK. Or, at the very least, better than this.

The old woman's last words echo, a delayed reaction.

"I don't matter?"

"Didn't say that. Said 'it' don't matter."

"How's that different?"

"Look. How much of that story you want me to tell out the window of some movin' truck? For that matter, how much of that story do I even know? I keep thinkin' you'll open up in time if I just lay off it. Beginnin' to doubt that system."

Carly falls silent. She does not open up.

She also does not shake the feeling that Delores said what she really meant. Carly is nobody. Carly isn't worth explaining. Carly doesn't even matter. Maybe everybody thinks that about Carly. Maybe Carly is even beginning to agree.

"This should be Chester's place right up here a piece. You see a blue sign?"

"I see a sign," Carly says. "It's too far away to see what color."

"Should be it round about now."

"There are three big dogs running out into the road."

"Yup. That's Chester's."

"Slow down! Don't hit the dogs!"

The three dogs, one beastly yellow mutt and two German shepherd types, are running straight at the grill of the pickup, barking their fool heads off. Delores isn't slowing down.

"Tell me when we get to the driveway. I'll slow down, and you turn us in."

"You're gonna hit the dogs!"

"I ain't gonna hit no dogs. Chester's dogs know how to duck. If they didn't they'd be dead a long time."

Before she finishes the sentence, the dogs split like water flowing around the truck. The two German shepherds flow to the driver's side. The ugly yellow mutt appears right under Carly's open window, leaping and snapping.

Carly rolls the window up, fast, her heart hammering. Why are Navajo dogs so mean? They're not, they're just doing their job. It echoes back into Carly's head, a scene from their long journey. She hasn't thought much about the walking part of their trip. She's been trying to think ahead. Are these Wakapi dogs just doing their job? Aren't they doing it a little too stridently? Can't somebody drive by without getting this treatment?

"Slow down. Right here. I mean, right turn. Here."

Carly has to hand-over-hand the wheel nearly a full turn. Then she corrects too fast, almost running them into the fence along the driveway.

"Tell me when to stop," Delores says, heading straight for a rough barn.

"Now," Carly says.

They're a good thirty feet from it. But a margin for error never hurts.

An old man comes wandering out from the barn, wiping his hands on a blue rag. Not old like Delores. Medium old. Maybe in his fifties. He has hair down to his waist, tied back in a ponytail. And a truly enormous potbelly. It rivals any Carly can remember seeing. He's wearing just jeans and a white undershirt.

"Well, well, well," he says. "Delores Watakobie. You haven't made it out here for quite the while."

"Best I don't drive too much these days. Just be glad I made it out here this time. Borrowed a pair of eyes."

The dogs are still circling and barking and snarling.

Chester comes around to the passenger side and stares right in at Carly, which makes her surprisingly uncomfortable. She smiles tightly, then looks away. He just keeps staring.

"This one of your great-granddaughters?" he asks Delores. As if Carly can't hear or speak for herself.

Delores is easing herself down from the driver's seat, seemingly right into the gaping maws of two vicious canine killers. She pushes one aside with her knee.

"Chester, you been out in the sun too long. That girl look to you like she got one drop of native blood in there, anywhere, in any corner of her body?"

"Well, I don't know," Chester says. "I guess not. But you never can tell."

Carly leans over and pulls the driver's side door closed behind the old woman. Fast. So the killers can't come right in after her.

"Who is she, then?"

"Don't know," Delores replies. "Still waitin' on her to tell me."

"Huh," he grunts. Like it's a mystery he can live without solving.

He begins to rummage around in the truck bed. Carly can feel the truck rock as he moves things around back there.

"Nothin' worth much," Delores says. "Maybe some scrap worth meltin'. What you gimme for the lot? We don't wanna haul none of it home."

"This all of it?"

"No, we got maybe two more loads."

"Well. Hmm. If they're both like this load, maybe ten, twelve dollars all told. Gotta get it off here, though. See what we got."

Delores knocks on the back window, startling her.

"Get on out here and help the man unload," she hollers.

Carly swallows hard.

"Not with those dogs out there. I don't want to get eaten."

Delores and Chester laugh. At her. It's clear, just to listen to it, that they're having a good laugh at Carly's expense.

Chester whistles sharply, and the dogs fall silent. Carly didn't realize how much noise they were really making. Until it went away. Until the world sounded so different without it.

"Barn!" Chester yells.

The dogs slink away.

Carly climbs down carefully. She really would have liked to hear a door close behind those dogs. But obviously that's more than she's going to get. So she just looks over her shoulder at the barn, then jumps like she's been shot when Chester clears his throat.

They both get another good laugh at Carly's expense.

Carly spends a good twenty minutes helping unload the truck she spent two hours loading.

For her trouble, Chester pays her a whole three dollars and twenty-five cents. That's the bad news. The good news is, he accommodates her request that the entire sum be paid in quarters.

By the time she navigates them back to Delores's house, Carly feels like she's been through a small war. Her thighs are shaking. When she steps out of the truck, she has to test them briefly to see if they'll hold.

Jen is working on the corral that contains the goats. Hammering in a couple of broken slats that used to be tied up with rope.

"Go on 'n load up again," Delores calls. "I think I got one more trip in me for the day."

She hobbles into the house.

"You didn't ask if *I* did," Carly mutters under her breath.

She walks slowly and carefully to where Jen is hammering.

Jen looks up. Stops. Says, "You survived."

Then Jen pulls a set of earbuds out of her ears. The wires lead into her shirt pocket. Like she was listening to music on an iPod or something. But Jen doesn't have an iPod.

"Barely."

Jen drops the hammer in the dirt and takes off her cowboy hat, mopping her face with her sleeve. Her face is red and wet with perspiration. The bright red bandanna Delores gave her is rolled into a thick headband and tied around her forehead to sop up sweat and to form a shelf to keep the hat off her eyes. The bandanna's soaked through.

"Pretty brave, going for a ride with a blind woman. Why didn't you drive?"

"It's a stick shift. Where'd you get that?"

She points to the wires leading into Jen's pocket. Jen lifts up on them. It's an iPod all right. A nice, big, new one. Over a hundred gigs maybe.

"Just about to tell you," Jen says. "Guess what happened while you were gone?"

"An iPod fell out of the sky and landed in your ears."

"Close. That guy came back."

"Alvin?"

"Yeah. Alvin. And guess what? He really is a policeman. With the Wakapi Police."

Carly's stomach and chest ice over lightly. Just what they don't need is a cop coming around every morning, like clockwork. Asking questions.

"How do you know? Was he in a cop car?"

"Sort of."

"OK, Jen. What's a *sort of* cop car look like?"

"Well. It was a pickup. Jacked up kind of high and all. But not the pickup he was driving the other day. Light blue. And bigger. Higher off the ground."

"Did it say anything about Wakapi Police on it?"

"I don't think so. But it had that thing on top. You know. That bar with the lights. For pulling people over. And he had on a uniform."

The uniform part hits home. Makes it all feel real. So Carly heads in a new direction entirely.

"I bet there's no such thing as the Wakapi Police. In fact, I bet there's no such thing as the Wakapi. I never heard of a tribe called the Wakapi. Did you?"

"Nope, I never did, and I told Delores that, and she laughed. She said most people haven't heard much about them, and they like it that way just fine. She said there's more than ten thousand Navajo for every Wakapi. She said the Hopi people are getting smaller and so is their land, and they're still dozens of times bigger and better known. She said the Wakapi have lots of kids, but they go off and live in the city and don't come back. So there just aren't that many of them left."

"Will you please stop talking for a minute, Jen? I don't care about any of that."

"Well, you said you thought there was no such thing as a Wakapi. But they must be real, because they have a police department and Alvin's in it, and I saw his uniform with the patch on it."

So there it is again. The uniform. There's no ducking the uniform.

"What kind of uniform?"

Carly is determined to prove this cop observation false. But her weapons are wearing thin.

"I don't know. A uniform-uniform. Short sleeved. I think he was wearing jeans, not uniform pants. But it was a uniform shirt. It had this patch on it that said Wakapi Police, and then this...I don't know. Design."

"What kind of design?"

"I don't know. I don't know, Carly. Geez. What's with the twenty questions? I kept looking at it, but I couldn't really figure out what it was. It was just a design. Some circles and some lines, and...well, what difference does it make? What if I said it was an eagle or a horse? And then you'd say...what? Yeah, that's the Wakapi Police all right. You don't know. So why are you even asking?"

Carly looks over her shoulder to see where the old woman is. She can see her through the window into the house, puttering at the kitchen sink. But Delores has phenomenal ears. To be safe, she grabs Jen's upper arm and walks her around to the back of the henhouse.

"Ow. What?"

"Did you tell him *anything*?" she asks, with an ominous shadow on the last word. "Anything about our situation at all?"

"No. He didn't ask me anything. The only thing he asked was whether you still needed to make your phone call, and I said no, Delores was driving you to the junk man and when you'd done a few trips and had enough money, you'd stop at the village store while you were out. So it was OK. And he said, 'Delores is driving?' and I said, 'Yeah, but it's OK because Carly's along to watch the road.' And he said, 'It's a good thing I didn't hear that,' so I said it again, but he just said the same thing. 'It's a good thing I didn't hear that.' So that's when I knew what he meant. That he was *pretending* he didn't hear that. And then we just talked about Delores and what a character she is, and then he left. That's all."

"Don't tell him anything about us, Jen."

"What if he asks? What am I supposed to say?"

"Nothing. Pretend you're stupid or something."

"Well, he already knows I'm not stupid. But anyway, most times you'll be here when he comes. How much money did you make?"

"Only three twenty-five. But we got a couple more loads we can do. If I live that long."

"He seems nice, Carly. I saw this iPod sitting on his dashboard, and I said, 'Wish I had one of those while I was out here working,' and he said, "How long you here with Delores?' and I said six more days. And so he loaned it to me. He's nice. Not exactly what I listen to, kind of new-agey, but it's OK. You get used to it." She stops. Waits. Braves a look at Carly's face. "He's nice."

"He's a cop!" she barks, way too loud. Delores might have heard that from all the way in the house. She lowers her voice. "He's probably got some kind of oath to turn us in. He's a cop."

There. She admitted it. She didn't want it to be true. She wanted him not to be. But he is.

Sometimes even Carly just has to buckle under to what is.

After lunch, Carly heads right back out to finish up that second load.

"It's still siesta," Jen says. She's on her back on the couch, the cowboy hat over her face.

"Mad dogs 'n Anglos," Delores says from the kitchen area.

"I just want to get done. Hey. Jen. Can I take that iPod?"

Carly wants to take the measure of this cop. If he were here, she'd study him. On the sly, while he wasn't looking. Instead she'll hold something that belongs to him and listen to what he likes to listen to. She has no idea what that will tell her. But it makes her feel as if she's in control. Of something. As if she has a plan.

The truck's been loaded up for nearly an hour. Jen and Delores are still indoors on afternoon break.

Carly squats in the shade of the henhouse, listening to music and staring at the big mesa. Watching waves of heat rise up off the ground, turning the horizon into waves. Like something that's only true until you move your hand and disperse it. Like water when you make a ripple. It bends everything you thought you could rely on. Nothing's what it seems.

Out of the corner of her eye she can see the thin white curtain from Delores's kitchen, sucked out the open window and fluttering lightly in the afternoon breeze.

The music is interesting. Like a meditation or something. No words, just a melody played by instruments she can't picture.

Something touches her shoulder. She gasps and falls face-first toward the rocky dirt, catching herself on the heels of her hands. Scraping them up pretty good.

Picturing mean dogs or scorpions, she flips over, backing away as she does.

It's Alvin, his hand out. Like to politely tap her on the shoulder. Which, she now realizes, he just did.

"Jumpy," he says.

"I'm scared of snakes and dogs."

"I'm neither snake nor dog."

She pulls herself up into a squat again and leans back against the henhouse, her heart still hammering. Trying to disguise her breathlessness.

Alvin squats in the dirt, a respectful five or six feet away.

"Like that music?"

"It's OK," Carly says.

Then nobody says anything for a time. And still Carly's heart won't stop hammering. She wraps the earbud cord carefully around the iPod and slides it into her shirt pocket.

"Well," Alvin says. "Let's go."

Carly's heart falls into her boots. First he'll take Carly to jail. Carly and Jen both, unless Jen made a run for it. Then he'll call the authorities…

"Go where?" she says, mustering her best acting skills. They aren't any too good. She can hear that with her own ears.

"Take that second load over to Chester's."

"You? Why not Delores?"

"Now you look like a smart little girl. Do I really have to answer that question for you? You got some debating to do with me on the wisdom of a driver who's nine-tenths blind?"

He's squatting with his arms wrapped around his knees. His feet flat. Carly wonders how he does that. She could never put her heels down flat in a squat. He's wearing jeans and a short-sleeve uniform shirt. She looks at the embroidered patch. It says Wakapi Police all right. Carly can't describe the design either.

He's wearing a shiny gold wedding ring on his left hand. Carly wonders why she bothered to look.

"Do I really have to go?" she asks. "I mean, you can see the road without me."

"I'm just the driver. You got to come and haggle with the man. It's not my load. It's your load."

"His dogs'll eat me."

"Chester's dogs wouldn't bite their own fleas."

"Wouldn't know that to listen to them."

Alvin looks straight into her face. She turns her eyes away.

"You put up a pretty tough front yourself, little girl. But I'm not afraid you're gonna bite me. I been around long enough to know the difference between a bark and a bite."

Carly just stares at the wavy horizon. If it's not what it seems, maybe the rest of this isn't, either.

Alvin rises to his feet. No hands.

"C'mon," he says. He kicks the toe of her boot lightly.

"I'm not a little girl."

"No? How old are you?"

"Eighteen."

"Uh-huh. Know how old you look? Fourteen."

"I am not fourteen! No way! I—"

It was about to become the word *I'm*. Halfway through, she puts on the brakes.

"Almost got you there. C'mon. Got to be on duty soon. Let's get this thing done."

Slowly, gravely, like following an executioner to the guillotine, she walks behind him. They climb into Delores's fully loaded truck. Where he can ask her anything he wants. Whatever's on his mind. Whatever makes him curious about her situation.

If there's another way, she doesn't find it in time.

Alvin careens down the road at a blinding twenty miles an hour or so. A couple of weeks ago, it would have seemed slow. But when you spend enough days going places at three miles an hour by foot, or five by car…

Both windows are open to keep the cab from getting too hot. Carly has to hold her hair down so it doesn't blow into her eyes and mouth. So it doesn't tangle.

"You know," Alvin says, "Delores is pretty darn proud of her electric wires, so don't be making her feel like that's not much.

She's a long way from the village to have electric. Only had it four years."

"What'd she have before that?" Carly asks, only half caring.

"Oh, we built her that wind turbine long time ago. Out of an old truck alternator and a convertor box. That was just like uptown at the time. She still won't let us take it down. Says she might need it if the power ever goes out. And it does. From time to time. But a phone. Way out where she is. That's asking a lot."

Carly only grunts.

"You don't seem to get what I'm saying. I'm saying power lines and a well is a pretty good thing. She used to just have a cistern, and the water had to be hauled. We got that dug for her, on account of she was getting older. And it might be nice if you didn't act like it was nothing. Like the one thing she doesn't have is just purely to inconvenience you."

"I didn't mean it that way," Carly said. "I'm sorry. I just never met somebody so stuck in the old ways."

"*Old ways?* Little girl, you don't know anything about old ways. If Delores was traditional Wakapi, she'd have no power and cook everything over a fire. She's one of the least traditional elders I know."

Carly has no idea how to dig her way out of these totally foreign concepts. So all she says is, "I didn't mean anything by it. I'm sorry. It's just that most people I know have phones."

They ride a good half the way without talking.

Then Alvin says, "Want to stop by the village store on the way back? Make that call?"

"If I have enough money."

"Two full loads ought to get you a phone call. I mean, you're calling California. Right? Not Sri Lanka."

"Yeah, but I don't know how many times I'll have to call information."

Speaking of information, until the silence falls, Carly has no idea that was too much.

"You don't know your stepfather's phone number?"

Carly turns her face away and looks out the window. She just won't answer. She watches the fence posts of a field of horses go by. Flashing in rhythm.

Then it hits her.

"How did you know it was my stepfather? How did you know he was in California?"

"Just a matter of asking the right questions."

Now that Carly thinks about it, she told Delores it was her stepfather she needed to call. Did she say he was in California? She doesn't think she did. Maybe Jen said more than she's willing to admit.

Suddenly Chester's dogs are in the road, barking. Alvin plows right through them, and of course they duck aside. He makes a left, not a right, into Chester's driveway. He came a different way.

He pulls within inches of the barn and shuts off the noisy engine.

She looks over at him. He's staring at her.

"Level with me, kid. Just how much trouble are you in?"

"I'm not in any trouble at all," she says. Her heart hammering. Her gut clenched. "Not if I can find my stepfather. He just moved away after my mom took us and left. He just doesn't know we're looking for him, that's all. If he knew, he'd be here as fast as he could drive. He just doesn't know we need him."

"OK," Alvin says.

"OK?"

"Sure. OK. I know you're not eighteen, but let's figure for now he'll take you in. We'll go that way. That doesn't work out, we'll go some other way."

Before she can even answer, Chester comes wandering out from the barn.

"Shut up!" Chester yells at the dogs, who slink into the barn without further instructions.

Alvin gets down from the truck. Carly sits, frozen.

"I'll help you unload this," Alvin tells Chester. "We'll get 'er done quick."

"That's interesting," Chester says.

"What is?"

"You seem to know that little interloper, too."

"You mean this lovely young lady?"

"Yeah," Chester says. "Yeah. That's what I meant. That's the one."

She can hear them saying more to each other as they off-load most of the car parts, then the bedsprings. But with all the banging of metal, she can't make out anything more for sure.

Carly is silent for most of the ride to the village store. There's something building up in there, but she wants to keep it in. But then it gets by her, suddenly, like a dog who bursts out through the door when he catches a glimpse of daylight.

"Why do I have to be an interloper? Why can't I just be someone who's visiting?"

Alvin chews on the inside of his cheek for a couple of seconds, then says, "Well, an interloper just means—"

"I know what it means," she says, more harshly than intended. "And he never talks to me. He looks at me like I'm a desk or a lamp. Like I don't even see him looking. And he never talks to me. First trip he talked to Delores. Second trip he talked to you. He treats me like I'm not even there."

She doesn't add that so many people do, she's begun to wonder if they all know something she doesn't.

Alvin sighs. "Chester's just a little notional is all. Little set in his ways."

Carly turns away. Looks out the window. The sun is on a slant. She doesn't know how late it is, but she hopes there's still time to call a business in California. If an answering machine or voice mail picks up, she'll lose the money she paid for the call. She only has eight dollars in quarters. That might not go far.

"OK, I'll level with you," Alvin tells the back of her head. "Chester's got a little chip on his shoulder around the subject of Anglos."

She turns to look at him. He looks more humble than he did before.

"I'm not *the subject* of Anglos. I'm a real, living, breathing example of one."

"That you are. Look, I'm not saying it's right, but I'm not going to apologize for the man, either. It's always wrong to judge a person by the actions of their whole people…but…the ones around here who feel the way they do…well, they tend to have their reasons. I'm just saying it's a story with two sides."

He steps on the brake, and Carly looks up to see a plain brick box of a store with two other pickup trucks and three motorcycles parked out front. The sign above the door—made with a slab of wood and a wood-burning tool—has a name Carly could never read or pronounce. But it has seven syllables. Seven. She counts. The windows are covered with a fine metal grating. In front and to the left of the place is an old-fashioned phone booth. The kind you can step inside. Close the door behind you. Some of the glass is intact, some broken out. The glass that remains is cloudy with scratches, as if it lived through a sandstorm.

"Be right back," she says.

She climbs down and walks in the direction of the phone booth. Three big men come out of the store and swing legs over their motorcycles. One of them smiles at her. She smiles back, but she's not sure it was much of a smile.

She steps inside the phone booth and closes the door, but there's no glass in the door. So there wasn't much point.

She knows you need the area code to call long-distance information, and she doesn't know the area code of Trinity. She starts by dialing the operator.

"I need the area code for Trinity, California," she says.

But just at that moment, the three motorcycles roar to life. The operator says something, but she can't hear it.

"Can you wait a minute?" she yells into the phone. "Just wait a minute. OK? Till these motorcycles drive away. So I can hear you."

She holds her hand over the mouthpiece of the phone. Watching the men put their helmets on. Their gloves. Finally they notice that she's waiting. They click the bikes into gear and roar off down the road. How they can stand all that noise wherever they go Carly can't imagine.

"Sorry," Carly tells the operator. "Sorry. Now what was that area code?"

"I have nothing for a Trinity, California."

Carly just hangs in that moment, not quite knowing what it means.

"Every place has an area code," she says.

"True. But I'm looking at every city or town in California. There's no Trinity. There's a Trinity National Forest ranger station…"

"Oh." Carly's throat tightens. "Could you look again?"

"Honey, there're just no other places to look."

"OK. Thanks."

She hangs up the phone. Opens the useless phone booth door and walks toward the truck. And she's fine. She does everything just fine. She opens the passenger door like everything is just fine. Slides up into the seat. Pulls her knees up and wraps her arms around them. She doesn't fasten her seat belt.

"Get what you needed?" Alvin asks.

She opens her mouth, and that's when the dam breaks. The tears come, and there's no stopping them. No amount of resistance will hold them back.

Alvin just sits there in silence and lets her cry.

A few minutes later, he hands her a cloth handkerchief from his jeans pocket.

A minute after that, he says, "I'll take that as a no."

The same light tap on her shoulder makes her jump almost as high. Though there isn't anybody it could be besides Alvin. Her closed eyes have been pressed hard against her knees, and when she looks up, the light makes her wince. Plus there are dark spots floating in front of each eye.

They're back in Delores's driveway.

Carly knew the truck had been moving. And she knew it had stopped. But she hadn't thought it out much more clearly than that. She hadn't processed those simple bits of sensory input.

Now she feels a little surprised to be here.

Tears are still running on her face, but her hitches and sobs have quieted. Not as though things are better. More as though they got tired of trying. Ran out of steam. She's careful not to look at Alvin. But out of the corner of her eye, she sees him push something across the seat in her direction. She looks down.

It's a yellow pad of lined paper, with a pen clipped on.

"Write down your stepfather's name. And what he does for a living. And the name of that town where he's supposed to be. In the morning I'll make a few inquiries. See if I can find out what's what."

Carly sniffles hard and wipes her nose on her sleeve. Which she knows is disgusting. And which she doesn't want to do in front of Alvin. But the drip method strikes her as even worse. Then she looks down and realizes she's holding Alvin's handkerchief. As if she didn't even know what it was for.

She wants to open her mouth and say something. Like maybe thank you. But it feels too hard. So she just nods.

She takes the pad and writes.

Theodore Thackett. Trinity, California, except the operator says there is no such place. But it's supposed to be on the coast up by Eureka. Works for contractors, doing construction.

She opens the truck door and slides down, leaving the clean handkerchief on the seat. Takes three steps toward the trailer, then turns and waves.

She wishes she'd never seen the look on his face. Boy, does he ever look sorry for her. It's a pathetic feeling. She must be utterly pathetic. Not that she didn't know. More that it's a shock to have the sheer extent of it mirrored back in his eyes.

He waves back. Even his wave is sad.

She doesn't go into, or even near, the house. She doesn't go anywhere near Jen, who's hanging wash on a clothesline at the far back of the property. She doesn't get close enough to see if it's their laundry or something she had to do for Delores. She's curious whether the old woman has a washing machine, or whether Jen washed things out by hand. Then she remembers Delores only has well water that doesn't run through a pipe. So that pretty much answers the question.

She opens the trailer door, startled all over again by that loud squeal. She thinks she should be used to it by now. But it got her again.

She sees Delores through the living room window and quickly turns her face away so the old woman can't see she's been crying. As she hurries inside and shuts the door behind her, she remembers. Delores can't see well enough to tell.

She lies on the little bed, facing the wall. Not actively crying anymore. Not actively anything.

After a while she puts the earbuds back in her ears and turns on Alvin's music again. Just to fill her head with something. Anything better than what she's already got. Which would be anything.

After what might be a couple hours of that—Carly doesn't have much sense of the time, but the music has cycled around and begun to repeat—she feels some movement in the trailer. Like something was bumping into it lightly, repeatedly. She pulls out the earbuds and waits. First nothing. Then another round. Without the music in her ears, it's obviously someone knocking on the door.

"Come on in, Delores."

"I would if I was, but Lord knows there's only one Delores." Alvin. "You decent?"

"Yeah."

"Come on out, then."

Carly stretches. Her muscles feel weird, as if she hasn't used them in months. Must be soreness from all the work she's had to do. She feels like this day has been a year long. Earlier this morning feels like last week.

She walks stiffly to the door and pushes it open, wincing at the sound.

"Yeah?" she says, squinting into the light.

Alvin has changed out of his uniform shirt into a plaid one. The light is on a long slant, and it's cooler. Must be almost dinnertime. Carly's stomach aches vaguely.

He's holding an unusually large road atlas of the United States, folded back to a page. He turns it around so she can see it.

"Take a look here," he says.

It's open to Northern California and has two small sticky notes on it. One on the coast, another a hair farther south and much farther east, deeper into the state.

"There's a Trinity County." Alvin points at the mid-state sticky note. "And a Trinity River. And a Trinity National Forest. And if you put Trinity, California, into a map search, it gives you back something. Points somewhere near the forest. But when you zoom in closer, it's not so much of a town, exactly."

Carly looks closely at it, then shakes her head.

"Ralph said it was on the coast. Up by Eureka."

"OK, then. Try this."

He points to the other sticky note. The one on the coast. It has a little pencil arrow drawn on it. It points down to a tiny town called Trinidad.

"Trinidad!" she says. Actually, she shouts it. "That's what he said! Trinidad!"

"Thought that might be the case, on account of here's Eureka right down here. So just dry your tears for the night, 'cause it's too late to call any businesses today. I already tried directory assistance up there, and there's no listing on him. But I can call some contractors in the morning. Pretty small town. I expect somebody ought to know him if he's there."

Carly rushes in and throws her arms around him, causing him to drop the atlas. Then, shocked that she would do a thing like that, she lets go and backs up suddenly.

"Sorry."

Alvin only laughs and picks up the atlas. "No need to be. Good to see you feeling better. Hope you're hungry. Smells good in that kitchen."

He tips his hat to her and walks back to his truck.

She watches him until the corner of the trailer blocks her view, nursing a feeling that's the closest thing to love she's felt since last time she saw Teddy.

Carly is washing her face in the sink when Jen comes bounding in.

"You OK?" Jen says, stopping suddenly.

"Yeah. Fine."

"Oh. Good. So, I have to tell you this. When you were gone, this lady came by. Her name is Virginia, and she's Wakapi. She's a grown-up. But not old. Maybe like Alvin. Well, older than Alvin. But not old. And she's pretty. She has this black hair that goes all the way down to the bottom of her butt. You never saw hair like this. She must have to pull it out of the way before she sits down. Can you imagine having hair you could actually sit on? Anyway, guess what? She has six horses, and three are paints. Three! And the old one, she says he's really sweet, and if I come by I can even ride him. And she brought meat."

"Meat? What kind of meat?"

Carly actually wants to focus on the horseback riding. When does Jen think she'll have time to ride some Wakapi woman's horse? They have to work all week, and then they're getting out of here as fast as their feet can carry them. But that feels like too big a subject. So she focuses on something simple. Like meat.

"It's mutton."

"Oh." Then she wonders why she even cared what kind.

"She brought it for Delores and took a bunch of eggs in trade. And Delores made mutton stew with potatoes and onions. And turnips. I'm not so sure about turnips. But it smells really good. You should come in the house now. It's almost ready."

"I'll be there in a minute."

Jen bounds right back out again. Like a windup toy with plenty of wind left. Like a regular little girl. One who's perfectly normal, and…there's really only one way to say it. Happy.

By the time Carly gets into the kitchen, there are three bowls of stew on the table. All she has to do is sit down in front of one. The smell floats up and fills her nostrils, maybe even her whole brain. She feels as if she hasn't eaten in days. As if she has never seen anything so appealing sitting in a bowl on a table in front of her.

Jen is already seated.

Delores is pouring goat's milk into cups in front of the open refrigerator. Carly can feel the cold air waft over her. It feels good. Everything does. All of a sudden, everything feels OK again.

Carly slips the iPod out of her shirt pocket and slides it across the table to Jen's place mat.

"Here. Thanks."

"Well, it's not like it's mine," Jen says.

"But he loaned it to *you*."

Maybe he likes Jen better. Or maybe…just maybe…Jen is better at asking for what she wants.

"Eat," Delores says. "Don't let it get cold."

Carly picks up a spoon and stirs the stew around, looking at the colors. There are chunks of fresh tomato in there and carrots that look more orange than any carrot she can remember seeing. And the potatoes are gold instead of white. And there's one vegetable she doesn't recognize. That must be the turnips.

"Where'd the tomatoes come from?" she asks Delores absently.

In her head, she enjoys picturing vegetables maybe hand-watered from a watering can. How does something so delicate come out of such arid, sandy red soil?

"Where do they come from?"

"Yeah. Where did they grow?"

"Now how would I know that?"

"I'm sorry. I thought you'd know where they're from."

Delores places her hands on her ample hips. "They come from my neighbor Virginia. Who works in Flagstaff three days a week. Where there are supermarkets. So that's where they come from. The supermarket. Where they grew from, well…feel free to go into Flagstaff 'n ask."

"Oh," Carly says. "The supermarket." She feels oddly disappointed. She looks up to see Delores staring at her intently.

"You must just think we're awful quaint around here, don't you, girl?"

"Um. No, ma'am. I didn't mean it that way at all. I was just interested."

She looks away. Lifts a chunk of it onto her spoon. Looks up at Delores, who's still watching her closely. As though she's yet to figure out something crucial.

"Is this a turnip?"

Delores seems to hear the question as a potential challenge. "Yeeeaaaah…" she says, drawing the word out. As if bracing to hear what argument Carly is about to hammer home next.

Carly pops it into her mouth and bites down. It's a little spicy but also savory, because of the gravy. Because of being cooked with the meat. It makes her close her eyes, in order to better taste it.

"It's good." She opens her eyes. Delores looks surprised. "Thank you," Carly adds.

The old woman's bushy white eyebrows arch up a little higher. "OK…" Delores says. Like there might be more to that sentence. But then there isn't.

"And thanks for what you did for my boots. They're so much better. And for leaving more of that salve in the trailer while I was working yesterday. It helps. And that oil you left with it, we used it on our lips *and* our sunburns. Works just as well for both. That was nice. Thank you."

Delores closes her mouth. Also the refrigerator door.

"You're welcome," she says. Like it's the last thing she ever expected to have to say.

Delores sits at the table, tucking a napkin into the collar of her sacky dress.

Carly looks down to see Roscoe staring up at her hopefully, tail swishing.

"Roscoe!" Delores bellows. "Go 'way. We don't stare at you while you're eatin'."

Carly thinks that should be enough volume. Even for Roscoe. But he just swishes his tail. Oblivious.

"Tell 'im, little one," Delores says to Jen. Probably because Jen is closer to the dog.

Jen reaches over and lifts one of Roscoe's enormous ears. Puts her mouth right under the great, soft flap of it. "Roscoe! Go lie down!"

Roscoe lowers his head and slinks into the living room, where he circles six times before lying on the one woven rug. The house falls strangely quiet.

They eat together in what feels almost like a stunned silence. Something that works without any of the parties seeming to know why.

WAKAPI LAND

May 16

"Bet there's nothing even left to do," Carly says. "What are we supposed to do for the rest of the week?"

She's proudly standing by the fully loaded pickup, one elbow leaning on the edge of the truck's bed. There's no junk left on Delores's property. Carly can look around in any and every direction, and nothing offends her innate sense of order.

"Hah!" Delores spits the word out hard. She's sitting in the shade, on a webbed nylon lawn chair. She seems not so much to be supervising as breathing in the day. "You ain't seen the inside of that shed yet."

Carly sighs. Looks over to Jen, who's milking goats, nearly obscured by the oversize cowboy hat, earbud cords dangling.

"What time do you think it is?" she asks Delores.

"That's the third time you asked so far this mornin'. Got an important appointment? Hot date? What?"

"Just wondered."

She knows by now that Delores doesn't wear a watch. Probably couldn't see to tell the time if she did. But twice already the old woman has been able to make a good estimate by stepping out into the sun to get a sense of where it sits in the sky.

"Might be near on eleven."

"Isn't this late for Alvin to come?"

"Oh. So that's what you're waitin' on. Why so anxious to see Alvin all of a sudden?"

"No reason. I mean…he just said he'd try to find something out for me is all."

"Must've had some official business to see to," Delores says. "Want some cold water?"

"Yeah. Sure. Thanks."

While Carly's waiting, she wanders over to the shed and opens the door. Something scurries out of the utter, fully entwined chaos. Carly doesn't even see what, it's traveling so fast. Doesn't even want to know.

She shuts the door again, ready to pretend, at least for the moment, that she never peered in at all. It's a problem she's all too happy to postpone.

Right around the time she and Jen finish their water, Alvin's truck pulls into the driveway. The off-duty truck.

Carly feels a strain ease and untangle in her gut. She's shocked by how big it was. She's been ignoring, denying, the stress of not knowing yet. It's quickly replaced by the terror of being about to find out. In many ways, that's worse. Certainly more acute. More impossible to ignore.

The truck stops in the dirt near the henhouse, and a woman steps out. Carly's heart falls again.

"Who's that?" she asks Delores.

"If it ain't Alvin it might be Pam and Leo," Delores says. As if that's all the explanation the situation requires.

It's not the woman who brought the mutton yesterday. Because her name was…Carly can't remember. But something else. Something longer. It wasn't Pam. And this woman's thick black hair only extends a few inches below her shoulders. Nowhere close to the bottom of her butt.

The woman is leaning back into the cab of the truck, like there's something on the bench seat she needs to untangle. A moment later she lifts a little boy out and sets him on his feet in the dirt. He's somewhere between two and three, as best Carly can figure. Then she lifts out a basket, drooping from its handle, looking loaded and heavy.

The boy runs straight for where Delores sits. Hugs her around the knees. He's not quick to let go, either.

"Howdy there, Leo," Delores says, patting him on the head in hard pats that Carly would think he would mind. But he doesn't seem to.

"Alvin had a call this morning," the woman says. "He and Ray had to go into the village. Help take care of a…situation. You know. That usual situation. Here, I brought you a basket of apples. Figured you got more mouths to feed and all."

Carly immediately wonders if that means he's had no time to look into *her* situation.

Pam sets the basket of apples by Delores's chair.

Delores says, "Thank you kindly. Maybe I'll make us a pie. You mean the situation that goes by the name Rodney?"

"That's the one," Pam says.

She's pretty, Carly decides, but in a way that's totally natural. Almost accidental. Pam seems like a woman who couldn't care less if she's pretty or not. But as luck would have it, she is.

Leo lets go of Delores's knees and strides up to Jen, like a gunfighter trying to keep his holster up. Like those old caricatures of bowlegged cowboys.

"Who're you?"

"Jen," she says.

"Jen." He repeats the word as if it had a flavor. "I'm Leo."

He points to himself with a hook of his thumb. As though Jen might not know which Leo he had in mind without explicit directions.

"Pleased to meet you, Leo."

"Sure," he says. The way he'd say "you're welcome" after doing something nice. Then he swaggers up to Carly. "Who're you?"

"I'm Carly. And you're Leo."

He's looking straight up into her eyes. Fully unguarded. In that odd moment, Carly suddenly knows she wants one of her own. Not now. Not soon. But she does. And she never knew that before. His jet-black hair is so soft looking and so shiny in the sun. It's all she can do not to reach down and stroke his head.

"How'd you know I'm Leo?" he asks. Half-surprised, half-challenging.

"I heard you tell *her*."

"Oh. Right."

Then he scampers away. Runs behind his mother and looks out from between her jeaned legs, one arm wrapped around each of her thighs. He smiles shyly, and when Carly smiles back, he buries his face in the back of his mom's leg.

It strikes Carly odd that any living being could act so confident and so shy in such a short space of time.

"Alvin asked me to come by and see to you," Pam says to Delores. "And he wanted me to meet your two new friends. Which I guess I'm about to do. Or maybe I'm doing it right now, already. And to take that last load in to Chester, if it's loaded and ready to go."

"Oh, it's loaded," Delores says. Implying some level of understatement. "She had that done first thing this mornin'. Before I even got breakfast down her. If there's one thing this girl won't put off"—she indicates Carly with a motion of her chin—"it's anything might get her out of here."

"Well, you can't blame her for that," Pam says. "Can you? Everybody always wants to get home. I bet both these girls are homesick like crazy."

"No," Jen pipes up. "Just Carly. I like it here."

That stops the conversation for an uncomfortable length of time and makes Carly burn in a place deep in her chest, where a resentment, already smoldering, is suddenly fanned. But she clamps down on it and says nothing. She does her best to put it away again. She has no idea what else to do with it but keep stuffing it back into makeshift storage.

"Oh, and one other thing," Pam says. "I got a note for Carly. That's you, right? The homesick one?"

"Yes, ma'am. A note? From Alvin? Where is it?"

"Dashboard of the truck."

Carly does not walk. She runs. Throws the truck door wide. Mangles the envelope tearing it open. Unfolds it without even closing the truck door.

It's on a sheet from a yellow legal pad, folded into quarters.

It starts with the name of a contractor. Mel VanNess. And an address and phone number. Carly's heart morphs into a flock of birds, all startled to the limits of their cage, suddenly, and at the same time.

Maybe Pam will take her to the pay phone on the way home.

But her heart folds its wings on the next line.

Carly Girl. Don't get your hopes up too high reading that first part about Mel. I couldn't find where your stepdad's working. That name and address is just a place he used to work. But not now. The guy said Teddy hurt his back, and as far as he knows, he's not working now at all.

I was hoping it would be a workman's comp case, but Mel says he hurt it on his own time. I tried to track him through disability insurance, but it seems like he wasn't working long enough to qualify. His car is registered to an address in Tulare. Is that where you all moved from? If so, I don't guess that helps.

Mel says he knows Teddy's still in town because he sees him at the market. He's always with this woman named Linda, who Mel knows to say hello to. But he doesn't know her last name or where she lives. Or anything else about her, really. But he says he's seen Teddy in the past two weeks or so. So I'm thinking he's still in town. I just don't know where.

Sorry, girl. Wanted to do better for you.

Oh. And Mel says to check the bar. I guess that means there's only one. Make of that what you will.
—Alvin

Carly leans on the truck for a few minutes, digesting what she just swallowed. She can see Jen and Pam and Delores and Leo interact, but she's too far away to hear them. It's like watching a movie with no sound track.

Teddy's with a woman?

That holds a surprising sting. He wasn't supposed to be. He was supposed to be missing them. All of them. Nothing should have been able to replace them. Or at least…not so fast. Then she decides this Linda is probably just a friend. Teddy always did get along well with women as friends. Yeah. That feels more like the truth. That feels better.

She folds the note and tucks it into her shirt pocket.

A strong, sure thought emerges from the pile of conflict. Comes right up out of the middle of her and makes itself at home. As if to stay awhile.

"That's all I really needed," she says. Out loud but under her breath. "I can find him with that."

Pam drives the dirt roads faster than Alvin. And she doesn't slow down for the bumps. She hits them full on at twenty-five or thirty miles per hour, sending the suspension of the truck a foot higher off the road. Leo, who's strapped into a car seat between them, giggles each time. Carly braces and winces, thinking Delores's rusty old truck will hit the road in a thousand pieces each time it lands.

When they pass over a rutted, washboard section of road, Pam slows some, and Leo makes a low humming sound out loud, just to hear it warble as the truck bumps along. He saves the laughter until the road smooths out again.

Carly hasn't said a word to Alvin's wife or vice versa.

It's Pam who finally breaks the silence.

"Not sure I've ever seen Alvin so heartbroken as he was on his way out the door this morning. He wanted so bad to find your stepdad. He knows you need some kind of good solution, and he just can't stand that he didn't rope it in for you."

"It doesn't matter," Carly says.

She listens to the words as they come out of her mouth, and then later as they echo around in the cab of the truck, leaving a print of themselves, as if they hadn't blown out the window yet. They sound terribly wrong.

"How can it not matter?" Pam asks at last. "I thought it was important to you girls."

"It's important to me to find him. And I will find him. I got enough to go on now. I'll find him. You'll see. I got all I need."

Carly stares out the window, watching a cloud of dust follow some vehicle she can't even see, in a far-off field that doesn't even seem likely to have a road. They pass two girls riding bareback and double on a fine-boned gray horse.

"How?" Pam asks.

"We'll just go there. We'll go there and find him. Go to the market or ask everybody in town. It's a small town. We'll find him."

"Awful long way for two young girls on your own."

"We came all *this* way on our own."

"And almost died doing it, the way I hear."

Carly decides she's done talking to Pam. She's done talking, period. There's nothing written into this work contract that says she has to tell her story to anybody. Justify her position to anybody. Get anybody's permission for anything she wants to do.

She looks up to see Chester's dogs in the road.

"I'm not going in there," she tells Pam. "You let me off right here."

Pam brakes in the middle of the otherwise deserted road. In the right-side mirror, Carly watches the cloud of red dust kicked up by the truck. Watches it settle behind them.

"Here?"

"Anywhere. I don't care. Just not in there with that awful man and those awful dogs. Leave me far enough away that the dogs won't mess with me."

"Chester's just—"

Carly stops her in midsentence by throwing open her door. She steps down into the road, feeling freer already. She slams the door behind her.

"What should I say you want for all this stuff?" Pam asks through the open window.

"I don't care. Whatever he pays. I don't care. I'll be right here."

A long pause, then the truck moves forward again, slowly, as if to spare Carly the bulk of the dust. It's still plenty of dust. It settles over her like a red cloud. She brushes it off her shirt, then wipes her face on her sleeve.

Chester's dogs follow the truck into the driveway, barking. Carly watches for a moment, but they don't come back out.

She leans on a fence post, staring out at a long line of mountains. The sky looks bluer at the edge of them than it looks overhead. It's a color of blue she's never seen in a sky before. Almost a royal or a navy blue. She thinks of Jen's pronouncement that the sky is somehow better here, then pushes it away again.

She's still surprisingly angry. Even though she can't put her finger on anything Pam did wrong. There's a buckskin horse grazing on scrubby weeds in the distance, halfway between the fence and the mountains. In his general direction, Carly says, "If anybody thinks they can stop me from going to California to find him, they got another think coming."

They ride home in absolute silence. It isn't until the truck stops in front of Delores's henhouse that Pam speaks to her again.

"Promise me you won't make any decisions until Alvin comes by to talk to you. Promise me you won't do anything. He's not going to let you walk out of this place without a cent to your name. Without anybody looking after you. Alvin's not like that. Besides, he has a responsibility now. To make sure you're OK."

Carly breathes in silence for a moment, realizing the sheer scope of her mistake. Alvin is the police. Carly just told the policeman's wife that she and Jen are moving on alone. All the way to California. She should have known better. She should have known Alvin wouldn't let her.

She gets down from the truck without answering.

Delores is nowhere to be found.

Jen is playing with that baby goat. The one they watched tormenting the barn cat, back when they were sitting across the road a few days earlier. Before they'd ever set foot on this property. It takes Carly back to a time when they were on their own. Unencumbered. Somehow it feels as though there was less to worry about then.

She walks up to Jen and the goat, both of whom take a minute to notice her. When they do, the goat startles. Bolts straight up in the air and then bounds three or four steps away. He stops there and looks over his shoulder at Carly. Carly is scary somehow. Jen is to play with. Carly is to run from.

"We don't have time for foolishness," Carly says.

Jen's mouth drops open at the sound of her tone.

"What's left to do, anyway?"

"We have to clean out that shed."

"OK, fine. Let's clean out the shed. Geez. What're you in such a bad mood about?"

"Nothing. I mean, I'm not. I just want to get done with everything and move on. I'm just so done with this place."

Jen follows her to the shed without comment.

"Careful opening the door," Carly says.

"Why?"

"I don't know. There could be something in there."

"Like what?"

"I don't know, Jen. Just be careful, OK?"

Jen opens the shed door. Nothing runs out.

Inside they see gardening tools, pallets, a manual mower, plastic milk crates, metal gas cans, glass bottles, more paint cans, plus dozens of items Carly can't even categorize in her brain.

"Damn," Jen says. "This'll be a big job."

"Why do you think I wanted to get started?"

Jen looks up to see the baby goat wiggle back into the enclosure and try to nurse from his mother, butting hard underneath her.

"You won't get anything from her," Jen shouts. "I took it all this morning. Besides, you're too old to nurse. Grow up."

They set about hauling things out into the light.

Carly says, "How do you know how old a goat is supposed to be before it stops nursing?"

"Delores told me. Said she didn't start milking that goat till it was high time for her little one to stop." Jen sticks her head into the shed again. "Hey. Look. Work gloves!"

Jen tosses out three and a half pairs of heavy leather gloves. Which is good. Not everything in that shed looks like something you'd want to touch with your bare hands. It's all been sitting a long time, and mice and insects and God only knows what have left their marks.

It takes probably the better part of an hour just to get it out where they can see it and sort it.

Jen shakes off her gloves, then takes off her hat and wipes sweat off her face with her sleeve. Carly just lets it drip.

"You're awful quiet," Jen says. "What's wrong with you today, anyway?"

"Nothing," Carly says. "I'm just thinking is all."

Alvin comes around near the end of dinner. Just as Delores's apple pie is being served. It's big enough to feed an army, made in a deep, square baking dish, with a second crust covering the mountain of its top.

"Good trick on that timing," Delores says.

"I smelled it from home," Alvin replies. He pulls up a chair and sits. His eyes look red and tired, like he hasn't slept enough. "So, I hear you girls met my two favorite people today."

He's trying to catch Carly's eye, but she won't allow it.

Jen says, "Leo is so cute!"

"That's how I look at it, but I don't guess I'm what you might call impartial."

Alvin waits for some comment from Carly. Everybody does, it seems. But Carly isn't talking. Talking has caused Carly enough trouble for one day.

"You want me to cut that and serve it?" he asks Delores.

"My hands ain't broke yet," Delores says.

He doesn't argue with her.

She serves Alvin first. Sets a square of pie in front of him. It's enormous.

"Holy cow, Delores. That's a whole dinner."

"Do your best with it."

More silence. A square of pie appears in front of Carly. She starts in on it immediately.

When everybody has pie, Delores sits back down at the table again. They eat in silence for a few bites.

Then Alvin says, "Miss Carly." In a big, solid, definite voice.

Carly jumps.

"What?"

"You're being awful quiet."

She shrugs. Nothing more.

When the dishes have been swept off the table and into the sink, Alvin reaches out and puts his hand on Carly's elbow. She pulls her arm away again.

"Take a walk with me," he says.

"What for?"

"Give us a chance to talk."

"I don't feel like walking. All I've been doing is walking and working for as long as I can remember. I'm sick of it. I'm tired. I just want to sit still. Do nothing for a change."

Alvin sits back and sighs. Folds his arms across his chest.

"Well, we do need to have a talk. One way or the other. I just thought maybe you'd rather do it in private."

Carly sits still, silent, feeling her skin and bones set like plaster of Paris. Feeling heavier and more dead in that chair with each second that passes. She doesn't want to move forward into the next part of her life; she can't move backward in time even if she tries. And she doesn't much like where she is.

Almost without realizing she's about to, she jumps to her feet and walks the seven short steps to the door. There she stops and turns around. Alvin is still sitting at the table with his arms folded. Watching to see what she'll do next.

"Well?" she says. "You coming or not?"

It's nearly sundown as they scuff along. Not on the road, but in a straight line toward the big mesa, though Carly can't imagine why. Just right into the heart of nowhere. Alvin is wearing brown cowboy boots. She watches them kick up dust.

She looks up to see a thin, grayish dog with a narrow muzzle loping along through the weeds. The animal spots them, stops, puts its head down. Watches them with suspicion.

"Get on, then," Alvin shouts.

He picks up what only amounts to a handful of dirt, but when he aims it, the animal spins on its heels and takes off. As if anticipating the hurling of large, painful rocks.

"Whose dog?" Carly asks.

"Dog? That's no dog. That's a coyote." He pronounces it as two syllables. Kie-oat. Without a long *e* at the end. "You never seen a coyote before?"

"I don't think so."

It scares her, after the fact. Even though the animal is gone now. But then she remembers that Alvin is here. No coyote would dare come after her when Alvin is here with her.

"Don't want you and your sister leaving this place on your own," he says.

So there it is. She knew it was out there. Waiting for her. She felt it. She's been braced for it, seemingly forever. And now it's landed.

Carly stops walking. It takes Alvin a step to notice.

"I thought you were my friend."

The urge to cry bends her lower lip around. Causes it to tremble. But she doesn't cry. She holds firm.

"I *am* your friend," he says. "What kind of friend would I be if I let you and your sister go all the way to Trinidad, California, on your own? You know how far that is, girl? I bet you don't. I looked it up. It's nearly twelve hundred miles."

"No way. Couldn't be."

"It could be and it is. I looked it up. Can't drive over the Sierra Nevada. Can't walk over them, either, in case you were getting any big ideas. So you have to go south to the Interstate 40, then drive all the way into Bakersfield or so. Then you have to go north for the better part of the length of California. California's a long state."

Carly's still rooted to the spot, an odd cross between stubborn and scared.

"I know California's a long state. I lived in California all my life."

"Oh, that long, huh?"

She turns away from him and begins to walk back to the relative safety of the pink trailer.

"Hey. Hey. You," he says, catching up fast.

"What?"

"Notice I never asked you about your mother? I never asked you if you ran away from her. Did you notice that?"

She stops. But she doesn't look at Alvin. She keeps her gaze leveled at about their boots. Maybe the bottoms of the legs of their jeans.

"What about it?"

"Know why I didn't?"

"No. I don't know anything." It strikes Carly as an expansive statement. Maybe more so than she meant it to be.

"Because a runaway, now that's a kid somebody wants back. A mother of a runaway, now she goes to some lengths. Provides photos to the police. Calls a million times a day. I checked to see, but there didn't seem to be anybody wanting you and your sister back. Now a throwaway, that's another thing altogether. A mother who would do such a thing, you want to make sure not to get kids back into a home like that. Because that mother doesn't deserve to have them."

"Unless she died."

Then she kicks herself for saying it. Hard.

"I see," Alvin says. "That would be a whole different story. I'm sorry."

"What are we supposed to do, then? Just stay here the rest of our lives?"

"You're supposed to give me some time and trust me to figure something out."

But Carly doesn't trust much of anybody anymore. Just Teddy. And herself. And she's pretty sure she was wrong to even begin to trust Alvin. He'll try one more time to get an address or phone number for Teddy. Then he'll turn them over to the authorities and let it be somebody else's worry. That's pretty much what everybody does when the chips are down. They say they care. Until you get to be too time-consuming. Too much of a bother.

"Fine," she says. "Whatever."

She strides for the safety of the trailer.

"That's not what I wanted to hear you say."

She stops dead in her tracks. Suddenly. A sundowner wind is coming up, blowing hot on her face and through her hair. Tears are leaking out no matter how hard she clamps down on the seal.

"What do you want me to say, then?"

"That I can trust you to stay put."

"You can trust me to stay put."

Then she stomps all the way back to the trailer. He doesn't seem to be following. Then again, she doesn't look back.

Without a watch or a clock, it's hard to know how long she waits for Jen. It feels like three hours. Carly guesses it's half that.

The longer she waits, the madder she gets. Here she is, sitting in this trailer by herself, while her sister chooses to sit inside with Delores. Are they talking? And if so, what about? What could they possibly have in common? What about all the years she and Jen have been family? What about everything Carly's tried to do to get them both to safety? Isn't that supposed to count for something? Isn't that supposed to be almost impossible to breach?

By the time Jen walks though the squeaky trailer door, one look at Carly's face stops her in her tracks.

"What?" Jen says.

Carly sniffs the air. There's a new smell. Jen brought it in with her. For a split second, Carly thinks Jen has been smoking pot. But that's not quite it. It's smoky and pungent, but not quite that.

"What's that?" she asks Jen.

"What's what?"

"That smell. Like you were smoking something."

"I wasn't smoking anything."

"Then what is that?"

First Jen seems unwilling to answer at all. But Carly just keeps staring. And the weight of her stare seems to be wearing Jen down.

"It's white sage. But that's all I can tell you."

"What do you mean that's all you can tell me? Who says?"

"It's just the way it is, Carly. It's…it's personal. It's a ceremony. There's nothing wrong with it. It just protects me and helps for grief. But it's between the person who gives it and the person who gets it. And that's all I can say."

"So Delores was doing some kind of magic on you?"

"Not magic. More like…religion."

"Not your religion."

"Can be if I want it to be."

"Get your stuff packed," Carly says. Nice and calm. "We're leaving tonight."

"But—"

"No," Carly says. "No buts. That's the only way it can be." She keeps her voice low, because of Delores and her amazing ears.

Carly gets up and begins to gather her belongings. Toothbrush and hairbrush from the counter in what they laughingly call the bathroom—the space behind the partition in the back of the trailer. Her jacket and spare shirt from the tiny half closet.

She stuffs everything in her backpack.

Meanwhile Jen sits down on the bed.

"It's already dark," Carly says. Barely above a whisper. "Get a move on."

"I'm not going," Jen says.

Then she starts to cry.

Carly walks to the bed and stands over Jen, making herself as big and as tall as she needs to be to get through this. She feels as if it's somebody else's body she's standing in. As if she's watching a movie. As if the ending doesn't have to matter so much. Not the way it would in her real life.

"So, you're splitting us up?" Carly asks. "After everything we've been through?"

And, with that, Carly starts to cry, too.

"Stay, Carly. Don't go. If you don't go, we won't have to split up."

"We have to go find Teddy. Teddy'll take us in. You don't know Delores will let you stay here."

"You don't know she won't," Jen says, sounding stronger.

Carly says nothing. Because she's suddenly seized with a sick feeling in her gut. Maybe Jen isn't just making assumptions. Jen's spent a lot of time alone with the old woman. Maybe these things have been discussed.

"I'm not going back to live with Teddy," Jen says. "I don't know why you're so sure about that. I don't know why you think that's such a perfect plan. Like all our problems'll be solved the minute you get him on the phone. He'll just drop everything and come save us, and we'll live happily ever after. He's not even our stepdad. You keep calling him our stepdad. He's not. They never got married. He's just a guy Mom used to live with."

"I won't stay here, Jen. You know that. I hate it here. Delores doesn't even like me."

"Well, maybe if you wouldn't be so snotty to her, she would."

Carly gets up. Picks up her loaded backpack. Makes one final sweep to be sure she hasn't forgotten anything. Then she walks to the door. Places one hand on the latch. Still crying.

"I mean it. I'll do what I say. I'll go. Right now."

She looks out through the little round window. It's nearly full-on dark. Just the slightest tinge of light still glows on the western edge of the sky.

All the lights are off in the house. Delores turns in early.

She can hear Jen crying. But nothing else.

"I'll walk right out and leave you here. Now come on, Jen. This is not a game. This is our life, our actual life. And it's time for us to move on from here."

She watches Jen cry. Listens to it. Listens to herself cry. Then she gradually eases the door open.

"Wait!" Jen calls. "Don't go yet. You have to take this. It'll keep you safe."

Jen levers to her feet and runs the three steps to where Carly is standing. She slips something off from around her own neck, something that was hiding under her shirt. A black-and-white feather, three or four inches long, with some kind of symbols painted on in red. It has a thin strip of leather wrapped neatly around the shaft and formed into a loop on top. It's on a leather thong.

She slips it over Carly's neck.

"Keep it under your shirt. Against your skin."

"I don't believe in that stuff."

"Maybe it'll protect you whether you do or not."

"Or maybe it won't do anything at all."

"So it can't hurt anything."

Then Jen goes back and sits on the bed. Knees drawn up tight. Arms wrapped around them. Refusing to look at Carly again.

Carly opens the trailer door again. Carefully. Slides through before the part where metal contacts metal.

She's out into the night.

She walks down the driveway to the road, looking over her shoulder five times. Waiting to see Jen run after her.

She stops at the road. Squats on the balls of her feet and waits.

It's barely cool, and the dark feels enveloping but not entirely safe. She thinks of snakes and coyotes. Angry dogs. She touches the tips of her fingers to the red dirt, as if for balance. But she's not really sure that's why. Maybe more to ground herself. She crouches like that for a time. Long enough for her leg muscles to ache. Fifteen, twenty minutes, maybe. The feather tickles her chest. It's not an altogether unpleasant feeling.

Jen never follows.

We've got ourselves a situation here, she thinks. She remembers those words, in Teddy's voice. And remembering Teddy's voice floods her with homesickness. But at no time did she ever actually intend to walk off Wakapi land without her sister. It's just not a possibility she's set to accept.

She walks back to the trailer and lets herself inside.

Jen is lying facing the trailer wall, her back to Carly. Carly strips down to her T-shirt and climbs into bed. They lie in silence in the dark for a minute or two.

"I'm glad you came back," Jen says. Clearly still crying.

"I'm leaving tomorrow night," Carly says. "I'm just giving you a little more time to come to your senses. Better get to work on that."

She almost slips the feather necklace off and gives it back. But then Jen might think she really is staying. That's why she doesn't. Probably why. Unless, somewhere inside her, Carly's thinking she needs all the protection she can get.

Neither says another word all night. But Carly sleeps very little. And she gets the impression that Jen is awake for most of the night, too.

Situations are like that. They take up all the time you used to use for working and eating and sleeping. They soak up your whole life like a black hole in space soaks up the sunlight. And then, where you used to have a life, all you have left is a situation.

WAKAPI LAND

May 17

Carly slips out of bed while her sister, Jen, is still asleep. Her eyes are burning and sore, as if she tried to keep them open in a sandstorm. She feels a little sick to her stomach.

She dresses quietly and slips out of the trailer, careful not to wake Jen. It's after dawn, but not much after. She lets herself into the unlocked house. The house is always unlocked. People don't lock their doors around here. Or, at least, Delores doesn't.

Delores is in the living room, making her bed. It's the first time Carly has gotten a look at where and how Delores sleeps. Her bed drops down out of a cupboard in the wall, the way some people's ironing boards do. It's built in. Carly has heard of beds like that and might even know what they're called. It might be in there, in her, somewhere. But she can't get her brain to work.

"Little one. Good," Delores says. "Help me get this darn Murphy folded back up. My grandson the carpenter made this for me, and he was so proud, but it's gettin' to be more trouble than it's worth. I swear, might come a time I have to just leave 'er down. Gettin' harder ever' day. Not sure how long I'll manage."

"OK," Carly says.

The old woman's face changes.

"Oh," she says. "You. Thought you were your sister."

"Sorry to disappoint you," Carly says, not bothering to hide her feelings.

"Just that she tends to bounce up earlier. Usually."

"We had a rough night."

Carly takes hold of the end of the bed and lifts. Once she gets it partway up, it seems willing to go the rest of the way on its own. She closes the cabinet door behind it.

That's how you put something away, she thinks. Nice and neat. Now you see it, now you don't. She used to be able to do that with everything. But now she knows. Some things don't store so easy.

Delores nods twice. Carly assumes she's to take that as a thank-you.

"You can't have my sister," Carly says.

It would have been easy to cry in the middle of saying that. But she doesn't. She closes a cabinet door on at least that much emotion.

Delores crosses her arms across her chest. Lifts her chin.

"Know how long I been on this earth, little girl? Ninety-two years, that's how long. In all that time I had a lot of strange things said to me. Thought I'd heard it all, matter of fact. But you might of just won the prize there. You think I'm takin' her against her will?"

"No," Carly says. "Just against mine."

"Uh-huh? That so? Well, maybe your will for what your sister ought to do ain't the be-all 'n end-all. Maybe your sister's will for what your sister ought to do is more to the point. Can you blame her for not wantin' to go back and live with that man?"

Carly realizes her mouth is open. Hanging wide.

"Yes! I can blame her! And I do!"

"You got blame trouble, then, if you could blame some poor child for not wantin' to go back to a man tried to force himself on her."

The room turns a bit unstable. Carly finds herself reaching out and touching her fingers to the cabinet. Just to be on the safe side. She has to run a path in her mind. Trace it back. Delores never met their mother. This can't be happening. This is not the way things are supposed to be happening.

"Who told you that?"

"Use your head, girl. *You* didn't say it. Who's that leave?"

"Jen told you Teddy tried to force himself on her? That's a total lie!"

"Why would she lie about it?"

"I don't know. I don't know. That's the whole question," Carly says, winding more deeply into the panic. "Why did she tell you that?"

The circular motion of her thoughts is accelerating. Making her dizzy. Why is Jen acting like this? Why is everything that used to be solid suddenly fluid? Why are the few things that used to be dependable suddenly upside down?

"I don't think that *is* the question," Delores says. "Here's what I think's the question: Why *didn't* she tell *you*?"

A pause that feels like an age, an era. It's probably two or three seconds. But some two- or three-second spans are longer than others.

Carly marches out of the house. Stomps across the dirt to the trailer. Throws open the trailer door with as much noise as possible. She wants Jen awake. But Jen is not even there.

Carly steps out again and looks around.

Jen is carrying a pail and the milking stool into the goat corral. She must have woken up when Carly did. Either that or she was never asleep. Maybe she was only pretending to be asleep. Maybe Jen pretends a lot of things. Maybe Carly doesn't know Jen at all. But if she doesn't know Jen, she doesn't know anybody. And that's a possibility right now. Anything is. Carly's life could be anything right now. Since it obviously isn't what she thought.

Carly strides over and ducks between the rails of the corral.

Jen notices. Turns her head toward Carly. Takes in the look on Carly's face. But she doesn't react in any special way. Maybe things were bad enough last night that Jen figures they're still just that. Just that bad and no more.

Jen pulls the stool up to the oldest momma goat. "You're up early."

"Never got to sleep. You told Delores Teddy tried to molest you."

It's not a question. So she doesn't put a question mark on the end of it.

Jen begins milking the goat. Carly can hear the distinctive light ringing sound of the stream of milk hitting the side of the pail.

"You're not answering me," Carly says.

"Didn't think it was a question. Are you asking me did I or didn't I?"

"Sure," Carly says. "Let's start there."

Jen milks for a long time without answering. Carly wants to grab her sister's shoulder and forcibly turn her around. A second later she wants to strangle Jen.

"I said it," Jen says. Still not looking up from her work.

"Why? Why, Jen? Why would you do a thing like that? Tell me. Why?"

At first, Jen doesn't.

Then, after a time, she does.

"Because he did."

The world spins on its axis for a brief time without much of anything happening. No one speaks. Carly's brain doesn't put out much activity. It's just a fallow period, in which everything holds still. For a change.

Then Carly awakens. Suddenly.

"How could you lie about a thing like that? How can it be so important to stay here that you'd lie? It's been, like, four days. Not even four days. How can this place mean so much to you? Why would you lie?"

"I wouldn't," Jen says.

Carly walks around to Jen's left side and sits down in the dirt. Cross-legged, right in all that potential filth. Just to make sure she doesn't fall down instead. Just to preempt disaster. The baby goat comes around and nibbles at her hair. She shoos him away.

Jen is refusing to look at her.

"It was while you were away at the lake," Jen says. "I was sleeping, and then he was in the bed with me, and he had his hand clamped down over my mouth. He was real drunk. He said he wouldn't hurt me, but I had to be quiet. Mom wasn't home anyway, but maybe he didn't want the neighbors to hear me scream. I kicked him where it hurts, and then I jumped out the window. And I ran in my pajamas all the way down to the bar. I went over hedges and cut through yards so he couldn't see which way I'd gone. So he couldn't follow. It was cold."

"You jumped out the second-floor window?"

"Yeah, and it hurt, too. Really bruised up the bottoms of my feet. Like bone bruises. They were just getting almost completely better when we started walking."

"You were dreaming."

"I don't think so."

"You said you were sound asleep when it happened. You dreamed he was there. And then you woke up when you jumped out the window."

Jen's hands stop moving. The goat kicks out lightly with one back hoof.

"Fine. Believe what you want, Carly. You always do anyway."

And on that line, the tears come back. For both of them. At almost exactly the same time. It's tedious to have so many tears. Tiring. Carly keeps expecting to run out of them. It's discouraging to keep waiting to touch the bottom of a bottomless well.

"Why would you tell that to Mom and not me?"

Jen's tears come faster now, and she wipes her eyes furiously on the back of her sleeve.

"Because...well, why do you think, Carly? Look what happened when Mom tried to tell you. You called her a liar. You turned on her. You hated her. You never forgave her. You wouldn't have believed me anyway. You only believe what you want. So it wouldn't've done any good. I didn't want you hating me, too."

A movement catches Carly's eye. Apparently Jen's, too. Because they both look up.

A woman is riding up the driveway on a white horse, towing two saddled, riderless horses behind her. Pulling them along on lead ropes attached to their bridles. One is a big bay, the other an old mostly-brown paint.

"Virginia's here," Jen says, sniffling. Wiping her eyes again.

But Carly already knew it was Virginia. Because of the woman's hair. It's so long that she had to gather it all up and wear it over her left shoulder to keep from sitting on it. It trails over her thigh and onto the saddle.

The woman rides right up to the fence. Her white horse leans his head over the rails. Stretches out his neck. As if he'd always wanted to meet a goat.

"I think maybe I came at a bad time," Virginia says.

Jen shakes her head vehemently. "No, it's OK, Virginia." But she doesn't try to hide the fact that she's crying.

It strikes Carly that maybe nobody would expect otherwise from them. Their mother is dead. Teddy is not quite findable. They have no father. They are very far from home. Their tears must not be much of a surprise to anyone.

Usually when you see two girls crying, you ask them what's wrong. But in their case, nobody even needs to ask.

Virginia says, "Delores told Alvin you girls were all caught up on your work, that there wasn't much left for you to do. So I thought you might like to go riding. But if I came at a bad time…"

"Yeah," Carly says. "We were sort of in the middle of something."

Jen jumps to her feet, startling the goats and knocking over the milking stool. "I want to go riding."

"I'm not in the mood," Carly says.

"Well, I am. I'm going." Jen marches to the fence and ducks through the rails. "Can I ride the paint?"

It's an ugly replay of last night. Carly always thought when the chips were down, Jen would do what Carly says. But this is the second time she's seen through that lie. When the chips are down, Jen does what Jen thinks is best. Carly's judgment doesn't even get its day in court.

It strikes Carly, all at once, that she really might have to choose between leaving without Jen or not leaving at all.

She struggles to her feet and dusts off her jeans.

"Fine, OK," she says. "I'll go for the ride, too."

It's a decision made purely for expedience. She wants nothing less than to climb up on a horse and not get the answers she needs from this conversation. But Jen is going. And Carly doesn't want to let her go alone. She wants them to have a chance to talk some more. And she doesn't dare let that fine thread break. The only thing that's held them together for days.

If she lets her sister go now, Jen might really be gone. Gone gone. Out of Carly's life forever. Or, anyway, that's how it feels.

It's a real enough feeling to get her into a saddle.

That's pretty damn real.

The big bay horse carries her along through what must be the life of someone else entirely. There's a rocking motion to the bay's gait. It's almost hypnotic.

Carly feels around for that place in herself that's deeply agitated. The way your tongue feels for a sore tooth, unable to leave that pain alone. But she can't entirely find it. She's too disconnected. The pain she's rooting around to find is in her life, and she's…well, she doesn't know where. Somewhere else.

Jen is riding beside her, so close that their wooden stirrups occasionally bang against each other.

Virginia is riding a few lengths ahead.

Jen is eating the last of her breakfast. Delores scrambled eggs and folded them in fry bread, like a breakfast sandwich. Handed one up to each girl before they rode away. Carly finished hers before they got to the end of the driveway. Jen has been savoring hers. Eating with both hands. Riding with no hands at all, the paint horse's reins resting on the horn of the saddle.

As Jen takes a tentative bite, a crumble of egg gets away from her. Bounces off the saddle and lands in the dirt.

"Ahhh," Jen says, half standing and twisting around in the stirrups, as if that will help to locate it. Seeming not to worry about unbalancing herself. Seeming not to notice that the ground is a long way down.

Then again, she jumped out a second-story window.

Carly pushes the thought away again. It's just a thing she heard. She doesn't know for a fact that anything like that ever happened at all.

Jen pops the last bite into her mouth.

Carly takes an even tighter grip on the saddle horn.

"Now I don't know what to believe," Carly says.

It seems like such a reasonable thing to say. But it's met with utter silence. Long and…utter.

Then, suddenly, Jen says, "Screw you, Carly." She drums on the paint horse's sides with her heels.

The horse breaks into a trot and catches up with Virginia's horse.

Carly rides behind them for a time, a little unsure as to what just happened. Then a light dawns. Things come a little clearer.

It seems so obvious now.

Jen thinks Carly was supposed to believe Jen.

They ride up a dirt road, past a schoolhouse. There are horses tied under an awning in the shade and a few cars and trucks parked out front. Bikes lean on the fence. Some parents are just delivering their kids for the morning. Other kids are just delivering themselves.

A group of five girls runs in a circle around them as they pass.

"Hi, Virginia," they all say, almost all at once. Only the littlest one misses the rhythm.

"Who're your friends, Virginia?" a girl in a bright yellow shirt asks.

"They're visitors. Say hi to them."

"Hi, visitors," the girls say, a little less simultaneously.

It feels good to Carly to be called a visitor and not an interloper.

"Bye, visitors," the little one says.

They ride on up the road. Past a herd of cattle with no fences to keep them in. Past a fenced yard with five cars in various stages of dismantlement. Past a little white wooden house with a porch swing. With a woman on the porch swing. Who waves as they go by.

Carly waves back, but she can't shake the feeling that the greeting was for everyone else. Jen is still riding next to Virginia, leaving Carly to feel like everyone fits into this landscape except her.

The trail begins to climb, and then Carly can see that it winds around to the top of the mesa. The sun is higher and stronger now, and sweat begins to creep down her collar, run down her back.

She nudges the bay forward, but he's in no hurry. He makes up maybe one length of the ten they're trailing, then falls back again when she stops nagging.

A solid decision forms in her head. She's leaving tonight. If Jen is going to be pigheaded, Carly can't afford to be weak. If Jen does what Jen thinks is right, Carly has to do what Carly thinks is right.

She'll take off after dark and not look back this time. And when she gets to Trinidad, she'll be able to see the ocean. Ralph said it was right on the coast. So there will always be water, and all she'll ever have to do to see water is just look. She won't be hot anymore, like she has been all her life. She won't spend every day baking. Feeling herself sweat. And for the rest of her life, she won't go anywhere dusty and dry and hot and empty. She'll always be where it's tree-lined and coastal and cool.

It's a perfect, perfectly welcome plan. There's really just one problem with it.

She only has about twelve hours to convince Jen to change her mind.

"You can ride over to the edge," Virginia says, when they're up on top of the mesa. "It's quite a view. You can see almost as far as the Interstate 40. Well. More than halfway there, anyway."

Jen nudges her horse forward. Carly holds back.

"Isn't it dangerous to take them right up to the edge?"

"A horse has enough sense not to step off a cliff. They're not stupid. They want to live, too."

Carly pretends the view is just as good from where she sits. She looks all around, trying to see something familiar. She sees a road that looks like a real road. Paved. It heads south, or maybe southwest, in a straight line, disappearing to a point at the horizon.

"What's that road?" she asks Virginia. "I thought there were no paved roads around here. Where does that go?"

"That's this road," she says. "The one we rode up on. The one with the school. If you take it the other way from the road Delores lives on, it's a dirt road for about a mile. Then it turns into pavement. Goes all the way down to the I-40. Dumps you down between Winslow and Flagstaff."

She remembers Alvin convincing her that Trinidad was too far away. He said you'd have to take the Interstate 40 all the way into California. Now Carly knows which road to take to meet up with the highway that will take her home.

She squeezes her boot heels against the bay gelding's side. He takes a few dozen lazy steps, and then she's right beside Jen. Right at the edge of the bluff.

They look off into the distance together.

Carly knows she's looking down on Delores's house, but she can't figure out which one it is. Everything is too small, too unfamiliar from this distance and angle. The few tiny homes are scattered so far apart that they look to Carly like pins on a map. The sun has gone behind a pebbly, perfectly mottled blanket of clouds. She can see a mountain in the distance with traces of snow on its peak.

"Those clouds look just like popcorn," Jen says.

It's the first she's spoken to Carly since Carly admitted the truth of what she does and does not believe.

"I really am leaving tonight," Carly says. "No bluff. This time it's real."

"I know it."

"Come with me."

Jen only shakes her head. She doesn't cry. Carly waits for her to cry. But apparently Jen found the bottom of her bottomless well.

"Then I'll go on ahead and find Teddy. I'll find out what's what."

Jen says nothing for a time. Carly's horse shifts his weight under her, rubbing his face on the inside of his knee. Like scratching an itch.

Jen says, "I already know what's what."

"I'll come back for you. As soon as I've got things squared away."

"If you don't die."

"I'm not going to die, Jen."

"I sure hope not. But you can't say for a fact."

"No. I guess I can't. But, anyway…I'm going."

"I know it," Jen says.

There's a calmness in her words. No less pain but no more agitation. It's all accepted, apparently, as just the way it's going to be. Apparently it's just that easy. If you're Jen.

They stare out at the view for a while longer. The gathering clouds form a nice break from the normally relentless sun.

"I just don't get how you can look at all this and not think it's beautiful out here," Jen says.

Carly tries to look at the vista with new eyes. She really tries. It may be the only way to stop this split that's about to happen. If Carly could suddenly fall in love with the Arizona desert…Love it enough to stay…

"I don't see it."

"I know you don't," Jen says. "And I just don't get it."

"There's nothing out here."

"See, that's the problem with you, Carly. You think if it wasn't made by a person, then it's not anything at all. You just want malls and cars and cell phones. You look at a sky like this and think it's nothing."

Jen reins the paint horse around, as if she'd been born on his back, and rides back to Virginia. Carly sits her horse a minute longer, wondering how long there's been a problem with her in Jen's eyes. She always thought they fit each other fine. Funny how wrong a person can be. And how little time it takes to pull the covers off someone's biggest mistake.

They lie in bed that night for maybe an hour. Carly is fully dressed. She even has her boots on. She tells herself she's just waiting to be sure Delores is asleep. But she doesn't share that thinking with Jen. Because she's not even sure she believes it herself.

She rehearses the sentence maybe twenty times in her head. Opens her mouth twice, only to hear nothing but silence come out.

Finally she pushes harder. Forces the issue.

"I'm going now."

"Be careful."

"I wish you'd change your mind, Jen."

"I wish you'd change yours."

Carly climbs out of bed. Reaches for her backpack. The realness of everything settles in on her hard and fast. She almost wavers. But she thinks about Teddy and a place with an ocean. A cool place, with a nice big house. And him. He'll help her understand how this whole horrible misunderstanding could have happened. He'll lead her to a truth she can live with. She couldn't stay here anyway. Never could have. But now, especially, she can't stay here and not know. She has to know.

She threads her arms through the straps of the pack. Hoists it onto her back. It feels familiar, but not in a good way.

"I'll come back for you."

She doesn't cry. She feels too scraped out to cry.

"And we'll be right back to where we are now. You won't stay and I won't go."

"No, I'll fix it. I'll find out what really happened. It'll be OK. You'll see. I think you just had a dream that night."

"I don't think so. It felt real."

"Dreams do sometimes."

"I feel like I might never see you again. Like you'll go out there and get yourself killed."

"No, I won't. Look. Say I left while you were sleeping. That you don't know where I went."

Jen snorts. "Right. Like they won't know where you went."

That makes Carly feel the need to get going. Get a head start on Alvin. Be so far away by morning that he won't be able to imagine she could have made so many miles. Then he'll be looking in all the wrong places. Too close to here.

"I'll see you soon," Carly says.

But it sounds a little bit like whistling past the graveyard. She doesn't say it like she fully believes it. Or like she expects Jen to.

The moon is still more than three-quarters full. And Carly's eyes have adjusted to the light. It's enough light to allow her to walk normally down the dirt road, due south, until it turns into pavement. Which it does, sooner than she expected.

It feels weird to walk on asphalt. Like she'd already forgotten such modern inventions existed.

Carly is nursing an unpleasant feeling in her gut. Like that weird unsettled feeling you get right before the nausea of a stomach flu hits. Oh, God, don't let me be sick, she thinks. Just what I couldn't afford to dump on top of all this.

Her jeans pockets are heavy with quarters. Eleven dollars in quarters. It jingles and weighs her down as she quickens her step, ready to make time, now that she can see where she's going well enough. Now that the road is smooth.

For a while she actually runs. Jogs down the road. Her blisters are nearly healed, her boots feel fine. She's in the best shape of her life. The road is a gentle downhill slope, which gives her a sense of power. Like when you're walking on one of those moving walkways at the airport. It makes you feel like you're a better walker than you really are. Like you can do anything.

Before she wears down from the running, she hears a motor behind her.

Her stomach goes cold. She spins around, expecting to see Alvin coming after her. But it's a different truck. A good twenty years older. It's a flatbed, with wooden slat railings on the sides of the bed.

She stands, frozen like a deer, lit up by its headlights.

Suddenly, and without even thinking, she sticks her thumb out. The truck passes her, then rumbles to a stop.

Carly runs to catch up.

Sure, she said no hitchhiking. But that was when Jen was along. It was her responsibility to make sure nothing bad happened to Jen. But now it's just her. And she doesn't worry so much about herself. Or maybe she doesn't even still care.

A middle-aged native woman leans out the passenger window. Points to the bed of the truck. Carly runs around to the back, steps on the trailer hitch, and pulls herself up. Drops onto the flat wooden bed.

She crawls up nearer the cab as the truck rolls on again. Takes off her backpack. Flops on her back and uses the pack for a pillow. That funny feeling in her gut is still there, but she tries to focus off it. For the first time since arriving on Wakapi land, she looks straight up into the night sky. It's alive with stars. Billions of stars, bright and clear. Even the strong moonlight can't wash them out completely.

She thinks of Jen saying the sky is better here than anywhere else. But she convinces herself that the sky will be at least as good in Trinidad. Better.

Within minutes, she's asleep.

The native woman is shaking her by the shoulder. She sits up suddenly. The truck is standing still. The moon is down. It's dark. Truly dark. Just a thin path illuminated by the headlights of the old truck.

"We turn here," the woman says. "You going to the 40?"

"Yeah," she grunts, still shaking off sleep.

"That way."

Carly thanks the woman for the ride and climbs down. The truck turns right onto a dirt road. Carly watches it until it's gone.

Then she looks up.

Now that the moon is down, the stars are surreal. They surround her like a dome, and she feels as though she can see into the depth of that field. Like the stars are really in three dimensions. She can even see an eroded-looking band of mass that could be the edge of the Milky Way.

Somewhere in the distance, a dozen or more coyotes strike up a chorus. Yipping and howling. It sends a shiver up her spine. Makes little hairs stand up at the nape of her neck. That's when she knows she's never been so alone in the world, or so aware of her aloneness.

That sickening feeling slices through her gut again, leaving her thighs trembling, as if she can't hold herself up. She falls to her knees in the dirt, wondering if she's about to be sick. But when she turns her gaze fully to it, she finds it's not sickness at all. It's fear. She's been terrified ever since leaving on her own. But she couldn't let it stop her. So she couldn't let herself admit it.

She thought she knew what it felt like to be on her own. But back then, she had Jen. But it's as if she didn't even know it. She thought that was alone, just her and Jen. But it wasn't.

This is.

It's about four miles later, as best she can gauge miles, and Carly is more or less sleeping on her feet. Walking and sleeping at the same time.

Suddenly, the world lights up in red, and Carly jumps fully awake, heart pounding. About fifty feet down the road in front of her, red lights flash. Cop cars, she thinks. What else could it be?

She has no doubt it's her they're after.

Then rhythmic bells start clanging. *Ding ding ding ding ding.* And the red lights move down in an arc, toward the road. First she thinks she might be dreaming with her eyes open. Then the lights drop into context and make sense. They're railroad gates. That's all. A railroad track intersects this road. And the train is coming. She can see it, off in the distance. She can hear one long whistle from its engine. Carly starts to run. Right in the direction of the clanging gates.

The train is coming. And it's headed west.

It's like a wind at her back. She's getting help. She's out on the road, making a beeline home to Teddy, and something in the universe is helping her get there. Paving a smooth road. First a truck picks her up and takes her practically to a railroad track. Then a train comes by headed west.

She sees the light on the engine of the train clearly now, off in the distance. She runs faster. Then she trips on something in the dark and goes flying. Lands on her belly and the heels of her hands. It knocks the wind out of her, as well as the burst of sudden confidence. But she struggles to her feet. The heels of her hands are stinging and wet, probably with blood. She leans on her knees, bloodying her jeans, until she can breathe again. Then she takes off trotting.

By the time she ducks under the clanging, flashing gate, the train has almost passed. She sees one final box car go by, but the door is just a crack open, barely enough to get a hand in. She knows there's such a thing as jumping a train. But she has no idea what you grab on to. How you grip the thing.

The caboose lumbers by. In the flashes of red, Carly thinks she sees a ladder on the back of it. She runs after the back of the train and leaps on pure faith. If she's wrong about what she thinks she sees, or if she misses, she's in for another hard fall. She braces for it. Her bleeding hands grab on to something metal. A metal rung. Thank God the tops of her hands are dry. So her fingers can take a good hold. Her feet swing around for purchase. Then they land on a rung as well.

She slides one arm through the ladder and wraps her arms tightly, so she can't lose her grip. A moment at a time, her heartbeat calms, and her breathing returns to almost normal. She's headed west, watching the dark shapes of whittled rocks and giant cactus flash by, dark silhouettes. Now all she has to do is hold on tight. And resist the urge to fall asleep.

She thinks about Jen. Is she sleeping soundly or lying awake worrying? What will Delores say in the morning when it's clear Carly is gone?

A startling thought descends. Maybe Delores and Alvin will turn Jen over to child protective services. After all, Jen had nobody except an older sister, and then even Carly ran out on her.

But Jen will say it wasn't like that.

But maybe no one will believe her.

Carly almost lets go, thinking she can make her way back down the tracks in the direction of the Wakapi. Then she realizes they've passed a dozen of those little roads. Just like the one Carly came down.

It's too late to find her way back now.

PART FOUR

Seems So Long Ago

NEW MEXICO

Christmas Day

"Christmas is supposed to be a day you wake up early in your warm house and run downstairs in your pj's to see what's under the tree with your name on it, damn it."

"Hmm," Jen said. "Well. We don't get that. So let's go see what we get."

They'd just woken up shivering in a tent at a KOA campground. Who knew it could get so cold in New Mexico? Carly thought. She'd expected it to be hot. Hotter than Tulare even. But they'd been climbing in elevation.

She'd wanted to ask if their new home was in the mountains. But then she would've had to talk to her mom. Or, God forbid, Wade.

"You ready?" she asked Jen.

"Ready as I'll ever be."

They stepped out into the freezing absolute silence.

Wade and their mom were sleeping in the bed of Wade's truck, which was parked behind their mom's car with a big rented trailer attached. No one moved in or near the cars. No one moved anywhere. Not many people were camping here. Most were home with their families for the holiday. Those who were here were apparently still asleep.

Jen pointed up at the pine trees. "Christmas trees," she said. Without much enthusiasm. Like it was just a thing she figured might be worth a try.

"I miss Teddy's millions of dumb decorations," Carly said.

Jen said nothing.

"Still not speaking to me?" Carly's mom asked.

They sat at a booth in a cheap roadside pancake restaurant. Carly watched Wade try to find a spot to park his mega-truck, along with the trailer containing most of their stuff. What they still owned, that is. The place they were moving into was small. Or so Carly had been told. Over and over, the whole time they'd packed. They'd had to leave a lot behind.

Thank God he was driving a separate vehicle, Carly thought for about the twentieth time.

"Carly," Jen said. "It's Christmas."

Like that hadn't gone without saying. But of course Carly got Jen's point. You can't not speak to your mother on Christmas. Silently, inwardly, Carly disagreed. Potentially right down to the suggestion that this day deserved to be honored as a Christmas.

A car pulled out of the parking lot, giving Wade a chance to park his long load across three spaces. Too bad, Carly thought. Now he'll be joining us.

"Wade says we should get there later today," Carly's mom said. "So it might not be much of a Christmas morning, but at least we can have a decent dinner. I mean, not a turkey or anything. But at least we can stop and buy a canned ham and some rolls or something. Eat in our new place."

She stared at Carly and waited. Carly could see it in her peripheral vision. She didn't look back. Instead she watched Wade pace down the sidewalk to the restaurant door. She could hear the clicking of his boot heels from inside.

"When do we get to open our presents?" Jen asked.

An awkward silence.

Then her mom said, "Little bit of a problem with that."

Jen sighed. "You were busy moving, and you didn't us get any. We got yours."

"No, I got them a long time ago. Weeks ago."

"Then what's the problem?"

Carly felt like Jen was half being herself and half channeling Carly. Saying what Carly would have said, but toning down the vitriol in the translation.

Wade sat down at the table. Jen said good morning to him. Carly said nothing and was careful not to look his way.

"I...got you girls gift certificates to your very favorite store," their mom said.

"Oh," Jen said. A downbeat "oh."

Jen had filled in the blanks already. So had Carly. Their very favorite store was, of course, in Tulare.

"You don't say good morning when I sit down?"

Wade. She heard the darkness in his voice. She could match it to a glare in his eyes from experience. From memory. She did not look up to confirm what she knew.

"Leave the girl alone, Wade. But what we'll do, we'll give you girls a little bit of cash. Can't be much. You know. Things being what they are. But you can go into town—the new town—and get to know the place by looking around and picking yourself out presents. Won't be anything too big, but then I'll get my money back on those gift certificates and we'll have more presents later on."

"OK," Jen said.

Carly said nothing. Just watched a woman with a leashed collie let the dog out of the car to sniff around in the parking lot. Watched it lift its leg on a bush.

"This is getting old," Wade said.

"I told you leave the girl alone, Wade."

"No. I'm gonna speak my piece here. This is Christmas morning, and your mom just told you what she's doing to salvage Christmas for you girls in a tight squeeze, and you got nothing to say at all?"

"Wade, butt out. She's my girl. Not yours. Get off it."

"Damn her!" Wade pounded the heel of his hand on the table. Hard.

Everybody in the restaurant fell silent. Every neck craned to see. Carly watched the cook come out of the kitchen, a middle-aged man with broad shoulders. He stood watching Wade until it became clear that nothing more was about to happen. Then he shook his head and pushed back through the swinging door.

"Wouldn't let *my* daughter treat me like that," Wade said.

"Well, now there's a surprise. I never would have known that if you hadn't already told me about a hundred and fifty times. And what do I tell you every time?"

"That I can treat my own daughter how I want, but this one's yours."

"Right. Good job listening."

The waitress appeared at their table, pad and pencil in hand. "Merry Christmas. What'll you folks have?"

She looked to Jen first.

"Two eggs over well with pancakes, please."

The waitress turned to Carly next.

"Bacon and scrambled eggs with rye toast. Please. And merry Christmas to you, too."

"Ah," Wade said. "It speaks."

"Enough, Wade," Carly's mom said. "I'll have the short stack. Wade, what do you want, honey?"

"Steak and eggs. Over easy. And a new stepdaughter."

The waitress pretended to smile. Or tried to, anyway. "Well, I'll bring you the steak and eggs, anyway."

She hurried off.

"Steak and eggs?" Carly's mom turned her irritation fully onto Wade. "Steak and eggs? You just *had* to order the most expensive thing on the menu? I was about to give the girls twenty-five dollars each for Christmas, and you just single-handedly cut it down to twenty."

"I like steak and eggs. I wanted steak and eggs. Damn it, it's Christmas, and what have I got here? Steak and eggs isn't asking so much."

A few heads turned again.

"Fine, we'll talk about it later. Just shut up before you get us kicked out of here. Probably the only place open for miles. Maybe the only place open in the state. So shut up and don't blow this for us."

The energy around Wade turned so tight and so dark that Carly involuntarily twitched her shoulders as a way of letting it move through her.

Later, after breakfast, as they trudged out through the parking lot together, Wade leaned over close to Carly's mom and spoke, his voice measured but chilling.

"And you don't *ever* tell me to shut up again."

"Oh, my God!" Jen shrieked as they drove through the gate in the white picket fence. Following Wade and the trailer. "You call this *small*?"

Carly looked up. The house was twice the size of their old rental in Tulare.

"This is Wade's brother's house," their mom said. "He's letting us use the guesthouse until we can get it together to afford something better."

"Oh," Jen said.

They stopped behind Wade in the driveway. Wade honked. And waited.

A few minutes later, a man stepped out of the house. Carly figured he was literally Wade's identical twin.

"Oh, crap," she whispered to Jen. "Two of him!"

"I heard that."

Carly caught her mother's eyes in the rearview mirror, then looked away.

Jen rolled her window down. The air felt light and cold. Carly briefly wondered if it ever snowed here.

She watched Wade walk up to his brother, arms out as if to embrace him. Wade Two, as she'd already named him in her head, stuck his right hand out to shake. But what kind of brothers shake hands? Carly thought. Especially twin brothers. These two, it turned out. Wade dropped his arms and shook.

"Just wanted to say hi," Wade said. "But we'll get right out of your hair again. Let you enjoy Christmas in peace."

"Yeah, that'd be good," Wade Two said. "It's not locked."

Then he turned and walked back into the big house.

"Runs in the family," Carly whispered to Jen.

"That one I didn't hear," her mother said. "But I don't want you whispering to your sister. I got a good idea I wouldn't like it."

"Who's he going inside to have Christmas with?" Jen asked their mom. "Has he got a whole big family in there?"

"I don't think so. Wade said his wife and kids left him. I don't know why he wants to be by himself."

Carly exchanged a look with Jen but said nothing. Because it all pretty much said itself.

"It's *one bedroom*?"

Carly blasted the words out to no one in particular. Then, realizing she'd just scraped close to speaking to her mom, she sat on the floor in the corner and said nothing more.

Jen stood in the middle of the one main room, looking around. "So, I'm guessing you guys get the bedroom. Right?"

"Well, of course, honey. You know we need privacy."

"And we don't, of course," Carly barely breathed. It was not meant to be heard by anyone but herself. And it wasn't.

"Where do *we* sleep?" Jen asked, her tone riding the edge of exasperation.

"Wade's brother is loaning us a fold-out couch."

"I have to share a bed with Carly?"

"It won't kill you, Jen. It's just for a while."

"Shit, this ain't gonna be easy," Wade said. "We'll have to put a TV in our bedroom. I'm gonna feel like a prisoner in there, and if I sit out here with these two kids, I'm gonna feel like a whole other kind of prisoner. This place would fit us great if it was just the two of us."

Jen came and sat on the floor, her hip bumping up against Carly's. Ducking the gathering storm.

"Well, it's *not*, Wade. When I met you, did I lie and say I was childless?"

"No, but—"

"Then just shu—" Carly's mom stopped herself. It was unlike her. But the tone in Wade's voice when he'd said she was never to tell him to shut up again—that was not easily forgotten. "Let's just have a nice Christmas," she said. "Much as we can. What's left of it."

"You want to have a nice Christmas? Give those girls their money and send 'em into town. I already need room to breathe."

"What do you think'll be open today?"

"I don't care. They can window-shop."

"Well, get their bikes out at least. It's too far to walk."

"Bikes are buried. All the way at the front end of that trailer."

"Well, they can't go into town, then. Can they?"

"I'm gonna go nuts trying to unload with them standing right here. Every place I walk they'll be right in my way."

"They live here, Wade. I'm telling you, they live here, too."

"And I'm telling you I wish they didn't."

Jen jumped to her feet. "We'll walk," she said. "Just go ahead and give us our Christmas money. We'll walk into town."

"It's like three miles, honey."

"I don't care."

"Each way."

Jen looked down at Carly. To see if she was game. Carly nodded. Of course she was willing to take a six-mile walk. Even though she never had before. The trick was figuring how not to end up back here.

"OK. It's your life." She doled out a twenty-dollar bill for each of them. "Give this to your sister who isn't speaking to me. And tell her merry Christmas."

Jen walked over to where Carly was still sitting. Cross-legged on the hardwood floor in the emptiness. It was hard for a place to look small with nothing in it, Carly thought. But this place managed.

Jen held the twenty down to Carly. "She says—"

"I heard her."

As they were walking out the door, Carly heard Wade say, "Thank the Lord they're gone. Not a moment too soon."

"What'd you get?" Jen asked when they met up again on the corner near the ice-cream store. "How'd you know already what you wanted?"

Carly took it out of her pocket and showed it to Jen.

"A phone card?"

"Yup."

"They have prepaid calling cards for only twenty bucks?"

"They even had cheaper ones. But I wanted all the minutes I could get."

"You going to call your friends back in Tulare?"

"Yeah," Carly said. "That's what I'm going to do."

"I'm going to have a great big chocolate sundae with my money while you do that. I don't know what to spend the rest on. Yet. But I sure want that sundae. Give me the energy to walk all that way back."

"I'll meet you in there," Carly said.

She walked to the pay phone at the end of the block. Her feet were already swollen, making her shoes uncomfortable. They weren't meant for that kind of walking. And she didn't have anything better. It was going to be a long walk back.

If she could even bring herself to go back.

She punched the numbers on the card into the pay phone, then touched Teddy's cell phone number by heart.

Six rings.

"Hi, this is Ted—"

"Teddy?"

"—I can't pick up right now, but leave a message."

"Oh," Carly said. "I thought it was really you. Oh, crap. Teddy, this is Carly. I just called to say merry Christmas. I'm in New Mexico. We're in the new place. Should've brought the address, but I don't know it yet. I'll call again. So…that's all, I guess. Just to say merry Christmas. And that I miss you."

Carly hung up the phone. Stood in front of it, staring at it, for a time. As if it might have something more to offer. Then she hobbled back to the ice-cream store. Jen stood outside, staring through the window. Steaming up the glass.

"Should've known they'd be closed," Jen said. "You were fast."

"Nobody was around."

"Oh. Yeah. Christmas."

"This is the worst. Worst. Christmas. Ever."

"It's pretty bad. But she tried. You know? She didn't know we wouldn't be living in Tulare by Christmas when she bought us those gift certificates. She tried, at least."

"She failed. How're we supposed to live in that little box with her and Wade and no room and no privacy?"

"Maybe it's not for very long."

"How are we supposed to live there even tonight?"

"Oh, crap, I don't know, Carly. She's trying."

"She's failing."

"You've got to talk to her sometime, Carly."

"That's what you think."

For lack of anything better to do, they began the long walk home. At least, it seemed like a long walk at the time.

NEW MEXICO

February 28

Carly sat at the table, eating cereal for dinner because nobody had cooked. And reading the box. Despite the fact that there was nothing interesting on the box. In fact, if someone had asked her what was written there, she wouldn't have been able to say. Wade emerged from the bedroom and plugged in the coffeemaker. Strange, she thought, how much of a morning routine they seemed to have in the evenings.

He sat down at the table. Carly carefully kept her gaze glued to the cereal box.

When she finally looked up, he was staring at her. It felt alarming.

"What? I'm eating cereal."

"Seems like you're always here. Wherever I go in this house, there you are."

"This *closet*, you mean? Besides, I'm never here. I ride my bike from school to the Internet café, and I sit there for hours because I don't want to be here."

"Every time I look up, you're looking back at me. That's all I know."

"Look, it's not my fault that we're still living in this sardine can two months later. If you'd go out and get a job like you keep saying you will…"

Then she pulled back, wondering if she'd gone too far. She risked a glance at Wade's eyes. They said yes, she had. But his mouth said far less.

"Nobody's hiring in my field."

"Then work in some other field."

"I'm not gonna do just anything."

"My mom does. You think she likes ringing up groceries and taking breakfast orders? She works whatever two jobs she can get."

The dark of Wade's eyes darkened. "Liked you better when you were a mute."

Carly's mom came striding out of the bedroom.

"Where's Jen?" she asked.

Carly just kept staring at the cereal box. Reading the same part for the third time. About how the cereal was baked with love. She pictured a big factory where everybody's feet hurt and nobody could wait another minute to take their break. Love. Sure. We all buy that.

"Your mother is talking to you," Wade said, a thin veneer of calm brushed on over his dark rage.

"Forget it, Wade. Leave it alone. I'm going in to the market early so I can grocery shop before work. When I get home tonight, I expect help carrying the groceries in."

"Tell your mother you'll help," Wade said.

So much for leaving it alone.

Carly nodded.

The door slammed behind Carly's mom. Carly heard her car start up.

All of a sudden Wade had her by the left wrist.

"Ow!" she yelled. "Hey! Ow!" The more she yelled, the harder Wade twisted. "Hey! You're hurting me!"

"I've just about had my fill of you," he said. Eerily calm.

They were on their feet now, Carly moving backward, trying to pull out of his grasp. The harder she pulled, the tighter he held and wrenched. Carly waited for the sickening crack of a bone break, but it never had a chance to happen.

"Let. Me. Go!"

He did. Too suddenly. With a sharp push that sent Carly stumbling backward into the brick of the fake fireplace. The corner edge of the brick struck hard against the right side of her back. Her head missed the same fate by inches.

She looked up to see if he was coming after her. But Wade wasn't even looking at her. He was looking at the front door.

"How long you been standing there?" he asked.

Carly followed his gaze to see Jen frozen in the open doorway. Letting the cold in. Her mouth open but no words coming out. Her eyes wide.

Carly seized the moment to escape, jostling Jen on her way by. She grabbed her bike from the spot where it leaned against the guesthouse, mounted it at a run, and pedaled fast in the direction of town. It hurt every time she pushed with her right leg. It hurt a lot. But she just kept pushing. She could see her breath as she peddled.

She got her tears out of the way on the ride. So that, on the off chance Teddy picked up his phone this time, he wouldn't have to hear her cry. It wasn't likely he'd pick up. He hadn't any of the other nine times she'd called. But somehow she thought he might this time. Because she so desperately needed him to.

Then she realized she hadn't brought the phone card with her. But it didn't matter. Because she knew the card number and the pin by heart.

"This is Ted—"

Everything fell inside Carly. Sagged into the lowest possible position. She sat on her bike, feet down on the pavement, in front of the pay phone. Absorbing the letdown. Shivering slightly. It took her a couple of beats too long to realize she should have been hearing the second sentence of the outgoing greeting.

"Hello? Ted here. Anybody there?"

"Teddy?"

"Yeah. Who's this?"

"Teddy, it's me. Carly."

"Carly? Why didn't you say anything? Why didn't you say hello?"

"I thought you were your voice mail. That's exactly what you say on your voice mail message. It sounds exactly the same."

"Oh. Really? I didn't know. Just a habit, I guess."

A silence. One of the young women from the ice-cream store waved at Carly as she walked by, her heels clicking on the concrete. Everybody knew Carly in this town because of all the time she killed here. Trying not to go home.

It was already dusk, she realized. She'd have to ride home in the dark. If she dared go home at all.

She spoke. Since Teddy didn't.

"I'm sorry I called so many times. I don't want you to think I'm a freak. I'm not a stalker. Normally I'd just tell you to call me back. But you can't call me back."

"No, that wouldn't be too smart. I got your new address. Thanks for leaving that on my voice mail. I'm worried, though. About all the calls you're making to here. What if your mom sees these on the phone bill?"

"I'm calling from a pay phone. I'm using a prepaid card."

"Ah. Good. Smart. She'd make trouble for me if she knew you were calling."

"I know she would."

Another silence.

"Are you OK, Carly? You don't sound so good."

"I can't stay here," she said. Her voice cracking on the word *here*. "It's not even safe here. I can't even go back there tonight, Teddy. I don't know what to do."

She couldn't not cry, so she cried quietly.

"God, Carly. I don't know what to say to help. I wish I could help. But if you run away from home, you can't come here. This is the worst place you could come. This is the first place they'd look for you."

"Oh," Carly said. "Right."

Another loss to absorb. She'd really felt somehow, at some deep level, that if Teddy answered the phone, he'd save her. She could just pour herself over the phone line to Tulare. And he would never let bad things happen to her again. But he was right. She couldn't go to him. They'd find her. Bring her back. They'd make trouble for Teddy, and it would be all her fault.

And yet…somehow she felt just a tiny bit saved. Anyway. Even his voice could save her. At least, for the moment. For as long as it lasted. She didn't even feel cold anymore.

"So…where are you living?" she asked.

"Oh. Nowhere."

"How can you be living nowhere?"

"Well. I'm somewhere. I mean, I sleep somewhere. But it's not my place. I'm sort of couch surfing right now. Freeloading."

"Are you working again?"

"Yeah. I have to. I have no choice."

"How's your back?"

She didn't like her own questions. They felt like small talk. But she didn't know how to change that.

"Not good. But I can't afford not to work. So I'm back with Ralph. He's throwing me a couple or three days work a week. That's pretty much all he's got to give me right now anyway. You know. With the economy so bad."

"Right. Right."

"You sure you're OK? Is this, like…an emergency?"

Carly shifted on the bike seat. Stretched her back slightly, as if to assess the damage. The pain stopped her cold. A little cry escaped her.

"What was that, Carly?"

"Nothing. Something just surprised me."

She couldn't tell him. It wouldn't be fair. He didn't have his own place, and she couldn't stay there even if he did. He wasn't in any position to help her. So it wasn't fair to tell him how badly she needed help.

"You know…it's only another year and a half until I turn eighteen. And then I'm coming back to Tulare. I mean, the day I turn eighteen. The same day. I'm moving back. And I'll get a job, and we'll live pretty close together, you know? And then maybe I can see you all the time."

"I'd love that, Carly." Said with depth. With genuine feeling that oozed through the phone and blanketed her. Soothed her.

"You would?"

"Yeah, that'd be great. I'd love to hang out with you. I'd come by after work and say, Hey, you. Want to go get a burger? And we could complain about our days or our crappy bosses or something. Well. Not really. Ralph's a nice guy. You could complain about your crappy boss. I could complain about something else."

"I just miss you so much, Teddy."

Something caught Carly's eye in her peripheral vision. She shifted carefully on the bike seat to see Jen sitting on her bike. Maybe ten feet away. Close enough to hear everything. Jen had that same look on her face. The doorway look.

Teddy? Jen mouthed the word.

Carly waved the question away. Then she realized she hadn't heard Teddy's answer. Had he said he missed her, too?

"So, listen, I should go," she said, "but when you get a real address, e-mail it to me. OK?"

"You still have that crappy dinosaur of a laptop?"

"No, that crashed. But there's an Internet café. And the library has computers. So I can check my e-mail, and they'll never know."

She glanced at Jen's shocked face again, then back at the concrete.

"OK," Teddy said. "It's a deal."

"Promise?"

"Yeah. I promise."

"I love you, Teddy."

"Hey, you gonna be OK?"

"I guess. I have to be. What choice do I have?"

"It's not a real emergency? Because I can hear something's wrong."

"Nope. Not a real emergency."

"Well. If it ever is, I'm your guy."

"I know that, Teddy. I know you are. That's why I love you."

"Take care, Carly."

"Bye, Teddy."

She hung up the phone gently. Cradled it back into position. As if it were tender. Easily wounded. As though it were the phone receiver that needed love and protection. Not her.

She looked up at Jen, who scooted her bike closer.

"Mom would kill you if she knew you were talking to Teddy."

"I know. Don't tell her."

"You OK?"

"No."

"How's your back?"

"Bad."

"Can I see it?"

"No."

"Please?"

Carly sighed. Leaned forward. Jen lifted the back of Carly's shirt. Carly heard Jen's breath suck in. A deep gasp.

"It's all scraped up, and it's got your shirt all bloody. And it's getting really bruised really fast."

"Don't tell Mom."

"About Teddy?"

"About anything."

"Oh. Um…I'm sorry, Carly. I already told her you got hurt. I called her at work and told her. She wants us to come there. Not go home. I'm sorry, I didn't think you wouldn't want me to tell her. Why wouldn't you want me to tell her?"

"I just think it might make things even worse with Wade."

"But *I* told on him. *You* didn't. I'll tell him it was me. She'll tell him it was me."

"I guess."

"Come on. Let's go over to Mom's work."

Carly pedaled behind Jen, trying to keep up. But the pain on every push overwhelmed her. Was she in a lot more pain now than on the ride into town? Or had she really managed to keep that down, where it couldn't get in her way?

That's when she looked down at her left wrist. It had swelled to two or three times its normal size. She could see the perfect prints of Wade's fingers in a fresh purple bruise.

Carly's mom towed her into the break room in the back of the Stop-n-Shop Market. By the elbow. Jen tumbled along behind.

"I'm sorry, Lara," she said to the only other employee in the room. "I know she's not supposed to be in here…"

"It's OK," Lara said. "Do what you gotta do."

"It's her back," Jen said.

"And what about this? This is nothing?"

She held Carly's left arm up for Jen to see.

"Oh. I didn't know that part."

Carly felt herself turned around. The back of her shirt lifted. Again.

"Shit," her mom whispered on a long exhale.

Carly heard Lara suck in her breath. Pretty much the way Jen had.

"Carly." Her mom spun her back around and grabbed her hard by both shoulders. It hurt. Her shoulders and her back. Both. "Listen up. Do I need to be taking you to a hospital?"

Carly shook her head.

Her mom's eyes snapped shut.

"My eyes are closed, Carly. I can't see you. I can't see you nod your head or shake it. So you have to talk to me. You want to stop talking to me again a minute later, fine. But right now, talk to me. Do we need to get you to an emergency room or an urgent care place?"

"No," Carly said.

"You sure?"

"No."

Carly's mom opened her eyes.

"You're not sure?"

"I think it'll be OK, but I'm not sure."

"Then I'll ask you again tomorrow. OK?" Carly nodded.

"Shit. Lost her again."

"You need to go home, Jocelyn?" Lara asked. "Take care of this? We'll get by."

"That's not fair to you and Tom."

"We'll manage. Really."

"I can't afford that, though."

"Jocelyn. I think this might be more important."

"Oh. Yeah. Yeah, of course. You're right. This is more important."

"They just keep going around and around in a circle," Jen said.

They lay close together on a twin bed in the corner of the tiny house. Behind a standing screen. Both the screen and the bed were on loan from Wade Two. The fold-out couch hadn't panned out because it wouldn't fit behind a screen.

Carly didn't know how long they'd been listening to the fight in the bedroom. Twenty minutes maybe.

"Why don't they just stop if they can't say anything new?"

"Because she's not going to leave him over this," Carly said. "So she has to make it into something she doesn't have to leave him over. And she's not there yet."

"Did you do what he said? Bait him about being unemployed?"

"He started it."

"Geez, Carly. Are you trying to get killed?"

"*He* was baiting *me*. Until I couldn't take it anymore. Just like he says I did to him. But when *I* lost *my* temper, all I did was talk."

"I know he was lying about how you just fell back. I saw him push you."

"Did you tell her that?"

"Yeah. But she kept saying it might be hard to tell the two apart. You know. Just by looking."

"Great. See? What did I tell you? She's not going to leave him over this."

After another half hour of muffled shouting and a few moments of ghostly quiet, Carly's mom stomped into the room, pulled aside the blind, and turned on the lamp by their bed.

Carly winced and covered her eyes.

"I'm considering this half your fault, Carly. I don't know what the hell you were thinking, talking to him like that about his job situation. Don't you know a man doesn't feel like a man when he's not working? When somebody else has to provide? This is at least half on you, girl. But I made it real clear he's never to lay a hand on you again. And if he does, we're out of here."

"We know," Jen said. "We heard every word of it."

"You keep out of this, Jen. But I know you, Carly. And I know you'd use that as a way to get what you want. So here's the deal. You never say a word to Wade again. Ever. About anything. Got that? You break that rule, you're on your own. You keep your mouth shut, I'll protect you. OK?"

Carly said nothing.

"A nod will do."

Carly nodded. Barely.

"Right. Should've known. Keeping her mouth shut is what Carly does best."

She stomped away again.

"Turn off the light, Jen, OK? It's in my eyes."

"OK, Carly. You want some aspirin?"

"Yeah. Thanks."

"Funny Mom didn't think of that."

"Not really," Carly said. "I don't think it's so funny. Mom thinks about men. And not too much else."

NEW MEXICO

April 30

Carly woke suddenly. Sat up in the dark. She looked over to find Jen already awake. Sitting on the edge of the narrow twin bed.

Something had gone crash in the bedroom.

"How long have they been fighting?" Carly asked.

"I think it's a new record. I can't believe you slept through it."

"Can you tell what it's about?"

"Not really. All I've got so far is Mom thinks Wade's a bastard, and he thinks he's totally justified. I still can't really tell *why* she thinks he's bastard."

"Was it ever in doubt?"

Jen didn't answer. Or laugh. Or even smile.

"What time's it? Do you know?"

"Last time I went in the kitchen it was one thirty. So maybe two."

Carly sat up on the edge of the bed next to her sister and listened.

The bedroom door flew open, banging against the wall. Both girls scooted straight backward on the bed. They couldn't see through the screen, so they had no idea what was hurtling in their direction. But they could hear.

The screen flew away and fell to the floor with a startling bang. Their mother stood over the bed.

"Get dressed, girls, and get your things together as fast as you can. We're leaving."

"No," Wade said. "I don't think you are."

They all three looked up to see him standing with his back to the door, that look of eerie calm in his eye. Carly could see just enough of his face in the spill of light from the bedroom to ice every inch of her torso.

Nothing moved, and no one spoke for a long time. Or at least it seemed long. Carly looked at her mother's face and saw fear. She tried to remember if she had ever seen her mother visibly afraid of anything. Nothing came to mind.

"Is that a threat, Wade? Are you telling me you're going to do something bad to me or my girls if we try to walk out that door?"

Time slowed to a crawl, leaving Carly unable to tell if five seconds or five minutes had passed. Probably five very slow seconds.

"Jocelyn," Wade said. "Baby. This is me, baby. This is us. Don't walk out on us. After all we've been for each other? I can't believe you'd walk away. We just need to talk is all."

"We been at it for hours, Wade."

"Yelling. Gimme an hour talking. Lemme remind you what we mean to each other. Then—I swear—you wanna walk out that door, I won't stand in your way."

Another time freeze.

Don't do it, don't do it, don't do it, Carly thought. She almost said it out loud. But she stopped herself because it might set him off. She could feel the frozen energy of Jen just inches from her right shoulder.

Carly watched the air go out of her mom. Watched her grow smaller and less rigid. She slumped down onto the couch.

"Talk, then."

"Not in front of them."

"Then where'd you have in mind?"

"We'll go for a drive. Like we used to. Remember how we used to go out for a drive and just talk?"

Nothing moved for a long minute. This time Carly counted off the seconds. So time couldn't play any tricks on her. She counted to fifty-seven.

Their mom rose to her feet.

"Girls, I'm going for a drive with Wade. Be back in an hour. While I'm gone, you gather up all your stuff. Get it ready to go. I know we don't have boxes and nothing much in the way of suitcases, so use some kitchen trash bags, or just stack it all together so it's easy to take out to the car. OK?"

"Sure, Mom," Jen said.

"OK," Carly said.

Wade and their mom walked out the door.

"God, that's so depressing," Jen said. "I can't believe that's all our stuff. What happened to all the stuff we used to have?"

"A lot got left in Tulare. And I think Wade threw stuff away. I heard him tell Mom once that when we leave stuff around, he throws it away and we never know the difference."

"Geez. Thank God we're getting out of here."

"Maybe," Carly said. "I'll believe it when I see it."

"She wouldn't be having us get our stuff ready if we weren't going."

"We'll see."

"I'm so sleepy I can't stand it. I'm going back to bed."

"Yeah, go ahead. What time's it, anyway? It feels like more than an hour already."

"I don't know. Look in the kitchen."

Carly squinted at the clock above the stove. It was nearly four thirty.

Carly sat bolt upright in bed. Light poured through the front windows. The screen still lay flat on the floor. The bedroom door hung open. Carly could see that the bedroom was empty.

She shook Jen by the shoulder. Hard.

"Huh? What?"

"Jen, wake up."

Jen sat up blinking. "What? What time is it?"

"I don't know. But it's light. And they're still not back."

Nothing happened for a long time. Neither spoke. Carly didn't know about Jen, but she needed time for possibilities to click together in her brain.

Jen spoke first. "You don't think they just took off and left us, do you?"

"No. Mom wouldn't do that. Would she?"

"I don't think so. But then, where are they?"

"I don't know, Jen."

"What do we do?"

"I don't know."

"Do we go to school?"

"I'm not going. Not unless they show up between now and then."

They didn't.

It was after noon. They sat at the table, eating peanut butter sandwiches. Well, Carly was eating her sandwich. Jen was mostly playing with hers. Peeling the top slice of bread back and watching the way the peanut butter separated. Over and over.

Jen hadn't been talking much. So when she spoke up suddenly, it made Carly jump.

"What are we going to do if they never come back?"

"I don't think we should talk about that yet."

"OK," Jen said. "I'm sorry, Carly."

"Maybe we should call the hospitals. Or the highway patrol or something. See if there've been any accidents. Maybe they're in the hospital and can't get back."

Jen had taken to biting her right thumbnail. She went at it again the minute she'd finished talking.

"They'd call us from the hospital, though. Wouldn't they?"

"If they could," Jen said.

"I thought about calling. But it scares me. Because let's say we call. And it turns out there was an accident. We're letting them know we're underage and we're here alone without them. They might come over and put us in a home or something."

"You could call and pretend to be older."

"But on the phone, everybody thinks I'm even younger than I am."

"Oh," Jen said. "That's true."

"I think we should just wait."

"How long?"

"I'm not sure yet," Carly said. "But longer."

"Oh, my God, here comes Wade!" Jen shrieked.

She'd been sitting by the window for hours. Many hours. It was after seven in the evening. The sun was nearly down. Carly was in the bathroom and couldn't get out there as fast as she'd have liked.

"But I don't see Mom. What's he doing back without Mom? Oh, wait. That's not Wade. That's Wade Two. His hair is much longer."

"Wade Two?"

Carly zipped up fast and ran to the window without washing her hands.

Together they watched Wade Two walk down the path to the guesthouse door. Neither said a word. Both girls knew something that did not need to be spoken out loud. In the four months they'd lived in this guesthouse, Wade Two had never come to the door. Not once. Not for any reason.

They watched him raise a hand to knock.

"I've got a bad feeling about this," Carly said.

He knocked.

"I bet they just got hurt."

"I hope so."

"Well, let him in, Carly."

Carly opened the door and stared into the face of Wade's twin brother, who stared back. He did not look like a happy man. Then again, he never had, all three of the times Carly had seen him from a distance. But in that moment he seemed less happy than ever before.

"You girls sit down," he said. With close to no emotion at all.

They did. In unison. They sank onto the couch, facing the door. Bizarrely, Wade Two did not come in. Just stood in the open doorway.

"I have to tell you bad news. I hate to do it. But somebody has to. I'll cut right to it. There's been an accident."

"What kind of accident?" Carly asked, a tingly electric heat spreading in her chest.

"Wade's truck. Went off the road up in the high mountains."

"Are they OK?"

"No."

Just for a second, Carly thought she was a statue. That she had turned to stone. A voice in her head said, You knew. You already knew. But there's knowing, and then there's *knowing*. This was the worse of the two.

"It was on the edge of a big drop-off," Wade Two said. "Or anyway, that's what they told me on the phone. The police, or whoever just called me. Hard to pay good attention at a time like that. You just hear the bad news and not much else."

Something rose up in Carly. Some kind of voice to speak.

"So what you're saying is, Wade took our mom up high in the mountains and drove them both off a cliff."

Wade Two's face tightened down. The look of loss suddenly armored over with a pestered expression. As though Carly were a gnat or a mosquito, hovering too close to his face.

"He didn't do it on purpose."

"How do *you* know?"

The only reaction was a deeper solidification of his features. It rattled Carly to look into the face of a man who looked exactly like Wade.

"I've done my part here. I told you." He turned away. Marched two steps toward his house. Then he stopped and looked at Carly over his shoulder. "I'll make the phone call to get you girls taken care of."

Carly ran to the open door. "Wait. What do you mean? Taken care of how?"

"Well, I don't know. The authorities will know. There has to be a procedure. You girls have a father you can go live with? Well, never mind. Don't bother telling me. I'll call whatever agency takes care of children. You tell them."

"It's too late," Carly said. Blurted out, really.

"Too late?"

"Their office'll be closed."

"Well...I don't think it matters," he said. "If a child is in danger, and it's an emergency, somebody will come sort it out."

"But we're not in danger, and it's not an emergency. I mean, not tonight. We're old enough to stay alone. We stay alone all the time. I'm old enough to babysit. Why drag them out here at night when we can just go to sleep in our own bed? Like we always do?"

Carly could see him chew on the inside of his cheek for a moment. She had a sudden dizzying sensation, like a tightrope walker. A sense that one mistake in balance would lead to the final fall.

"I'll call in the morning, then. You girls try to get some sleep."

He walked away. Carly watched him go, knowing she had to turn and face Jen. And not wanting to. She put it off as long as she reasonably could.

Jen was still sitting on the couch. Doing nothing. Jen, it seemed, really had turned to stone.

"Jen?"

"What are we supposed to do, Carly?"

"We're going to go live with Teddy. Now come on. Get your backpack, and go through your stuff and put together only what fits in the backpack. Like just the stuff you'd take camping. We're leaving tonight."

Carly was halfway across the room to her backpack when she heard a small, muffled thump. She turned to see Jen sitting on her own crumpled legs in the middle of the floor.

"Come on, Jen. Get up."

But she didn't.

"Here, I'll help you."

But Jen's bones seemed to have turned to jelly.

So Carly sat in the middle of the floor, shoulder to shoulder with her sister. For about an hour. Thinking how nice it would be to collapse. But she couldn't afford to. Somebody had to stay upright. And the job had fallen to Carly.

There wasn't much Carly could do, under the circumstances, but she figured at least she could do a decent job of being the one who didn't collapse.

PART FIVE

Now Again

ARIZONA

May 18

It's undoubtedly the small hours of the morning, though Carly has no way of knowing which ones. She only knows it's getting harder to stay awake.

She's been holding on to this metal ladder for what seems like two or three hours now, one arm hooked through so she doesn't have to trust her hands. So her hands can't slip.

Funny how something can start out heaven, then so quickly turn to hell. The dark scenery has grown tedious. Over and over she's startled by a sudden rock face springing up just a few feet from her right or left shoulder. Or a tunnel. It's hard to know what's happening when the train suddenly plunges into a tunnel.

But that's not what makes it hell. It's the fact that there's no way to rest. And it's getting harder to stay awake.

Actually, it's getting almost impossible to stay awake.

She tries climbing up higher on the ladder, thinking maybe she can pull herself up onto the top of the railroad car. But she can't see what she'd be stepping onto, and she can't stop thinking about how much clearance there might be between the top of the train and the roof of the tunnels.

She thinks about letting go and giving up on the ride, but she can't see what she'd be falling onto, or into. The train might be a couple of feet from the edge of a cliff for all she knows. Besides, where would she go then? She doesn't know her way to Highway 40 from here, wherever here is, the way she would if she'd just kept walking down that paved road. She could get lost in the middle of nowhere. Forever. Well. The point being that forever, for her, would only be a couple of days in that case.

So she's stuck. No going up, no going down. Too late to turn back. But she's not quite sure what's in front of her if she just hangs on. Do westbound trains just keep going west? Or do they bear north or south at some point? She has no way to know. It's never affected her life before. So she never cared.

She tries to sit on a rung, but it leaves her feet dangling. But she's desperate enough to give that a try.

A few moments later she snaps awake, hanging by nothing but the bruised crook of her right arm. She has to use her left to grab hold again, and while she does, nothing but her rigid refusal to relax her bent right arm is keeping her from falling. She takes a good hold with her left, but her whole body is still trailing free, swinging. She eases her right arm straight, then grabs the side of the ladder with her right hand. Both of her arms shake with the strain, and her heart is pounding. She has to pull herself up to get her feet back on the ladder. Her arms are ready to fail her. To just let go. The backpack isn't helping. It's weighing on her, pulling her backward. She looks down. Just blackness. No way to know what will happen if she falls.

She gives it all she's got. Pulls up, arms trembling, muscles screaming with overuse. Then her foot hits a rung. She steps in close to the ladder again and wraps her arms around it, shaking. Calming her heart.

She has to stay awake.

It's now officially a life-or-death situation.

She thinks about Jen saying, "I'm afraid you're going to go out and get yourself killed." Or words to that effect.

She was so sure Jen was wrong about that.

Now she has to prove it.

The train stops. It seems almost too good to be true, but Carly can hear the scream of the brakes, the metal on metal. And then they're standing still.

She climbs down onto the tracks.

Her arms are shaking, not so much with fear—though she has plenty of that, too—but from overexertion. Like they couldn't lift a leaf without five or six days to rest and regroup. But she doesn't have time to think about that. There's no way to know how long the train will remain stopped. They don't seem to be anywhere. And she has to find a way to get into this train, rather than on it. So she can relax and sleep.

She picks her way in the dark up to the last boxcar. The one with the door that was open just a crack. She grasps the door with both hands and tries to slide it, but it's heavy. Her arms are all but useless. She uses the weight of her body instead. Holds with her fingers and throws her body in the direction she wants the door to go. It gives a few inches. She uses the same maneuver five more times, getting another few inches on each pull.

The train starts to move again.

She slips off her backpack and throws it into the boxcar, then immediately regrets the decision. If she fails in her attempt to jump the train, it's gone forever.

She has to get on.

She takes a three-step running start and throws her body through the opening, hitting one hip hard on the edge of the sliding door. It's not enough. She barely has her whole upper body on the floor of the car. She's falling back again.

"Oh, shit!" she says out loud.

Her waist is bending, the weight of her legs pulling down and inward, and rather than falling back and away from the train, she's about to fall in a hook motion, right under the wheels. And there's no way to stop it. She has nothing to grab on to.

Jen was right.

In that tiny fraction of a second, she processes the inevitability of her own death.

This is it.

From inside the boxcar, two hands grab her wrists.

A little noise something like a scream escapes her throat. She instinctively tries to pull away from their grasp.

"Don't let go!" a voice says. It's a male voice, but young. Teenage boy young. "I'm gonna pull. Let me pull you. Try to shimmy up on your belly."

He pulls hard, and it hurts Carly's midsection, which is scraping along the edge of the boxcar floor. She straightens as best she can, lifting her legs with great effort, then inchworms along the boards.

When her knees touch wood, she knows she's not going to die. She collapses, trying to breathe again.

She has no idea who's in this car with her, but since she was dead a minute ago, it doesn't seem to matter.

"Thank you," she says. "Whoever that is."

"Yeah. You don't wanta fall like that. That's the worst. You could end up right under those wheels. People lose both legs. Or if it goes right over the middle of you…well…why talk about that? You made it."

She wants to say something else appreciative, but nothing comes out. She doesn't have enough strength left to find and form words.

A deep male voice says, "What's going on, Davis? What's all the noise?"

"It's nothing, Dad. Go back to sleep. It's just a girl. A girl jumped the train is all."

"A girl? All by herself? What's a girl doing jumping the train all by herself?"

"I don't know, Dad, but it's OK. Just go back to sleep."

A second or two later, Carly hears a deep, rumbly snore coming from the front of the car.

"He never really woke up," Davis says. "He's nice when he's awake. But he sleeps like rocks. So he'll say stuff like that, but he's really asleep the whole time. He's real nice and polite when he's awake. So, where are you headed?"

"You seen my backpack?" Carly asks. It's not what she meant to say. It's just what comes out.

"Yeah, it's right here."

She hears it sliding across the wood floor, feels it bump her hand. She pulls it in close. Sets her head down on it.

"California," she says, failing to enunciate the word clearly.

"Oh," Davis says. "We're going to Lake Havasu. Supposed to be real nice there. We might even stay for a while. All summer. If it works out, I might do a semester of school there in the fall."

Carly tries to say something in return, but the words don't quite form. She's so spent she feels almost drunk, and the words are just a slur, whatever they were about to be.

A minute later she's asleep.

It's still dark when she wakes. She sits up. Davis's dad is still snoring.

The door on the other side of the car has been slid partway open, and Davis is sitting on the edge of the car, swinging his legs and watching Arizona roll by. The sky shows just a hint of dawn off to the left. Carly can almost see the shapes of things.

From the silhouette of him, Carly thinks Davis is a couple of years younger than she is. Older than Jen but younger than Carly.

The wind coming in feels bracing and cool. That classic cold desert night. But…clearer. Or something. Like they're somewhere else entirely. This is not Wakapi land. She can feel that.

She thinks again about Jen and what will happen to her when they find out Carly is gone. She calms her gut by convincing herself that even if Jen gets put in a home while she's gone, Teddy can get her back again. There are more nagging fears, but she squashes them as hard as she can.

She levers to her feet, nearly falling to the floor again when her arms fail to hold her. She teeters carefully over to the partly open door and sits cross-legged on the floor, safely back from the edge.

She knows exactly why she does this. It's because she remembers that feeling, standing under the stars last night. That complete aloneness. And she wants not to be alone. If only for a short time.

"Hi," she says.

"Oh. Hi."

He seems surprised that she's awake.

"I think you saved my life back there."

"Maybe. Or you might've grabbed on by yourself."

"I don't think so. I think I was falling. Anyway, I meant to say thanks. You know. At the time. But it was weird. I was just so used up from all that. It was like I didn't have the strength. But anyway, thanks."

"You did."

"I did what?"

"Say thanks."

"Oh. Did I? I don't remember that."

"I think so. Anyway, you're welcome. No problem."

They sit quietly for a time. Carly is unsure of what else to say. If anything. She thinks about Jen again, and whether she's in trouble where Carly left her. It strikes her suddenly that Jen is the one who should have the feather necklace to protect her. Not that Carly really believes it will. But still.

She takes it out from under her shirt and examines it in the dim light, to see if she damaged it. The shaft of the feather is a little crooked, but she straightens it out as best she can.

"Pretty," Davis says. "Looks Native American."

"It is."

"Genuine?"

"Yeah."

"Navajo? Zuni?"

"Wakapi."

Carly expects him to say he never heard of such a thing.

Instead he says, "Oh! That's so rare. Did you really meet a Wakapi? That's amazing. They're almost gone."

"You've heard of them."

"Yeah, I did a report on Native American culture for school. About how important it is to keep it going. Like, the Wakapi are a perfect example. They teach their kids this oral history, but then if the kids leave the reservation, maybe they don't teach it to *their* kids. And then what if it just stops? Can you imagine what a loss that would be?"

"I guess. Yeah."

"You *guess*? It's a whole *culture*. But it's not just the kids leaving the reservations, it's us and the way we tried to erase their culture, taking kids from their parents and putting them in boarding schools and changing their names and not letting them speak their language. I have an apple. You want half?"

Carly is surprised by the sudden shift in conversational direction. She was just getting interested in the culture issue. Was Delores teaching Jen the Wakapi oral history? Can Jen pass it on to her kids, even though they're not Wakapi? Or maybe Jen would say they can be if she wants them to be.

"Um. Sure. If you think that's fair. I mean…it's your apple. If you want it all."

"I don't mind."

Carly moves a little closer to watch. Davis opens what looks like a small penknife and cuts the apple into two equal halves. He seems to be working very hard to make them exactly even. In fact, he ends up bringing the knife up through the stem and slicing it vertically in two.

"Here," he says, extending the gift in her direction.

"Thanks. That's really nice."

She takes it from him and takes a bite. It tastes like a Red Delicious. But more to the point, it tastes like the best bite of apple Carly has ever held in her mouth. Ever crunched into with her teeth. And she knows why, too. Because she wasn't supposed to be alive to taste it.

She looks out at the dawn, and it's a more beautiful dawn than she ever knew existed. And for the same reason.

It strikes her that this feeling will wear off in time, and she hates knowing that. She wants to hold it. Frame it. Bronze it. Title it "This Is How It Feels to Be in Your Life." But she's been in her life all along. She just didn't see that as anything worth noting.

She takes another bite.

Then she leans back a little and reaches into her pocket for one of her many quarters. Sets it on the floor between her sore hip and Davis.

"Here," she says.

He looks closely to see what it is. Picks it up and holds it.

"You don't have to pay me for that apple. I gave it to you. For free."

"I know. I wasn't. Really. I wasn't trying to pay you. I just wanted to give you something. Because you gave me something. But I don't really have anything else but that."

"Oh," Davis says. "OK. Thanks."

He slips it into the breast pocket of his denim jacket.

"Kind of stupid," she says. "A quarter isn't much."

"Well. It's a lot to you, I bet. You probably don't have much."

That's so true that Carly doesn't even want to comment on how true it is. So she says nothing at all.

They sit quietly for a time, finishing the apple and watching the world go by in the dark. The sky is taking on a coppery glow off to the east, and Carly can see the lights of some kind of civilization. Like they're getting close to a town. She pulls her jacket tighter around herself with one arm.

"I'm practically biting right into the core," Carly says. "Because I don't want to waste any."

"I eat the core," Davis says.

"Really?"

"I eat everything but the stem. The seeds are sort of chewy, but it's not bad."

Carly pulls out the severed stem and pops the rest into her mouth. The texture of the core is hard to bite down on, but it still tastes like apple. They launch the stem halves out into the world at the exact same moment, then laugh at how perfectly accidentally timed that was.

"Any idea where this train goes?" she asks him.

"My dad and I are jumping off as soon we see the Colorado River. That's the state line, you know. Arizona turns into California right at the Colorado River. Right in the middle of the river. I don't know where the train goes after that. On into California, I guess. My dad would know. We're going to go see Lake Havasu."

"Why by freight train?"

"We go most everywhere by freight train. Or we hitchhike. One or the other."

"Always? All your life?"

"Not always. Just the last couple years. Since my dad lost his job. Since we lost the house. Well, not the whole time since he lost his job. Just since we lost the house. He lost his job, and then for a few months he was trying to get another one, but nobody was hiring in his field. And then he decided if we couldn't have a house, we should at least see the world. He said he could stand to raise me poor, but not on a street corner or in some shelter. He said at least we could be free and have some real experiences."

"You like it? Traveling around all the time?"

"It's OK. We've seen some really nice places. It's just different than having a house. Not as good in some ways. But it's OK, I guess."

"What did your dad used to do?"

"Engineer."

"Train?"

"Aerospace."

"Oh."

"How 'bout you?"

"Oh. Yeah. Me."

Carly takes a minute to decide what to tell him. She starts at the beginning, when they had to leave Teddy. Then the story gets more and more detailed. And by the time she's told him everything, the sun is up over the mountains, pouring onto their faces.

Davis has shaggy hair and bad skin, but his brown eyes are big and nice.

"I hope you find him," he says.

"Me, too."

"You think he did what they say he did?"

Carly opens her mouth to answer and is struck by a complete thought. If he did, that explains everything. Jen's incomprehensible behavior is completely understandable. If he did.

"Maybe," she says.

She's a little stunned to hear herself say it. It's almost as though her opinion on the subject has changed retroactively. Without bothering to notify her.

Then again, that would mean Teddy really did. And that's equally incomprehensible. That requires every bit as much explaining.

"Will you stay with him if he did?"

"Oh, no. I don't think I could do that."

"What would you do then?"

"No idea."

They stare out into the dawn in silence for a few minutes. It's not an uncomfortable silence. Just a moment when nothing needs saying.

Then Carly says, "I don't even know why I told you all that."

"I do. It's because you'll never see me again. Strangers tell me and my dad stuff all the time. Big stuff. Stuff they don't even tell their own families. It's easier with a stranger. They don't even know who you are, so what could it hurt?"

"I think I'm going to try to sleep some more," she says. She's feeling a little off-balance now, and that's part of why she says it. But she's also just really tired. She's probably had two or three hours sleep in the last two days. "Maybe when I wake up, we'll be in California."

"Maybe. If you wake up and we're gone, you're over the state line."

"Nice meeting you, if that happens. But it'll be nice to be back in California."

But not as nice as it would have been a few minutes ago. Before she figured out that Jen was probably telling the truth.

Carly dozes for a minute or an hour. It's hard to tell.

Then she sits up, nursing an uncomfortable feeling. A lot of what she's stored lately is working its way loose. That can't be good.

Davis is still sitting in the open door of the boxcar, watching the morning go by. Or waiting for the river. Or both.

It's warmer now. She struggles to her feet. Her whole body is sore, either from impact or overexertion. In some areas, both. She feels as though she was hit by a speeding car in her sleep.

Davis looks partway over his shoulder as she sits down next to him.

"As long as I'm never going to see you again," she says, "there's something else."

Then she stops a minute. Wondering what the something is. She's literally about to tell Davis something she hasn't shared with herself yet.

"OK," he says.

"I have to think how to say it." She knows a little about what it is. Because she knows how it feels. But training a collection of words to contain it might prove tricky. "I think however I say it, it's going to come out wrong."

"Just say it however you can."

"Why did he pick *her*?"

"You mean...not somebody else's sister?"

"I mean not me."

In the silence that follows, Carly has a chance to experience just how wrong that really sounds.

Davis says, "You didn't want him to..."

"No! Of course not. I didn't mean that at all. If he did that, which I'm not sure now if he did, he shouldn't have picked anybody.

I mean, anybody young. But he picked her. Why her and not me? Oh, crap. That's not what I mean. What do I mean?"

"Maybe you just wanted him to like you best? Even though... probably you wanted him to like you in a better way than that."

"Maybe. It sure sounds better than what I said. I bet you think I'm the sickest person on the planet."

"No. I don't. Really. You should see some of the stuff people have told us."

"Don't tell anybody."

"I won't."

"I'd deny it."

"Who would I tell? I don't even know who you are. That was the whole point, remember?"

Then, as Carly is settling back into that more comfortable reality, Davis shouts out suddenly. Loudly.

"There it is! Dad! There it is!"

"Hmm?" his father mumbles.

"The Colorado River! I can see it! Dad! Get up! We have to jump off in a minute."

And Carly already misses Davis. And maybe even Davis's father. Even though they're still on the train.

Silently, and as bravely as possible, she adjusts back to that place of being alone. Her consolation prize is knowing that's the California state line she can see from here.

Davis's father leans over her. He's a big man. Tall. Heavily built.

"The train'll probably stop in Needles," he tells her. "There's a train yard there. If the train stops in the yard, jump off. Fast. Security man'll go all down the train opening the doors of the box-cars. You don't want to get caught in here. Look out both doors. See which side he's on. Jump out the other side. Head for the main drag."

"How do I keep going west, then?"

"Hitch a ride. The main drag of Needles is right next to the train yard. Broadway, I think they call it. It's a business loop on the I-40. So hitch a ride right there on the street. Just about everybody going down that street'll be merging onto the interstate."

"Dad, come on," Davis says. "We have to go."

"Don't hitch on the highway shoulder," the dad says. "Because cars can't stop there anyway. Hitch on Broadway."

"Thanks," she says.

But she's not even sure if he heard. He's already over to the wide-open door of the car, timing his jump. Trailing a huge back-packers' multiday pack from the end of his right hand.

Davis disappears. Davis's dad throws the pack after him. Then the dad disappears.

Carly runs to the open doorway, but the train is on a curved section of track, and she can't even see where they've gone.

They're just gone.

Carly wakes to the loud banging noises of boxcar doors being slammed open.

She jumps to her feet and looks out the door she came in. The side of the train that almost killed her. The door is still only open a couple of feet. She peers out toward the engine and sees the security man. Fortunately, he's still way up at the front of the train. He has a long way to go to get back here.

She grabs her pack and leaps out the other side, forgetting how battered and tired her muscles are. She ends up on her face in heavy gravel, scraping her chin and her already-scraped hands and further bruising the front of just about everything else. She has to regroup a moment before pulling to her feet. She can still hear the banging of the doors as they slam open.

She manages to trot across the yard, looking both ways as she stumbles over a series of tracks. There's a shiny silver Amtrak train waiting at a station a few hundred yards down. Facing west. Carly wishes like hell she had enough money in her pockets to board it.

She forces her attention back to crossing the yard.

She stops, considers briefly. Decides to head toward the Amtrak station.

"Hey! You!" a big male voice yells.

Carly turns and looks behind her, across the yard. The security man is looking right through an open box car at her.

She takes off running. Problem is, she keeps running into trains. There are so many trains stopped here, on parallel tracks. It's like running in a maze. When she finally gets to the end of the last train blocking her from the street, she heads for freedom. But between her the main street of town is a fence. A chain link fence. About six to eight feet high. Topped with barbed wire.

Davis's dad forgot to mention that.

For a moment, she has that feeling again. Like the one she had as she began to fall under the wheels of the train. That feeling of, After all I've been through, it's just going to end like this.

"No," she says out loud. No. This is not how it ends.

She sprints around a building, puffing with the exertion, and comes out into a parking lot, in view of an open gate. She blasts through to freedom. Runs all the way to a corner on the main drag of town.

There she stops and looks back. And sees that the train station is not fenced in any way. Somehow she had boxed herself into some private, adjacent area. Somehow she had found the only fence around. It seems too much like a symbol of the way her life is flowing these days.

She also sees that the security man apparently didn't care enough to follow.

It's hot. Needles is in the Mojave Desert, she seems to recall.

She walks stiffly down the street, headed for the first gas station. A lighted display on a bank she passes says it's 9:23 a.m. and ninety-six degrees.

She still doesn't have a hat. She never thought to bring Delores's old gardening hat. If she'd thought of it, she still wouldn't have. Because that would have been stealing. But she never thought of it.

She hobbles into the gas station and uses their ladies' room. It's unlocked. And filthy. But it doesn't really matter. She washes her hands and face at the sink. Looks up into the mirror. Her chin is scraped and bloody from that header she took into the gravel. The soap stings her chin and the heels of her hands when she washes them. She has fresh blood on her shirt. Dried blood on the knees of her jeans.

She takes some toilet paper and paper towels and stuffs them into her backpack. Holds one paper towel to her chin to try to stop the bleeding.

She leans into the sink and drinks water from the tap until she can't possibly hold another ounce.

Then she walks around to the convenience store and buys a chocolate bar and a packet of peanuts. She adds it up in her head. It's about 20 percent of her life savings. Then again, she might be nearly halfway there. Maybe. Or maybe only a third, but she hates to think that. She wants to stay with the half.

The woman at the counter rings her up with the tips of long pink fingernails.

"West," Carly says, still holding the paper towel to her chin. "That way?"

She points.

The woman nods. Like talking is too much trouble.

She walks back out into the oven of the Mojave. Throws the paper towel in the trash on her way by.

She wants to eat the peanuts first, but then she remembers that the chocolate will melt in her pocket or pack. So she walks to the street. Peels the paper back on the candy. Looks carefully for cops or the highway patrol. Takes one bite of candy and sticks her thumb out just as a huge old bus of a motor home roars by. It stops a few yards up ahead. It's teal and white, two horizontal stripes of each. Twenty years old maybe. The covered spare tire says Lazy Daze. It has a ladder on the back, a sickening reminder of the worst of last night.

She hasn't even been hitchhiking long enough to chew and swallow one bite of chocolate, and she already has a ride.

As she jogs up to the big, silly vehicle, she thinks about this wind she's had at her back the whole trip. The truck is there, the train is there, the motor home is there. Just exactly when she needs them.

Then she remembers she almost died jumping that train.

Then she remembers Davis grabbing her wrists and pulling her on. She decides she has to count her near-death experience as wind at her back, too.

Before she can reach the motor home, it moves forward a few yards.

Damn, she thinks. I was wrong. They're not stopping for me.

It stops again.

An older woman leans her head out the window.

"Come on, honey," she yells to Carly.

Carly runs again.

The motor home jerks forward a few more yards.

This isn't funny, Carly thinks, stopping in her tracks on the sweltering sidewalk. She can feel the sun baking down on her scalp at the part of her hair.

The engine of the big motor home shuts down, giving way to silence. A moment later, the side door opens, and the woman leans out, a ring of keys jingling in her hand.

"Come on, honey," she says. "I'm sorry about my husband. If I don't take the keys from him, he just keeps on driving."

Carly takes a few steps. Not sure if any of this is for real.

"My goodness," the woman says. "You're so young. Don't you know it's dangerous to hitchhike when you're so young? And what did you do to your chin? You shouldn't be out here by yourself."

It causes Carly's hackles to rise. But she moves a few steps closer. She can feel coolness pouring out the door of the rig. She doesn't want to miss this chance. If it's really a chance. If it's real.

"Did you just stop to tell me that?" she asks the woman.

The woman is white-haired, maybe in her seventies. Bright-blue eyes with laugh lines at the corners. Like Teddy's laugh lines, only more so. Only a couple of decades later.

"No, honey, we're giving you a ride. Come on."

The woman backs up the three inside steps, into the living space of the motor home. Carly follows her in. It's gloriously cool.

"It's nice in here," Carly says. "Thanks for the ride."

"We never pick up hitchhikers, honey, but you're so young. I was worried about you. You can sit down here on the couch if you want. Or even lie down and take a nap. You look tired."

"I am."

"You thirsty?"

"No, ma'am. I just had a drink. Thank you, anyway."

"OK, then."

Like that's all the business they could possibly have with each other.

The woman carefully closes and locks the side door. Carly looks at the husband, behind the wheel. He hasn't even turned around to see who's joined them. He's just staring forward, through the windshield. As if anxious to keep going.

When Carly's hostess is fully settled into the passenger seat and has her safety belt fastened, she hands the ring of keys back to the driver.

"OK, Malcolm," she says. "*Now* you can drive."

Just as Carly is dropping off to sleep on the surprisingly comfortable couch, the woman's voice jolts her awake again.

"Before you take your nap, hon, better tell us where you're headed."

Carly sits up. Her head feels thick and muddled, as if she's been sleeping for twelve hours.

"Far west as you'll take me. Where are *you* headed?"

"We go west and then north."

"Me, too!" Carly says, excited now.

Wind. At her back. Right?

"Where exactly?"

"Trinidad."

"Trinidad?" the woman asks. "Trinidad? Where's that? Never heard of it."

Malcolm, the driver, mumbles something too quietly for Carly to hear.

His wife leans over and swats him on the arm.

"Malcolm, sometimes you just piss me off something royal. You know that?"

"What'd I do?" Malcolm asks, a little louder.

He still hasn't taken his eyes off the road. Carly still hasn't seen his face.

"One day in three I have to wake up in the morning and remind you my name is Lois after forty-nine years, but you remember the name of some little pissant town nobody's ever heard of up by Crescent City. Damn you."

"Eureka," Carly says.

"Eureka what, dear?" Lois replies.

"It's near Eureka."

"Oh. I thought you meant you had an idea or something."

Malcolm mumbles again.

"He says it's in between," Lois says. "North of Eureka, south of Crescent City. Damn it, it pisses me off that you know that. You don't even know my name."

"Lois!" he proclaims proudly.

"Well, sure. Now that I tipped you." Then she turns around in her seat to address Carly again. "You go ahead and take your nap, dear. If you're still asleep, we'll wake you up when we get home to Fresno. We ought to be there by dinner."

Fresno. By dinner.

Carly stretches out on the couch and tries to remember the details of how long she's been on the road. She left last night…no wait, the night before. No. It really was just last night. It only seems longer. And by dinner she'll be in Fresno, California.

Now that's a tailwind.

If Malcolm doesn't forget how to find Fresno, things are working out better than she could ever have imagined.

Carly wakes up, blinks. Sits up on the couch in the big old motor home. It's afternoon. Maybe late afternoon. She's been asleep a long time. Her stomach is growling. Her bladder is straining with all that water she drank this morning.

The motor home is not moving.

Lois and Malcolm are sitting at the dinette table, eating sandwiches. It's the first time she's gotten a look at him. He's as old as Lois, or older, seventies at least, but he seems big and almost handsome. His hair is full and dark except for a little gray at the sideburns. He looks like he was a strong man for most of his life. But his eyes are faraway. He never bothers to look at

Carly. Maybe he's been watching her sleep and has gotten his fill. But somehow she doesn't think so. She thinks probably he just doesn't care.

Carly can see and smell what they're eating. Tuna fish on wheat bread. It smells great. Her stomach cramps painfully. But at least she has that pack of peanuts.

Lois looks over, sees that Carly's awake, and immediately jumps to her feet. Still chewing, she bustles over to the little refrigerator. She extracts another sandwich, already made, on a stiff paper plate and garnished with pickle spears and potato chips.

She sets it on the dinette table.

"For me?" Carly asks, hardly willing to believe such a thing could be true.

"Well, of course for you," Lois says. "You think we're going to eat in front of you while you starve? If you don't like tuna fish, Malcolm will eat that and I'll make you peanut butter and grape jelly."

"I like tuna fish. A lot. Thank you. That was very nice of you."

"You want some lemonade?"

"Yes, ma'am. Thank you. Think I could use your bathroom before I eat?"

Lois points. Though, really, there's only one little boxed-off area in the motor home that could possibly be a miniature bathroom.

Carly stumbles over and opens the door. It actually looks big to her because she got used to the one in Delores's trailer.

She sits down gingerly on the toilet—every muscle and bruise still aches—her knees nearly brushing the door. Wondering how Malcolm fits. There's a mirror on the inside of the door, and it makes her uncomfortable. The scrapes on her chin look almost black. The sunburn blisters on her forehead and nose are peeling. Her hair looks as though it hasn't been brushed in weeks.

I look homeless, she thinks. Then it hits her. She is.

She flushes the toilet with a pedal on the floor and washes her hands in the sink. There's a shower in here. She wonders whether her hosts would allow her to use it. A shower sure would feel good. Delores only had a bathtub in her house, and Carly only used it once. They had to fill it with buckets of water from the pump at the well. They had to heat two of the buckets on the propane stove. Most of the time they took sponge baths in the trailer.

She sits down at the table with Lois and Malcolm. Lois smiles at her. Malcolm doesn't look up.

She sips the lemonade first. It delivers a blast of flavor she was not expecting.

"This is homemade," she says.

"Well, of course. You think I'd serve you that powder out of a jar?"

"I don't know. Everybody else always did. Where are we?"

"Bakersfield," Malcolm says. Still without looking at her.

They eat in silence for a few minutes. The food is making Carly feel more grounded.

Then Lois says, "We don't feel comfortable letting you hitch-hike all the way to Trinidad."

Like it's her decision, Carly thinks.

It's that sinking feeling that's become so familiar. It takes her back to Alvin, saying, "I don't want you and you sister leaving here on your own." That definitive moment when an adult decides to take over your life.

"I have to get there, though. And it can't be much farther."

"It's almost another five hundred miles."

Carly's heart falls. The half-eaten sandwich sinks in her hand until it's back on the plate.

"Oh, no. It couldn't be. From Fresno? Or from here?"

"From Fresno."

"Couldn't be."

Lois gets up and brings her a giant road atlas that looks almost exactly like the one Alvin showed her.

"This looks like…" She was going say "Alvin's" but she decides she doesn't want to bring up Alvin. Though she's not sure why not. "A friend of mine had one just like this." And, in the sting of the word *friend*, she knows why not. Some friend she's been to Alvin. Promised him to his face he could trust her to stay put. And she knew the whole time it was nothing but a lie.

She looks up Northern California. Finds Fresno. Runs her finger up the coast to Eureka and beyond.

"Holy cow, that's a long state," she says. "But…Anyway, I've got to get there. I didn't come all this way to give up now."

"We'll take you to the bus station in Fresno."

"Oh," Carly says. "OK."

That allows her appetite to function again, and she picks up the sandwich and takes a few more bites.

That'll be fine. She hasn't got enough money for a bus, of course. But Lois doesn't need to know that. Maybe she can spend the night in the station. In the morning she'll be on her own again. She can just keep going. And there will be no one around to take over. No one to tell her what she can or can't do.

If there was anything she couldn't do, she wouldn't be here right now.

If only other people knew that as well as she did.

Lois insists on coming into the bus station. Which is not the way Carly planned it at all.

"I'll be right back," Lois tells Malcolm. "Give me the keys."

Malcolm just sits in the driver's seat for a moment or two, hands at ten and two on the wheel. The engine is still running. Then he pulls back out into traffic, watching carefully in the side mirror.

"Malcolm, stop. No, wait. Don't stop. We're too far now. You'll have to circle the block. Where did you think you were going, Malcolm?"

"Home," he says.

"We're taking the young lady to the bus station."

"Oh."

"And we were already at the bus station."

"Oh."

"Make a right here."

"I know how to circle a block."

Two more right turns, then they pull up on the other side of the station. The sun is well off to the west. It's past dinnertime. Probably seven or seven thirty.

"Now stop, Malcolm," Lois says. "Turn off the engine."

Malcolm sighs. Shifts into park. Turns the key to off.

Lois reaches over and grabs they keys out of the ignition. As though she's been practicing for years.

"Come on, honey," she says to Carly. "Let's go see what's what."

They step out the side door together. It's the remains of a hot day in Fresno. It's the kind of hot she knows from Tulare, which isn't far away.

Carly thinks maybe she'll just take off running. Get this over with. She looks both ways. Makes a decision.

She sticks. For the moment.

Maybe Lois will just come in, see when the bus is scheduled, then leave her there. That would be better.

They walk along the sidewalk. Round the corner together.

Carly says, "I don't mean to be rude, but…is it safe for him to be driving?"

"Oh, my goodness yes. Malcolm's a great driver. Never takes his eyes off the road. Never gets lost."

"You're not afraid he'll forget how?"

"Honey, I should be so lucky that man could forget how to drive. It's everything else he's forgotten."

She holds the door of the bus station open for Carly. A blast of cool hits Carly in the face as she walks inside.

"He's forgotten me a time or two," Lois says. "Until I got smart and started taking the keys. Left me once in a gas station in Seligman, Arizona. Remembered how to drive away but forgot me, and when I called him eight hundred times, he forgot what you're supposed to do with the cell phone when it rings. That was a mess, let me tell you. But in sixty years, he hasn't gotten so much as a parking ticket. If there's one thing that man can do—and there may be only one thing left that man can do—it's drive that rig."

Lois marches up to the counter.

Carly sits down on a hard bench. Turns her back to the business being done. After all, it really isn't her business. She's not the one who thinks she can't hitchhike. That's a grown-up stranger's decision.

It takes a long time. She can hear Lois talking to a man behind the counter. But she purposely stays too far away to hear what they're saying.

She looks behind her once and thinks she can just slip out the door. But Lois might call the cops to get her picked up. Better she should wait. Lois will probably leave her here to wait for the bus. Maybe she can get herself locked inside for the night. In the morning she'll be on her own. And on her way.

She looks up to see Lois standing over her again.

"OK, here's your ticket, hon. Bus doesn't go all the way to Trinidad. Goes to Arcata. That's about sixteen miles away. Or maybe he said fourteen. Anyway, he says there's a regional bus you can pick up right there at the same station. Almost like a city bus, but it goes up and down to those little towns on the coast.

Just ask in the station in Arcata, they'll tell you. But the bus from here doesn't leave till morning."

Carly just stares at the ticket for a long moment.

"You bought me a ticket?"

"Well, how else were you gonna get there?"

"How did you know I didn't have money to buy my own?"

"Honey…really…what kind of fool stands in the hundred-degree heat in the full sun in the Mojave Desert hitching a ride if they have enough money to buy *any* ticket to ride *anything*?"

Carly nods a few times. All that bravado about how she can handle herself for another night, for another five hundred miles, melts away, leaving her overwhelmed with gratitude that she doesn't have to.

"That's very nice," Carly says. "I appreciate it. But you have to write your name and address down in my little book. And how much you paid for the ticket. So I can send you the money back when I can."

She opens her backpack and begins to rummage around, looking for the book.

"It doesn't really matter, honey. We can manage."

"No, really. It's important to me. I want to give it back when I can."

Lois shrugs. "OK, if that's what you want."

Carly wraps her hand around the book and pulls it free. Lois sits beside her and writes down the information in the tiniest, loopiest, neatest script Carly has ever witnessed.

Lois folds up the book and hands it back.

"Now come on back to the rig, and we'll all get a good night's sleep."

"I can sleep here in the station."

"No, you can't. Man locks up at ten."

"Don't you want to get home, though?"

"Honey, we *are* home. That *is* home. When we get home, we just park it in the Crestview Trailer Park. Still home inside the rig. Only difference is what we see out the windows. Now come on."

In her dream, Carly leaps through the narrow doorway into that boxcar a second time. Just like she did the first time. She makes it just as far in. Hits her hip just as hard. Then she's falling back again, under the wheels of the train.

No one grabs her wrists.

She lands hard on her back on the metal rail. She can see the wheel that will take her life, that will cut her in two, bearing down on her in the dark.

She sits upright, belting out a gigantic noise.

Eyes open, she looks around. She's in the old motor home with Malcolm and Lois. Sitting up on the couch across from the dinette table. She looks toward the bedroom in the back to see if she woke them. But nothing stirs. Maybe that huge noise she made in the dream was nothing but a rush of air in the real world.

It's the second time in two days that she's died—not in truth, but in her own head, her own perception. She's getting tired of dying. She's getting tired of that moment in which her life is supposed to flash before her eyes. Because both times it contained nothing at all. Her heart calms easily, but she can't stop shaking. It's an actual trembling, a shudder, as if it were below zero in here. Her teeth even chatter. It feels as though her nerves have been stripped bare. Like life is touching them. Even in the middle of the night, in the dark, with no actual life events in sight.

She berates herself, reminding herself that it was only a dream. But the minute she does, she knows the dream has nothing to do with it. She's not scared of what's behind her. It's what's ahead of her that's causing problems.

She never gets back to sleep.

CALIFORNIA

May 19

Lois gets up at four in the morning. Before it's even light. Carly knows it's four because there's a little battery-powered clock mounted over the dinette table. It ticks.

"What are you doing up so early?" Carly asks.

"Oh, I always get up at four. Always did. All my life. Well, my adult life, anyway. Used to get up at four to go to work. Been retired twelve years, but I still can't seem to kick the habit. How about you? What are you doing up so early?"

"Never really got to sleep."

"You OK?"

"Oh yeah," she says, though she's not. "I think I just have my days and nights turned around." Which is half the truth, anyway.

Lois sits on the couch next to Carly. Fairly close. She still hasn't turned on a light. She presses her hand against Carly's palm. At first Carly thinks the old woman is trying to hold hands with her, which feels mildly alarming. Then she feels it. Cash. Some folded bills.

Carly doesn't know what kind of bills or how many. Maybe three or four from the feel of it.

"It's going to be late when that bus gets in tonight, and I want to make sure you have someplace to stay."

"I can stay with my stepfather," Carly says.

But she's not 100 percent sure that's true. She's been up all night thinking of a hundred reasons why Teddy might not be able to take her in. Or why she might not want him to.

"I just worry that it'll be late and maybe the first night you won't have any place to go. I'd just feel better if you have enough on you to get a room."

So now Carly knows the bills are not ones. Or fives.

"OK, thanks," Carly says. "But I'm writing it down in my little book. And I'm going to pay you back."

"Fair enough," Lois says.

Then they sit without talking for a moment. Carly wants to say something, but she can't imagine how to phrase it. Can't imagine what words will not completely misrepresent her feelings. Then she realizes that she has that trouble a lot. Nearly all the time.

"I really, really appreciate that you're being so nice to me," Carly says. "But I don't know why. I appreciate it, but I don't know why you'd want to. You don't even know me."

Carly hears Lois sigh in the mostly dark. Her eyes are adjusted enough to the low light to see that the older woman's hair is down, long and white and wispy and thin. It makes her look even older. And a lot more vulnerable.

"Both my parents died when I was young," Lois says. "Younger than you."

Immediately the tears come to Carly's eyes. Because her mother died. It hits her that every time she's cried since leaving

New Mexico, no matter what she thought she was crying about, she was really crying because her mother died.

"I went to live with my granddad. And that was OK, I guess. I'm lucky I had him. But he was already pretty senile. So it felt a lot like being alone."

It strikes Carly as a cruel trick for life to play on poor Lois. Twice.

"Bet you must feel the same way now," Carly says. Then she immediately regrets saying it. "I'm sorry. What a stupid thing to say. I'm really sorry. I didn't mean that to come out the way it sounded."

"It's OK," Lois says, neatly wrapping up the moment and putting it to rest. "You're absolutely right. I'm just saying my heart went out to you. You can understand that, right?"

"Yes, ma'am."

"Lois."

"Yes, Lois. I can understand that. I don't like being alone, either."

"I don't think anybody does."

But Carly thinks some people are better at it than others. Like Jen. Jen can rely on her own wits and be OK. But Carly doesn't say so.

Thinking about Jen brings a great pang of missing Jen.

It strikes her that she hasn't even told Lois she has a sister. It strikes her that this older woman, whom she inwardly accused of taking over her life, has actually asked very few questions about Carly's situation.

"Well, sit tight," Lois says. "I'll make you some bacon and eggs and fried potatoes and pack you a lunch for the bus."

The suggestion that Lois would do all that for her—no, the very fact that someone is even around to be able to do all that for her—makes her cry all over again.

They walk into the station together, Carly feeling fresh and revived from the shower she took in the tiny motor home bathroom. Lois hands her what's supposed to be her lunch in a brown paper bag. It feels more like dinner for six.

Carly doesn't know what to say.

So she says, "When you get home, will he still try to drive away?"

"Oh, no. When he's home, he's home. He'll hook up the sewer drain. Hook up the water. Rinse out all the tanks. Plug into power. Cover the tires. All the stuff you're supposed to do after a trip. He knows not to drive away after that."

"So…then…what does he do?"

Lois thinks that over for a moment.

"Absolutely nothing," she says.

Now Lois seems uncomfortable. They both do.

"You don't mind if I don't wait with you, do you?" Lois asks. "'Cause, you know, he's awake now, and he'll be wanting to go."

"No," Carly says. "Not at all. I'll be fine. You've done plenty. Thank you."

They stand awkwardly for a moment.

Then Carly dives in and gives Lois a hug. It wasn't exactly premeditated. It just happened that way. Lois seems surprised. Unbalanced. She just stands there, with her hands at her sides. But in time, she gives Carly a pat on the back, then on the head.

Carly lets go.

"You travel safe, now," Lois says.

She hurries out of the station.

Carly hears the noisy engine of the motor home roar to life. She crosses to the window and watches it drive away.

Now she's alone. Just as surely as she was alone out on Wakapi land in the middle of the night, under the stars. It's light in the bus station, and there are a few people around. But that doesn't matter. Carly knows by now how it feels to be alone. And this is it.

She digs the money out of her pocket and looks at it in the light. She's wanted to count it a dozen times since Lois gave it to her. But it seemed rude, with Lois right there watching.

It's four twenties.

It strikes Carly that if she's going to be alone, it's better to be alone with eighty dollars, a bus ticket, and a big bag of food.

She knows she's had worse.

A few hours into the long bus ride, Carly wakes suddenly. Her neck is sore, and her face feels smashed and sweaty from pressing up against the glass of the window. But the rest of her face is cool because the air-conditioning blows up from the base of the window. Right onto her face.

The bus has left the more flat and hot inland sections of Highway 101 and is winding up through a forested section. Carly looks out the window, wishing she'd sat on the other side. The left side. She doesn't know how soon they'll see the ocean, but she knows the best views of the ocean are on the left side when you're heading north. She should have thought of that.

She's never seen the ocean before. Until recently, she'd never thought much about it. But now she feels her life will change when she finally sees it. Whenever that might be. She tries to look out the windows on the other side of the bus, hoping to see a glimpse of it, but the man sitting next to her keeps acting as though she's looking at him, which is making them both uneasy.

Carly opens Lois's bag.

In it is a sandwich on a big French roll, cut in half and wrapped in plastic film. On closer investigation, it turns out to be home-made chicken salad. It's easily big enough for two meals. Under that is an orange, a banana, a bottle of apple juice, and a sealed cup of store-bought chocolate pudding.

There's also a plastic spoon and two paper napkins.

It makes Carly cry again.

Are the tears still because her mother died? She asks herself that.

Turns out that's partly it. It's also the fact that, even when her mother was alive, she never did anything like this. Never took this good care of her. Maybe gave her money to buy lunch at school. But only if Carly reminded. Insisted.

She wonders if Lois's mother packed her lunches like this before she died. She wonders how Lois's parents died.

Suddenly, in one big rush, she wonders if Lois would take her in if Teddy won't. Or if she can't let him. And Jen. She could go back and get Jen and bring her to Fresno. Lois doesn't want to be alone. And Carly has her address.

Then the truth rolls over her and sets her back to where she started. Lois and Malcolm live in a motor home. It's barely big enough for two people. Besides. What a weird thought to have about strangers. What's happening to her?

No, it's Teddy or nothing. There is no plan B.

It causes the trembling to start again. Now she's trembling and crying. In public. On a bus. With a grown man sitting right beside her. She thinks he's going to ask her what's wrong. And she doesn't want that. He averts his gaze. Pretends he can't hear or see. Then Carly wishes he'd asked her what's wrong instead.

Carly is sleeping on the backseat of the bus, which is all one long bench seat, from one window to the other. Because the bus is not so crowded now. Lots of people have gotten off, but not so many have gotten on.

She wakes and sits up. Looks out the windows. It's dark. She wonders if they're almost there. Or if she passed her stop. But no, Arcata is the last stop.

Isn't it?

But she knows she couldn't have overslept. Because that tailwind would never allow it. It's just so clear now. She's getting help. Something or someone is looking out for her. Otherwise, how was she supposed to cover twelve hundred miles in two days, with barely a cent in her pocket?

And another thing. It dawns on her quite suddenly. If she's getting help to go home to Teddy, then home to Teddy must be the right place to go. Would the universe help speed and ease her way back to a child molester? Of course not. She's on a good road. She can tell by the smoothness of it.

She knows this in a way she's never known anything before. A sureness she always thought was reserved for anyone else in the world besides her.

Then, in her half-asleep state, it dawns on her that the bus is not moving. She stands up and looks through the front windshield.

They're on a small, two-lane stretch of highway. In their lane, the northbound lane, nothing but red taillights as far as the eye can see. Thing is, it's a twisty road. So the eye can't see very far. Maybe seven cars. But they're definitely all standing still.

In the southbound lane, nothing. That lane is empty.

No matter how long Carly stands at the back of the bus watching, no cars come by going south.

She can only see a half-dozen heads of other riders on the bus, and they all seem to be asleep.

She makes her way up to the driver. He jumps. As if startled to suddenly see her standing there. As if he, too, was asleep.

"What going on?" she asks.

"Overturned truck a couple of miles up ahead. One of those big logging trucks."

"Any idea how long we're stuck here?"

"No idea at all. Pretty remote where we are. Depends how long it takes to get some emergency equipment up here to clear the highway. First they gotta clear the logging truck. Then they gotta clear the logs. Ever seen the logs those things carry? Whole trunks of old growth redwoods. I've seen 'em where six logs is a full load. They weigh tons. No idea how they'll get 'em out of there. Probably they'll have to bring in an empty truck. And some kind of really big winch."

"How far are we from Arcata?"

"Depends on when we move again. We'd be there in probably an hour and a half if we could move."

It strikes Carly suddenly that the local bus up to Trinidad might not run in the middle of the night.

"Hope I don't miss the last bus up to Trinidad."

The driver shakes his head. Glumly.

"We've been sitting here for over an hour. Even if we started to move right now, I don't see you catching that last bus. I'm sorry."

Carly sighs. Thanks him. Walks all the way back down the aisle and sits down on the rear seat again. Her mind is clear. She's careful of that. No point thinking anything at all.

She looks out the window. A couple of the trees lining the road have trunks almost as wide as the bus. On her left is a sharp drop-off, with water below, glistening in the moonlight. But it's not the ocean. More like a wide creek or a shallow river. She wonders again when she'll see the ocean.

She lies down.

Some kind of emergency vehicle comes by, speeding the wrong way up the empty southbound lane. No siren, just lights. She watches the flashing red lights fire up the giant redwoods.

Then nothing at all.

CALIFORNIA

May 20

The bus driver shakes Carly gently by her shoulder and tells her this is Arcata.

She sits up, rubbing her eyes.

They're stopped in front of a small, squat tan building with a hanging wooden sign that says ARCATA MAD RIVER TRANSIT. Carly has never head of a place called Mad River. And she isn't at all sure she wants to hear of it now.

There's no one on the bus except Carly and the driver.

"Time's it?" she mumbles.

"Half past midnight. You got someplace to be tonight? I feel bad we got so far behind schedule. You got someplace to go? Station's already locked up."

She thinks about the eighty dollars. She could go to a motel. But it seems like a lot of money to waste just to lie awake all night. She's been sleeping all day. Her sleep schedule is officially backward.

"I'm OK," she says, grabbing up her backpack. "I just need a pay phone."

"There's a pay phone outside the station."

"That's fine, then. I'll call my stepfather. He'll drive down from Trinidad and pick me up."

The last thing Carly needs is another adult watching her movements.

She shuffles down the aisle and off the bus.

She looks over her shoulder on the way to the pay phone. The driver is still watching her.

She digs into her pocket for one of her many quarters. For one crazy, sleepy moment, she almost drops it into the slot on the phone. Like she was so lost in a dream, maybe she thought she really could call Teddy and get picked up. Instead she pantomimes putting several quarters into the slot.

A minute later she turns in toward the phone and away from the driver. As if somebody just answered. As if she wants to talk in private.

She reads the sign on the window of the bus station. It says, NO LOITERING. NO OPEN ALCOHOL CONTAINERS. NO SMOKING WITHIN TWENTY FEET OF BUILD—that's all, just "build"—no "ing"—NO PUBLIC USE OF MEDICAL MARIJUANA. That one feels especially perplexing. NO DOGS.

She looks over to see a line of homeless people sitting with their backs up against a low wall. Looking at her. They're all young. Not as young as Carly, but young enough. She wonders if she's just a step above where they are right now. Or if even that is flattering herself.

She looks over her shoulder at the bus driver, but he's gone.

She hears cars going by behind her back. Fast. Not all that regularly. Not constant traffic. But she can hear the highway from here.

She turns around.

Behind her and across the little street is a brick wall, two or three feet high, with a chain link fence above it. But it's not a high fence. Maybe five feet. And nothing on top to make it hard to scale. Just a horizontal wire to keep it from sagging. If someone climbs it.

She doesn't even hang up the phone. Just lets it drop.

She looks around one more time, avoiding the eyes of the homeless group.

Then she runs for the fence and scales it in four big movements. Her body is still sore, and it screams pain at every move, but Carly just absorbs that. Doesn't let it stop her. Doesn't let it change a thing.

She drops down into the weeds on the shoulder of the highway. It's two lanes in each direction, with a wide grass—well, weed—median down the center. Not very well lighted, unless a car is coming by. And when one does, Carly ducks into the weeds and crouches down. In case it's the police or the highway patrol. It's probably illegal to walk on the freeway.

She sets off in the only direction she can go without crossing the four lanes.

She doesn't even know if she's headed north or south. But in a few minutes she comes to a sign marking this the 101 South. So she has to cross the highway and start over in the other direction. There are no cars coming anyway.

It's cold. Surprisingly cold. And foggy. The longer she walks, the foggier it gets. And she still can't see the ocean. It could be right there, right below her and off to the left. She'd never know it. Her visibility has been cut to near nothing. The world is black until a car comes along. Then it's white.

But none of that matters. It's only sixteen miles to Trinidad. And if there's one thing Carly knows how to do, it's walk. Sixteen miles is nothing. Walking all night is nothing.

At least it's the final stretch. At long last.

A wind comes up. It's a wind unlike any Carly can remember. At least, from such an exposed position as outdoors, facing right into its wrath. It feels like a miniature hurricane.

Carly finds herself leaning forward to push harder against it. She needs to, just to keep moving. She might actually move backward if she stopped pushing so hard.

The fog is even more dense now, making her feel as though the world has disappeared, leaving nothing but a windy, white outer space. The wind is whipping fog mist into her face. Her face is wet. Her hair is wet. Her jacket is soaking through. Gradually, but it's wetting her to the skin. She can feel water dripping off the feather and down her belly.

It's cold. Really cold.

Her eyelashes are thick with moisture, and it hurts when the wind whips droplets into her eyes. It's getting harder to keep them open.

Carly reaches an abutment for an overpass and stands behind the concrete structure for a minute or two, blinking and catching her breath. It takes so much energy to walk into the wind, she feels as if she's climbing a mountain. She wants to stay here, hide here, and be safe from the fury. But she's probably only thirteen or fourteen miles from Trinidad.

She didn't come all this way to let a big wind stop her. She didn't come all this way to let anything stop her.

She thinks about Jen. Wonders if she's fast asleep in the trailer, or even in the old woman's house. If she's sleeping with a smile on her face. Or if she's not there anymore at all. That reminds Carly that she'd better hurry.

She steps back into the wind and whipping fog drizzle and walks more miles in that misery. She could be anywhere for all she knows. She could be nowhere.

She can't even prove for a fact that this is planet Earth.

In time, the road angles steeply uphill. A long, relentless, painful grade with nothing but redwood forest on either side. But at least she can see something besides a white curtain. She can barely make out trees. But they look more like the ghosts of trees in all that fog.

Still she plows on, sheer stubbornness replacing her normal energy. Nothing can hold her back. And yet it seems as though the whole world is conspiring to try. It's holding her back with all the force it can possibly muster.

As if somehow dreaming on her feet, she sees Alvin's face very clearly and suddenly in her mind. And he speaks to her. Or, at least, her mind speaks to her. In Alvin's voice.

"Face it, Carly girl. You lost that tailwind."

"That was bullshit," she says. Out loud. The wind snatching her words away. "That was stupid to act like I can know right from wrong by how long it takes to get to it."

"But you liked that theory fine," he says, "when it was going your way."

That knocks Carly fully back into the moment.

She rests again behind the abutment of another overpass. Shivering and cold and holding back tears of frustration. She pulls the remnants of Lois's bag lunch out of her backpack and eats the other half of her chicken salad sandwich.

Then she steps out into the wind and fog and keeps walking.

Something dawns on her suddenly. It's just a feeling. She never really matches it with words. But…all the grown-ups who acted like she shouldn't be out in the world on her own…that she was too young…that she was too small and the world was too big. All of a sudden it feels like they were right.

The wind has mostly died when she sees the exit for Trinidad. The fog is just as thick, though, so she's nearly on top of the sign by the time she sees it. Her whole body is shaking from exertion. But it really doesn't matter now.

Dawn is somewhere nearby. It's hard to track it through so much fog. But it's definitely getting lighter.

She walks down the shoulder of the exit and follows a sign toward Trinidad State Beach. Somewhere in the back of her head she knows she saw a sign that told the population of Trinidad, and it was only 311. But she can't remember how long ago she saw that or where.

How hard can it be to find a person among 311?

She walks down a curvy little street, through a town that feels too small to be real. The blank whiteness that masks each building until she's nearly right on top of it only adds to that otherworldly feeling.

She passes the Trinidad Trailer Court, where huge American flags blow in the wind. Please don't let Teddy live in the trailer court, she thinks. She wants to see him in a big house looking out over the ocean. But then she remembers he's not even working.

What if he left town to find a job?

She presses her mind back to the moment. She can't afford panic now. She's…well, she's here. But where is here? How does it help her to be here? When does she get to stop? What's she supposed to do next?

She comes around a curve in the road and passes an elementary school. It has a play yard, and Carly stops a minute and looks across the parking lot and through the fence. Pictures Jen playing in that yard. All by herself. Too clearly, really. Almost as clearly as she pictured Alvin on the highway. As though she's lost some grasp of what's still real.

She turns her face away again. Passes a tiny library that seems also to be the police station. Out front are statues of a mermaid and a dolphin surfing on individual metal waves, side by side.

She passes a bright red volunteer fire station. Really bright.

What she does not pass are people. It's early, and the town is deserted. Like a ghost town or a movie set. Just buildings and Carly and fog.

It's getting light fast now, and she looks up to the end of the street and sees what looks like the top of a lighthouse. A white lighthouse with a red roof.

She stops cold and listens, realizing she can hear the ocean. It's not crashing, exactly. It sounds more as if it's breathing. Drawing in and out.

She breaks into a run.

At the end of the street, she stands at the top of the stairs that lead down to the lighthouse.

The ocean is stretched out beneath her. Maybe 150 feet below this sudden cliff. A sleepy bay. Dozens of boats float down there, anchored in the fog. Rocks jut up out of the water, like rough pyramids. Some the size of a bus. Some the size of a house. Some the size of an apartment house. There's a dull, distant bell clanging. It seems to ring in time with the swell.

Carly pulls in a sharp breath, then presses her eyes shut.

Please, she says in her own mind. Please let it still be there when I open my eyes. She can't help feeling it's too breathtaking to be real. And yet she can't believe that her imagination could have created it, either.

She opens her eyes. It's all still there.

She sits on a bench for a while, watching the scene grow lighter. The bench is wet and cold. But so is she, so it doesn't seem to matter.

It's morning. She's walked all night, and she needs to sleep.

She thinks about getting a room with her eighty dollars. But maybe she should save that for more of an emergency. Anyway, first she wants to walk down the path, through the manicured little park surrounding the lighthouse. See what more there is to see.

She finds a long, steep stairway down to the beach. It's made with pieces of railroad ties and lined with green berry vines and trees. She takes it almost all the way to the bottom.

Before the last set of steps down to the beach, she stops. She can hear seagulls crying, that same bell clanging somewhere, the breath of the bay. She can see some kind of dock or pier far off to her right, but she can't see it well in all this fog. She could step down onto the beach, but then what? You can walk to one end, then you can walk to the other. But when you've spent the night walking sixteen miles in a small hurricane, taking a walk on the beach doesn't sound all that appealing. She just wants to sleep somewhere. Where she'll be left alone. Where she won't be seen.

She looks to her right, and without even thinking it out, dives into the berry vines and heavy understory. Tiny thorns scratch her hands and face, snag her hair, grab on to her jacket. But she just moves them aside as best she can and keeps going. The thorns just mean no one else will be brave enough to tramp into the same spot.

She curls up in the damp foliage and rests her head on her backpack, listening to the gulls and the breathing of the swell.

A couple of minutes later, she's fast asleep.

When she wakes, the fog is gone. The sky is blue. She can see snatches of it through the trees and berry vines. She looks west at the sunlight glinting off the ocean in a long, sparkly band. The sun's already on a pretty good slant. Which means she slept most of the day.

She claws her way back to the stairs, scratching herself up further on the thorns.

As she emerges from the foliage, she startles a young mother with a little boy. The woman draws in a sharp breath and yanks the child closer to her side. Then she hurries herself and the boy up the stairs double-time, glancing over her shoulder at Carly. Twice.

Carly can't help but feel offended. At first she assumes she just startled the woman by appearing suddenly and unexpectedly, and that was understandable. But everything after that seems like overkill.

She eases her way up a few stairs.

The woman with the little boy needn't have worried. The sixteen miles Carly walked, uphill and against the wind, has taken a toll. Her muscles have stiffened now and feel barely usable. It's not so bad where the railroad ties are set close together, creating short risers. But now and then there's a big step up. Carly can't make those big steps without easing her leg up with the help of both hands. She also can't do it without letting out a little whimper of pain each time.

When she gets back up to the tiny park around the lighthouse, she isn't sure what to do next. She figures she should go into a few businesses and ask about Teddy. Find someone who knows him. But—after that experience with the mother on the stairs—she decides she'd better find a public restroom and get a good look at herself first.

It's pretty shocking.

Carly stands in the gas station bathroom, leaning on the sink. Just staring at her own reflection in the mirror.

Her chin is a mass of blackened scabs. Her sunburn blisters have left a line of scars across her forehead and nose. She knew that. But then there are the scratches. They didn't seem like much at the time. But she has maybe thirty scratches on her face, and they're red with blood. And, even worse, they've become swollen. And her hair looks almost like dreadlocks, it's so tangled.

She reaches up and pulls a few stray bits of berry vine out of her hair.

Then she decides staring won't help.

She washes her hands and face. She pulls the hairbrush out of her pack and works the tangles out as best she can. It pulls, and she loses a lot of hair. But it has to be done. She looks in the mirror again. It's not much progress. But there's nothing more she can do. The rest is not immediately fixable.

"You know Teddy Thackett?" she asks the clerk.

She's at the check-out station in the only market in town—at least, the only one she's seen so far—holding a small bottle of orange juice.

The young woman tips her head, like a dog hearing a noise it can't understand.

"Teddy Thackett. No, can't say as I do. He supposed to live here?"

"Yeah, he lives here. He has a friend named Linda."

"Linda Litnipski?"

"I…I don't know her last name."

"I know Linda Litnipski. But I didn't think she was seeing anybody." She cranes her neck to yell to a guy in the produce aisle. "Hey, Kurt. Is Linda Litnipski seeing somebody these days?"

"I heard she was, yeah. Somebody told me a month or two ago she had a new boyfriend. But I haven't met him."

"Was his name Teddy?"

"I never knew his name."

"Sorry, kid," the clerk says. "Say, how'd your face get so scratched up? Are you OK?"

Carly doesn't answer. Just slides the bottle of orange juice closer to the woman, who takes the hint and rings it up. Carly pays her in quarters. It feels good to get rid of some of those quarters. They feel like lead weights in her pockets.

On her way out the door, she feels a hand slap down on her shoulder. She spins defensively.

It's the guy from produce.

"If you're looking for Linda and her boyfriend, go by the Whale Tail Lounge tonight."

"How do you know they'll be there tonight?"

"Well…Linda's there every other night of her life. Can't see why tonight would be any different."

Carly walks to the Whale Tail Lounge. Even though it isn't nearly night. It's out on Patrick's Point Road, a long paved road lined with giant redwood trees. She can hear the ocean breathing off to her left.

First it seems there's nothing out on this road at all except trees. But now and then she passes hidden driveways, usually with closed gates. And there are RV parks here and there, and cottages and inns. They surprise her a little every time. Because her eyes keep convincing her there's nothing here but forest.

She walks nearly a mile before realizing it's a long walk to this place. She wishes she'd waited in town until it was later. They probably won't even let her in, if it's a bar. She'll have to walk all the way back to town to get something to eat. Then she'll have to walk back to the Whale Tail again tonight. But she has no idea what hour constitutes "tonight." She doesn't even know what time it is.

In another half a mile, she finds it. The Whale Tail Cottages, with the Whale Tail Lounge attached.

She looks at the menu posted in the window and realizes two things: That she's very hungry. And that it's a restaurant that serves drinks, not just a bar. So she can probably go in.

Actually, three things.

She looks at the prices and realizes she can't justify eating here.

She walks all the way back to town.

"Is it always this windy around here?" she asks her waiter.

He's about twenty, with a face so gentle she wants to sink into his eyes and never come out into the world again.

"Does this seem windy to you?"

"No, not now. I meant last night. Well, this morning, early."

"It wasn't any more windy than usual last night."

"Wow. So that's, like, an everyday thing? It felt like a hurricane to me."

"Right here in town?"

"Well. No. I was walking up from Arcata last night. And the wind was so strong I could hardly walk in it."

"Hmm. We didn't really get it so much up here. I mean, that I know of. Maybe I slept right through it."

Then he moves off with her order. A bowl of clam chowder and a glass of iced tea. She promised herself she wouldn't spend more than the quarters in her pocket would cover.

While he's gone, she looks out at the ocean. The bay. She can see it from here. The café isn't exactly poised on the edge of the cliff, but if she looks across the street at the right angle, she can see a sliver of water between the cliff and the horizon. It feels good to be indoors. To see the ocean without the wind and the fog and the cold punishing her while she watches.

What do people do when they're homeless? she wonders. Do they ever get used to that? Could she ever get used to having no way to get indoors, out of the elements?

Her stomach ices over in fear, bordering on panic, and at first she doesn't know why. Then it breaks through. She's about to find out if she's homeless or not. Not even if she and Jen are homeless. Jen seems to have found a home. Carly seems to be the one out in the world alone.

The waiter comes back with her soup.

"I asked the cook," he says. "Because he drives up from Eureka every morning early. He said there was sort of a microburst. This little wind event, and then a couple miles later, it was gone. Weather is like that sometimes. You can have these little microclimates. Ten miles away it's all still. Oh. And by the way. He doesn't know Teddy, either. But since he lives in Eureka...you know..."

"Oh," she says. "Well...thanks for asking him, anyway. I never heard of a microburst. Or a microclimate. But anyway, I'm glad that's not what it's like here usually. Because I'm hoping I'll be living here soon."

"I hope that works out for you," he says and fills her glass with iced tea.

Her stomach clamps tight and then freezes up again.

She thinks, Yeah. I hope that works out for me, too.

She sits for hours, staring at the ocean and nursing iced tea after iced tea. Because she has no place else to go. The waiter keeps coming by and filling up her glass, and when she apologizes for taking up the table, he assures her that it's fine because they're not busy at all.

It means a great deal to Carly to have someplace she feels welcome. The fact that it's just a cheap, touristy seafood café is not the best part of that feeling.

Carly doesn't know exactly what time it is when she gets back to the Whale Tail, but she figures it's too early. If she had to guess, she'd say it was seven or seven thirty. What if this Linda—she can't bring herself to think "Teddy" somehow—doesn't come to the lounge until nine? Or Ten? Or later? Or...at all.

She doesn't think she can go in, because she doesn't want to waste money ordering anything. She'll have to find a place outside to sit where she can see the front door.

But first, she sticks her head inside.

Then she takes two steps in.

The bar area is on the left, but the angle of the line of patrons sitting at the bar blocks her view of most of the faces. So she walks right into the bar area for a better look.

She's busted immediately.

A waiter taps her on the shoulder and says, "Excuse me, miss. You have to be twenty-one to be in the bar."

But she doesn't answer him. Because there, in the mirror behind the bartender, is the perfect reflection of Teddy's face. She squeezes her eyes closed, the way she did when she first saw Trinidad Bay. When she opens them, Teddy's reflection is still there.

She opens her mouth to call out to him. She wants to say, Oh, my God, do you have any idea how far I've come to find you? Do you have any idea how many times I've watched this moment play out in my head?

The waiter taps her shoulder again, but she ignores it.

She calls out to Teddy. But all that comes out is just that one word. "Teddy!"

It's much too loud. Every diner, every bar patron, stops talking and turns to look at her.

"Miss, I'm going to have to ask you to leave," the waiter says.

"I just have to see Teddy."

And then, Teddy is there. Towering over her.

"Carly?" he asks. As if it might or might not be her. As if she might be some sort of cunning Carly imposter, sent to trick him.

She throws her arms around his chest and holds him so tightly he makes a wheezing noise.

"Carly, what're you doing here?"

But she can't make words happen. She can't even open her mouth.

"Ted, what the hell is this?" a woman's voice says.

Carly doesn't have to look up to know she's about to meet Linda Litnipski.

Catherine Ryan Hyde

The waiter is getting less patient. Carly can hear it in his voice.

"Take this outside, Ted," he says, "whatever it is."

Teddy peels Carly off and leads her outside. Back out into the misty cold air. How can anyplace be cold in late May? It's a thought out of context, but it's what she thinks.

Linda Litnipski follows. She's blonde, maybe as tall as Teddy, or taller. Built solid. With a long, horsey, not particularly attractive face.

"You better start explaining, Ted," she says.

"It's nothing," Teddy says.

The two words hit Carly like a torpedo.

It makes her think of Delores Watakobie, telling those little Wakapi girls the same thing about Carly. "It's nothing." Or… maybe Delores said, "It don't matter." But the feeling is the same. She can even see a flash of the old woman's face. Too clearly. Like Alvin on the freeway. Like Jen playing on the monkey bars at the Trinidad Elementary School.

"What kind of nothing, exactly?" Linda demands.

"Just the daughter of a woman I used to know. It's not what you're thinking, Linda. I swear."

"Well, what's she doing here, then?"

"Here's a thought," Teddy says. "Let's ask *her*. Carly, what are you doing here? Where's your mom?"

"She's gone, Teddy."

"She took off and left you guys?"

"She died."

A long silence. One even Linda Litnipski doesn't dare fill.

"She died?"

"She went out for a drive with that idiot. Wade. And now she's dead."

Another long silence. Carly can feel the fog creeping into her joints and bone marrow.

"God, I'm sorry, Carly."

"But…" Linda says.

"But…" Teddy says. "…what are you doing here?"

"I came to find you."

"Me? Why me?"

"*Why you?* Teddy. I had to find *somebody*. Who else could I find? Who else do I even *have* to find?"

Carly hears waves land on the rocks in the silence that follows. Something is forming in her gut, against her will. A clear sensation that this is not how the moment was supposed to play out.

Linda Litnipski is the one to break the silence. "If you think for one minute this kid is coming into my house, Ted Thackett, you got another thing coming. Tell me you know better than to think a thing that."

"Would you just chill a minute? We'll get her someplace to stay."

"Yeah? With whose money? I don't see you bringing anything in."

Carly watches them and listens to them and thinks, Why would Teddy be with somebody like that? Then it hits her: Carly's mother was somebody like that. Carly's mother treated Teddy just about like this. Not quite as harsh. But somewhere in the same neighborhood.

"I have money," Carly says. "I can get a room for tonight. I have eighty dollars."

"Eighty dollars?" Linda says. Like she's sneezing on something that belongs to Carly. Like she's saying twenty cents. "You're on the ocean, kiddo. You can't get much for eighty dollars."

"Now wait," Teddy says. "Wait. Let's just go to the cheapest place we can find and see what they charge."

"And who makes up the difference?"

"Stop!" Carly shouts.

Everybody does. Everything stops. It makes her feeler braver. So she goes on.

"Stop talking about me like I'm not here. Stop arguing over me. Fuck it. Fuck this. I'll be fine on my own. Just stay out of it. But I need to talk to Teddy. I'm not leaving town without talking to Teddy."

Carly waits for something to happen. Nothing happens. She really stopped the woman cold. She never dropped an F-bomb before. It felt pretty good.

"Teddy," Carly says. "When can I talk to you?"

"Come on, get in the car," he says. "We'll find you a place to stay."

"My car?" Linda asks.

Teddy sighs deeply. "Fine. Not your car. Fine. Carly, can you just sit tight and wait right here? I'm going to walk home and get my car. And then we'll find you a place to stay."

"Take my car," Linda says. "Who cares? I was just saying. I was just pointing out that you might want to ask my permission first."

Teddy sighs again. "Linda, mind if I use your car?"

She fishes around in her purse and then tosses him the keys. It's a wild, drunken throw. They land in the dirt a few feet away. Then she turns on one high-heeled red cowboy boot and teeters back into the lounge.

Carly looks at Teddy, and Teddy looks at her. She sees the beginnings of a smile form around his mouth and in the crinkly places at the corners of his eyes. But it's an unbearably sad smile.

"This is really off the wall," he says. "This is really out of nowhere."

What she thinks is, It wouldn't be. If you had told me where you landed. Like you promised you would.

What she says is, "Sorry. I didn't know where else to go."

Teddy retrieves the keys.

"Jocelyn died?"

"I wouldn't make a thing like that up."

"I know. I didn't mean it like that. It's just hard to take in."

"Tell me about it. I think that asshole killed her."

"You tell the police this?"

"No. What's the point? He killed himself, too. Too late to put him in jail even if I'm right. Drove them both off a cliff. Only question is whether he did it on purpose. I guess we'll never know. But she was leaving him. So I think he did it on purpose. I can't prove it. But that's what I think."

"Jesus," Teddy says.

He puts an arm around her shoulder and leads her over to Linda's car. It's an old vintage Jaguar XKE, perfectly restored. She has money. Linda has money.

He opens the door for her, and she plunks into the deep, low bucket seat.

"Ow," she says, as her thigh muscles have to try to support her weight.

Teddy walks around and gets in. But he doesn't start the engine. He just sits there, both hands on the steering wheel.

"Jocelyn always did have a broken picker. Everybody said so."

"She picked *you*."

"I rest my case." A long pause. Then he looks over at Carly. Studies her. "What happened to your face?"

"Which part of it?"

"I don't know. Start anywhere."

"Well. The scrape on my chin was from when I took a header into some gravel jumping off a freight train. The sunburn blister scars are from walking halfway across Arizona without a hat after we ran out of sunscreen. And the scratches are from some berry vines where I slept last."

Teddy sits another minute, then starts the engine. It has a beefy sound, a sort of growly rumble.

He does not appear to want to address anything she just said.

"I apologize for Linda. She has this thing about the house. She's very…private. Doesn't like anybody in the house. Or even near the house. And she's a little gun-shy on the subject of my exes. But she's not as bad as she came off back there."

"Didn't figure she could be," Carly says.

She's gone beyond the need to be polite. It's a relief.

He pulls out of the parking lot and heads out Patrick's Point Road, away from town.

"There's a place down here that has good rates. If it's more than what you've got, I'll cover the difference. Not that it's really my money, but I'll take the heat for that. She's going out of town tomorrow morning. So I'll come by where you're staying, and we'll talk. OK?"

"Yeah. I guess."

She's just too tired now. As if she's been hanging on to one skinny vine to keep from plummeting off a cliff. But she's been hanging on too long. It's worth the fall just to let go. It feels good to let go. She really couldn't have held on even a minute longer. Everybody has a breaking point. Especially if you're going to fall sooner or later anyway.

"If it was my house, it'd be a whole different story. I'm really sorry, Carly. If it were just me, what's mine would be yours. Hell, what's mine *is* yours. Only trouble is, that's pretty much nothing. But we'll talk tomorrow, I promise. I'll come by first thing. I don't know what I can do to help, but if I can, I will. OK?"

"Why can't we talk tonight?"

"Please, Carly. Wait till she goes out of town. If I don't get right back there, I won't get a moment's peace tonight. I'll come by in the morning."

He pulls into the gravel parking lot of the Redwood Inn. The sign says, BEST RATES IN TOWN. It also says, VACANCY.

Teddy walks with her into the office.

An old man with just a fringe of hair looks up from a loud TV show.

"Hey, Ted," he says.

"What's the cheapest room you can give my young friend here?"

"Well, seeing as it's you...that'll only be forty dollars extra. No, I'm kidding. Eighty-five, and that's a little better than ten percent discount."

"She'll take it."

Carly tries to go into her pocket for the cash, but Teddy grabs her wrist and holds it still.

"You hang on to that," he says. "In case you need it later on."

He pulls a credit card out of his wallet and pays for the room.

Carly's heart goes in two distinct directions at once. Teddy is taking over, taking care of things. Like she knew he would. That's one direction. But then there's the other direction. The one where he's telling her all her problems won't be solved after tonight. Which she was pretty clear on already.

He pulls her into his arms, and she buries her face in him. Wraps her arms around him and holds on tight, her eyes pressed closed. Breathes in that warmth. It's been away for so long. Or she has. Or both.

"I'll come by first thing in the morning. I promise. I have to get back now. But as soon as she leaves tomorrow, I'll come straight here."

He kisses the top of her head. Pressing his lips down hard and leaving them for a long moment.

Carly can feel the imprint of them long after he walks out the door.

Carly takes a long, hot bath and washes out her dirty clothes in the sink.

Her room is small but nice enough. She can't see the ocean, but she can hear it. Even with the doors and the windows closed. But she can hear it much better if she sits out on her little scrap of patio. So she wraps herself up in both blankets—the one from the bed and the one she finds folded in the closet—and sits outside for most of the night.

It's too foggy to see the moon, but she can see where it is in the sky because the fog is brighter right there.

She doesn't sleep much, and she doesn't think much. No more than she can help.

She does have two clear thoughts, though. At about three a.m. it occurs to her that Teddy never asked where Jen is.

That kicks off another thought. It's not completely new. It flitted through her mind when she chose to keep hanging on to the back of that freight train and not go back to Jen. But it's been held at bay for such a long time that it almost strikes her as something unfamiliar.

The original plan was to walk off the Wakapi reservation, down that paved road from Delores's dirt road all the way to the I-40. And to make a careful note of that intersection. So she could find the road back again. Instead she jumped a freight train in the pitch dark.

Now Carly's not even sure she knows where Jen is herself.

TRINIDAD, CA

May 21

Carly lies down on the bed at about seven in the morning and falls asleep without meaning to.

At ten after eight, the phone blasts her out of sleep.

She sits bolt upright, her heart pounding. It takes her a minute to remember what a phone is. What she's supposed to do with it. While she's sorting this out, it rings again, making her jump a second time. It's a loud ring. Loud noises spell trouble in Carly's mind. Like sirens. Like the way the police knock on somebody's door when nobody's going to like what happens next.

She picks it up. Doesn't even speak into it, because she's that unsure.

She hears an unsteady "Hello?"

"Oh. Teddy. It's you."

"Did I wake you up?"

"Maybe. I don't know."

"Look. Curveball, kiddo. Just as she's walking out the door, she tells me we're expecting a very important delivery and I have to be here to take it. It's really important. If I miss it, she won't just kill me. She'll kill me, skin the corpse, and set my entrails on fire. And let's just hope it would be in that order."

Carly rubs her eyes. As if that will help.

"You're not coming?"

Before she can even say "You promised," Teddy intervenes. But she definitely would have said that. Given a little more time.

"I know, I know. I promised. So here's what I'm going to do. I'm going to take my life into my hands and let you come here to the house. But don't ever tell her. And don't drop anything or leave fingerprints or look around too much or..."

"Can I breathe?"

Silence.

"I know this is hard, Carly, but work with me here. Help us get through this."

"Why do you always end up with women who push you around?"

The silence feels prickly. But she's not sorry she said it. Not at all.

"You're not supposed to ask questions like that."

"Why not?"

"Because grown-ups don't know the answers. Look. Can you walk down here? It's about a third of a mile."

"Gosh. I don't know. A third of a mile. That's an awful long walk."

"OK, fine, but stand out on the road—"

"Teddy. I was kidding."

"Oh. Right. I forgot. You walked halfway across Arizona. I guess we'll get to that part when we talk. So, just...gather up your stuff—"

"That shouldn't take long."

"—and walk out to the road and make a left, away from town. I'll stand out in the road. You'll see me. If anybody from town is out and around, we might have to abort the mission and try this later."

"OK."

She stares at the phone for a moment, wondering if she should say good-bye. Then she puts it back to her ear. Teddy is already gone.

It's like a dream. A little too much like one.

In a dream, she'd see Teddy standing in the middle of the road in an impossibly green forest of perfect, giant trees. And of course she'd be walking. Because when you walk fifteen or twenty miles a day, you dream about walking. And he'd seem too far away for too long, like Carly just couldn't make enough progress to reach him.

In a dream, something would happen before she got to him. He'd disappear, or the scene would change suddenly.

Apparently, this is not a dream. Because Carly walks right up to him and looks into his face. He averts his eyes. Then he looks all around and rushes her through the gate, locking it behind them.

Carly takes in the surroundings.

It's on the ocean side. Just like she was hoping it would be. But then she wonders why it matters. Since apparently she doesn't get to live here anyway.

It was a nice house, once upon a time. Natural brown wood shingles to blend in with the redwoods. Perched right on the cliff. But it's in bad repair. And there's junk everywhere. Old mattresses and a couch rotting outside, and bed frames and something under a blue tarp. And a tractor. Why would anyone need a tractor on this little lot? And old fencing. Why don't people just throw away their fencing when they tear it down?

The classic Jaguar is sitting in front of the garage, along with a newer Mercedes and Teddy's Firebird.

"This could be a nice house," Carly says. "Why doesn't she clean it up?"

"You'd have to ask her. But don't. Because you were never here."

"Why don't *you* clean it up?"

"She would not appreciate that. She doesn't like people touching her stuff."

"It's trash."

"She doesn't like people touching her trash. Now come on inside. We can still be seen from the gate if we stand here."

He opens the front door.

It's a little better inside. The furniture is a bit run-down. A coffee table in front of the saggy couch is covered with eleven beer bottles. Carly wonders briefly why he didn't just sweep them off into the recycling bin before she got here.

Then her eyes are drawn out through the big picture window. It's spotted with sea spray, so she walks closer, as if that will help her see through. Below her is an ocean not unlike the one she saw when she first came into town. Except without the boats anchored. Rocks the size of buildings, with waves foaming around their bases. One rock is so big it has trees on its crown, like an island.

Carly can't take her eyes off the scene.

Then she sees an old car fender on the cliff, marring her view. And she wonders again how people live like that, and why. If this were her house, she'd clean it up right. And wash the windows.

She reaches out and almost touches the tips of her fingers to the glass. Then she remembers Teddy telling her not to leave fingerprints. Maybe he was kidding. Or half kidding. Then again, maybe not.

She shoves her hands deep into her pockets.

"What did she go out of town in?" she asks, still looking at the sea. Still trying not to look at the junk fender. "Her car is here."

"She has three cars."

"Why doesn't she keep them in the garage? They're so expensive."

"Because…there are other valuable things in the garage. Look, this is why she doesn't like people around. I'll level with you. She has some things in this house that are worth money. That's why she's so weird about having people around."

"She thinks I'll steal from her?"

"No. I mean, she doesn't know. She doesn't know you. But she doesn't think everybody'll steal. She thinks everybody'll talk. And then, sooner or later, somebody'll steal."

Carly listens to the surf, in the pause, when there's nothing else to listen to. She looks around at Teddy. He's sitting on the saggy couch, faced away from her. She can see the top of the back of his head. That bald spot looks a lot bigger. Or maybe it's just that he's keeping his hair shorter now.

"Where did she get a house like this? Where does she get all her money? What does she do?"

"That's an awful lot of questions, Carly."

"Just three."

"That's an awful lot."

"Pick one, then."

"Her father left it to her when he died."

Maybe that explains why she doesn't take care of it. Maybe people only take care of things they had to work hard for. Maybe they don't take care of things that landed in their life for free.

She looks over her shoulder at Teddy just as he takes a long swallow from a half-empty bottle of beer.

"If you had a house like this, would you leave it to Jen and me when you died?"

"You're forgetting I have a daughter."

"Oh. Right. I did forget that. But you never see her."

"But she's still my daughter. Linda's father hadn't seen her since she was six. But she was still his daughter. There's something about blood. It lasts forever."

Carly watches out the window in silence, feeling the trajectory of those sentences as they settle into a place in her gut. Like bad food. Something that will need to come up and out later. So she can keep moving. Keep living.

"That's a pretty clear message," she says.

Nothing is what she thought it was. Carly was wrong about everything. Clearly. Everything. She's actually known that for a while. But up until this moment she thought it was everything except how much Teddy loved them. But she was wrong. It was everything.

Now Teddy is standing shoulder to shoulder with her at the window, except for the fact that his shoulder is much higher.

"If there was something I could do, I would," he says.

But that's not true. Because she just asked him if he would leave them a house if he could. And he said he wouldn't.

"What am I supposed to do now, Teddy?"

"Well. I don't know. Oh. I know. The state has agencies to help kids like you. You know. Foster care and stuff."

"Gosh, if only I'd thought of that."

A long silence. The sound of the waves is the only good thing about it.

Then Teddy says, "I don't know what you want from me, Carly."

She doesn't know, either, anymore. Until she hears herself say it.

"I want you to tell me what happened that night. When I was away up at the lake. And I want you to tell me the truth."

"Yeah. Of course. Absolutely, I will. Come and sit down."

He sits back down on the couch. Carly sits across from him in a stuffed wing chair with the fabric worn smooth on its arms.

She wants to see his face. To judge for herself if he's telling the truth.

He picks up his beer before talking and drains the last of it. Half the bottle, from the look of it.

"I'm just sick about that whole thing," he says. "But I appreciate that you want to hear my side. That you haven't made up your mind against me. It was a total misunderstanding, but I'm not blaming Jen. Jen's a great kid. It's not her fault. But she was having a dream. That's all. You were up at the lake and your mom was at the bar, and it was just me and Jen. And she was asleep in her room. But then I heard her make these noises, like she was having a bad dream. So I went in and sat on her bed and tried to wake her up. I put my hand on her cheek—I thought I could wake her up gentle, you know? But she opened her eyes and looked right at me and screamed. Like she didn't even know me. The only thing I can figure is that she was still dreaming. Then she went out the window."

Carly's watching him the whole time. To help her judge. And it looks and feels like the truth. She already knew it, she realizes. She knew it all along. Teddy isn't like that. He might be unfocused. And soft. But he would never do a thing like that.

"I *thought* that was what happened. I told Jen it was probably a dream."

"I tried to tell your mom my side of the story. But I think she wanted to believe Jen so she could leave me for that guy."

"Why didn't you tell me where you were when you got settled?"

Teddy gets up and wanders into the kitchen. As though he didn't hear the question. Or as though he's chosen not to answer.

He comes back out with another open bottle of beer and flops down hard.

"I thought you'd be better off without me," he says.

Before Carly can open her mouth to speak, a distant bell rings. Something that sounds like it's coming from the road out front.

"That's that delivery," Teddy says. "Please don't move. Please just sit here. Don't do anything. This is important. I'll be right back."

The minute he's out the front door, Carly walks through the house in the direction of the garage. Looking to see if there's a door that opens into the garage from the house. Yeah, he told her not to. But now she almost has to. She has to see for herself what's so valuable that no one can come near the place. She promises herself she won't talk about it. Whatever it is, she won't tell. If she doesn't steal, and she doesn't tell, there's no harm done.

She opens the door into a linen closet, closes it again. Opens the door into a dirty bathroom, with the toilet running. Closes that, too.

The third door opens into the garage.

Carly squints at the unexpected brightness.

Strung from the ceiling are fixture after fixture of long, bright, full-spectrum grow lights, gleaming down on about two hundred young marijuana plants.

Carly closes the door again. Leans her forehead against it.

That explains so much, she thinks.

She leans there, eyes pressed closed, until suddenly Teddy is back. Much sooner than she expected.

She turns around and absorbs the look on his face. Abject panic.

"Carly," he hisses, barely over a whisper. "You looked in the garage?"

"Don't worry. I won't tell."

"We have a full-scale disaster on our hands," he whispers.

"I'm not going to tell, Teddy."

"There's a cop here looking for you."

The words are a cattle prod to her lower abdomen, lighting her up with a painful jolt of electricity. Leaving her unable to breathe properly.

"A cop? What's a cop doing here? How did anybody know I was here?"

"I have no idea, Carly."

"Did you tell him I was here?"

"No. I told him you weren't. But he flashed a badge and insisted on coming in. He wants to look around for you. So I decided you're here after all."

"I'll go out the back."

"No!" he says. Too loud. He winces at his own volume. "No. Then he'll search the place. Get out there and see what he wants."

"You know what he wants, Teddy. He's going to put me in foster care."

Teddy grabs her hard by both shoulders. Looks straight into her eyes.

"Honey, I'm sorry. But you were going there anyway."

Just for a moment, Carly hates him. It's a strange feeling. A thing too far out of place to be possible.

She yanks her shoulders out of his grasp.

She takes a deep breath and walks into the living room, her heart pounding so hard she can hear and feel it in her ears.

There, in the middle of the room, is Alvin. Holding his hat in one hand.

"Alvin?" she says.

Alvin looks at Carly, then at Teddy, over Carly's shoulder.

"Thought you said she wasn't here."

"Yeah," Teddy says. "Funny story about that. Turns out I just temporarily misplaced her."

It's clear by the look on Alvin's face that he doesn't find that story funny. He turns his searing gaze back on Carly.

"You look like you been through a war. Thought I could trust you to stay put."

"I know. I'm sorry."

"You have no idea how worried I was about you. Especially after I saw this." He pulls a folded sheet of paper out of his shirt pocket. Waves it in her direction. As if she'll instinctively know what it is. "I was making inquiries all along, you know. To help you. Not to make trouble for anybody. To see if I could find this guy for you. Then I go into the office one morning and get this on my fax machine." He waves the paper again. "And I go tearing over to Delores's to tell you not to go near him ever again. And I find out you're already gone. Took off in the night like a thief, after lying and saying you wouldn't. Can you imagine how worried we all were about you?"

Carly is so struck by his worry that it bumps her curiosity about the paper out of its rightful place in line.

"You drove all the way out here because you were worried about me?"

Teddy says, "Wait a minute. You two know each other?"

Nobody answers him.

"Don't know why that's so hard to believe," Alvin says. To her. Not to Teddy.

Carly doesn't know how to answer. It's in there. But not in words.

"What is that? That paper you're waving?"

"It's his arrest record. Or, actually, this is the report the police took from the victim and her family last time they arrested him."

"For…"

"Child molestation."

"Wait. My mother had him arrested?"

"No. She did not. This was someone else's mother had him arrested for child molestation. He did twenty-two months in the state prison at Chino for it. And I'm still having a little trouble getting all the particulars…but…it doesn't appear to be a first offense."

The room goes silent except for an irritating buzzing Carly can't identify. A second later she realizes it's the sound of blood rushing inside her own ears.

"I can't believe that," she says.

"Try this on for size, then." Alvin shakes the paper by the top edge until it unfolds, then reads aloud to her. "'Victim says the suspect appeared in her bed in the middle of the night and woke her up with one hand over her mouth. He told her he wouldn't hurt her, but she had to be quiet.' That sound familiar at all?"

Carly sits down hard in the wing chair. She looks across the coffee table and its sea of beer bottles to Teddy's face. He's slumped back on the couch now, the fresh open beer in his hand again. She tries to look into his face, but he averts his gaze. Then he sets the beer bottle down and drops his head into his hands.

"Teddy. You lied to me?"

No answer. He just rubs his face with both hands.

"You looked me right in the eye and lied to me?"

"I didn't want you to think that about me." His voice is faint. Teddy is getting smaller and weaker. Carly is getting bigger and stronger. She can feel it. "I didn't want you to think I was somebody who would do a thing like that."

"But you are!" she shouts, half rising to her feet with the unexpected force and volume. Even Alvin jumps. "How could you do that?"

"I was drunk, Carly. Can you understand that? I'd just found out Jocelyn was actually sleeping with that guy I was hoping she was only flirting with. I was upset, and I got too drunk. I didn't know what I was doing."

Carly looks down at the full bottle of beer sitting in front of him on the coffee table.

"Then stop *drinking!*" she bellows.

On the word *drinking*, she draws her right arm back and then slaps the bottle off the table with the back of her hand. It hurts. A lot. The bottle bounces off the wall but doesn't break. It lands on the carpet, beer foaming as it soaks into the dirty gray pile.

"How can you sit there drinking at nine o'clock in the morning while you're telling me you're not responsible for what you do when you drink?"

Teddy never answers. He just goes to tend to the spilled beer, picking up the bottle and carrying it into the kitchen. When he emerges again, he's holding a towel.

"Am I under arrest for something here?" he asks Alvin. "I did my time for that thing you've got in your hand. There's nothing new, right? You came here to get Carly because you think it's not even safe for her to be around me. So could you just take her now and go? If there are no specific charges, I'd just like to be left alone now. Please."

Carly looks at Alvin, and Alvin looks back.

"Ready to go home now?" he asks.

Carly nods. Though she thinks it's an odd use of the word *home*. As if Carly has one. Sometime she'll have to ask him about that. But for the moment, she just follows him to the door.

Before it closes behind them, Teddy says, "I loved you, Carly."

She sticks her head back in.

"What?"

She heard, though.

"I loved you. And I loved Jen."

Carly notices his use of the past tense. But she doesn't mention that.

All she says is, "Then how come you didn't you ask me where she is?"

No answer. Which doesn't feel all that surprising.

Carly follows Alvin through the yard like a puppy who's just been punished with a rolled-up newspaper. The gate is hanging partway open, and she follows him to the road, expecting to see his blue pickup. Instead he walks to a car, silver and two-door, with a convertible top. He unlocks the passenger door and holds it open for her.

"Why does everybody have so many cars?" she asks, knowing it probably won't make much sense to Alvin.

"This is Pam's car. I think it's impractical as all hell, but she loves it. And she has a long drive to work, so who am I to say? Pickup truck bench seats weren't made for long rides. Have to admit this is a little more comfortable."

"Is Jen..." But then she can't bring herself to finish.

Alvin is still standing there with the door open wide. And Carly is still not getting in.

"Is Jen what?"

"You know."

"I don't. Actually."

"OK? Is she OK?"

"Just the same as she was when you left her. Looks OK to me."

Carly plunks stiffly into the soft bucket seat, and he closes the door behind her. Just for a minute she's flooded with relief. Because Jen is right where Carly left her. And because it's a long drive back to Delores's. Maybe two days. Maybe more. And somebody else is in charge now. Carly doesn't have to be the one to figure out what comes next.

South of Eureka, on one of the many bridges where the Eel River snakes under the highway time after time after time, Carly breaks a long silence.

"How could I have been so stupid?" she asks Alvin.

"Really want me to answer that?"

"Probably not. But go ahead."

"Way I see it, you're one of those people with set opinions on how you want the world to behave. Always trying to bend the world to fit your liking instead of the other way around. So then, once you make up your mind how you want something to be, you start losing the eyes to see what it really is."

"I believe what I want to believe."

"That would be the short version. Yeah."

"Jen always tells me I believe what I want to believe."

"It's not stupidity. In my opinion. I think you've got a good mind. Your trouble is, you think you know the difference between a good thing and a bad one. But you don't."

They're over the bridge and moving into a forested area now. Carly stares out the window for a minute, waiting for what he said to make sense. It never does.

"Everybody knows the difference between a good thing and a bad thing."

"Wrong. Hardly anybody does. You thought Teddy was a good thing."

"Well. Yeah. I was wrong about that, but—"

"And you thought the night you stumbled onto Wakapi territory and ran afoul of Delores Watakobie was one of the worst nights of your life. You may not even know yet how wrong you were about that. But you will. In time."

She waits for the old Carly, the old indignation. That natural sense of something in her gut rising up to champion her worldview. When nothing happens, she searches for it. And finds only emptiness. That old Carly is either dead or just too wounded and tired to defend itself.

"It was good for Jen," she says.

"Because Jen *let* it be."

They don't talk for a long time.

Then Alvin says, "You must have at least tried on the idea that it was true."

"Not really," Carly says.

"Not even once?"

"Not really."

"Can you explain to me how a thing like that works?"

"Not really," Carly says.

All she knows is that it probably won't ever work again.

Carly wakes up in the passenger seat and looks around. The highway is two-lane here and twisty. Alvin has to slow down for the curves.

"Welcome back, sleeping beauty," he says.

"I have my days and nights all turned around. Where are we?"

"We seem to be…just about exactly in the middle of nowhere."

She's struck again with disbelief that Alvin would care enough about whether she lived or died to drive twelve hundred miles to fetch her back. But she still can't get words around that.

So she says, "I'm sorry I lied and said you could trust me to stay put."

"Did you know it was a lie when you said it?"

"Yeah. I'm sorry."

"Would you be sorry even if you never got caught at it? Even if you never had to answer for it?"

"Yeah. I would. I know I would. Because I already felt bad about it. This woman who gave me a ride in her motor home had a big road atlas just like yours. I told her my friend had one just like it. And then I felt really bad. When I said you were my friend. Because I wasn't a very good friend to you."

Silence. Maybe he's just pausing to see if there's more.

Then he says, "If you're waiting for me to argue that point, I hope you brought something to read."

It's a glimpse into how angry he is with her, and it feels lumpy in her stomach, an icky sensation. One she can't quite shake.

"So you got a ride," he says. "I was wondering how you got there so fast. You must've been awful lucky with rides to get there so quick. I thought I had a good day or two before you'd show up. If I'd thought you could beat me there, I'd have called the Trinidad police so fast…"

"I'm surprised you didn't anyway. Just to save yourself the long trip."

"They'd have turned you over to child protective services."

"I know it."

"I've been trying to get you a better ending to your story than all that. In case you hadn't noticed. Because I know you're scared they might not keep you and Jen together, and I know how much that means to you. Tried to tell you so. But you didn't believe me. You didn't trust me to give a damn about you."

"No," she says.

"Why not?"

"Because nobody else ever did."

"And because you always think you know better than everybody about everything."

"No," she says. "I don't. Anymore. Used to, I guess. But I couldn't think so after everything that happened. That would be impossible. Now I think I don't know anything about anything."

"That's good," Alvin says.

Carly snorts. "How is it good to know nothing?"

"It's good to *know* you know nothing. You don't know any less than you did before. But now you know what you don't know. That's an improvement."

She chews that over for a minute. Then she says, "Maybe. Yeah."

They drive in silence for a few minutes. Now and then Carly sees yellow warning signs that show the outline of a truck tipping over on a tight curve. It reminds her of the overturned logging truck.

Just as she thinks that, she sees a loaded-up logging truck sweep by in the opposite direction. Northbound. The trailer is just two steel brackets on wheels, to hold the giant trunks of trees. Maybe eight trunks on this load. Carly wonders how many they can cut before all this beauty is gone forever.

"You ever going to forgive me for that?" she asks, surprising both of them.

Alvin doesn't answer right away.

Finally he says, "Not just like that. Not like throwing a switch. Words don't cost much. But if you keep standing behind some of the things you've said so far this trip, I expect we can get from here to there."

Going through Sacramento, Carly wakes up again.

"How much longer can you drive?" she asks him.

"I'll have to stop over at least one night."

"I can drive."

"Nice try."

"What am I going to do now, Alvin?"

Alvin sighs.

"You got a couple options, it seems to me."

"Like what?"

"You could be an emancipated minor. Sixteen's old enough for that. You'd have to prove you can put a roof over your own head and feed your own self. Thing is, you got nobody to argue against it. So I'm not sure anybody's trying to get in your way on that anyhow. What you're not old enough to do is be a legal guardian for your sister. But in a year and a half you can. And she's doing fine where she is now."

"Think Delores would let me stay?"

"You'd have to ask Delores about that."

"She'll say no. She hates me."

"No. She doesn't. Not at all."

"She acts like she does."

"You act like you hate her, too. Do you?"

"I sort of thought I did at first. But no. I don't hate her."

"Trouble with you and Delores is you're too much alike."

"Is that a joke? We're nothing alike."

"You're so alike it's funny. That's why you two get along worse than a cat and a dog. Both so headstrong. Two stubborn women, both trying to out-stubborn each other. Now don't you ever tell anybody I said that because she's an elder and I'm supposed to look on her with nothing but respect. And I respect her plenty, but I still got eyes. And it doesn't help you acting like you know everything. Oh, but that's right. You don't know anything about anything anymore. Maybe that'll make things a little better between the two of you. They sure as hell couldn't get much worse."

Carly chews on the inside of her lip a little. She pulls the feather necklace out from under her shirt. Examines it again for damage. It looks a little worse for wear. Maybe less so than Carly. But they both survived.

She looks up to see Alvin watching her.

"Where'd you get that?"

"Jen gave it to me."

"And where'd Jen get it? No, never mind. Stupid question. When we get back on Wakapi land, don't let anybody see you with that. A traditional Wakapi would take that away from you."

"Why? It was a present. What's wrong with that?"

"It's Wakapi medicine. It's not for just anybody. No offense. There's a system in place for bringing somebody into the circle, and then they can be privy to the old wisdom. But that Delores…Well, she's one of a kind. You know her Wakapi name means something along the lines of 'Stubborn'? Well. It's kind of hard to translate. Best I can tell you is it means, 'She who relies on her own counsel.' The unwritten second half of that thought being 'and pretty much ignores everybody else's.' Now you see why I say you two are birds of a feather?"

When she wakes up again, it's nearly dark. They're not moving. They're parked at a highway rest area, and Alvin is standing outside the car, stretching his back.

The outside of Carly's right hand aches. Where she hit that beer bottle. It's strange to have the pain break through suddenly like that. She knows it didn't just start. It's been aching all day. But she just now took that in. It's strange not to feel what you feel.

Or maybe it's that other parts of her have been hurting worse.

She turns on the overhead light and looks at it closely. It's deeply bruised and swollen enough to worry her.

She looks up to see Alvin dropping into the driver's seat again.

"That hand doesn't look so good," he says.

She holds it out to him so he can take a closer look.

"Might be some little fractures in there. Couldn't say. When we get home, we might need to get that looked at."

There he goes again with the word *home*. But Carly needs a home so badly she chooses not to question it.

"You tired?" she asks him.

"Very. Trying to decide whether to look for a motel or just put this seat back and take a nap. Think I'll do that second one for right now. See how far that takes me. And maybe...just maybe...when daylight rolls around, you can spell me for a bit. You got a license?"

"No, but I've got a learner's permit."

"California?"

"Yeah. California."

"Well, we'll do it early, then. Before we get over the state line."

He levers his seat back with a sigh. Sets his hat over his face.

Carly holds and rubs her right hand a minute longer.

Then she asks, "Why did he pick *her*?"

"Teddy?" From behind the hat.

"Yeah, Teddy."

"Why did Teddy pick Jen?"

"Yeah."

"As opposed to…"

"Me."

She doesn't even bother with the shame. She's too tired. It feels like too much trouble.

He tips the hat up with one hand.

"I know you must mean that in a general sense. Like maybe referring to whatever liking-her-better sort of thing you think must've been behind his picking her and not you. Because I know you didn't mean you wanted him to try some stunt like that on you."

"Right. No. I didn't mean that. Thanks for knowing I didn't mean that."

"Kind of stings anyway, though, huh?"

"Kind of. Is that the sickest thing in the world?"

"More or less human, I suppose."

Then he lets the hat down again.

Carly watches him. Though there's nothing really to watch. He's just lying there with his hat over his face. Apparently he's not going to answer the question. But that shouldn't surprise her, she thinks. Probably it's an unanswerable question.

Then he tips the hat up again and says, "Teddy is a child molester."

"That's not answering my question, Alvin."

"Yes, it is. You just don't get what I'm saying yet. Teddy is a child molester. And Jen is a child."

Carly says nothing. Because nothing more needs to be said.

CALIFORNIA

May 22

"That was a nice little town," Alvin says. "Pretty."

The waitress is setting breakfast in front of them. Carly's bacon and scrambled eggs. Alvin's omelet with vegetables inside and salsa on top. He picks up the bottle of Tabasco, unscrews the lid, and shakes about twelve drops of sauce onto the salsa.

"Who puts Tabasco sauce on salsa?"

"People who like their salsa hot."

"What town was nice?"

"*What town?* That's a weird question."

"Well, we've been through so many."

"I don't mean the ones we went *through*. I mean the one we went *to*."

"Oh. Trinidad."

"Yeah. Trinidad. It was nice up there. Didn't you think?"

Carly takes a bite of scrambled egg. It tastes fine. There's nothing wrong with it. It just tastes like scrambled egg. But she wants it to taste like more. So she opens the ketchup bottle and tips it over her plate. Waits. Nothing comes out.

"I guess," she says. "I liked it a lot when I first saw it. Didn't look as nice on the way out, though. Besides. I couldn't get warm. The wind and the fog just cut right into my bones, and I could never get warm."

"And when you were on the Wakapi, you were always complaining how you could never get cool."

"Oh. That's true. I guess that's a problem, huh?"

Carly hits the end of the bottle with the heel of her hand, and about three times more ketchup than she wanted lands right on the bacon. Right where she didn't want any.

"Yeah, for *you*," Alvin says.

They eat in silence for several minutes.

Carly watches people through the window as they get out of their cars and make their way into this roadside diner. An old couple who stop to buy a newspaper from a dispenser on their way in. A family with three little kids who have to fold up two strollers and leave them in the entryway. Trade them for booster seats.

Seems like they all have routines. Which Carly figures is another way of saying lives. She can't help wondering how that would feel.

"I appreciate how you've been buying my food," Carly says.

"Can't let you starve."

"But I've got to tell you something about that. I've actually got eighty dollars. This nice old lady who gave me a ride loaned it to me. But she was very specific about what it was for. She gave me the money in case I needed a room. You know, if it was night and I didn't have any place to stay. But I didn't need to use it for that. And I didn't feel right using it for anything else. Because it wasn't *for* anything else. It was for a room. So the reason I didn't tell you I had that money is because I think I ought to send it back to her now."

"OK," Alvin says.

She waits, still half expecting him to say more.

"Maybe we could even stop in Fresno and I could give it back to her."

"We're past Fresno."

"We are? I didn't see us go through Fresno."

"We didn't. We took the I-5. It's faster."

"Oh," Carly says. "OK." She eats a few more bites. "Only thing...I sort of wanted to tell her it meant the world to me how she did that. But I guess I can write her a note and wrap the money up in it and mail it."

She waits to see if he has anything to add to that. Apparently not.

"And I wanted to tell you it meant the world to me how you drove all the way up there to get me. But I haven't figured out the right words just yet."

"Those'll do," he says. Without looking up from his plate.

"But I don't just want to keep eating on your dime. I want you to write down what you spend on my food. In my little notebook. And I'll pay it back. When I can. When I've figured out how to earn some money."

"Shouldn't be hard," Alvin says. "You're a good worker. Seem to be. If you're willing to work, you can always make a little here and there. Speaking of which. I need to put some new fence in over at my place. You show up and help me, we'll get her done in a day and we'll call it even on the food."

"Yeah, OK. Thanks. I'll still owe her for the bus ticket, though. Even after I give her back her eighty dollars."

"Ah. More details coming out about how you managed to beat me there. And here I thought you were magic. Just flew through the air or closed your eyes and beamed yourself from one place to the other. Just all neat like that."

"That would've been nice," Carly says.

"Don't argue. You ran into some unexpected kindness. That's a type of magic all its own. That's like magic wearing a disguise, like a false nose and glasses, so you think it's something more everyday than all that."

She waits for him to open the car door for her. The way he always seems to want to do. Instead he's holding the keys in her direction.

"You want to drive from here to the state line?"

"Hell, yeah!"

She climbs into the driver's seat. Buckles up. Alvin climbs in beside her.

"Think we could put the top down?" she asks.

Alvin pushes a button on the dashboard. A little motor whirrs somewhere, and the top goes back. All by itself. Just like that.

"Everything changes," he says. "Huh? When I was going off to college, I had a convertible. Not a new one or anything. You wanted the top down, you had to *put* it down. You know. With your hands."

Carly shifts into drive and then checks all around the car. In both side mirrors. And in the rearview mirror, even though she plans to go forward. She does it to impress Alvin with how careful she can be.

"Only problem is, you still don't have a hat," he says as she pulls out of the lot. "You'll get all sunburned again."

"Might be worth it."

Alvin just shakes his head.

A few minutes later, when they're doing sixty-five on the I-40 East, the wind in Carly's hair, he says, "We'll have to stop and get you a proper hat. That floppy old-lady thing is just not you."

Carly grunts her disgust.

"I think she did that on purpose. Just because she knew I'd hate it."

He doesn't say anything for a moment, so she glances over at him. Catches a wry half smile.

"Answer number one, I'm sure that was the only hat she had to give you. Answer number two, I have to allow for the possibility that you might be right about that all the same."

"If you buy me a hat, you have to write it down in my notebook."

"Tell you what. I was gonna stop tonight at a real live motel. Get us each a room. Which would you rather? Sleep in a real room? Or sleep in the car again and have the hat?"

"I'd rather have the hat. But you still have to write it down."

"Carly. It's a gift. I'm offering you a gift. When somebody offers you a gift, you just take it and say thank you. See, this is what I mean. About how you and Delores are so alike it's funny. If you two ask for some help, or act like you could use some, or like you're grateful for some, I guess you feel like it means you're admitting you needed it. Why do you think she's so happy having Jen around the house? She's going blind, in case you didn't notice. But she can't bring herself to say she shouldn't be living on her own anymore. But just look how happy she is now that she doesn't have to. Somebody wants to give you what you need, just say thank you. Especially if you didn't have to ask."

"Right," Carly says. "OK. Thank you."

"You just keep practicing that," Alvin says. "I expect it'll get easier as time goes by."

WAKAPI LAND

May 23

Just as Alvin turns into Delores Watakobie's long dirt driveway, Carly says, "Maybe we should've called. You know. Let somebody know you found me and you were bringing me back. And then somebody could've told Delores."

Alvin is wearing that knowing half smile that Carly sees on so many faces and never quite understands. He brakes in front of the henhouse, shifts into park. Pulls on the hand brake.

"Wish I'd thought of that," he says.

"Meaning…you thought of that?"

"I called Pam that first morning and told her we were on our way back, and to drive over and tell Delores so she could stop worrying."

"Where was I?"

"Sleeping."

"Oh. Yeah. I had my days and nights turned around."

"You might've mentioned that a time or two. Or ten."

"Was she really worried?"

"Ask her yourself."

He flips his head in the direction of the house. Delores is standing in the open doorway. As if trying to decide whether to go to all the trouble of meeting them halfway.

Carly steps out into the dry oven of the desert. Sets her wonderful new hat on her head. Saves Delores the trouble by walking to where she stands.

"Well, well," Delores says. "The prodigal loudmouth."

Carly doesn't know what to say. So she says nothing at all. In the silence, she hears and feels Alvin step up behind her.

"What's that?" Delores asks, and reaches up to touch Carly's new hat. "Mind if I take a look close-up?"

Carly takes it off and hands it to the old woman. She still hasn't said a word. She can't help being painfully aware of that.

Delores holds the hat up close to her face. Runs her hands over the felt. Feels the shape of the crown, the weave of the band.

"This's a nice piece of goods. Couldn't of been cheap. Where'd you get a nice hat like this?"

"It was a gift from Alvin," she says.

Delores hands it back to Carly, who snugs it back onto her head. It feels good. She likes who she is when it's up there.

"Damn," Delores says. "Now I got to wear that old floppy thing myself. Hate that hat. Pretty fancy present, Alvin. Don't remember you ever gettin' me anythin' that nice, and how long've we known each other? All your damn life, isn't it?"

Alvin speaks, and Carly notices how much his voice has become a comfort to her. She feels that, deep in her gut. Like a hot water bottle, or the first sip of a hot drink going down when you're cold. When the fog and the wind has gotten into your bones and you just can't get warm.

"You want a better hat, Delores? I'll be happy to get you one."

"Don't you dare, young man," she says, pointing one spotted finger in his general direction. "You know I can do for myself.

Always done for myself, an' if I want a new hat, I'll weave my own. I can still weave, you know. Don't need to see good to weave. Day somebody got to gimme a new hat's the day I let my creator put me six feet under."

She turns and shuffles back into the house.

Carly looks at Alvin. He's smiling that same little wry half smile he uses on her.

"See what I mean? Birds of a feather."

"Except I shut up and took the hat."

"That you did. Say, day after tomorrow for that fence work, OK? I'll come by, pick you up."

"OK."

He tips his hat to her. Which means he's leaving.

She rushes in and throws her arms around him, knocking her new hat into the dirt. Holds him tight, the way she grabbed Teddy in the Whale Tail Lounge. But Alvin doesn't make a wheezing noise. He doesn't make any noise at all. He seems to be able to take it. He hugs her in return. Which, if she's remembering right, Teddy never did.

Then she steps back, embarrassed. Picks up her hat and brushes red dirt off its crown.

Alvin tips his hat again. Climbs into Pam's car and backs all the way down the driveway. Carly stands in front of the house and watches him go. She raises her hand in a wave, but Alvin never looks back.

Carly stands and looks around. Breathes deeply, as if smelling the Wakapi landscape. As if allowing the dry air to fill more than just her lungs. Just for a moment, she notices the way the sun lights up the big mesa behind the house.

Something is different in just these few days. Delores's old truck is parked out behind the henhouse, covered with a giant blue tarp. It's not in its usual spot under the carport. And there's some new fencing, a semicircle at the open end of the carport. Thin metal posts with three strands of plain wire strung between. And there are three strands of wire stapled to the posts of the carport, too, so the whole thing is like a partly covered paddock. So now you couldn't drive the truck in there if you wanted to. Carly notes this but doesn't understand it. In fact, she doesn't try.

Instead, she joins Delores inside the house. It's nice in there. Cooler. Not cold, like air-conditioning. But a lot nicer than outside. The old woman is standing in the kitchen, pouring a glass of cold water from the fridge. It doesn't occur to Carly that Delores might be pouring it for Carly, not for herself.

Carly takes off her hat and holds it in her hand.

Roscoe thumps his tail against the rug but doesn't get up.

"Have a sit," Delores says and sets the glass of cold water on the table. In front of the chair Carly always used at mealtimes. Back when she ate her meals here. Seems like a long time ago now.

"Thanks," she says. She sits. And sips. Hat on her lap. "It's nice in here. Cool."

"Got the swamp cooler goin'."

So that's what that noise is, she thinks.

"Where's Jen?"

"Still at school."

"School?"

"Don't tell me you forgot what that is."

"I didn't think Jen would be going, though. I mean…this soon. I just can't believe you even got her signed up for school so fast."

"Signed up…well, maybe not exactly. But she's goin'. And the teacher don't mind if she sits in for now. We all tried to tell 'er wait for next year. This year's good as gone. But she wanted to go. No talkin' 'er out of it. Said she wanted to catch up what she missed. Really I think she's wantin' to make some friends 'er own age. Tide 'er over the summer, you know?"

"Oh. Yeah. That's good. That's nice, if she can make some friends."

Delores says nothing. She's still at the kitchen counter, but she's not doing anything special there. Just leaning. As though thinking. As though she's putting Carly's words on a scale to see how much they weigh.

When Carly gets tired of waiting for the old woman to speak, she says, "Were you really worried about me?"

"You could of got yourself dead a dozen diff'rent ways, you know."

"I know. I almost did."

"Well, you're OK now. Guess that's what matters."

Delores waddles off into the living room and sits down on the couch, emitting a noise that's a cross between a grunt and a sigh. Roscoe lifts his head briefly, looks over his shoulder at Delores, then sets his chin down on the rug again.

"Mind if I take my water into the trailer? I'll bring the glass back. It was such a long drive and I'm tired, and it would be nice to lie down."

"Swamp cooler's fixed in there now. Chester came over 'n fixed it. Got a chain hangs down in the middle of the room. Just give that chain a good hard pull. Noisy, but it should cool off in there right quick."

She wants to question the idea that Chester would do such a thing. But it seems pointless. Since he already did.

Carly wakes from a long nap to find that the trailer is cool. Cooler than the house. Maybe because it's so much smaller.

She sits up.

The window that used to have no glass has been mended with what looks like a scrap of Plexiglas, cut to fit just right and sealed with duct tape around the edges. So you can still see through it. But the cold can't get in. Or out.

Just for a minute, Carly thinks she hears a distant sound like the slow, gentle clopping of hooves. Then she decides it was only in her head.

She gets up and washes her face in a bucket of water that's sitting near the sink. Behind the partition in the back of the trailer. When she comes back out, the sound is louder now. And definitely real.

She looks out the window to see Jen riding up the road on Virginia's old mostly brown paint horse. Carly sinks into a sit on the bed and watches. Jen is riding bareback. Nothing but a woven blanket between her and the horse. Her reins are a loop of rope tied to a rope halter. Her legs swing free. She's still wearing that straw cowboy hat Delores gave her. It still suits her. Carly always knew it did. She just wouldn't admit that at the time.

It's a sight. Really. A sight.

Carly grabs her hat up off the counter and steps out into the heat. The big creak of the door doesn't surprise her, nor does it feel like a problem. It's just something she remembers.

She stands at the top of the driveway.

At first Jen is looking off in the direction of the mesa. But then she turns her head to the house. Carly can spot the moment when Jen sees her. Even though they're too far apart to see each other's face. But she can still tell.

Jen drums her heels lightly on the paint's sides. She's still wearing those cross-trainers Carly took—borrowed—for her in New Mexico. The paint breaks into a rough trot, and Jen holds on with one hand woven into his mane.

Then she pulls back on the rope reins and just sits her horse for a second or two, maybe twenty feet from where Carly is standing. All in one motion, she throws a leg back over the paint's butt and drops to the ground. Runs up to Carly. And she doesn't stop when she gets there. She hits Carly like a moving train, nearly bowling her right over into the dirt. Her arms wrap around Carly's ribs. Squeeze tight.

Jen knows how to turn her head just right so that her hat, which curls up tight at the sides, doesn't get knocked off. Carly wonders if that means she's been giving a lot of hugs since she started wearing it.

Carly wraps her arms around Jen in return, the stiff straw of the roper's hat rough against her scarred chin. After a while she thinks it might be time to let go. But Jen doesn't. So neither does Carly.

After a few more seconds of this, Carly says, "Shouldn't you tie up that horse?"

"Anoaki won't go anywhere. He's real good." But she straightens up and lets Carly go. "Nice hat!"

"Thanks. Alvin gave it to me."

"Looks good! You look like you belong here."

Jen waits to see if Carly has anything to say about that. But Carly chooses to let it go by. Well, not chooses so much. It just goes by. And she doesn't know what to do with it. So that's the way things stay.

Jen walks back to her horse, who hasn't moved. Takes him by the reins and leads him to the new fence built onto the carport. Peels back a section of wire that Carly didn't even notice has been set up as a gate. Then Jen slides the blanket off his back and drapes it over the fence. Unties the rope halter and lets it fall. It swings from the reins still clutched in her hand. Jen steps back, and Anoaki walks through the gate and into the shade of the carport. Jen hangs the halter on a fence post and hooks the gate closed. Walks around behind the carport, emerging a moment later with a flake of hay. She throws it over the fence to the horse, then walks back to where Carly is standing in the afternoon sun.

"So Virginia gave you that horse?"

"Not exactly. She called it a loan. But I don't really think she's gonna ask for him back. 'Cause he's retired. She doesn't use him much anymore. But he can take me to school and back. That's not too much for hardly any horse. I'm so glad you got back, Carly. I was scared to death. I thought you might die."

"Well, I didn't," she says.

She decides she can—and should—keep her close calls to herself.

"Stay, Carly. Please. Just for a couple of months. Do it for me. So I can show you how good it is here. Then if you still want to go, you can. Please?"

"I don't know if Delores will *let* me stay."

"Will you ask her?"

"Yeah," Carly says. "I'll ask her."

Carly ducks her head down going through the door into the house. And she still doesn't know why.

Delores is sitting on the couch, weaving strong, stiff tan grasses around a frame of thicker straw. She's not looking at her work. Her eyes are trained off in the distance. As if looking out the window. But Carly doesn't think that's the case. The old woman probably can't see that far. She's probably staring into space.

Carly sits in the only chair, across from her. Roscoe thumps his tail.

"Making a basket?"

"Makin' myself a new hat."

Then neither says anything for a time. This is that moment Alvin told Carly to practice. Admitting she needs something. And would appreciate getting it.

So she pushes harder. Puts a figurative shoulder behind the words.

"Jen wants me to stay a couple months. She thinks I'll get to like it here. She thinks if I give her a month or two, she can show me why she loves this place so much."

Nothing happens at first. The silence makes Carly's heart fall. Her poor heart, she thinks. Not really in a self-pitying way. More like she finally has some empathy for the poor abused organ. How many more falls can it take?

"'N what do *you* want to do?" Delores asks, finally.

"I'd like to stay. If you'll have me. God's honest truth, I need to stay. I don't have any place else to go."

"Surprised," Delores says. Her hands still moving. Still building that hat. "We thought you'd pick the live-on-your-own plan."

"Scary being on your own," Carly says. Seems like once she opens up that faucet of honesty, it flows without much effort. "Turns out I'm not so big and strong as I thought. Maybe I really am too young."

"Got news for you," Delores says. "I'm ninety-two, and I'm not so big 'n strong as *I* thought, neither."

A long silence. Carly's gut can't quite relax. Because Delores hasn't exactly said yes.

When she can't stand it anymore, Carly says, "So…"

"I can always use another hand around the place."

Carly empties her lungs of breath she didn't even know she was holding. "I'll help. I will. I'll work hard. And I'll be nicer and more cooperative."

"Nah, you'll still be what you are," Delores says. "But it's OK. I won't be nicer 'n more cooperative, neither. Just got to put up with each other. Somethin' you could do would be a real big help. You could learn to drive stick. If you could drive my old truck, wouldn't always be at the mercy of people bringin' stuff out here to me. We need somethin', you could just drive out 'n get it."

"I could do that. I'll go easy on your clutch, too."

"Was gonna try to talk Alvin into teachin' you on his truck." She pauses, but before Carly can open her mouth to answer, Delores says, "No, scratch that. Learn on my old truck. Ain't no earthly good to me unless you can drive it. I got no business gettin' behind that wheel ever again, and we both know it."

Carly rises to her feet. With effort. Her body still feels pounded and overused.

"Thank you," she says.

Delores only nods.

But anyway, Carly said it. And it went down a little easier the second time. Just like Alvin said it would.

After dinner, Carly sits on the bed in the cool trailer, looking out the window. Watching the light change on the mesa. Lighting it up redder as the sun slants.

She tries on the idea of this place as home, and it still doesn't fit. But it makes her remember sitting in that tourist restaurant in Trinidad, drinking iced tea and wondering how it would feel to never get in out of the elements. No matter how bad those elements got. Now she's indoors, and it's cool. And there's electricity. And water, even if you do have to walk out to the well and fetch it. And a bed. And a place to store what few belongings she owns. That strikes her as the most fundamental elements of a home. Maybe, she thinks, you have to do the rest on your own.

She sits another hour or more, wondering when Jen will come in, so they can go to bed. Jen is in the house with Delores. It makes Carly feel a little left out. Though she knows she could be in the house, too, if she wanted. All she'd have to do is walk in and join them.

She makes up her mind to try that tomorrow.

It's after dark when Jen bounces in.

"Just wanted to come say good night," she says.

"You're not sleeping here?"

"No, I sleep on the couch in the house. That way I'm there if Delores needs anything in the night."

"Oh. OK."

"Well…good night."

"Good night," Carly says.

But Jen doesn't leave straightaway. Carly feels like not enough has been said. She wonders if Jen feels the same.

Carly decides it's her turn. That she's the one who never says enough.

"I'm sorry I didn't believe you."

"Oh. That. Did you really, like…not *ever* think maybe it happened?"

"Not even once. Not even a little bit. It's kind of hard to explain."

"Oh," Jen says. "That's OK. You don't have to explain. I mean, not OK. It hurt me. But it's OK because…I sort of knew why. And I know it wasn't really about me. I could tell. I know how much you loved him."

"Thanks," Carly says. Thinking she's gotten good at that word in a short time. "Here's the thing, though. I'm sorry I didn't believe Mom, too. And it's a little too late to make it up to Mom."

A long silence. Carly realizes she's been hoping Jen had some kind of answer for that. It feels funny, to look up to your kid sister like she has the missing piece to something you can't make fit together yourself.

"Maybe she sort of knew why, too."

"Hope so," Carly says.

"It was partly my fault. You thought she was lying because I was afraid to say she wasn't. It's my fault, too. I feel bad, too."

"I can forgive you easier than me."

"Same here."

Carly doesn't know what to say. So she says nothing at all.

"See you in the morning. Unless you sleep in. In which case I'll be at school."

"You makin' friends?" Carly doesn't realize until it's out of her mouth that she just dropped a *g*. Like Delores. It's almost funny, after the fact.

"Tons," Jen says.

"Good. That's good." She reaches under the collar of her shirt. Pulls out the feather pendant. "Here, I should give this back to you now. It did its job, you know?"

"No, it's OK," Jen says. "You keep it. I'm doing fine."

Then she slips out the noisy door again.

And Carly is left alone with just this. Just a little pink metal trailer with bare utilities and a view of the moon rising, more of a crescent now, over a long mesa.

It's not much. But it's more than she's had for a long time.

She sleeps long and well.

WAKAPI LAND

May 25

"Can I use that fence post pounder thingy?" Carly asks Alvin.

"Be my guest."

She nearly falls over when she takes it from him. It's heavy.

She's at Alvin's place, where she's never been before. It's about two miles farther down the same road as Chester's. In fact, Chester's dogs barked at them as Carly drove by.

Yes, Carly got to drive Alvin's truck. Once she got it into first and then second gear, with a bit of instruction and a lot of practice, it was pretty easy.

She lifts the fence tool with great effort and positions it.

It has a handle on each side. You slip it over the top of the T-post. And then you lift it up and slam it down, and the weight of it drives the post into the ground. A little deeper each time. At least, that's how it worked when Alvin did it. He made it look easy. He said it has a big spring in it, so it doesn't jar you right down to your toes on every hit.

Carly is determined to make it work, though part of her knows she's clearly in over her head.

She slams it down a few times, hard. Careful not to cry out each time it hurts her right hand. The T-post doesn't move much. Despite the fact that Alvin soaked the dirt in this spot for a long time with a hose.

Then she stops. Because she needs to.

She's breathing like she's just run a marathon. She takes off her hat with one hand and wipes the sweat off her face with her sleeve.

Alvin sets the hose down and walks over to where Carly is standing. Grabs one handle of the heavy tool.

"Trade you," he says.

"Yeah, OK."

"That hurt your hand?"

"Yeah. Some."

"Sure we don't need to get that looked at?"

"But the swelling's going down."

"Well, give it a break then. Least you can do for it. I should've thought of that. I'm sorry."

"It's not your fault," she says.

"I just forgot, is the thing. Or I never would've had you try it."

She picks up the hose and Alvin's tape measure. Measures off six feet from the post he's working on. Soaks the next spot.

"Hotter than it was when I left," she says to him.

"Yup. Summer's coming on, all right. Nothing you or anybody else can do to change its mind."

"I feel really bad about my mom. I can't stop thinking about that."

Alvin stops pounding. Carly just keeps looking at the dirt, refusing to make eye contact. In her peripheral vision, she can feel him watching her.

"Come on," he says. "Let's take ourselves a break."

They sit on the porch together in the shade. In two straight-backed wooden chairs. Carly takes off her hat and sets it on her knee. Where she can look at it.

A Wakapi woman Carly never met goes by on a bicycle down the dirt road, a thin cloud of red dust following. The woman raises one hand in a wave, and Alvin returns the gesture.

"Hey, Alvin," the woman calls. "Hey, Carly."

Then she rides on.

"How does she know my name?"

"Oh, you got to be quite the legend around here while you were away. Now what's this about your mom?"

Carly lets out a long, unhappy sigh.

"I thought she was lying about Teddy. So she could leave him for this guy. Who she was already sleeping with. I wouldn't speak to her. I said I hated her, and I called her a liar. I told her I'd never forgive her. And then I didn't speak to her for months. Literally. Like, four or five months. And then she went off with that guy and got herself killed. And now I come to find out she wasn't lying. She did a lot that was wrong, my mom, but not that. Not that one thing. And I didn't know that was the last chance I'd ever have to speak to her. And now I feel like I'm going to have to live with that for the rest of my life."

"You are," Alvin says.

"Gee, thanks. You were supposed to say something comforting."

"Want me to lie to you?"

"No."

They sit quietly for a time. Carly puts one hand on her hat, where it sits on her knee. It looks just right there. When it's not on her head.

"We took off out of there so fast, I don't even know where they buried her."

"Want me to see if I can find out?"

"Yeah. That would be good. Thank you."

"See? You're getting good at that. Told you a little practice's all it takes."

Alvin gets up and wanders into the house. Comes back out with two pottery cups of ice water about the size of small buckets. Hands one to her.

"Thanks," she says and takes a long draw.

"OK. I'll try to say something comforting. We got a different relationship to our ancestors than the people you grew up with. We still get some help and guidance from those who're gone. Like they're gone in one way, but not in every way. We're not taught to be cut off from our ancestors, like they're just dead, and that's that."

"Wish I'd been taught like that."

"Never too old to learn," Alvin says. "Question is whether you'll stay around here with us long enough to pick up something new."

Carly never answers that question.

She just looks off at the line of low mountains in the distance, liking the way the sun hits them. Liking the way the breeze blows patterns in the dry grasses between here and there. Liking the way the horses graze in a field across the road. And the way the clouds scud across the navy-blue edges of the sky.

It's a good sky.

The reason she doesn't answer the question is because she still wants to reserve more time to think. Before she makes any big commitments.

But she's pretty sure she already knows.

AUTHOR'S NOTE

There is no such thing as a Native American tribe called the Wakapi. They are fictional.

The land on which I have depicted them living is very real. It's in Arizona, just where it appears in this novel. It contains the Painted Desert and some of the most impressive landscapes I know. It is haunting and simple, pure, and, in my eyes, achingly beautiful. It never ceases to make me feel awed, insignificant, and inspired, usually all at the same time. I have been both through and to this area on a number of occasions.

In the real world, these lands belong to the Navajo, Hopi, and Apache tribes.

My initial vision for this book was to depict a few fictional members of a real tribe, and I set off to research this tribe with much the same zeal as I set off to research transplant surgeries when I wrote Second Hand Heart.

Here's what I learned:

A surgery is a finite thing. And, when all is said and done, it is only that: a thing. It is not a human being, a rich history, or a culture. It has limits. It follows the same basic guidelines each time it occurs. Its complexity is nothing compared to a people.

As a result of this realization, I created the fictional Wakapi tribe as a way to show my immense respect for the Native American culture and way of life. Because I ultimately decided it was far more respectful to openly admit that I do not know any Native American tribe well enough to take on their story, or even the story of one or more of their people. A great deal of harm has been done to Native culture by outsiders. My hope is not to contribute to that harm in any way. Ultimately, I decided my goal would be best accomplished by remaining on the outside.

I do realize I am still depicting a version of Native American life in a very general way. I don't suppose I can have done so perfectly from my outsider position, but I hope I have done it reasonably well, and that my respect shines through.

ABOUT THE AUTHOR

Catherine Ryan Hyde is the author and co-author of nineteen books, including *When I Found You, Second Hand Heart, When You Were Older,* and *Don't Let Me Go. Her novel Pay It Forward* was included on the ALA's Best Books for Young Adults list, translated into twenty-three foreign editions, and turned into a major Warner Brothers motion picture. Her short stories have received honorable mentions in the Raymond Carver Short Story Contest, nominations for Pushcart Prizes and the O. Henry Award, and citations in the *Best American Short Stories* anthologies. Along with Anne R. Allen, she recently co-authored *How To Be A Writer In The E-Age...And Keep Your E-Sanity.* An avid traveler and amateur photographer, she has hiked the Grand Canyon, the Inca Trail to Machu Picchu, and many more of the world's most beautiful places. She currently resides in Cambria, California.